THE HEYWARD SHEPHERD CONSPIRACY

BY

MAP V. RYAN

First Edition, January 2014
11th Eye Press

ISBN-13: 978-0615949444

TO TOM,
INERTIA NOT SPEED

Blumenthal v. United States (1947):

"For it is most often true, especially in broad schemes calling for the aid of many persons, that after discovery of enough to show clearly the essence of the scheme and the identity of a number participating, the identity and the fact of participation of others remain undiscovered and undiscoverable. Secrecy and concealment are essential features of successful conspiracy. The more completely they are achieved, the more successful the crime. Hence the law rightly gives room for allowing the conviction of those discovered upon showing sufficiently the essential nature of the plan and their connections with it, without requiring evidence of knowledge of all its details or of the participation of others. Otherwise the difficulties, not only of discovery, but of certainty in proof and of correlating proof with pleading would become insuperable, and conspirators would go free by their very ingenuity."

* * * * * * * * * *

CONTENTS

I. Wednesday, April 19, 1995

From the Washington Post, page D5.

The man slain in a brutal attack on a Mount Pleasant street Saturday Morning may have met his killer a few hours before he died, D.C. police investigators said yesterday. Detectives said the death of Nathaddeus Jerome Smith, who was stabbed more than 50 times, was characteristic of other so-called pick-up slayings involving homosexual men.

Smith, 26, who police said was openly homosexual, was stabbed repeatedly in the face and chest and found lying between two parked cars. Residents of the area reported hearing Smith cry out for help as he was attacked.

"To look at a morgue photo of him, it is hard to tell it was the same person," one detective said.

A few blocks from where Smith was attacked, police found a silver Dodge compact driven from the scene by the killer. The detectives determined that Smith had borrowed the car from a friend and had been using it over the weekend while he was visiting the Washington area.

The savage nature of the killing, on Kenyon Street, also left residents horrified. Neighbors jammed police emergency lines with numerous calls during the attack.

No arrests have been made.

~ Chapter One ~

4:37 a.m.

The rolled-up newspaper crashed against the aluminum patio door, waking Annie from a fitful sleep. She sat up and stole a glance at her husband, his white pockmarked face illuminated by the bed-side clock.

Even in his sleep, he was wearing that self-satisfied, almost smug grin that had been grating on her as of late.

Clearly, the idea of being a father suited him.

Annie, not so much.

"Triplets, triple, three," she whispered as she ran her fingers across her dark, distended stomach. "Girl, what have you got yourself into?"

She knew she was re-entering the mental loop that had kept her tossing and turning night after night, but she was too tired to resist. It always started with the money. The tens of thousands of dollars spent on *in vitro* fertilization. And for what? To bring a child – or rather, children – into such a cruel and base world? So small, so vulnerable....

In the Metro section of the morning paper, in the local news broadcast every night, it was plain as day. The body count did not lie. Year in, year out, Washington, D.C. beat out much bigger cities like Detroit and New Orleans for the dubious distinction of being labeled The Nation's Murder Capital.

As a prosecutor in the U.S. Attorney's Office, Annie had seen much of it up close. Toddlers killed by stray bullets, robbery victims shot dead for *buckin'* their assailants, domestic quarrels ending in body bags. Homicides over dice games, murders over women, killings on account of the Superbowl,

5

bloated black bodies washing up on the shores of the Anacostia. Wanton death and destruction such a common reaction to slights so imperceptible, so infinitely small, that the *casus belli* often faded from memory by the time of the police interrogation:

"So, you shot him?"

"Yeah."

"You shot him with the gun?"

"Uh-huh."

"The one we found in the car?"

"Mmmmm."

"How close were you when you shot him?"

"Right up on him, you know, right there."

"Did you bring the gun with you so you could shoot him?"

"Yeah, pretty much."

"Why'd you shoot him then?"

"Well, you see ... that's a good question. I dunno, we was just beefin'. He done said something, you know, a minute ago. I don't really remember. My other baby's mother, she know. He her cousin. Why don't you axe her?"

The tart smell of rotting magnolia flowers broke Annie from her trance. She slowly rolled out of bed, and tip-toed across the room. At the window, the streetlight bathed her in a sickly yellow hue, and the old Iranian couple from down the street, out for their morning walk in matching Nike track suits, recoiled at the sight of her as she waved nauseously.

Annie closed the window and returned to bed. She tried to distract herself by making a mental list of household chores and errands she would have her smirking husband run.

Baby-proof the electrical outlets. Convert the guest room to a nursery. And, for the last time, replace that flimsy patio door!

She had almost fallen asleep when the telephone rang.

She picked up on the first ring. "Hello?"

"Annie Fairbrother?"

"Who's calling?"

"You'll never guess who just got picked up B and E at St. Nick's."

Annie looked at the clock as her husband stirred. "I asked, who's calling?"

"Jamal, Jamal Stancil."

She froze when she heard the name. Then the phone clicked dead.

"Who is it," her husband groaned.

"Nothing. A cop, I think."

"What's – ?"

"It's nothing, Steve. He said – Jamal Stancil got arrested."

"Stancil? Wasn't he the Ba – ?"

He stopped short.

Annie said nothing.

"I thought he got sent down to Lorton, what, a couple of years ago?"

"Yes. He did." Annie got out of bed, slid into her robe, and wrapped it tightly around her mid-section. "But now he's out."

"Babe, where are you going?"

"The office. I want to be there at papering, make sure it's done right."

"Papering? Oh, you gotta be kidding. It's not even five o'clock."

"Who's kidding?" she said as she hurriedly dressed. "Some asshole – some cop just called me, here, at our home, and I aim to find out who it was."

"OK, whatever."

"Plus, it's my job. It's what I do. Or do you think we could live in this pretty house on your government paycheck alone?"

"Annie, you know, you're going to have to slow down pretty soon. Like, take it easy?"

"Have to?" she snapped. "Nothing 'have to' about it, Steve. Life's all about choices. You make your choices for you, and I make mine for myself."

5:03 a.m.

The regular contingent of whores were ambling about the payphone, caterwauling at the burgeoning commuter traffic, when De La Suggs, laboring and out of breath from his run up North Capitol, managed to roar, "You Bins bitches clear the fuck out!" and every one of them did, except for a dark skinned girl with glaring yellow eyes.

"Who da' fuck think you is?" she demanded. "AT&T?"

"Don' mine her, Mister De La," one of the retreating whores cried out. "She still new."

"Come on, Shameika!" another one added. "Better leave Shorty be!"

De La could see that the yellow eyed girl was still grittin' him. "Bitch, I said clear outta here. I got a call to take."

Now the woman gave him a slant eyed smile and a toothy grin, as if she suddenly recognized him. "Lil' man, watchu lookin' for? You be liking that poo-poo?"

Not wanting to touch the skeezy bitch with his bare hands, De La retrieved a leather-bound book from the side- pocket of his fatigue shorts and whacked the woman across the head with it, sending her sprawling.

Then he spit on the woman as she tried to crawl away.

"That's the Book of Divine Principle, bitch!" he laughed. "Minister said this little jump would come in handy one day, and Gotdam, if he wasn't right!"

De La quickly commandeered the pay phone. But as the

minutes passed and the sun began to peek up over the pauper's cemetery across the street, his mirth turned to worry.

"Can't believe I jeopardized this once-in-a-lifetime gig with a trifling little Sursum Corda combo," he mumbled as he checked his watch. "Whateva. In this business, it's either feast or famine. When you're bumping curbs, you jes gotta take what jobs come calling."

Then, the phone rang. De La pounced. "Whodis?"

"Heyward Shepherd is out of the train."

"Oh, man! It on?"

"Heyward Shepherd is *out* of the train," the nasally white-man voice repeated. "The crimes of this guilty land will now be purged with blood!"

6:08 a.m.

Central cell is the most crowded place for a black man to feel all alone. Dozens and dozens of brothers, some old, most young, a few particularly vicious, but most just truly scared. And the rules are simple: don' look at nobody, don' talk to no one.

So when the young 'Bama stepped up to Mal, saying he knows him from round the Gardenz, there was but one thing to say in response: "You don' know me, nigga."

Mal could see the kid was terrified. Shoot, he'd been this kid once himself. Every juvenile that's ever been locked up in Oak Hill will say he's hard, but put him in adult lock-up for the first time, and you'll quickly see how soft he really is. For the one thing that most distinguishes Central Cell – the underground cage that connects the police department to the courthouse – is the smell: you know it's a step-up from juvi when multiple dudes be shitting-in-pants scared.

So maybe this be the kid's first time, Mal thought. But

fuck him. I got my own problems here.

The cage was crowded, constantly moving and swaying, hard words, hands pushing up in faces. Mal reached to steady himself, but when he got ahold of the cold iron bars, the despair that had stalked him from childhood began its seductive whispers. *Don't listen to them, listen to me.*

The voices were soon joined by the familiar visions. His mother – eyes rolled back in her head. The faceless old man in an orange jumpsuit. The dead baby in the oversized bonnet. All of them repeating in a sing-song voice, "Never shoulda been born, never shoulda been born!"

Mal closed his eyes tight, and tried to focus. Try to go the quiet place, he thought, jes like the Imam say.

He tried to paint a mental picture of the ladybugs, thousands of them, ascending from below, a shimmering red curtain of life, washing away the darkness, empowering his people, saving the unborn –

"Yo, Doo?"

It was the Gardenz kid tugging on his shirt.

"Doo, how much longa d'ya think we godda be up in dis joint fo' we get outta 'ere?"

"Step off, young 'un," Mal said in a garrulous voice. "I toll you I don't know you."

But the kid persisted, and he was soon joined by others, kids saying they know him, devils pretending to be children. When the single ladybug dropped from the sky and landed on the young devil's shoulder, Mal couldn't tell if she was real or not, so when the kid reached up to brush it off, Mal grabbed his wrist and held fast.

But the devil would not be denied. A stream of roaches raced out of the little shitass's ears and down his neck, flipping the ladybug over on her back, taking turns savaging her. Now the whole room around him was gangin' on.

A voice called out, "Hey! You OK, man?"

And another: "Shit, nigga, stop that shaking!"

And then the young devil, the 'Bama, literally crying, "Sum'n help! Nigga breaking my arm, yo!"

8:52 a.m.

Shuffling past the newly black-topped street, idling taxi cabs, and steaming hot dog stands, Liam McNaughton took his place in the nervous, sweaty line of humanity waiting to get into the D.C. Superior Court's H. Carl Moultrie Building.

Liam loosened his tie, slung his suit jacket over his shoulder, and began to compulsively check the time – the face of his watch glistening with sweat – until he noticed the date.

Exactly nine months earlier, on the first day of his first job as a lawyer, his boss Dorsey Jamison, Esq. had given him the following sartorial advise: "Don't get nothing but a worsted wool suit!" And ever the eager associate, he had complied, maxing out his Filene's Basement charge card with five tailored Jones New York suits ("One for each day of the week," as Dorsey had further suggested).

But now that Liam was out solo, hustling court appointed criminal cases in the abysmally hot Moultrie building instead of settling small ball personal injury claims in Dorsey Jamison's air-conditioned office, he wished he had bought just *one* of those seersucker suits he saw all the courthouse old-timers wearing.

As the line inched forward, tantalizingly close to the long shadow cast by the courthouse's entrance, Liam could begin to hear the security guards barking out their orders from just inside.

"Follow me easy, don't carry me greezy!"

"Coats, purses, and bags on the belt; everything else go

11

in the bowl!"

"Set off the alarm, you will go back to the end of the line!"

When it was finally Liam's turn to press through the tinted glass entry doors, he took a quick inventory of the objects in his pockets. Then he greeted the security guards with his most obsequious smile, making a big show of placing his metallic baubles – his keys, asthma inhaler, his Mont Blanc pen and gold-plated card holder – one by one into *their* avocado green Tupperware bowl.

Then, after taking his place in line for the metal detector, Liam craned his neck in quiet desperation as his most important belongings, tucked neatly behind his briefcase, rattled along the conveyor belt, disappearing into the mouth of the x-ray machine.

At this point, Liam found a disheveled old man wearing a JUROR badge holding up the line, fumbling about with a cup of McDonald's coffee.

"Just put it on the table, sir," Liam suggested. "Or take it with you through the metal detector."

Looking startled, the old man started ambling back towards the x-ray machine.

"No, sir, not there! Just put your cup – "

But the man wasn't listening, so Liam quickly stepped forward in line, and when the security guard gave him the subtle nod, he walked stiffly through the metal detector, and with no alarm sounding, he bounded forward, relieved to find the Tupperware bowl and his briefcase intact, waiting for him at the back-end of the x-ray machine, just ahead of the old - man's tipped-over Styrofoam cup.

"Ah, Jesus!" one of the security guards screamed at the sight of the coffee spilling over the sides of the conveyor belt. "Which one of you geniuses put this through?"

Liam gave the guard a look of *sorry-wish-I-could-help-ya*

as he scooped up his belongings and made a beeline to the crowded down-escalator. As was his custom as of late, he immediately took to the right – the business-suited lawyers and furtive young black men whizzing by him – and began staring up into the warm light that flooded in from the atrium ceiling, admiring the floating escalators that crisscrossed the center of the building, six stories up, two stories down. He allowed himself to daydream that he was on the steps of the Supreme Court, staring into the klieg lights, about to give an admiring Connie Chung or maybe even that hottie Greta Van Susteren an exclusive interview about his newest quixotic challenge to the legal system. *"Well, of course, Greta, we're the underdog in this thing, but it's a fight that has to be fought, you know what I mean?"*

Liam snapped to when the escalator steps suddenly disappeared from beneath his feet, and he stumbled forward into the long basement foyer that lead to Courtroom C-10 – the arraignment court – where he joined the trenchant mass of humanity wallowing about in the darkness.

A shiver ran through the crowd when a voice rang out, "9 o'clock list is up!", and the business-suit clad men and women surged forward like spawning salmon, desperate to see who had received a Criminal Justice Act appointment to represent one of the indigent riff-raff, thugs, or deviants arrested the night before.

The CJA lawyers, as they were known, were a diverse and desperate lot: elderly black men, all tweed vest, pocket watch and bejeweled walking stick; the Caribbean women with their high hats and saucy smiles; West Africans with their English schoolboy accents and dubious bar credentials. Pakistanis hunched low and furtive, Indians and Sikhs, dark and assertive. Dowdy widows and divorcees trying to supplement their meager Social Security allowances shoulder-to-shoulder in the mosh pit with the newly minted cubs, mostly from B-list law schools, still smarting over their failure to land a real job with one of the Big Firms. A daily act of penance and self-loathing, even the blind, the hard-of-hearing, and guys with catheter bags pushed their way forward to the list.

In <u>Gideon v. Wainwright</u> (1963), the United States Supreme Court ruled that the U.S. Constitution required the states to appoint lawyers to all persons of limited means who were facing criminal prosecution, and no place in the country took that mandate more seriously than the District of Columbia, where indigents became entitled to a virtual buffet of free legal services. Need a divorce? The court will pay for a lawyer. Wanna adopt a foster kid? The city will pay for that too. Got busted selling PCP? Don't sweat it – you're gonna get yourself a CJA lawyer!

Liam tried to move in closer to the shredded cork bulletin board where the 9 o'clock list would be posted. "My name's gonna be up there today," he said, tightening the knot in his tie. "I can just feel it."

His optimism, however, wasn't entirely justified. While there were usually over a hundred cases posted on the 9 o'clock list every morning, there would be over 900 lawyers vying for them (or for whatever was left over after the high-and-mighty Public Defender Service cherry-picked the two dozen most juicy and loathsome cases for themselves). The CJA Office would post two more lists later that day, placing another thirty cases or so up for grabs. But if you didn't make the 9 o'clock list, it was hardly worth waiting around for the late-afternoon dregs – the fugitive warrants, the hospital cases, the ones headed for the mental observation calendar. The 9 o'clock list was *the* list. If you didn't get picked for the 9 o'clock list, you might as well go home.

"Outa the way, you twenty-three one tens!" an angry voice

bellowed behind Liam.

It was Marlton Stove, the oversized *eminence grise* of the CJA bar, unofficial leader of the Fifth Streeters – the baker's dozen fat old sponges who believed that their seniority and rumored kick-backs entitled them to each and every court appointed case that came in through the courthouse door.

"The ink ain't even dry on yer tickets!" Stove growled as the crowd parted before him.

Following in Stove's wake were several other Fifth Streeters, including the white-bearded Robert E.L. Stucky, who elbowed past Liam with a guffaw and a glare. "Some of these pimply faced boys ain't got their pants dry neither!"

"Fat ass Colonel Sanders," Liam said under his breath.

After bullying their way to the bulletin board, Stove, Stucky, and the other Fifth Streeters began calling out names:

"Derrick Jenkins! He's mine! Anybody here for Derrick Jenkins? Follow my investigator to the Lawyer's Lounge."

"Anybody here for Cyprian Tate? How 'bout Sammy Clemonts? Joseph Boone? Jones, Remy Jones? All you there, go to the Lawyer's Lounge."

"Any of you we didn't call? Any mommas or sisters or brothers? You want your boy out and can pay a cash money retainer? Same thing! Meet us at the Lawyer's Lounge. Otherwise you'll be stuck with one of these losers!"

9:21 a.m.

De La Suggs took the Styrofoam container out of the plastic bag and balanced it on the plumbing behind the toilet. He opened its lid and dug through an overflowing mound of French fries until he got ahold of the hamburger underneath.

Holding his position, he put his ear to the door of the toilet stall. When he was confident that he was still alone, he removed the heavy zip-lock package from in-between the hamburger buns, shook off the stray pieces of shredded lettuce, and pulled out a tiny pistol.

"Just how Captain done planned it," he said, slipping the little gun into his pocket, right next to his Book of Divine Principle.

On the way out the stall, De La checked himself in the mirror. Dark aviator shades, toothpick, and a wicked scowl – he liked what he saw.

"Heyward Shepherd," he said to his reflection, "today's just not gonna be yo' day."

Then he flung the lunch container into the urinal, and strode out.

Back in the foyer, he waited for the crowd of suits to dissipate before strolling over to the cork bulletin board where the list was posted. Unable to find the name he was looking for after the first pass, he quickly retraced his finger over the entire list and was half-way done when a white man in a seersucker suit stepped up behind him and began giving him the sigh treatment.

De La turned to face the man. "You need to see the list?"

"Yes, I do."

"Are you a lawyer or sumpin?"

"Suit, tie, brief case," the man said sardonically. "Uh, yeah?"

"Hmmph." De La felt like breaking out his Book of Divine Principle and giving the man a proper reading, but he had business to attend to. "Lemme axe you a question. What if a guy's name ain't up here?"

"Well, it could be he's not on there," the white man said, stating the obvious. "You talking about someone arrested last night?"

"Last night? Yeh, that's right. Or more probably this

morning."

"Maybe he's on the afternoon list. Why don't you come back then?"

De La contemplated a bright, oily spot on the white man's temple for a moment. Then he took a step back and said, "Oh, am I in you way? My bad."

The lawyer moved into the space without looking back, but De La had one more question. "Hey, mista. What time that other list come out?"

Now it was the lawyer's turn to play hard. "Oh, you're talking to me now? *My* bad," he said after the requisite pause. "Afternoon list goes up at one thirty. Another one comes out around three."

"Three o'clock?" De La could feel his own eyeballs bouncing from side to side. "But my man 'sposed to be here right at nine."

"Looks like fate dealt you a bad hand," the lawyer said with grin. "I guess you'll just have to wait around here like the rest of us schmucks."

~ Chapter Two ~

9:20 a.m.

Liam walked away from the 9 o'clock list muttering to himself, wondering how much longer he could go on like this.

He'd been calling in for CJA cases since the beginning of the year, and for his efforts, the Court had appointed him to a mere twelve cases: three fugitive warrants, two shoplifting cases, six prostitution busts, one aggressive panhandling. Worse, the court had yet to pay him for any of the vouchers he'd turned in; so here it was in April, and his total income year-to-date was still zero.

In this heat, in a worsted wool suit, there was no way he would be up for the arduous walk home, so he pored through his briefcase for the buck twenty it would cost to take the subway. When he couldn't find enough change, he rifled through his wallet and – score! – he found an old Metro ticket with 35 cents left on it, and within minutes he was boarding a cool, spotlessly clean, and near-empty Red Line train at Judiciary Square.

Liam tried not to make eye contact with any of the other passengers, while at the same time, studiously avoided looking at his own reflection in the window. As he deboarded at Union Station, he could not shake the feeling that he was lost.

Fighting his way through the giddy throngs of child-tourists and harried Amtrak travelers, he joined the scores of other well-dressed young twenty-somethings rushing through the traffic circles and taxi lanes towards the U.S. Capitol like determined ants.

At Constitution Avenue, in the shadow of the Capitol dome, Liam ordinarily parted company with this well-heeled crowd in order to head for home. But on this day, as he waited for the light at the cross-walk, a confident young woman walked by, her skirt inadvertently pinned up under her designer back pack.

Liam looked around to see if anyone else had noticed, but the sidewalk was empty, so he decided to get a closer look at those orange sherbet-colored panties.

He closed to about ten feet when a shabby black man stepped out of the shadows in front of the woman. The man took two quick steps towards the girl and then, almost involuntarily, one step back.

"Little change for the homeless?"

The startled woman passed by without comment, and when she did, the homeless man – after doing a double take – started trailing after her.

"Hey, Missus," he called out. "You dress! You dress!"

The woman stopped for a moment, looked around angrily, then snapped her skirt back into place.

The black man then did another two step forward–one step back hitch, extending his crusty palm towards her.

"Buy me a baloney sandwich, Missus?"

At this point, Liam had caught up with the two of them. He tried to sneak past un-noticed, pretending to look at his watch, but the woman smiled as if she knew him.

"Hey!" she said, picking up his lanky pace. "What's going on?"

"Oh, me? Uh, nothing. I... I was going to say something, you know, about – "

"Come on, slow poke," she chirped. "We're late!"

Leaving the skip-stepping beggar behind, Liam and the woman continued side-by-side until they reached the polished marble entrance of the Russell Senate Office Buildings.

"Thanks," the woman said with a nervous giggle. "He kind

of scared me."

Liam's tongue felt thick and dry. "Uh, yeah. Me too."

The woman sprang up the marble steps but stopped half-way when she saw that Liam wasn't following. "Are you in the Hart building?"

"Hart?"

"What member are you with?"

"Member? Oh, no, I don't really work for the Hill. I'm a lawyer – a criminal lawyer. You know, CJA?"

"Don't work on the Hill?" she said, curling her lip. "Well, uh, have a nice day, I guess."

Liam watched as the woman disappeared behind a set of ornate golden doors. Then he trudged off, head down. He felt nauseous and woozy.

Must be the heat, he thought to himself.

9:45 a.m.

Annie Fairbrother opened the top drawer of her dead-file – the cabinet where she kept what she called her "scalps" – and pulled out the thick folder she was looking for.

United States v. Jamal Stancil.

She removed the jacket that contained the very core of the case: the defendant's mug shot, the Pretrial Services Agency's biographic report and drug test results, the detective's affidavit in support of the arrest warrant, the five-page grand jury indictment, and the prosecutor's goldenrod copy of the judgment and commitment order.

She looked at this last document and shook her head.

The case represented everything Annie hated about domestic violence prosecutions. Brandy Carey – Stancil's girlfriend – had not been the model complaining witness. Some days she said she wanted "Mal" locked up forever, other days she would invoke what she called her "material privilege" and vow not to testify.

To Annie, this reticence was unconscionable. Maybe a woman like that has the right to protect her abuser, Annie remembered thinking at the time. After all, she chose to live with him for all those years. But there had been another victim in the case: Brandy's unborn child, just days away from delivery, murdered at the hands – or rather, at the feet – of her father.

It would have been an unconventional murder case, no doubt, but those were the kind Annie excelled at. Motive, premeditation – she'd have no problem with that.

What presented more of a challenge in Stancil's case was that the D.C. Criminal Code defined "homicide" as the intentional killing of another human being. Annie had felt confident that she'd be able to prove that the nine-month old stillborn was a "human being"; in fact, she kind of relished the idea of the defense attorney having to argue to the jury otherwise.

But her hope of getting yet another 25-to-life notch on her belt evaporated just weeks after Stancil's arrest, when the newly appointed United States Attorney called her and the chief deputy of the homicide division up to his 14th Floor suite and in no uncertain terms forbid them from pursuing a murder charge in the case. The order had come directly from the Attorney General.

"But the grand jury already heard from the Medical Examiner," Annie had protested. "They've seen the autopsy, and I've already read them the murder instruction! They can't wait to indict this guy!"

"Elections have consequences," the U.S. Attorney said, conspicuously directing his comments away from Annie and towards her supervisor. "The President has a lot of women to thank, and that starts now."

Annie remembered standing up, pushing her supervisor's hand off her shoulder, and screaming, "Women? Who do you think was the victim in this case? What about *this* woman?"

She also remembered the man's cold response: "You are free to proceed with the counts alleged to have been committed against *that* woman. The A.G.'s office will be studying the ramifications of any prosecution relating to the death of her fetus. It's their case now."

Thus, with her case gutted, and her best leverage gone, Annie had been forced to make what she considered a far too generous offer to Stancil: plead guilty to felony aggravated assault for kicking Brandy in the stomach, and the other counts – the threats, the unlawful entries, the stalking – would be dismissed. And with a little arm-twisting from his CJA lawyer, Stancil eventually accepted the deal.

Annie had taken some solace in the fact that Stancil would certainly be sentenced no less than eight years of actual prison time. But astonishingly, the judge – the silver-haired Vincent DeMaglio – suspended all but two years of the ten-year sentence he imposed.

It was one of the few times Annie remembered losing her cool in court. "Probation?" she had screamed. "This guy will be out in less than a year with the time he's already served!"

And even now, almost three years later, remembering the judge's response made her sick to her stomach: "Miss Fairbrother, with *these* people, in *their* relationships, a certain level of violence is … accepted."

Annie felt the acid rising in her throat as she put Judge DeMaglio's judgment and commitment order back in the folder.

"God rest his racist soul, but I'm glad that man is – "

Before she could finish her sentence, the dry-heaving

began anew, and as she grabbed for the nearby trash can, she knocked Stancil's accordion folder off her desk, spilling its contents across the floor.

After wiping her mouth on her sleeve, Annie got down on her hands and knees and began picking the myriad of papers off the floor.

"I've been waiting for you to slip up, Stancil," she said to his mug shot. "Breaking into a school might only get you six months. But you'll do eight years of back-up time after I get done violating you."

9:52 a.m.

Liam walked down the steps to his apartment, unlocked the metal security gate, and stepped inside.

Officially a "furnished one-bedroom," the apartment was really a studio divided by a chest-high wall. On one side, there was just enough space for a twin-size bed; on the other, everything was cheery white Ikea – the obligatory dresser, wobbly entertainment center, and cock-eyed side table.

And with a trash-strewn patch of sidewalk ivy the only thing visible from his dirty little window, he didn't even bother to close the mangled Levolor blinds before stripping off his sweat soaked clothes and sinking into the cheery white foam chair.

There, he picked up the motivational book he had begun a few days earlier and removed and unfolded the piece of paper that had served as a book mark. The paper contained a pie chart he had drawn up according to the book's instructions, dividing the 168 hours contained in one week into four sections: 56 hours to SLEEP, 52 hours to WORK, 20 hours to EDUCATION, and 40 hours to PLAY.

Liam sighed. It all looked great on paper, but here it was,

ten o'clock in the morning, and his workday had largely evaporated – begun and ended with nary a penny to show for it. PLAY and SLEEP were definitely getting more of the pie than WORK and EDUCATION.

Liam yawned, eyed his bed, and thought about the sticky Gallery magazine he had stowed underneath. Then he saw the blinking red light on his answering machine.

Maybe I should check my messages, he thought. After all, I do have a law office to run here.

The first message was from a prosecutor in the U.S. Attorney's Office who quickly outlined the government's plea offer in one of his few remaining cases – United States v. Shameika Masterson (or the case of the "Poo-poo Prostitute," as Liam liked to think of it).

As with every other prostitution bust he was involved with, it began with an undercover officer pulling up to Ms. Masterson and asking her "What's up?" "Nothing," was her reply, according to the police report. Then:

"You working?"

"You know it. You looking for the poo-poo?"

"Yeah, how much?"

"Twenty dollars."

"O.K., get in."

After which the officer gave the predetermined signal (flashing his lights, hitting the brakes three times, whatever), causing the police to swarm in and arrest the poor whore.

Upon getting his client released on her personal recognizance, Liam had asked if she'd sit down with him so that he could get some basic information from her – working phone number, place to receive mail, interest in pleading guilty, that kind of thing – and Ms. Masterson had agreed on the condition that he buy her three hot dogs from one of the vendors in front of the courthouse. Liam only had enough money to buy her one chili-cheese half-smoke, which she promptly shoved down her mouth whole before waving "Bye bye."

Liam deleted the prosecutor's message without memorializing its contents. Frankly, he never expected to see Shameika Masterson again, so why worry about the details of the plea offer? Every one of the women in the six prostitution cases he had been appointed to – including Ms. Masterson – had self-reported to the Pretrial Services Agency as being HIV positive. Moreover, to date, none of the women had bothered to show up for their trials.

"Easy money," Liam said to himself.

The second message contained a happy voice that was sadly becoming more and more familiar. "Yes sir, this is Mrs. Jones at the John Adler Rental Agency. Mr. McNaughton, your March rent is overdue. And your April rent is now officially overdue, as well. Please call us to let us know when you will be bringing over your payments. And, sir, please don't forget to include the $50 late fee for each month. Have a blessed day."

Liam deleted that message as well, and continued onto the next one.

"Hey, Yum," a husky female voice laughed. "It's J."

There was a pause, and Liam thought he could hear the sound of her breathing.

"I was just calling to see how you were doing and all... there in your law office."

Another pause, and he began to feel his ears buzzing.

"O.K., I just had a question ... a legal question. Well, you're not home, so ... you know, no need to call me back. "

Liam immediately reached for the rewind button. He wanted to hear her call him "Yum" again, just like the first time.

~ Chapter Three ~

10:43 a.m.

A white man dressed as a doctor squeezed Mal's shoulder. "Ah, you are up! My name is Dr. Zeidenberg. The Marshals asked me take a look in on you, see how you're doing."

Mal tried to speak, but his jaw was swollen shut. When he tried to lift himself off the bed, he discovered he was held fast by thick leather straps.

"I'll see if I can't get them to loosen those," the man dressed as a doctor said. "Maybe I can get a nurse to take a look at your mouth."

He then turned his attention to the clipboard that hung over Mal's head.

"So, let's see here. Mr. Stancil…. Malcolm X. Stancil. By any means necessary, huh?" the man chuckled. "So what we're going to do here is perform what's called a forensic evaluation. I just need you to answer a few questions. Better to not try talking right now, so you just give me the thumbs up for yes, and the thumbs down for no, OK?"

Mal looked out the corner of his eye at his own shackled hand, and raised his thumb.

"Good, good…." The doctor began scribbling on his pad. "OK, let's start with an easy one. You are Malcolm Stancil, correct?"

Mal suddenly realized that he had given the police the wrong name. He desperately tried to mouth the words "Heyward Shepherd" but nothing but bloody spittle came out.

"Now, now, just use your hand. Thumb up, yes; thumb down, no." The man dressed as a doctor gave Mal a quick demonstration. "OK, so do you know where you are?"

26

THE HEYWARD SHEPHERD CONSPIRACY

Mal turned his thumb down.

"You're in the Central Cell infirmary." The man was speaking loudly and slowly, as if to a foreigner. "You were arrested, remember? You were being processed, you know, waiting to go into the arraignment court, and some sort of altercation broke out." The man pushed his glasses up on his forehead, holding the clipboard close to his face. "I see. Oh yes. Says here you started a riot. In the cell block. The Marshals had to subdue you. For your own safety." He pushed his glasses back on his nose, raising his hairy eyebrows. "Yes, well, they always say that, don't they?"

Mal gave the doctor the thumbs up.

"Alright kiddo, last question. Isn't it fair to say that you're not currently or recently experiencing any hallucinations, hearing voices, that kind of thing?"

Mal watched the ladybug hovering around the doctor's head and thought to himself, Yes, I am 'speriencing dem 'lucinations, so he gave the doctor the thumbs up.

"Excellent! Survey says, competent! Besides, no sense wasting bed space at St. E's when you're only looking at an Unlawful Entry."

Mal tensed against the restraints.

"Oh, now, don't worry," the man dressed as a doctor assured him. "Unlawful Entry, it's just a misdemeanor. Nothing serious. Like trespassing. I just don't see any reason to do a full forensic at this time, that's all I'm saying. Just promise me you won't hurt yourself or anyone else, and we'll have you out of here in no time."

Mal nodded and gave the thumbs up.

27

11:03 a.m.

Annie had been staring at the blurry images of her first sonogram when the phone rang. It was a lieutenant at the Fourth District finally getting back to her.

"Hey, Lieutenant," Annie said, "I got a call from one of your guys about an arrest this morning. You know how the Hell he got my home number?"

"Don't know nothing about nothing, ma'am. We don't usually call youse'all at home 'less you give us your number first."

"Hmmph. Well, I want someone to look into it."

"Uh, sure, Mrs. Fairbrother. Is that it?"

"No. I need to know if you show anything on a Jamal Stancil. DOB in '66 or '67; an AKA of 'Mal.' Arrested last night."

"Stancil? Lemme check. Yeah, here he is on the list. Stancil, Malcolm X."

"Malcolm X.?"

"Says here, 'Malcolm X.'"

"Not Jamal Stancil?"

"First name Malcolm, middle name X."

"Well ... that's probably my guy. Where's he now?"

"Already gone downtown. Olsen got him."

"Dennis Olsen?"

"The same."

"Tell me he wasn't in on the arrest."

"Oh, no," the lieutenant laughed. "James McCoy – you know, Supercop – he's the one who caught your man. Climbing up the walls of that Catholic school up there on North Cap, I think he said."

"Where's McCoy now?"

"Where's McCoy?" the lieutenant repeated dryly. "I'll tell

you where he is. He's out doing police work, ma'am. Didn't you hear about the double we had this morning at Sursum Corda? We got everybody on that – McCoy included."

"What about my case? Who's going to do the probable cause affidavit? My guy's on probation and I want him held!"

"Look, ma'am, I don't mean no disrespect or nothing, but honestly, we got bigger fish to fry over here. Two teenage girls killed execution style, OK? And you want us to drop everything for an Unlawful Entry just cause he's on papers?"

"Lieutenant, we *all* have jobs to do. So if it's all the same to you...."

"Right," the cop answered, drawing out the word. "We all have jobs to do. Look, ma'am – Mrs. Fairbrother – things are just a little hectic down here right now. You know Supercop – I'm sure he took care of things. In fact, now that I think about it, I believe McCoy narrated P.C. to Olsen, and Olsen will be available to do the affidavit for you guys after booking."

Annie sighed. "Well, if McCoy pops up, tell him to call me here. Or if I'm not here, down at papering. Who knows what Olsen is going to leave out?"

She hung up and immediately began drafting the motion to show cause – the government's formal request that the court strip a criminal defendant of his probation and put him behind bars. She pulled up the computerized template and, in the prompt that asked for the alleged probation violation, typed in the words "April 19, 1995 Unlawful Entry."

"Wait a second," she said, taking her hands off the keyboard. The man who called that morning told her that Stancil was picked up for "B and E." Annie had never heard the District's cops use the term "B and E" – presumably short for "breaking and entering." Maybe that's what they called it in Maryland or Virginia, but here, it was always "U/E" for unlawful entry or perhaps "B1" or "B2" for first or second degree burglary.

Then another thought crossed her mind. The caller had also said that Stancil had been arrested at St. Nick's, a location that didn't immediately register any significance for Annie. But now, searching through the Stancil file again, she found the folder marked "Bootsy Henson." Bootsy was the mother of Stancil's girlfriend Brandy Carey, and her witness intake form confirmed Annie's vague recollection: Bootsy Henson had worked for the St. Nicholas' Interparish School.

"Going after the girl, going after the mother," Annie mused. "Just like old times, eh, Stancil?"

Annie took a quick sip of her now cold hibiscus tea. Gagging, she dumped the rest of the red liquid in the dead plant on her desk. She hated taking shortcuts, but she was determined to get the motion filed by the end of the day, so she went to print it out – just to see what it would look like on paper – but the keyboard stopped working and a gray pop-up message froze her computer screen. She read the message quickly:

ALL FEDERAL BUILDINGS ON HIGH ALERT.... ALL NON-ESSENTIAL PERSONNEL TO BE EVACUATED IMMEDIATELY.... INFORMATION TO FOLLOW.

"What's this all about," Annie wondered aloud.

She rolled her chair to the door in order to peek down the hall. Several people were gathered around the break-room, and over the sound of the CNN news loop that blared 24/7 from the overhead television, she thought she heard several people crying in anguish.

11:17 a.m.

After listening to Julianne's phone message for a third time, Liam dialed her number. Then, just as quickly, he hung up. The buzzing in his head intensified. "I'd better lie down," he thought. "Think this one over."

Almost a year earlier, Liam had taken a break from studying for his law school finals to go to the El Rey Lounge, a downtown Albuquerque nightclub where his friend's Latin Boogie band sometimes played. What he found instead was a mass of Cinco de Mayo revelers inside, and a hot black chick – all cowboy boots and mini-skirt – sitting alone on the patio.

Her name was Julianne Montross. A native of Philadelphia, she was perpetual grad student, with prior stops at UCLA's Graduate School of Oceanography and the Thunderbird Business School in Phoenix. Now, at age 32, she had just dropped out of the University of New Mexico's Master's Program in Archaeology and had come to the El Rey for the going away party her friends had thrown for her.

Those friends now long gone, Liam had her all to himself, and three margaritas later, with his hand comfortably working its way up her thigh, he caught her studying him.

"Tell me your name again?"

"Liam," he said. "Sort of like William, except its L - I - A - M."

"William," she repeated. "William."

"Yeah, but without the 'Will' part. It's Irish, don't you know?"

"Oh, I get it!" Her eyes brightened as she smiled. "Yum! Like, yummy!'"

He drove her home in her emerald green Miata, and they made love with the lights on, conscientiously exploring each other's body – black hand on white skin, white hand on black skin – enmeshed in the goose down sleeping bag she used as a bed.

Two people without tethers, they remained so intertwined for most of the next eight weeks, sport fucking to his Bob Marley, Nirvana, and Allman Brothers cassette tapes, with

31

Liam emerging from her apartment only to take his law school finals, buy groceries, and re-stock his lamb-skin condom supply. No long talks about mothers, fathers, or other hang-ups; just dinner on restaurant patios, talking politics and the weather, holding hands in public.

And so, as spring gave way to summer, their "no-strings-attached" fling quickly developed into a "why-say-goodbye" romance. Julianne was planning on moving to Washington, D.C., nominally to get a job in the Clinton administration, and with little reason to stay in New Mexico, Liam decided to join her.

When Liam announced to his mother and brother that he was packing up and moving, neither lodged even a cursory objection. He tried to call his father to let him know he'd be on the East Coast too; but the phone number that he pried from his mother just rang and rang. His law school buddies wanted to know who this woman was he was following across the country to Washington, D.C.; his law professors warned him that it would be awfully difficult to get a job there.

Julianne left first, arriving in her convertible Miata just in time to watch the Fourth of July fireworks exploding behind the Washington Monument. Liam, meanwhile, completed his bar exams in mid-July before loading up a Ryder truck with all of his earthly possessions (packed neatly into one suitcase and a milk crate) along with Julianne's living room/dining room set and then leaving New Mexico for good.

Five days later, as he helped Julianne lug her furniture to her 11th floor Pentagon City apartment, Liam began seeing stars. He stumbled out on her balcony and tried to catch his breath. With the Washington skyline flickering in the distance, and the scorching, silent heat sucking the air from his ears, he was overcome with the enormity of what he had just done – he had moved to a city where he didn't have a job, dependent on the kindness and hospitality of a woman he barely knew.

"Hey, Yum," she purred, sneaking up on him. "I bet we could have some fun out here. Hope you brought that Nirvana tape with you, if you know what I mean."

When he didn't respond, she asked him what was wrong.

"It's just that – I can't believe you're going to be working for that guy," Liam pouted.

Julianne's uncle – some kind of Philadelphia alderman – had arranged a job for her as an administrative assistant for a freshman Pennsylvania Congressman best known for displaying the body of his miscarried son in all of his campaign literature.

"Well, one of us has to have a job," she said, lighting up a joint.

"But I just don't get it – why would an inner-city pol like your uncle be trading favors with a pro-life right-winger from the sticks?"

"Oh, Yum! You're so country! That's just the way Washington works!" Julianne exhaled a cloud of smoke. "And you best learn that quick, fast and in a hurry."

Without his own well-placed uncle, Liam would go on to spend the rest of the summer trying to find a job, but by early September, he had yet to receive a single response to any of the 239 resumes he had sent out. Julianne kept telling him about a second cousin she had in the area who made a decent living as a banquet waiter for a mega-catering company. Her cousin could easily get him an interview, she said, and he didn't need any experience. "In fact, all you need is a white collared shirt, and Lord knows you've got plenty of those hanging in *my* closet."

Liam was starting to feel the walls of Julianne's cramped apartment cave in on him, so one day, with his meager savings nearly depleted, he took her up on the offer, and her cousin

33

made the call. But as he was heading out the door for his first training session, the phone rang.

Ever the optimist, he decided to take the call.

"Hello?"

"Looking for a Lee – Liam… McNa – McNugut – "

"McNaughton. This is he."

"You sent me a resume, right? Law Offices of Dorsey Jamison and Associates. You're not black, are you?"

"Ah, no. I mean, yes. Yes, I sent you a resume."

"Good," the deep, gravelly voice continued. "Come by this morning, I'll let you write me a memo. If it's any good, you got a job. Ten bucks an hour."

The job at the caterer paid more than $10 an hour, but Liam hadn't come to D.C. to be a waiter. "OK, I'll be right over."

It turned out that the Law Offices of Dorsey Jamison & Associates consisted of only one office – the basement floor of Dorsey's Lincoln Park townhome – and upon his hiring, Liam would become the one and only associate. But a job's a job, and a week later, Liam almost broke into tears when Dorsey presented him a sheet of pre-cut business cards with the words "Liam McNaughton, Trail Attorney" printed on them.

(It took him several weeks to catch the typo, but by then, he had learned that Dorsey was not one to suffer fools gladly, especially when it was his own mistake).

On the occasion of his first paycheck – meager as it was – Liam had decided to surprise Julianne and take her out for lunch. The House Office Building where she worked was impressive: high-ceilings, marble walls, columns everywhere. He had hoped for a tour, and maybe even a chance to meet the Congressman, but when he showed up unannounced, presenting his new "Trail Attorney" business card, Julianne hustled him out without introductions.

Walking silently through the lunch-time crowd on Pennsylvania Avenue, she pushed away his hand as he reached for hers.

"Not here, Yum," he remembered her saying. "I might see somebody."

11:45 a.m.

De La Suggs was hanging behind the herd of people filing out the courthouse when a shrill female voice called from behind him, "Court be closed! Y'all got to go! Now!"

He drifted to the left of the woman – some sorta security guard – and let her pass.

Schedule gonna be way off now, he thought. Captain can't be blaming me for the court being all closed down and shit. I'm jes a soldier following orders. Can't be 'spected to improvise. Muthfucka wasn't even on the list like he was sposed to.

"Hey Shorty!" the shrill voice called out from behind him. "I toll you keep moving!"

De La saw that the female security guard was approaching fast, and he instinctively reached in his pocket for the tiny gun. Switching off the safety, he formed the intent: *Put that gun up in da bitch's mouth, push her into da 'bafroom 'fo anybody notice we gone, then turn her face down on the dirty pee covered floor and make her regret ever calling me Shorty.*

"Nigga," the woman screamed in his face, "I ain't be telling you again!"

When she tried to push on him, De La stepped back deftly, causing the somewhat overweight woman to stumble forward. Then, just as she was about to hit the floor face-first, he snatched her by the back of the collar and held her aloft.

"Watcha step, miss," he whispered in her ear. "You

coulda got hurt *bad*."

De La quickly disappeared among the last of the crowd evacuating into the moist spring air. In that one second, he had changed his mind – he no longer had the intent.

Can't be jeopardizin' no mission, he thought. Orders is orders when you out bumpin' curbs.

~ Chapter Four ~

11:55 a.m.

The Marshal held up the bandaged black man like a lost playground toy. "This yours?" he boomed.

MPD Officer Dennis Olsen gave the Marshal a long look up and down. "One twelve? Yep, that's the guy."

Though he didn't like the man's attitude, Olsen admired how the "U.S. MARSHAL" t-shirt hugged his pecs, and he wished he could wear a tight muscle shirt for work instead of his starched baby-blue uniform.

"Don't I gotta sign something?" Olsen asked. "I mean, he didn't look all fucked up like this when I brought him in here this morning."

"No, sir, just take him," the Marshal replied. "I'm serving you with the body. You want to let him go, let him go. You want to bring him back tomorrow, then bring him back tomorrow. The Court don't really give a fuck one way or the other."

Then the Marshall held his hands up high as if he had scored a field goal and called out, "One-one-two, clear!"

"Police releasing criminals," Olsen muttered, grabbing his arrestee by the cuffs. "Only in D.C."

Like most of the 134 men and 15 women scheduled to be brought through the arraignment court that morning, Malcolm X. Stancil – Number 112 on the lock-up list – was being regurgitated to the officer who had arrested him. With the news of the Oklahoma City bombing, Washington D.C. – the very embodiment of the federal government – became just a tad *jumpy*, with the Secret Service barricading Pennsylvania Avenue in front of the White House, bomb-sniffing dogs patrolling the U.S. Capitol, and a muddled FBI warning causing thousands of federal workers to flee for the safety of the suburbs. To make matters worse, when a suspicious bag containing an unknown powder was found near the police officer's entrance to the Superior Court, Chief Judge Armstrong Cummings hastily issued the following order:

SUPERIOR COURT OF
THE DISTRICT OF COLUMBIA

In re.   )
Admin. Order No. 239.   )
_____)

ORDER

Upon consideration of the recommendations of the Metropolitan Police Department and the U.S. Marshal's Service, the Superior Court, by the Chief Judge Armstrong Cummings, hereby:

ORDERS: that the Superior Court be and is hereby CLOSED, effective immediately; EXCEPT that Courtroom C-10 shall continue to hear all felony presentments, probation or parole holds, and arraignment of misdemeanants *currently* before the Court; and

IT IS FURTHER ORDERED: that *all* other cases currently before the court are hereby EXCUSED until 9:00 a.m. Thursday, April 20, 1995 or until further notice; and

IT IS FURTHER ORDERED: that the U.S. Marshal's Service be and is hereby ORDERED to transmit this Order throughout the Superior Court, including all judges' chambers, the U.S. Attorney's "papering office," and the Lawyer's Lounge, and effectuate its content FORTHWITH.

IT IS SO ORDERED.

Signed: Armstrong Cummings, Chief Judge

As Olsen guided his – or rather, McCoy's – prisoner out of the cell block, backwards as it were, over the invisible line that separates the D.C. Superior Court from the Metropolitan Police Department, he realized he didn't exactly know what to do next. So he decided to take a drive, and shoved his ward in the back of his double-parked squad car.

"Alright Mr. Malcolm X. motherfucker," he said, sliding into the driver's seat and pulling a Polaroid camera from the glove compartment, "you know the drill."

Olsen snapped a picture of his battered prisoner, just as he had done earlier that morning at the station-house. Flapping the Polaroid to make it dry faster, he laughed to himself. "Think you're gonna get me on some excessive force claim? Guess again."

Then he started the car and pulled off.

"So, what? You wanna go to the homeless shelter? Or are you one of those outdoorsy types that lives in the Bins?"

The man in the back seat said nothing, his chin down, causing Olsen to curse "Supercop" James McCoy under his breath. "Fucking guy, Mirandizes these assholes at the first fucking instance. Then you can't even hold a polite conversation without some fag lawyer suing you for civil rights."

"Alright, Malcolm X.," Olsen said, taking his eyes off the rear view, "have it your way. I'll just take you to where I found you."

And twenty minutes later, they pulled up to the Fourth District police station on Georgia Avenue, Olsen parking in the shadow of the Eifel Tower-like radio antennae that dominated the skyline overhead.

"Haven't used this in a while," he mused as he pulled his ticket-book from above the visor. When he finished writing and checking the boxes, he got out of the car and opened the back door; the prisoner stepped out and, as if on instinct, turned his back to him; Olsen, on cue, then took off the man's cuffs, and the dance was then complete.

"Lucky for you, you ain't getting another beating today," Olsen said, crumpling up the citation he had just written and shoving it in the man's shirt pocket. "You're hereby commanded to come back to court June 15th. It's all written down for you, right there. If you can even read."

The man didn't move.

"I'm warning you, too, if you don't come back, the court will issue a warrant for your arrest, and then I'll really be pissed. And make sure to wear a clean shirt when you come to court, O.K.? That shit you're wearing stinks." Olsen smelled his own hand and winced. "What'd you do? Take a bath in a tub of turpentine or something?"

The man didn't look up.

"Well, anyway, go on, you're free," Olsen said, taking a step back. "And you can thank your brutha-man, Judge Asshole Cummings."

"I wants my bag."

Olsen took another step back on his heels. "What'd you say?"

"My bag. The one the other police tooken from me."

"You say you want your property, huh?" Olsen stood up tall now. "Well, it'll take me a while to prepare the paperwork. Regs say I got till tomorrow. So, as your main man Michael Jackson says, 'Just beat it!'"

12:43 p.m.

The phone next to the bed rang in Liam's ear.

"Hello," he said, trying to sound awake. "Law Offices."

"Hey, Yum, it's me, Julianne."

Liam felt his skin go clammy.

"Did I wake you up or something?"

"No, yeah, I was just ... working. What's up?"

"Well, you called me, didn't you?"

"I called you? You called me."

"That I did. I called you from work."

"OK?"

"And *then* you called me. At home. I star sixty-nined you."

There was a long pause, and Liam thought he heard Julianne pulling on a joint.

"I'm guessing you're not at work then."

Julianne exhaled. "Of course not. I'm at home. Shit, Yum, don't you know what happened?"

"No. What?"

"Oklahoma City?"

Liam thought quick. In the process of carting all of Julianne's furniture across the country the previous summer, he had stayed overnight in a motel in Oklahoma City after the first day's drive. Lounging at the pool, he had chatted up a plump little girl from Arkansas who was on her way to start college in nearby Norman. The young girl marveled that Liam was going to Washington D.C., that he was a lawyer, that he was driving cross-country all alone, and when her parents took her kid brother off to the Denny's, Liam took her doggy-style in his motel room.

"What about Oklahoma City?" he asked cautiously.

"Oh, wow! You haven't heard? They shut down the

41

Capitol! The whole federal government is closed, I think. It's all over the T.V. Somebody blew up a federal building there. Hundreds of people have died, maybe thousands. And kids, little children .... It's just unbelievable. It's ... sickening. "

"Oh, I didn't hear about that." Liam paused for a moment, wondering if she could sense his relief. "That's terrible, I guess."

"You guess?" Julianne took another long draw on her joint. "Man, Yum, you are cold."

A few seconds passed before she started up again. "So, what's been going on? How's the law biz?"

"Going great. Just great."

"Settle up with any of those prostitutes? A little barter action, maybe?"

"Ah jeez, J, is that why you called? To start that shit again?"

"Sorry, sorry," she said, clearly enjoying herself. "Seriously, I called to see if you wanted a job."

Liam sucked in his breath involuntarily. He hoped she hadn't heard.

"There's a woman who knows my boss's wife," she continued, "whose pastor or some such thing needs a lawyer for a friend. Some kind of *criminal* thing, I don't know much more than that."

"Well hey! That's the kind of thing I do!"

"Weird how your name came up, really kind of strange. My boss asked me to look up the name of a local lawyer, and it turned out to be you. I told him that I, uh, knew you, you know, that I could call you for him. And, well, now here I am."

Julianne coughed a bit, then caught herself. "Maybe there's another lawyer named McNaughton out there. Bet you didn't think about that before hanging out your shingle, did you?"

"Sure didn't."

"Anyway. The Chief Justice of the D.C. Court or whatever is a friend of the Congressman, and – "

"You mean, Chief Judge."

"Right, whatever. Anyway, he – the Chief Judge – owed my boss a favor or something and told him he'd get him the right kind of lawyer for the guy. All I got is a name.... OK, here it is. He's supposed to be in court today, this morning, I guess. Some kind of breaking and entering charge."

"Unlawful Entry?"

"Yeah, Yum, whatever. I'm just telling you what's on this piece of paper here. His name is Shepherd Heyward, Heyward Shepherd, something like that. It says here, Number 112. That's underlined, but I don't really know what that means. Anyway, he needs a lawyer, and the Congressman asked for you, so – "

"Thanks, J, I really appreciate it." Liam was positively giddy. "I'm sure I can help the guy out and all. It's kinda cool, you know, getting a case referred from a Congressman."

"I'll bet."

"You know, I've been meaning to call you, you know, just to see how things are since we last –"

"Look, gotta go now. Should I call my boss and let him know you'll do it?"

Liam could feel his face flush with anger. "Well, is the guy going to pay me, or what?"

"It's all been worked out, I guess, for you to get the case. You know, the public defender thing you do. Isn't that what happens? You go down there, you get the case?"

"No, what's supposed to happen is that you call in when your name comes up in the alphabet and then the cases are sort of randomly assigned and each attorney gets three or four cases." He looked up at his empty wall calendar. "At least that's the way it's supposed to work."

"Well, do you want the case or not? My boss says it's all been worked out. If you don't want it, I'll tell him to give it someone else."

"No, no, that's great. I'll take it. I just got back from court, but it's no big deal to turn around and go back, just as soon as –"

"Alrighty then. So, thanks, I guess. From the Congressman and all."

"No, thank you. Sorry if I sounded pissed off or whatever there. It's just – it's been a while since we talked, and ...."

Liam listened to her breathing in his ear for a few more seconds.

"So I guess I better get going," he finally said.

"Sure. Good luck, Yum. Maybe I'll catch you later."

2:12 p.m.

Annie Fairbrother's phone kept ringing, but she didn't pick up. She knew it was her husband checking in on her, wanting to know when she was coming home. But he'd been with her long enough to know that given the horrific news coming out of Oklahoma City, there would be no way she'd be leaving a job half-done, pregnancy or no pregnancy.

When she heard through the grape-vine that the Superior Court had closed for all business except felony lock-ups, she had decided to lobby the papering office for a felony charge against Stancil. She knew it would be a tough sell. This kind of thing was usually charged as an Unlawful Entry, a fairly routine misdemeanor. But Annie believed a case could be made for Burglary Two – that Stancil had unlawfully entered an uninhabited building with the *intent* of committing some other crime.

Of course, she had no real evidence of the man's intent. And with all that had gone on that day, the judge sitting in the arraignment court would probably give the government hell for trying to charge the crime as a felony. Still, it was worth a try, especially if she could find an excitable newbie to do it for her.

She began dialing the number to the papering office again, but hung up when she saw Josh Boltner, another AUSA on her floor, pass by. "Hey, Josh!" she called out. "C'mere a minute!"

"Hey, Annie. Crazy day, huh?"

The smell of Josh's fresh coffee hit her before she saw the green and white paper cup in his hand. Curse this pregnancy and this infernal hibiscus tea, she joked to herself. I miss my afternoon triple latte!

"Yeah, terrible news," Annie said, clearing her throat.

"My guess, it was the PLO. What do you – ?"

"I dunno. Listen, Josh, were you down at papering at all today? I've been calling them for the last hour or so and nobody's picking up."

"Sure was. I was all ready to start the Shane Yarrow trial. You know, the one with the fire-hose, over by the railroad tracks." He tied an imaginary noose around his neck and made a bug-eyed tongue-out face.

"Sure, Josh, I remember," she said with almost motherly tenderness. Like all of the AUSA's on her floor, Annie felt bad that Josh could never get a case with a good nickname.

"Anyway, I was prepping my civilian witnesses, and then boom! Total fucking chaos down there. Can you believe that asshole Cummings closed the whole court? You should see his order – what a joke! I knew they made a mistake making that guy Chief."

Annie winced. It pained her to hear words so demeaning of the Chief Judge – a former colleague of theirs, for goodness sakes – especially when the same things would never have

45

been said if the man was white. "Well, Josh," she said defensively, "elections do have consequences, as they say. Besides, I heard the Haz-Mat team found a suspicious bag of powder just outside the courthouse."

"And you close the whole thing down on account of some powder?"

"Come on! Ever hear of anthrax? Why just a couple of years ago, an anthrax hoax just about shut down Old Town Alexandria. Case went all the way to the Supreme Court."

"Yeah, well. Any-who, I heard it was just some kind of chocolate protein powder, for weight-lifters or whatever. You know, steroids? Word is that knucklehead Olsen left it there, had his name written right on the bag, so –"

"OK, never mind that. What does the Chief's order say about the ones that got arrested? I got a guy I'm waiting for, picked up last night, probably just a misdemeanor. But I'm going to violate his probation. Maybe I can even stick him with B-2. Remember the guy I had in here a few years back, domestic case, the guy, you know, with the pregnant girlfriend?"

"'The Baby Stomper?' You mean he's out on the street?"

"Yeah, DeMaglio only gave him two years on a split sentence."

"DeMaglio? Really? I always liked that old guy."

"Yeah, well, believe it or not. Anyway, he got picked up today on something petty, and I wanted to jump on him."

"Well, unless he picked up a felony, he's walking back out the way he came in."

"Even guys on papers?"

"Ah, the order did have something about – like those guys were going to be processed if – something, something, and something – I can't remember. Sorry. Things were pretty crazy down there. You shoulda seen it. When word came down that the Marshals were rounding up all the cops in the building and sticking them with the bodies, I never seen the police move so fast to get back to their cars."

"And what are the police supposed to do with them? The bodies, I mean."

"Give 'em citations, I suppose."

Annie looked at Josh with skepticism.

"Yeah, I know," he said, angling for the door. "But I guess that's better than just letting them go. Still, I'd be surprised if you ever see your guy again."

Annie sighed as she swiveled back to the computer. It had taken the IT guys almost two hours to get it up and running again after the security alarm crashed the server; then she had to draw up the Stancil motion from scratch since all the computerized templates had been corrupted. Now, before printing it out, she decided to review it one last time, and quickly realized she would have to make one final change.

Stancil's original court-appointed lawyer – R. Bunning Goodwine – had become some kind of domestic relations judge in neighboring Prince George's County. Annie thought Goodwine had been an excellent attorney, unusually so for a CJA lawyer. Realizing that someone else would have to take his place, she smiled for the first time that day.

"Now let's see if you don't get the plead-and-porter attorney you deserve," she said as she moved her mouse to the "Certificate of Service" section of the motion.

Annie deleted Goodwine's name and address; then she silently read the string of words familiar to every trial lawyer: "I hereby certify that on this __ day of _____, 1995, I mailed, first class postage prepaid, a true copy of the foregoing to:"

And here, she typed in the words "Criminal Justice Act Office, Basement Level, D.C. Superior Court, Washington D.C. 20001 (Defense Counsel To Be Appointed)."

II. Tuesday, May 16, 1995

From the Washington Post, page B5.

Like a determined unit from an aged army, 40 elderly people gathered yesterday morning in front of their drug-plagued Capitol Hill public housing complex and formed, more or less, two marching lines. Accompanied by several Nation of Islam security guards, observed by reporters and monitored by police, the elderly residents of Potomac Gardens, at 12th and G streets SE, twice walked slowly and quietly around the perimeter of the complex, which encompasses a city block.

Their mission: to support the guards, who last week engaged in a series of skirmishes with drug dealers and their sympathizers. The battles left casualties on both sides and the D.C. police on alert. The Nation of Islam guards have an emergency contract at Potomac Gardens that expires today. Most marchers were women in their sixties, seventies and eighties, joined by a few men. Some used canes. One woman was pushed along in her wheelchair. She and others held handmade signs praising the Nation of Islam guards and expressing their desire to oust drugs from Potomac Gardens.

The elderly marchers provided a low-key but sharp counterpoint to the dozens of teenagers and young adults, many of them residents of Potomac Gardens, who profanely jeered the Nation of Islam guards Thursday. One guard was hospitalized with a stab wound in the chest, and another was hit in the ear by a thrown bottle. A teenager who was beaten during the melee was hospitalized with a gash on the back of his head.

Residents, police and guards seemed to agree that much of the tension stems from the fact that the unarmed guards have challenged and disrupted open-air drug dealing at the complex. Despite the installation of a wrought-iron security fence in 1993, sales of crack and heroin have continued in and around the complex.

~ Chapter Five ~

Liam punched in his personal I.D. number and then the "QUICK CASH" button, and the bank machine hummed and clicked before giving its answer: INSUFFICIENT FUNDS.

He tried again, requesting just forty dollars, but out came the same answer: INSUFFICIENT FUNDS. He tried one last time, requesting the bare minimum, and this time the machine spit out a crisp twenty-dollar bill.

Liam snatched the twenty, tossed his crumpled receipt into a nearby cardboard box, and stalked out of the glass vestibule. But something made him stop short. Would a legitimate banking institution really use a ragged cardboard box for a trash can? Curious to see if an account number or some other identifying information was on his receipt, he went back to check.

Cigarette butts, lint balls, aluminum gum wrappers, and perhaps a dozen crumpled bank receipts filled the box, which was crisscrossed with a drizzle of brown spittle. Liam delicately pulled out the receipt and began smoothing out the wrinkles. But when he saw the balance – $4,566.20 – he completely forgot about account numbers and the potential for criminality.

As he tossed the receipt back in the box, Liam came face-to-face with his own reflection in the glass door. He thought he looked the part of a lawyer – nice suit, nice shoes, handsome knot in his tie – but staring back at him was an impersonator, an imposter; someone capable of superficially befriending other outliers, bedding strange women, and charming petty bureaucrats; but incapable of paying the rent, unable to pay a phone bill, adrift in a city of transients, envious of someone else's ATM receipt.

Liam skulked out of the bank and into the neighboring bar.

In a mood like this, there was but one palliative – drinking with the Murder Lawyers.

§ § § § § § § § §

Liam met the Murder Lawyers – as he called them – on his very first day of picking up CJA cases. After completing all twenty minutes of the mandatory orientation, he had been assigned his first case. He was ecstatic, of course, but he simply didn't know what to do next. So he stopped the first lawyer he saw and asked for help.

"First thing – go back to law school and demand a full and immediate refund!" the white-bearded man responded.

Liam was left speechless. But as the crowd began pushing by him to get to the 9 o'clock list, a barrel-chested man smacked Liam on the back.

"Don't worry about him," chuckled the man. "I wouldn't hire Robert E.L. Stucky to fight a parking ticket."

Before Liam could respond, the man leaned in close, and in a conspiratorial whisper, asked, "You know what the 'E.L.' stands for, don't you?"

Liam shook his head no.

"'E. Lee,'" the man guffawed: "Robert E. Lee Stucky. What an ass!"

Liam thought that with his grey streaked blond hair falling over his eyes and his mischievous smile, this man – this lawyer – looked like a giant child, the big kid at the playground who sticks up for the littler ones, so he quickly stuck out his hand and introduced himself, and the man responded by shaking Liam's hand heartily.

"Name's Red Green."

"Red –?"

"Green. My friends call me R.G." Pushing forward to the

9 o'clock list, he asked over his shoulder, "So, you picking up?"

"Picking up? Oh, yeah! I got my first case today."

"Beats dancing at the Hanger Club!"

"The what?"

"Never mind that. You know what you're doing?"

"Of course I do. Actually, no, I don't."

"Well, then, follow me, son. Lemme show you how our thing works here."

Liam tagged along breathlessly as Red flowed through the courthouse explaining the very basics of bringing a defendant through the long slog of arraignment. First, pick-up your assigned client's Pretrial Services Agency biographic report and then check on the list of "no-papers"– the cases the prosecutors are dropping. Next, search for your new client, who will most likely be in the U.S. Marshal's "Bull Pen" or in the lock-up behind Courtroom C-10, and then interview him, but briefly, getting only the basic stuff – name, address, phone number – then get the hell out of the god-awful dungeon. And the last stop: the Lawyer's Lounge, where you check on your client's criminal history and verify the information in the PSA report.

"And then bill your voucher accordingly," R.G. said with a wink.

But as they walked into a dingy alcove underneath the escalator, Liam felt another rim shot coming. "You're pulling my leg, right?" he asked, looking around the room. "This is another lock-up, right? Or where you get the drug test results?"

"Au contraire," Red assured him. "This is in fact the lounge for us lawyers. But between you and me, the only reason I venture into this pit is this – the CCS computer."

The Criminal Court System computer, he explained, accessed a database of every person arrested in the District of Columbia since 1972: names, addresses, aliases, police report numbers, the crimes charged and their dispositions. To demonstrate, he began punching in the names of some of his more notorious clients – violent felons, all – when suddenly he jumped up. "Yikes! I almost forgot. I got this guy's murder trial starting upstairs."

"You're picking up cases *and* trying a murder case?"

"Sure, why not? They didn't have enough jurors for the pool, so I thought I'd check in down here and see if I got anything. Hey, they can't really start without me, can they?"

"I guess not."

"Stop by the National Grille after work," Red said as he dashed off. "It's just across the street. Park in the garage there in the morning and you can get your parking validated from the bar at seven."

"I don't have a car," Liam offered sheepishly, but Red was already off and running.

As it turned out, Liam's first case was eventually "no papered," but he still felt like the day had been a tremendous success: his first time in Courtroom C-10, his first time in lock-up, his first interview of a client. One thing bothered him, though: Why did so many of the other lawyers keep referring to him as a "twenty three one ten"?

He resolved to go to the National Grille that very evening and inquire of Red.

Walking into the air-conditioned steak house, Liam noticed a group of men – obviously lawyers – huddled around the bar. He asked them if they knew where Red Green was.

"He's looking for Little Boo," chortled a dark-skinned Pakistani. "In Edgewood Terrace."

Liam looked at him quizzically. The other lawyers chuckled.

"Maybe you know him?" the Pakistani asked.

"Who?"

"Little Boo."

The other lawyers gagged on their cigarettes with laughter. When Liam started to walk away, the Pakistani pulled out a bar stool.

"Name's Mo," he said, extending his hand. "Please, I meant no offense. You must be R.G.'s intern?"

More laughter.

"Ah, no. I'm a lawyer. Just started doing CJA."

"Well now, new blood!" the dapper Pakistani yelled. "Bartender, Dewars all around!"

Mo (real name, Mohammad Al-Quetta) went on to make introductions all around. With him were Nuggie Phelps, part-time CJA lawyer and full-time scion of a Newport News shipping magnate, and Bobby Conti, a chain-smoking, silver-haired man with dark circles under his eyes. Bobby was in the midst of a four-month long conspiracy trial in the federal court, while Mo said he had been at the U.S. Attorney's Office all day representing a snitch before the grand jury. Nuggie, on the other hand, had recently been suspended from receiving CJA appointments, but he wouldn't really say why.

Over the course of the evening, Liam learned that all of these men – including Red Green, who appeared several rounds later – were twice married and once divorced, with one set of kids in college and another still in elementary school. They all had houses in McLean or Falls Church or Potomac, with big mortgages, huge lawns, and long commutes to go with them. Red, Mo, and Bobby had all been doing CJA from back in the good old days, the mid-to-late 80's, when Reagan's war on drugs provided them with as many cases as they wanted, any day of the week. Now, with the lousy economy sending hordes of lawyers into the ranks of the CJA bar, even the Murder Lawyers were lucky to be assigned the ordinary allotment of four cases every third month. Clearly, they weren't in it for the money – after all, any one of them could have set up shop in Baltimore or in the Virginia or Maryland suburbs and made a fortune as a high priced criminal defense attorney. Nor were they picking up CJA cases because they were bleeding-hearts or true believers – for the most part, they privately despised their own clients and the perverted ghetto culture they came from. No, what the Murder Lawyers really lived for – what they drove an hour-and-a-half each way every weekday for – was the story.

For the Murder Lawyers, the District of Columbia Superior Court was a cauldron of black humor and tragicomedy, garnished with unbridled sexuality, depravity, and fleeting moments of kindness and dignity. With their tales of severed cocks, old lady rapes, and survivors of point-blank shots to the head, they were without a doubt the most sought-after guests at any cocktail party. Among themselves, however, the old war stories had begun to lose their luster, and lacking much new fodder for their nightly binge drinking, the Murder Lawyers had been reduced to trading courthouse gossip, complaining about the judges who cut their vouchers, and general familial kvetching.

So when Liam showed up at the Grille that night looking for Red Green and asking a million questions, the Murder Lawyers decided to take him on as their informal apprentice. In exchange, he was to pay them back in a most sought-after currency: a twenty-seven year-old's tales of sexual conquest and misadventure.

§ § § § § § § § §

As Liam stalked into the Capitol Lounge, the Murder Lawyers were in their usual perch, their cigarette smoke dancing in the beams of sunshine filtering through the dark wooden shutters. Liam ordered a Dewars on the rocks and turned his attention to the muted televisions overhead – all showing the CNN news loop of the caved-in Murrah Building being imploded into nothingness.

"You see the story on CNN about that Japanese cult that got arrested today?" Mo asked no one in particular. "The one that released sarin gas on the subway?"

"At least three times already," Red Green answered drolly.

"You laugh, but I'm telling you, Oklahoma City, international death cults, Newt Gingrich – all these things are connected! Young Liam agrees with me, I'm sure! It's the Jews, right Liam, who are –"

Mo broke off his explanation when Emmanuel Barstow, the only African American among them, walked up and took a stool.

"Brother Emmanuel," Mo called out with a smile. "Salam alaikum."

"Hey, guys," he answered dryly before ordering his drink.

"Hey, Manny, you know the Kid?" Red asked, putting his meaty hand on the back of Liam's neck.

"Yeah, sure, we met a couple of weeks ago."

"Hey, Mr. Barstow," Liam said meekly.

With those words, Nuggie jumped off his barstool, a drunken smile across his face.

"Oh, Mr. Barstow is it? *Mister* Barstow?"

The Murder Lawyers shot Nuggie a look, and he sat back down.

"Yeah, hey kid," Emmanuel said. "Whatever happened with that chick you were talking to that night?"

"That day I met you?" Liam thought about it for a second. "That was the day of the Oklahoma City bombing, wasn't it?"

"Yeah, that's right." Emmanuel threw down his drink in one draw, nodding to the bartender for another. "You all seen that chick in here once before, that blond lobbyist."

Blank stares.

"Works for MCI?"

More blank stares.

"One who drives the red Porsche?"

"Oh yeah," they all responded.

"Come on kid," R.G. commanded. "Give up the details!"

Liam tried to act coy, swirling the ice in his empty drink. "Girl who drives a Porsche.... Hmmmmm. Lemme see if I can remember." Then he moaned dramatically and put his hands on his head. "Oh, that one! The Sperminator? I can't tell you about her, guys. It's just too fucked up."

"Fuck that!" Mo said. "Tell us about the pussy!"

§ § § § § § § § §

"So I came down here that day, thinking I was going to get a case or something. A Congressman referred me the case, I'd like you all to know."

"Probably wanted you to do it for free," mumbled Bobby Conti.

"Pro bono is for suckers, kid," Manny said. "Don't forget that."

"No. No way. Never. No, this was a CJA case, but by the time I got down here, the courthouse was empty. The Marshals told me that the courthouse had been closed hours ago, but I was welcome to check C-10 for any stragglers. Of course, no one was there. Apparently my case had walked out the back door along with everyone else that day."

"Fucking Chief Judge," interrupted Mo. "He's going to drive us to the poor house!"

"If you don't get 'em in the front end, Liam, you might still catch him on the back," Bobby Conti counseled.

"Hmmm, I never thought of that. Anyway, so as I was saying, I came over here to see what's going on, and none of you were here, except for Emmanuel, I mean, Manny."

"Not *Mister* Barstow?" giggled Nuggie.

"Right Nuggie. Whatever. So we're just drinking, watching CNN and all that, and in comes this woman, dressed in this hot red dress, and she sits down next to us. She's like really upset about Oklahoma City, and starts going on about how we should just nuke the Arabs back to the Stone Age and shit. And she's really throwing them down, vodka soaked in pineapples, if I recall, one after another. Then, just like that, she starts giggling and laughing and wanting to dance. At first, she started hitting on Manny."

"Sheeet, kid. She saw that ring on my finger the minute she walked in. She was all over your skinny White ass."

"Well, she was all over everybody. Me, the bartender, the fucking valets. So I had to make my move pretty quick. I told her I was a criminal defense lawyer, and she was like, 'Oooohh, I bet you could get off a bad girl like me.'"

"There you go," offered Bobby Conti.

"Then she sorta started pulling me into the restroom."

"The women's room?" Nuggie asked nervously.

"Hell, I don't even know, to tell the truth. I mean, we were real fucked up." Liam downed the remains of his drink, before continuing. "All I know is she had promised that she gave the best head."

"To the kid!" R.G. toasted.

"So," Mo asked, practically falling off his barstool, "was she a spitter or a swallower?"

"Well that's the kicker, see? First, I gotta say, she did give good head. Best ever in fact. But before we started, you know, she had asked me to tell her before I cum."

The Murder Lawyers all laughed at that one. "Yeah

right!"

"I didn't say anything, of course, and just blew it right in her mouth –"

"To the kid!" R.G. cheered. "Vinny, another round over here!"

"She was kind of pissed, but she was pretty cool about it. In fact, and here's the funny part, she held it in her mouth, and as she was leaving the stall, she turns to me and – you remember that movie 'The Terminator?' Arnold Schwarzenegger? That scene where he goes into the police station, right before he smashes it up?"

"Yeah?"

"Well, so, this girl, she turns to me and says –"

"Oh wait, you told me this one yesterday," Nuggie said excitedly. Popping several pieces of ice in his mouth, he jumped off his barstool and began mimicking the big Austrian. "I'll be back! I'll be back! I am the Sperminator!"

And just that quickly, with Nuggie stepping all over Liam's punch-line, the Murder Lawyers turned their attention back to the CNN news loop.

§ § § § § § § § §

The emerging crowd of lobbyists, congressional staffers, and other front runners around the bar signaled that it was close to seven – time for the Murder Lawyers to get their parking validated. As Liam staggered outside to begin his walk home, he saw that he was not alone.

"Hey, Nuggie. You need a lift or something?"

"Yeah, if you don't mind."

"The Willard again?"

"Nah, take me over to the Hyatt. It's closer to your place."

Nuggie pulled a long chain of keys from his pocket and

weakly tossed them to Liam. The keys skittered loudly along the pavement, and when both men bent down to pick them up, they cracked heads.

"Damn, Nuggie, are you trying to murder me?"

"No intent! No *mens rea!*" Nuggie yelled, his eyes shut tight. "See! I know this stuff! I really do!"

Liam picked up the long key ring – a full set of miniature stainless-steel golf clubs – and handed them to the valet.

"Amigo, do me a favor? There's no way I'm driving tonight. Hold on to his car till tomorrow, and get him a cab." Liam handed the valet his still crisp twenty dollar bill. "Have him taken to the Willard Hotel, they'll know what to do with him there."

Liam then headed off by foot in the opposite direction, trudging up Constitution Avenue towards home. When he reached the apex of the hill, he decided to take a detour and walked onto the west side of the Capitol. There, he took a seat on the cascading marble steps, taking in the picture postcard view of the sun setting behind the Washington Monument and the Lincoln Memorial.

"Now this is what it's all about," Liam said to himself. "*This* is why I came to Washington."

There were numerous people about: several U.S. Capitol police shooting the breeze, joggers running up and down the steps, tourists gawking and snapping pictures, all in anticipation of a glorious sunset.

A man and a woman sat down arm-in-arm a few feet away and began nuzzling, and Liam suddenly remembered the real reason he'd come to D.C.

III. Thursday, June 15, 1995
Part One
From the Washington Post, page D3.

D.C. police arrested a man on a kidnapping charge yesterday after a woman said he and other members of a religious cult forced her to take part in a bizarre ritual on a Maryland farm.

The woman said that on Friday she was beaten and forced to roll in excrement and smear the blood of a duck on her clothes, according to court documents. She said she then was returned to the District and sexually assaulted.

Robert L. Floyd, 30, of the 500 block of Kennedy Street NW, was ordered held without bond at the D.C. Jail. Floyd, a self-employed mathematics tutor, is alleged to be the leader of a group called the Daughters of Yemoja. Authorities said they were trying to learn more about the group and hoped to identify and interview other members.

~ Chapter Six ~

Olsen looked over at his new partner, noting how his biceps barely filled out the sleeves of his starched and pressed uniform. Supercop, ha! he stewed to himself. I don't see what's so super about him.

Turning back to gaze out of the patrol car's passenger-side window, Olsen asked McCoy if he really was the one who found those two girls over in the projects.

"That was me."

Olsen whistled through his teeth. "Geesh! What kind of animal kills a kid?"

"Kids," McCoy replied, emphasizing the plural. "And no smoking in the car. Regulations, you know."

Olsen looked at McCoy – who had not taken his eyes off the road – then at the cigarette in his own hand. "Sure, whatever," he said, putting the cigarette behind his ear. "Regulations."

"Radio's quiet," McCoy said after a turn. "How bout we head over to the U.S. Attorney's Office? I got some business to take care of."

"You go on ahead. I'll be over at the Burger King getting breakfast."

"Most important meal of the day."

Olsen stared out the window, thinking about the indignity of having to "partner up" with McCoy while the Civilian Complaint Review Board investigated yet another excessive force complaint against him. Fucking lawyers, he thought. They just make the world a shitty place to be.

Tiring of the dilapidated scenery that was Georgia Avenue, Olsen turned back towards his partner, gazing at his profile. "Hey! You know who you remind me of?"

"No."

"You ever see that Beastie Boys video on MTV? The one where they dress up like cops and go running over the tops of buildings and shit? You look just like those guys in the video, with your hair, you know, and your mustache and your big sun glasses."

Shaking his head back and forth, Olsen began shrieking:

I can't stand it, I know you planned it!
I'm gonna set it straight, this Watergate!
But I can't stand rocking when I'm in here!
Because your crystal ball ain't so clear!
So while you sit back and wonder why
I got this fucking thorn in my side –
Oh my! It's a mirage!
I'm telling y'all – it's a sabotage!

McCoy smiled politely, eyes forward.

"You know," Olsen confided, "I think most rap is crap. But the Beastie Boys, right? They rock!"

"Sorry. Never heard of 'em."

"You never seen that video? Don't you watch MTV? It's on, like, all the time."

"Don't have cable."

"Don't have –?" Olsen couldn't finish his sentence. He hoped the excessive force investigation would be quick, cause teaming up with this queer dude was gonna be pure torture.

§ § § § § § § § §

Waiting for her computer to boot up, Annie Fairbrother read the Metro section of the Post and tried to sip her mint tea. Even here, after four months of pregnancy, nausea still bedeviled her. Her energy was down. Her mind wandered.

And she had to pee all the time. She was beginning to believe that pregnancy – especially a "high-risk" pregnancy like hers – was not exactly the great time of joy promised by well-wishers and their greeting cards.

When the computer sprung to life, she immediately checked her electronic calendar. Like virtually every prosecutor in the U.S. Attorney's Office, Annie might have as many as a dozen cases scheduled in three or four different courtrooms that morning. Most would be brief matters, such as felony arraignments and show cause hearings, the kinds of things that would be handled in the ordinary course by the AUSA assigned to the particular courtroom. Other matters – the motions hearings, trials, and sentencings – would require her personal appearance.

When she saw the name Jamal Stancil pop-up on her calendar, she froze.

"My lord! It would have to be before the Chief Judge, wouldn't it?"

Annie was in the middle of a jury trial and had completely forgotten about the Stancil matter. She hated going before any judge unprepared, but it was worse with the Chief – they had some history together. Armstrong Cummings had been involved in her recruitment to the U.S. Attorney's Office – at least indirectly – just a year or so before his own appointment to the bench by President Reagan, and their careers paralleled in other ways that Annie hoped were significant for *her* quest for a judgeship. Neither was a native Washingtonian – she grew up in New York, he in Detroit. And neither had any qualms about locking up a brother for life. Both had critics who challenged their "blackness," Annie on account of marrying a Jew, Judge Cummings for marrying a Korean.

And then there was that moment of intimacy – drunken groping, actually – at his swearing-in party.

"Get yourself together, girl," she said, popping out of her chair. "Gotta be the warrior still."

She yanked Stancil's thick case file from off the top of her cabinet, but immediately doubled-over with pain. Her nurse practitioner had warned her not to do a lot of bending or reaching, and now she found out why.

"Sorry, my babies," she said softly. "I won't do that again."

There was no way to adequately prepare for a show cause hearing the morning of, but Annie did what she could. Her paralegal had tracked down the affidavit in support of Stancil's April 19th arrest for Unlawful Entry, so she started there, reading it silently:

> *On 4/19/95, at approx. 0410 hours, undersigned responded to an anonymous 911 call for burglary in progress at 940 North Cap. N.E. Driving to Northwest side of building (Saint Nicholas' School for Girls), undersigned saw S-1, later identified at Malcolm X. Stancil, D.O.B. 11/10/67, climbing a downspout approx. 30 feet off the ground. Suspect was detained without incident. Further investigation revealed that fire-exit door on school roof was opened (no alarm triggered). Said open fire door leads to school cafeteria and then to auditorium, which then and there contained various musical instruments and electronic equipment.*
>
> *Upon arrest S-1 was found to be in possession of one (1) canvas bag (color yellow), containing misc. clothing matter, one (1) paint brush, two (2) empty cans (approx. 1 quart), various personal papers and drawings, miscellaneous magazine clippings and other paper matter, and one large matchbox.*
>
> *An official from the school reported to the scene, and found no visible damage to premises and no property*

unaccounted for. This same official stated that S-1 did not have permission to be on premises. S-1 was arrested and charged with U/E. S-1 read his rights, statement refused.

Annie read the report a second time, highlighting the name "Malcolm X. Stancil" and the date of birth "11/10/67." For a moment, she wondered if her "Jamal Stancil" was the same as this Malcolm X. fellow. She cross-referenced the Pretrial Services Agency's biographical report from the '92 case and found that the dates of birth matched.

"Maybe Supercop's not so super," she mused, "getting tripped up on a fake name like that."

Someone outside of Annie's door cleared his throat.

"Officer McCoy," she said. "Speak of the devil."

The man nodded politely and took a seat.

"Don't get too comfortable now. I only got a few minutes. I'm in the middle of a trial, that big fencing sting that Mike Fuller pulled off."

"The one in Petworth? Hmmph. I believe I gave Detective Fuller some intel on that one."

"Really? I didn't know that."

"It wasn't that big a deal, I guess. I just kept seeing the truck of a guy I had arrested a couple of years ago, coming out of the Hecht's Warehouse with a palette of CD players. I mentioned it to Mike, and after that, I don't know what happened."

"You remembered the car of a guy you arrested two years ago?"

"Not so much the car, just the license plate number. I mean, how many white box trucks are there out there?"

Annie was not sure if this was typical cop bravado. "Sounds like you ought to be sitting for the detective's exam," she said.

"Already took it. Back in November. I gotta make a

decision pretty quick, or else I guess I gotta take it again."

"You mean you passed?"

"Yes, ma'am."

"Why didn't you move up then? More money, right? Better hours?"

"Yep. More money, better hours."

Annie waited for McCoy to say something more, but he just sat there, an awkward smile barely concealed under his silly mustache.

"So I hear you're working on that double at Sursum Corda."

"Yes, ma'am."

"Those poor girls.... Any suspects yet?"

"Working on it."

"Hmmph." Annie sensed the cop's irritation; he obviously took his job as seriously as she did. "Well, I assume you're here on this Stancil thing."

"Correct. The officer who brought him down here on my arrest – Officer Olsen – wrote him up a citation to come back today. I brought you a copy of my affidavit, if you had any questions."

Annie smiled.

"So you're telling me I've got this guy in C-10 on the same day I got him before Judge Cummings for a show cause? How lucky is that?"

"Ma'am?"

"I'm violating him on his probation based on your arrest. We go before Judge Cummings this morning." Annie paused for a second before correcting herself. "*Chief* Judge Cummings. I'm in trial now. Ordinarily I'd let the Assistant in his courtroom handle it. But with this guy, I'm making it my business to be there."

"Think he'll show in either courtroom?"

"With the kind of back-up time he's got, who knows? But before I forget, I got a question for you."

"Shoot."

Annie leaned forward so that she was close enough to hear McCoy's breathing. "Who gave you my home phone number?"

"Ma'am?"

"On the night Stancil was arrested. You called me at home. Remember?"

McCoy leaned back in his chair. "Ma'am, I didn't know you were on this case until this morning when the Liaison gave me your name."

Annie continued to give him the hard stare. It worked.

"Really, Miss Fairbrother. It wasn't me. I didn't call. If I need to get an Assistant after hours, I'll usually just page them."

"I see."

She stared at him for a few more seconds.

"Well then, just one more question. Why do you list the defendant as 'Malcolm X. Stancil' in your report? How could you let this guy get away with giving you a false name? That might have led to his release when he was first brought down here, you know."

"Ah, ma'am ... that is his name."

"No, I don't think so. 'Malcolm X.'? I mean, come on."

"'Malcolm X. Stancil,' that's the name he had on his I.D."

"What I.D.?"

"Well...ah ...." McCoy took a sideways glance at his arrest report. "His baptismal certificate."

The look on Annie's face made clear she didn't like his answer.

"Mayor's Executive Order says we gotta treat that as good I.D. Ma'am, the document looked legit – I mean, it had a raised seal. It had been issued just couple of months earlier – issued by that guy who's been in the papers, Minister And-One."

"Who?"

"Minister And-One. Ex-communicated Catholic priest, the one who started that Moonie church?"

Annie shrugged her shoulders.

"Anyway, the certificate had his picture on it, it had a raised seal, and he didn't have anything else on him. Come to think of it, he did try to give me some other name. Haywood something. But I went with his ID, and he eventually gave it up as his. And the name came back clean, so ..."

"So you didn't know he was on probation."

McCoy grimaced.

"Yeah. This guy Stancil was on probation for Agg Assault. He beat his girlfriend real bad. Eight years back-up time. You gave him a citation when he should've gone through C-10 on a five-day hold. Based on a two month old Baptismal certificate?"

"Ma'am, I ran his name, it came up clean. As I recall, I narrated PC to Olsen, and he brought the body down here. What happened after that, I don't know. I mean, that's why I wanted to bring you a copy of my report myself."

"My paralegal tracked down your report, Officer. But thanks all the same."

"OK, but there's more. I've issued a supplemental. The head of security at the school has contacted me. He's pretty sure that they've had a second break-in. Nothing missing or anything like that. Just that they found that same door on the roof open about two days ago."

"Any surveillance cameras, witnesses, anything?"

"I'm on my way to check that out today. Didn't sound like there'd be anything, though."

"Curiouser and curiouser." Annie began writing some

notes on a legal pad. "Baby Stomper, what are you up to now?"

"Ma'am?"

"Nothing. Don't worry about it. So, anything else you want to add to your report?"

"Well, I gotta theory. There's been a lot of vandalism in that area, broken windows, graffiti, that kind of thing. And maybe you've heard about it, there's been someone spray-painting these swastika-like things on all the hydrants and pay phones around that area. When I see this guy Stancil climbing that drain pipe like some kind of Spiderman, I'm starting to think, maybe this guy —"

"I've got your property report right here, officer. It says he had empty paint cans with him. Right? In the knapsack or whatever he was carrying? And some brushes."

"I'm not totally sure they were paint cans —"

"Not spray paint, though? Right? You think this guy is Michelangelo? He's up there painting with a paint brush?"

"Right, but —"

"And did you find any of these swastikas in the school?"

She didn't wait for his answer.

"No, you didn't. Well, look here. I got a better theory, and it goes like this. This guy Stancil used to beat up his girlfriend real bad. A real asshole this guy. You're a cop. You know the type of guy I'm talking about. The kind that goes after his girl's mother too. Well, wouldn't you know where she works?"

"The girl?"

"No, the mom."

McCoy didn't say anything.

"St. Nicks."

"Oh."

"Look, McCoy, I gotta get going. I'll page you as soon as I get a break from my trial; then I'll just meet you in courtroom

315. That's the Chief Judge's courtroom."

Annie took a deep breath and pushed herself out of her seat.

"Need some help, ma'am?"

"Do I look like I need some help?"

"No, no ma'am," he stuttered. "Just that you look – you are – pregnant, and I thought I could get your bag for you."

"What do you mean, 'I look pregnant'?" she asked dryly.

Supercop looked at her a few seconds, studying her face, then broke out in a big smile.

"Almost got you," Annie said, and the two walked out of her office together, Officer McCoy pulling her rolling briefcase for her.

§ § § § § § § § §

Liam took a quick glance at the giant electronic bulletin board that contained the names of all the judges and their respective courtrooms. His trial – or rather, his client's trial – was scheduled before Judge Simon Wurchseat.

When Liam saw where to go – Courtroom 310 – he ran past the crowd waiting for the escalators and charged up the back stairway two steps at a time. Rounding the second floor, he began to smell an awful fecal odor. Stepping lively at the third-floor landing, he discovered its source: a pile of oozing poo, unmistakably human.

In just six months, Liam had seen virtually every bodily excretion in the hallways, bathrooms, and lock-ups of the Superior Court: blood, puss, piss, spit, vomit, snot, used tampons, used condoms, dirty diapers, soiled underwear. This, however, was a first for shit, or at least human shit (the seeing-eye dog for one of the blind CJA lawyers had crapped in the

Lawyer's Lounge and it was weeks before anyone cleaned it up).

He negotiated his way around this new mess and continued on to the third floor. A hand-written note on the door to Courtroom 310 stated, "All matters before Judge Wurchseat go to 315," so he continued down the dimly lit corridor to Courtroom 315, where, on the door, he found the computer printout of Judge Wurchseat's calendar. Liam's case, <u>United States v. Candy Ennist</u> was near the bottom.

Liam slipped in through the double doors like a ghost. The plan was to find a seat and act as if he'd been there all morning. But two things stopped him in his tracks.

The courtrooms of the H. Carl Moultrie Superior Court are usually crowded, writhing, nervous, sweaty places, with baby's mommas clicking their tongues, cops clipping their fingernails, old men hawking into handkerchiefs, prosecutors whispering confidently to each other. The doors to the courtrooms constantly swing open and closed with court reporters, law clerks, and probation officers coming in and out, and despite the sign that says, "Don't stand in front of the doors!" the lawyers do exactly that, having impromptu conferences, exchanging plea offers, or demanding long-since-produced police reports. The courtroom clerks, meanwhile, call out case after case in lackadaisical voices, followed by one broke-down lawyer after another, beckoning their shuffling clients to take up their respective positions at the defense table so that the judge can berate them for being late, being unready for trial, or for having dirty urine, only to then pass the matter so the defendant and his counsel might have a moment in the hallway to see if something couldn't be "worked out." Things moved even faster when the defendants didn't show up: the case is called, the lawyer – not seeing his client – walks briskly up to the microphone and, paying homage to the empty space next to him, says, "Your Honor, I have no representations." The judge then enters a bench warrant for the defendant's arrest, and the lawyer skips gaily out of the courtroom, happy to be able to turn in his CJA voucher for payment. But oftentimes, he doesn't skip fast enough, as some slow-moving, slow-talking young black man is liable to stand up at this point and say, "Yo Honor? Here I yam," and then, before the lawyer can trudge back to the defense table, the judge will ask, already knowing the answer, "Counsel, would you like some time to discuss the government's plea offer with your client? Maybe try to work something out?"

But this courtroom – Courtroom 315 – didn't have the usual hum of activity; to the contrary, it was eerily quiet. And in contrast to the dull cashew color of every other courtroom Liam had been in, the wood paneled walls of Courtroom 315 were stained a resplendent dark cherry and lined with some two dozen portrait paintings. The paintings all had gaudy frames and were illuminated by museum-quality halogens, and upon closer inspection, Liam could see that the portraits were of the former Chief Judges for the District of Columbia going back to the late 1800's.

He noted that all the faces were white save one: that of H. Carl Moultrie, Chief Judge of the Superior Court from 1978 to 1986, and the first African-American to serve that office.

"Counsel! This is not a museum!"

Liam looked up; it was Chief Judge Armstrong Cummings – the second black man to serve that office – and he was staring right at him.

"Take your seat," he snarled, "or wait in the hall!"

Liam quickly scanned the front rows of the gallery, by custom reserved for lawyers, and saw a single unoccupied chair in between two Fifth Streeters – Robert E.L. Stucky on one side, Ernie "Champ" Shavers and his colostomy bag on the

72

other.   Both men gave Liam satisfied smiles as Champ unstrapped his bag and laid it in the empty seat.

"Counsel!"

It was the Chief Judge again.

"Yes, Your Honor," Liam called out, half standing, half crouching.

"Counsel, maybe you and those other lawyers who snuck in here late – don't think I didn't see you three back there – maybe you don't realize that the Court is handling two calendars today, mine and that of Judge Wurchseat. Perhaps you've not been before me and don't know how I run things?"

"I'm sorry, Your Honor, I'm sorry." There was an empty seat in the middle of the second row, so Liam scooted in, trying not to fall in anyone's lap.

"Counsel!"

"I'm sorry, Your Honor, trying to find a seat here."

"Counsel, you will face the court when addressing it!"

"Sorry, Your Honor."

"What exactly are you here for, sir?"

"Candy Ennist, Your Honor." A few tight chuckles erupted from the courtroom gallery, and Liam felt his face turn red.

"What is your name again, young man?"

"McNaughton, sir, Liam McNaughton."

"McNaughton, eh? Alright, sir, take a seat and we'll get to you in a — Wait a second! McNaughton?"

Leaning over to the clerk, the judge asked his clerk, "Do we have that show-cause jacket? .... It's not on the calendar? .... They can't find it? .... Oh, here's chamber's file. Never mind Miss Macaby." The judge began reading something from the file, and when he was done, he said, "Counsel, please step forward."

Liam put down his briefcase, then bent to pick it up. He

had never been summoned to the bench before, and it took a tremendous effort to force his recalcitrant legs forward. The Chief had turned on the white-noise husher well before he was in earshot of the bench, and when he got close, he realized that the judge was already mid-sentence.

"– but he insisted, and here you are instead. I don't know how this happened. So my question is: how did you get this case?"

"I - I - I picked the case up in C-10, Your Honor."

"C-10? The arraignment court? You don't pick up show causes in C-10, sir. Did you represent Mr. Stancil before, in some other matter?"

"I'm sorry. Who?"

"Mr. Stancil. Jamal Stancil."

"Your Honor, sir, I'm here for Candy Ennist," he said robotically. "On Judge Wurchseat's calendar."

The judge turned off the husher and reclined back in his chair for a few moments, disappearing from Liam's view.

"Madam Clerk," Liam heard the judge say, "get the CJA Office on the phone. Forthwith!"

74

~ Chapter Seven ~

Mal shuffled down the courthouse corridor, clutching a bulging plastic grocery bag hard and tight to his body.

His beard was uneven and sporadic, his lips were cracked and chalky, and a slight tremor affected the right side of his face.   He avoided eye contact, and in a soft voice, repeated over and over, "Never shoulda been born, never shoulda been born."

When the double doors to Courtroom C-10 opened from the inside with a loud click,   Mal held back, watching the grandmas and baby's mommas jam in. A woman with a black mustache – the one who had opened the courtroom – taped a note on the door, and Mal could see that it was a list of ten names. His was number 9.

He took a seat on the long bench in the back, careful to keep his bag close. No one was sitting up where the judge sits, but Mal knew what to expect. He'd been in this spot before, waiting for a white judge to send another brother to jail.

But this time, Mal thought, it's gonna be different. This time, he was going to tell the judge the truth. Tell him, "You can't give me no time, cause I was doing just what I was told to do inside that school."

It's true, I ain't completely finished the job, Mal imagined himself telling the judge. But I dinnit know! When I got out, when I went back to the police for my bag, that's when I found that I still had one of them little Curtain of Life jumps the Minister done gave me.

"OK, OK, it's true. I know, that's not all I done did wrong. It's true I didn't give 'em that secret code name I was taught," Mal said out loud, to the consternation of a smattering of lawyers sitting on the bench next to him.

"Heyward Shepherd," he said, lowering his voice and

covering his face in his hands. "'Poxy fumes musta got to me. Made me forget. Still, ain't no excuse, I know. Lord knows I owe Minister And-One for getting me outta jail so quick that day. Had to be him, right? I mean, who else I know got that kind of juice?"

Mal recalled how Minister And-One used to brag on how all the judges knew who he was. So Mal figured that all he had to do was drop the Minister's name and this here judge would probably take some mercy on him.

On account of how the Minister been helping him stay out of trouble.

On account of the good works Mal'd been doing at that school.

On account of how as soon as he got the old yellow duffel bag back from the police, he had gone straight away to old St. Martin's to thank the Minister personally and give him the respect due.

And more importantly, ask him what to do with that last box of bugs.

Even now, sitting in the back of Courtroom C-10, Mal got the shivers just thinking about that moment of his return to Minister And-One's church. The victim of an ecclesiastical civil war and several tax liens, the gray gothic church was all cobwebs and rot, except for the yellow, gold and green signboard out front. The sign was made of hand-carved wood, and surrounded with crucifixes that were distinctively bent counter-clockwise at their tips, almost like swastikas. Mal himself couldn't read too good, but someone had told him that the church's new name – "St. Gerard Majella's New Moon Temple" – was spelled out there too, though most everyone still called it by its original name St. Martin's.

And while he hadn't exactly expected a hero's welcome at old St. Martin's, he damn sure hadn't expected to see a half-a-dozen of Minister And-One's disciples pouring out after him. Mal had spent many an hour in Bible Study at the church, so he knew these were the hardcore dudes from Cap'n Shubel's Prison Ministry. All dressed in black football jerseys, intent betrayed by wild eyes.

No one had to explain it to him, no one had to write it down – Mal knew to run and run he did.

He'd go on the next few days trying to escape his pursuers and figure out what he'd done wrong. But when the city-wide odor of the trash trucks told him it was Friday, he decided to take a chance and go back to St. Nick's school – the scene of the crime, so to speak. If nothing else, Mal had figured that he was still owed his last paycheck.

But when he got there, Mr. Kim, his boss, shooed him away. "You barred from premises!" he had shouted. "You go now!"

Mal had protested that he was innocent, that he didn't know why the police had arrested him, but Mr. Kim wouldn't hear of it.

"You good worker, but me just contractor," he said, pulling out a wad of hundred dollar bills and quickly peeling off fifteen of them to Mal. "Maybe get job back when court case ova'."

Mal would be the first to admit that being banished from the flock like that – first from the Minister and then by Mr. Kim – had knocked him down a peg or two.

"Surely Yo' Honor will 'preciate that," he practiced saying. "I mean, a nigga gotta be pretty far down to be staying at the Bins."

But what if the judge don't know about no Bins, Mal thought to himself. Well then, he'd have to explain that during his apprenticeship with Mr. Kim, Mal had learned that the brick silos that run along North Capitol Street used to serve as the water filtration and purification system for McMillan Reservoir – the longtime source of the city's drinking water. When the federal government abandoned the place in 1986, the brick sand bins started to crumble, and the area became a no-man's land, a dumping ground, mostly used for dog fights and prostitution, a great place to dispose of dead bodies and other dangerous secrets.

Mal'd been pretty run down before, but he never figured that he'd become one of those deranged bag men who hid themselves and their belongings in the Bins. But sure enough, that's exactly what happened. After his arrest and sudden release, he would spend the next six weeks shuffling between the Bins, a bevy of soup kitchens, and the pauper's cemetery off of North Capitol where his mother was buried.

But then Mal had figured out a way to make it all right again.

It all started on the tail end of the Number 32 Metrobus route, way up in Northwest. The 32 bus was a great way to keep out of the elements, on account of how it went from one far end of the city to the other, but the Metro police had caught Mal sleeping, so off he went.

Walking down Wisconsin Ave, over by American University, he had stopped outside a store selling pretty flowers and trees. A ladybug landed on his shoulder, and he momentarily felt at peace.

"Oh, look, you've got a friend," said a white woman wearing an apron. "Aren't ladybirds just wonderful?"

"Birds?"

"When is a ladybug not a ladybug," the woman mused. "Sorry. That's just what we called them growing up down South."

Mal laughed an insincere laugh. "You work here?"

"I do."

"You ever hear of sumpin called frozen ladybugs?"

"Of course. Organic gardeners use them to get rid of aphids and other bugs."

"For real? How long they stay that way?"

"You mean frozen? I'm not sure. I think they can stay frozen for weeks, maybe a few months."

"Nah, I mean, after you take 'em out."

"Oh. Out of refrigeration? I think you pretty much have to release them within a couple hours."

Mal remembered getting agitated at this point.

"What would happen if, you know, you didn't let them out?"

"You mean, you take them out from refrigeration and then you don't open the packaging?"

"That's right, the packaging."

"They'd probably all die, I presume. They're packed in there pretty tight, I think."

"Wait. Wait a minute. What – what if you had a special box? One that would open up, like, auto – automatic. With a timer, you dig? Say 'bout six months later? What about that?"

The white lady took a step back.

"I really don't know, sir. Why would you want to keep them in a box for so long?"

"For that speech –"

Mal had stopped short, realizing that he may have already said too much. After all, the Minister had told him time and again that the element of surprise was the key to the Curtain of Life.

So he smiled wide to put the white woman at ease.

"It's just real important, ya feel me? The bugs gotta come out alive, see? It's to help the children."

"The children, you say? Well, six months is an awful long time," the white lady said. "We have some catalogues I could

79

check. Maybe they can stay dormant for that long, I really don't know."

She went behind a counter and opened up a book, and after a few minutes of reading, told Mal that if he wanted something that would stay dormant for more than a couple of days, he'd be better off with praying mantis eggs, which took about four weeks to hatch.

"Or spined soldier bugs, or parasitic aphid wasps," she said. "All of which are commercially available. We can get them here tomorrow by Fed Ex, or thirty, forty-five days regular delivery."

"Dem praying jumps, how many can I git for a hundred fifty? I need bout twenty five."

Now, sitting in the courtroom, nervously awaiting his name to be called, Mal mentally corrected himself, remembering the box that was left over.

"I shoulda said twenty fo'."

§ § § § § § § § §

"So look," Olsen said, his voice cracking. "At some point you're going to have to let me do some driving."

McCoy slowly pulled the car to a halt, opened his door, and walked around to the passenger side.

"Scoot over," he said through Olsen's open window.

Truth is, McCoy hated driving – the street proved too distracting for him, and having Olsen drive might allow him go to full meditation zone. Thirteen years as a police officer had taught him to view the human horror stories he routinely encountered not as random events but as a part of a complex web that formed the basis of an ordered universe. He believed somewhat messianically that he was uniquely gifted with the ability to decipher these linkages, understand their intersections

80

and cross-currents, and, in his capacity as a law enforcement officer, use these skills to benefit society as a whole.

Olsen peeled off as soon as he got behind the wheel. "Now that's what I'm talkin' 'bout!"

McCoy quickly buckled himself in. He would have to have a talk with Olsen at some point, get him straight on some basic things. But right now, all he wanted to do was study the D.C. road map he kept in the glove compartment.

Spreading the map on his lap, he drew a big red dot over the intersection of North Capitol and H Streets N.W. – site of St. Nicholas' Interparish School. Then he did the same for the unit block of L Place N.W. – the heart of Sursum Corda. He examined the map, holding it out at various distances. Two crimes – one, a simple trespassing, the other, the cold-blooded murder of two teenage girls – committed within minutes of each other, less than a couple of blocks from one another, but otherwise unrelated in any meaningful way.

"So, whatcha doing there?" Olsen asked.

"Triangulation."

"Oh yeah? I heard of that."

"Hard to do with just two points."

"Just connect the dots, right?"

McCoy took a sideways glance at his partner, then did just that, extending the line to the edges of the paper.

Several things immediately jumped out at him: the line between these seemingly random points crossed directly over the Fourth District's Georgia Avenue Station (the last place Malcolm X. Stancil was seen) and through the massive Potomac Garden housing projects in Southeast Washington (Stancil's last known address, at least according to the probation office's records).

Of course, it all could be pure coincidence. McCoy imagined he could draw a line across any two points in the city and come up with some remote connection to this inconsequential mope. But if nothing else, the line served as a starting point to his extrasensory investigation. If the line between them doesn't connect these crimes, he concluded, then logic dictates that the space on either side must.

§ § § § § § § § §

"Citation case number nine. United States versus Malcolm X. Stancil."

Citation in one hand, grocery bag in the other, Mal staggered forward, unsure of where to go. A well-dressed black lady suddenly appeared next to him. "If you want to get out of here," she whispered in his ear, "don't say nothin' at all."

Then a well-dressed white lady stepped next to him on the other side and began telling the judge that Mal had broken into a school and should be held in jail because he was on probation. Mal immediately spoke up, explaining as quick as he could that he had been working at the school and, besides, he had gone back and fixed everything, all twenty four of them, but the black lady kept shushing him.

"Government's request for a five day hold granted," said the judge mid-yawn. "Counsel, when do you want him back?"

"I'm just stand-in counsel today, Your Honor," said the shushing lady. "Looks like the underlying probation case was Bunning Goodwine's case. CJA Single Representation Plan, Your Honor. This case should be assigned to him too. Set it for – whenever."

"Alright, we'll set this down on the misdemeanor calendar. Set it for next Thursday, that's the twentieth I think."

"Thank you, Your Honor," the two women said in unison as they turned and walked away from the judge.

Mal tried to follow suit but was quickly grabbed from behind by two muscle-bound white guys. "Right this way, bub," one of them whispered in his ear. "You're coming with us."

Mal jerked his arm away when one of the men tried to take his bag, and the other muscle-bound white man was on him in an instant, pressing that same arm up behind his back and causing him to involuntarily twist with pain.

"Stop resisting!" the man kept telling him, "and I'll let up!"

"Mister Stancil! Mister Stancil!" the judge finally yelled. "You have to go with the Marshals. You'll be back in court next week, alright?"

"But, Yo Honor!" Mal stammered. "I gotta get back to the Bins or they'll all die!"

"Tell your story to your lawyer, Mr. Stancil. I'm sure he'll be able to help you out."

"But they're in my bag, don't you understand?"

"The Marshals will take good care of your property, sir. You'll get your bag back once your case is –"

"No! Not this bag!" Mal screamed as the Marshals dragged him away. "The one I done left in the –!"

"Oh, these homeless guys and their bags," the judge said under his breath as the metal door clanged shut on Mal's protestations. "Alright, Madam Clerk, call the next case."

§ § § § § § § §

When the Chief Judge finished his muted phone call, he leaned his seat forward and said, "Alright, counsel, you've kept us waiting long enough as it is. Miss Macaby, call the case."

"On the court's add-on calendar," the clerk called out, "calling the case of the United States versus Jamal Stancil, case number ...." The woman's voice tailed off. "Your Honor, we still do not have that file."

The Chief ruffled the papers in front of him. "For the record, Miss Macaby, that case number is F1045-92."

A prosecutor with a military-style buzz cut barked out, "Sir, yes sir! Dan Gerson, for the United States, standing in for ...." The prosecutor quickly scanned a piece of paper. "Annie Fairbrother, Your Honor, sir!"

Liam, meanwhile, began wandering back towards the audience.

"No, no, no, counsel," the judge chided. "Your place is at defense table. This is *your* case, sir."

"Your Honor, I'm sorry. Like I said before, I thought the only case I had was on Judge Wurchseat's calendar, Candy Ennist."

"Mr. McNaughton, you are the assigned counsel in a show cause matter that appears on my calendar. I assume by your reaction you have not yet met with your client."

Liam looked at his shoes and bit his lip.

"Counsel, you must have received the show cause notice. My chambers mailed it to your office almost two months ago. I appointed you to take over the case from Mr. Goodwine. I was told you agreed to take the case."

"No, no sir," he stammered. "I don't think I received that notice. I mean, if I did, I certainly would be here."

Several of the Fifth Streeters in audience guffawed loudly, but the Chief Judge held out his hand to silence them. "Mr. McNaughton, your office is at 1616 Columbia Road Northwest, correct?"

"Ah, no sir, I'm on Second Street Northeast. Apartment Number – I mean, Suite Number –"

"Your Honor," a voice drawled from behind Liam. "I believe I can help." It was Robert E.L. Stucky, sidling up to

84

the defense table. "That must be *my* case you're talking about."

"Well now. Mister Stucky." The Chief Judge flared his nostrils. "You say this is your case, do you?"

"To be precise, Your Honor, it's William McNaughton's case. He's my law partner, of course. You remember Billy McNaughton! Bilko Billy? Well now, that's our address, Your Honor, right there on Columbia Road."

Liam raised his hand to get the judge's attention.

"One moment, counsel," the judge said. "Mr. Stucky, are you saying – ?"

"Yes, Your Honor, clearly a mistake has been made here. I am guessing that this case was supposed to be assigned to Mister William McNaughton, not this young man."

"You guessed wrong, Mr. Stucky. I've already confirmed with the CJA office that the court appointed Mister McNaughton here and we've checked the bar number. Notice was just sent to the wrong office. Have a seat now."

Liam raised his hand again, this time holding up a pen. "Your Honor – "

"No offense to counsel," interrupted Stucky, "it's just that he is, shall we say, of fairly recent vintage. A felony show cause is certainly no place for a rookie lawyer to cut his teeth."

Liam felt the hair rise on the back of his neck.

"Mr. Stucky, the court appreciates your concern," the judge said through a clenched jaw. "Be that as it may, the CJA office just made me aware – and let the record show that it is precisely 10:50 in the morning – that your law partner Billy McNaughton is no longer with us. That he died, what, three years ago?"

Stucky looked momentarily dazed. Then he mouthed the words, "Are we on the record?"

"We most certainly are on the record, Mr. Stucky. Most certainly are!"

85

"Well, ah, yes, judge, it's, ah, true. His death was – was a shock, a real loss for us all, Your Honor. Oh, how I miss old Bilko Billy. Anyway, I can assure you, Your Honor, that –"

"Mr. Stucky, I can assure *you* that as Chief Judge, I do not intend to interfere with the, ahem, smooth workings of the CJA Office, be that as they may. I give them the cases, they give me the lawyers. Of course, from time to time, I take the prerogative of assigning the cases myself, as was the case here. Am I making myself clear, Mr. Stucky?"

"Yessir."

"Now that I've been made aware of Mr. William R. McNaughton's demise, I assure you that the CJA Office will no longer burden you and your vast partnership with any more of his appointments."

"Just trying to help," Stucky said, retreating from the lectern and leaving a foul smell trailing behind him.

"Now, Mr. McNaughton," the Chief called down. "Are you willing to accept this appointment? This is a domestic case, and these cases can be very tricky. I see here that the defendant pled guilty to assaulting his girlfriend, or wife, I don't really know all the details. This was Judge DeMaglio's case. I suspect that you never appeared before Judge DeMaglio?"

"No, Your Honor."

"Her injuries must have been serious, since this was an aggravated assault." The judge read the papers closely now. "He kicked her."

"O.K."

"In the stomach, evidently."

"In … the … stomach. Yes, yes, Your Honor, I got that."

"Put your pad away, Mr. McNaughton," scolded the judge, "and look up here. I want you to keep in mind, sir, that the court is going to be watching you very carefully in this regard. A felony show cause is a serious matter, and Mr. Stucky may well have been right – I'm not so sure that this case wasn't meant for someone else. But for now, it's your case. There's a new arrest that has triggered this hearing, an Unlawful Entry, if I'm correct. You'll have to look into that. You would be well advised to seek out the counsel of someone –" and here the judge scanned across the sneering Fifth Streeters seated in the front row "– someone who can counsel you on how to proceed in such matters. None of this is as easy as it looks."

"Yes, Your Honor, I certainly will."

"Now then. Your client evidently isn't here, and you haven't seen the government's show cause motion, so I will issue a bench warrant for Mr. Stancil. And Mr. McNaughton, as for your other matter, the case on Judge Wurchseat's calendar, you should get down to Judge Malley's courtroom right away. I've referred all of those trial matters to him. Make sure on the way out you give Miss Macaby your praecipe with your correct address."

"Thank you, Your Honor."

"And counsel, here," the judge said, leaning over the bench. "Take this copy of the government's show cause motion."

Liam gingerly took the papers out of the judge's hand, then slid over to the courtroom clerk's desk.

"Here ya go, Honey," the kindly old black woman whispered, handing him the triplicate entry of appearance form. "You bring that back later. Soon as I can, I'll let Judge Malley's clerk know you're on the way down."

Liam mouthed the words "Thank you," and then bolted out of the courtroom, thinking, Maybe the learning curve has finally broken my way.

~ Chapter Eight ~

"So where to, Supercop?"

McCoy ran his finger along the line that crossed his map and noted how it intersected with the eastern-most corner of the McMillan Reservoir. "Right here on K. Then left on First Street."

"Aw," Olsen moaned. "Tell me we're not going into the Bins today."

"You said you wanted to drive. So we're gonna drive."

"Okey dokey, boss." Olsen jammed on the accelerator as they rounded the corner, the car fish tailing towards a group of transvestite hookers meandering in the curb lane.

"OK, just one thing," McCoy said, grabbing the armrest. "Well, two things really. First, don't let Sarge know you're driving."

"Sheeeet, you think I'd squeal on my own damn self?"

"Right. Second thing is you go the speed limit. Or slower. I get motion sickness."

"Motion sickness."

"So keep it slow."

"OK, I got it."

Olsen hung his left arm out the window and patted a tune on the car door. "Do we have a great job or what?"

"The best."

"You know, McCoy, I almost got in with the Maryland State Police?"

"Really?"

"Yessir. I'm from Maryland. Waldorf, actually."

"Mmm-hmm."

"Ever been there? To Waldorf?"

"Sure."

"Oh yeah?"

"My folks ran a couple of liquor stores in the city. The Black and White. We used to go out to Waldorf once in a while for wholesale."

"The Black and White? Not that the one over there on New York Avenue? The one that's all burned out?"

"Yep. That was the first one. Me and my brothers all grew up right upstairs."

"On New York Avenue?"

"Yep. My dad had other stores. H Street. Nannie Helen Burroughs. One on Capitol Hill. After the riots, though, my folks basically retired. They kept one store, up on Connecticut and Cathedral."

"Connecticut Avenue?" Olsen snickered. "Not a lot of people protesting 'Doctor' King so much up there, eh?"

Meticulously, McCoy began to fold the map back up. "You know, Dennis, my father taught me that if you focus on the color of a man's skin, you miss the eyes, and the eyes tell the whole story. My dad used to stand by the door and greet everyone as they walked in, white and black, looking each person in the eye. Maybe that served as some sort of deterrent, or maybe it just confused folks with bad intentions – I never did figure it out. But in all the years on New York Avenue, we were never robbed. Not once."

"Place looks like shit now. No offense."

"Yes, well, burned to the ground, now that's another matter," McCoy said reflectively. "After the riots, my parents plowed their insurance money into the one store that wasn't torched – in Upper Northwest. The one on Connecticut. AU Park they now call it. But my dad took the move hard. He started to sit at the cash register – nursing a bum hip, he would say – instead of standing by the door like he used to. And that's what I believe got him killed."

"What? Your dad was killed?"

89

"Yep. A kid, just fifteen years old. Pulls a gun on Da', robs him of the nine hundred and thirty two bucks in the register, shoots him in the chest on the way out."

"Fuck, dude. That's harsh."

"The kid who did it, caught just minutes later, trying to carjack a Metrobus for his escape."

"So you know who did it?"

"I was seventeen at the time, my brothers were both in the Army. You know how the juvenile proceedings are closed to the public? Well, imagine me and my grieving mother being subpoenaed to come to court every day for a trial we were never gonna see. Just sitting there in the hallway...."

"You mean the little fuck got away with it?" Olsen said after a moment.

"Well, yes and no. After a couple of days, we learned that he had pleaded guilty – 'involved' is what they call it for juveniles. And I'll never forget it – I caught a glimpse of him when he was led out of the courtroom. He was laughing, smiling. City prosecutor told my mom that the kid would go to Oak Hill for a long time. But something never seemed right to me about that whole scene, and years later, I found out why. You probably remember it from the text book – the case of In re. De La S."

"Ah, what?"

"'Even juvenile offenders must be read their Miranda rights.' Remember that? From the Police Academy text book?"

Olsen stared ahead blankly.

McCoy placed the map back in the glove compartment.

"Yeah, that was my Da'."

§ § § § § § § § §

"Look, man, I don' know what to tell you!"

De La Suggs lowered his voice. He realized he was speaking too loudly for a public payphone, particularly one in the middle of the courthouse.

"It's jes like last time. They got a hundred-sumpin names on the list, and the nigga ain't there. The next list don't come out till after lunch. Why we need him anyway?"

De La held the phone away from his ear. He could feel the blood rushing to his head, the feeling he got when he was being disrespected.

"OK, OK, you right, we each got our roles and whatever, whatever. I just tired of chasing a fucking ghost, that's all. He ain't back with his girl out in the projects. I been looking all round the Bins like the Minister says. I even done waited for him to come back to the school. Nigga ain't never gonna show up if you asking me."

De La waited for the voice on the other end to respond.

"Now? You coming down here now? Well whatchu want me to do?"

As the white man gave his answer, De La began calculating the numbers in his head.

"The Korean plumber? O.K. Standard price, ten G's. Just tell me the where and the when and the how, O.K., and I do it."

As he listened to the details of the job, De La admired all the fat booty in halter-tops going up the escalators. "Damn, girl," he said softly, "You thick!"

The stern white-man voice snapped De La back to attention.

"I got it, I got it. You want me to find out if the Korean told anyone bout Greek Fire. O.K., then, tell me what the fuck Greek Fire is?"

91

De La pulled the phone from his ear again.

When the screaming stopped, he said, "Yo, Captain, chill out. I'm a professional. You a professional. You say I don't need to know what Greek Fire's all about, that's cool. But if you want me to squeeze a man 'fore I kill him, that's gonna cost an additional ten. Specially if I ain't to know exactly what I'ma squeezing him for. Understand?"

De La smiled as he hung up the phone. Just as he had predicted, this job was turning into a real gold mine.

§ § § § § § § § §

Liam strode tall into Judge Malley's courtroom and craned his neck to look for his client, Candy Ennist. The only white girl prostitute he'd ever been appointed to represent, she should have been easy to pick out among the weather-beaten black faces looking back at him.

"Oh well," he thought, casually sitting down. "Looks like there won't be any trial today."

While he waited for his case to be called, he began reading from the show cause report the Chief Judge had handed him. In 1993, one Jamal Stancil had pled guilty to Aggravated Assault, with the court sentencing him to ten-years, with all but two years suspended, followed by four years of probation, and a thousand dollar fine. According to the government's motion, the man had picked up some new charge – an Unlawful Entry evidently – and as a result, the court had summoned him to "show cause" why his probation should not be immediately revoked.

When someone began coughing asthmatically behind him, Liam suddenly looked up to see an almost empty courtroom. Worried that his case may have already been called, he slunk up to the clerk and whispered, "Candy Ennist?"

The clerk gave him a look of disdain. "Where have you been? We called that case an hour ago!"

"But I thought Miss Macaby –"

"We'll be calling your case for trial momentarily, counsel. Your client is in the back if you want to speak to her."

Liam stood there in shock, thinking, Candy is here! Candy's in the back! There will be a trial after all!

He rushed over to the young white Marshal who guarded the door to the lock-up.

"Good morning! Here for Candy Ennist. I understand you have her."

The Marshal put down the karate supply catalog he was reading and looked at the list on the door. "Go ahead."

A thick iron door separated the cashew-colored courtroom from the steel and stench of the dungeon that lurked behind – two identical holding cells, one packed with a dozen black men in bright orange jumpsuits, the other holding a single white woman sitting with her head in her hands. She was in a blue jump suit.

The orange-clad men, standing shoulder-to-shoulder, began the predictable calls. *"You my lawyer?" "D'ya see Mr. Stucky out der?" "Dude, you gotta cigarette you can give me?" "Yo, what time is it up in here?" "Cun I barra ya ink pen, Mista?" "Yo mon, I ain't even sposed to be up in here. Cun you help me now?"*

Liam ignored them the best he could.

"Miss Ennist?" he said gently. "Miss Ennist, it's me, Liam McNaughton."

"Yeh?"

"Your lawyer?"

"Oh yeah," the woman said, looking up slowly. "I remember you. You bought me a scrapple-egg-n-cheese. That was real sweet." She smiled broadly, exposing her missing,

93

yellowed, and darkened teeth.

Liam tried not to look away impolitely.

"Uh, what are you doing back here? Didn't I get you out on PR?"

"I went and picked up another charge," she sniffled. "But Mister McNugy — McNugyton – Sir, they said that I was possessing some heron with intent, but they didn't read me my rights, so I didn't think I needed to go back to court."

"Wait a second. You picked up a new case after mine?"

"Yeah, right after we was in court."

Liam stewed for a moment. That should've been my case too, he thought.

"So why didn't you call me, you know, let me know what was going on?"

"The judge done sent me to the half-way house. But some P.A. bitch tried to pull some shit with me, so I called my old man Bennie, you know, the one they call 'Bennie No Thumbs,' and anyway he come and get me. The same officer who caught me tricking up round the Bins? Officer Gilroy? He the one that caught me with the heron in my purse. Now they got me over CTF."

"Well, whatever. Do you want me to see if there is a plea offer that will maybe take care of all your cases? Maybe they'll even send you back to the half-way house."

The woman put her hands over her face and began weeping.

"Miss Ennist? Miss Ennist? I mean, we can have a trial – if that's what you really want."

"Mister Lawyer, sir, I don't care 'bout no trial! Just look what they done to my leg!" She pulled back the left pant leg of her loose-fitting jump suit, exposing a bright pink stump.

"Oh my God! What –?"

"I jes wanna go back home," she sputtered. "I jes wanna

see my momma again. Why can't you get me outta here?"

The din from the neighboring male cell quieted, and Liam took a step back, knocking over a pair of tiny aluminum crutches.

Candy suddenly hopped up on her one remaining leg and wiped her nose on her sleeve.

"Could you give me those, please, sir?"

"Sure, Miss Ennist. Anything you need."

As Candy reached through the bars for the crutches, her shirt sleeve fell back, exposing the gangrenous sores and tract marks that dotted her milk-white arm. When she caught Liam staring, she began swinging the crutches wildly against the bars.

"Anything I need? God-damn jailhouse doctors stole my leg! I knows what you're thinking! But it was God-damn niggers!"

The momentary empathy from the next cell immediately ceased, with the orange sardines laughing and making jokes. *"How you gonna trick now, fuckin' skeezer?" "Go on, there, white girl, you still got yo' money maker!" "Bitch, I got yo' leg right ere!"*

The din quieted only slightly when the karate catalog Marshal burst through the door, followed by two black muscle-bound titans. "Counsel, get out now!"

Liam scurried back into the courtroom, and a second later, the big black Marshals thundered after him, one carrying Candy under her arms, the other with the aluminum crutches in his fists. Karate Catalog followed close behind, scanning the room until he locked eyes with Liam.

Liam quickly turned his focus on the judge.

With his Brylcreem comb-over, Judge E. Edward Malley bore a startling resemblance to Gerald Ford, the President who had appointed him. Judge Malley was known to attend Mass

95

every day at noon; and as the clerk called out the case of <u>United States versus Candy Ennist</u>, Liam caught him eyeing his watch.

"Counsel," he said tartly, "we were ready for you some time ago. But Miss Farmington has informed me that you had another matter before the Chief Judge this morning. Is that so?"

"Yes, Your Honor, that's right. A show cause. I thought his courtroom clerk, Miss Macaby, had –"

"Sir, you're fortunate I didn't just proceed without you."

"Proceed – without me?"

"It's your client who has business before this court, sir, not you. Whether you appear or not is a matter between you and the disciplinary committee."

"I'm so sorry, Your Honor. Please –"

"Next time you're in court before me, Mr. McNaughton, I want you to remember something. It is the policy of this court – the Superior Court – that trials come first. As counsel, you must appear in the courtroom where your trial is scheduled – first. That means before going to any other courtroom, regardless of who else you may have matters before, even if your trial is set on the misdemeanor calendar. First! Do you understand?"

"First, Your Honor, I understand. Yes, first. I apologize."

The judge now turned his attention to the prosecutor. "So, Mister Pledge, is the government ready for trial?"

"For the record, Your Honor, Jayson Pledge for the United States. We have one to two witnesses."

"And for the defense?"

Out of the corner of his eye, Liam saw his client looking at him plaintively. "If I may have a brief pass, Your Honor, to see if we can work something out?"

"No, sir, you may not. Today is trial. The time for discussing pleas was before today." The judge looked at his watch again. "I am going to certify this case for trial to ... ah,

Madam Clerk? Ah, yes, Courtroom 201. I believe Commissioner Corley is in there.... What's that? She's gone?"

The judge leaned over to his courtroom clerk and handed her the file. The dread-locked black woman and the Gerald Ford clone then shared a brief laugh between themselves, as the judge could clearly be heard saying, "Happy hour started early again, eh?"

Judge Malley cleared his throat before turning his attention back to the lawyers. "Well then, Miss Farmington has just notified me that Courtroom 201 is down and will not resume until one o'clock. Mr. Pledge, if you would be so kind as to take the court jacket with you. Thank you. And you there, counsel, what is your name again?"

"McNaughton, sir. Liam McNaughton."

"Well, Mr. McNaughton, if your client wishes to dispose of this case through a plea, I suggest you talk to Mr. Pledge on the way upstairs. Should you reach a plea agreement, notify Commissioner Corley. Court stands in recess until 2 o'clock!"

And with that, the judge spun off the bench and out the door.

Liam gathered up his briefcase, followed the prosecutor out of the courtroom, and then collapsed on one of the brown plastic chairs that lined the hallway. He exhaled deeply, then heard a voice close to his ear hiss, "Hey, counselor."

It was Karate Catalog, red-faced and clenching his fists.

"You're the one who gave your client those crutches, aren't you?"

"Yes. I just thought –"

"Well, don't do that again!" he screamed, drawing the attention of the other people in the hall.

"OK, OK, I got ya."

"I can get you barred from lock-up for doing stupid shit like that! No pens, no candy, no cigarettes! Nothing!"

97

Liam stood up, wiping the Marshal's spit off of his face, thinking, I'm the lawyer here, I'm not the one who is supposed to be fielding questions. About to lose his cool, Liam tried to flip the script.

"Hey look, I'm still sorta new around here. I just didn't know. They don't teach this kind of thing in law school." It was a trick he had learned by mistake, really. He had spent his first months of practice trying to create the impression that he knew more than he did – a charade that almost uniformly lead to bad results. What worked much better, he ultimately learned, was to swallow his pride and admit what he didn't know – then he got a lot of rookie play.

"Ah, it's alright," Karate Catalog said, backing off. "You didn't know. I just started down here myself a year ago, so I know what it's like. Just please don't do it again. I coulda got in trouble."

"You betcha. Again, I'm sorry."

Liam stuck his hand out to shake, but the Marshal had already begun to walk away. Liam waited for him to turn the corner before gathering his briefcase and heading the same way.

The once crowded hallway had emptied, except for one pot-bellied white dude sitting across the hall, eyeballing Liam. With his five o'clock shadow, ponytail, and Buffalo Sabres jersey, the man looked every bit the undercover cop, and as Liam walked past, the man gave him a shit-eating grin and a stiff Heil Hitler salute.

"Asshole," Liam said under his breath.

IV. Thursday, June 15, 1995
Part Two

I've got jungle fever
She's got jungle fever
We've got jungle fever
We're in love
She's gone black-boy crazy
He's gone white-girl hazy
Ain't no thinking maybe
We're in love

Stevie Wonder, Jungle Fever (1991)

~ Chapter Nine ~

THE COURT: Alright, Madam Clerk, hand me the jacket please. Thank you. Where are we with this case. And who are you, counsel, for the record?

MR. PLEDGE: Jayson Pledge, for the government, Your Honor.

MR. MCNAUGHTON: Liam McNaughton, Your Honor.

THE COURT: So this is not a plea? You couldn't work something out?

MR. PLEDGE: No, Your Honor. We are ready for trial.

THE COURT: Ok, are there any preliminary matters? Counsel?

MR. PLEDGE: None from the government, Your Honor.

MR. MCNAUGHTON: Your Honor, we do have a motion to dismiss filed.

THE COURT: You do?

MR. MCNAUGHTON: Yes, Your Honor. And the government hasn't responded. So I ask that that motion be deemed conceded.

MR. PLEDGE: We object to that, Your Honor.

THE COURT: Just one minute there. OK, here it is. Is this why this file is so thick? Your motion, sir, what is this, Yellow Pages ads?

MR. MCNAUGHTON: Precisely, Your Honor. It's selective prosecution for the government to go after street prostitution, alleged street prostitution, when the high end of the business – the escorts – advertise quite openly in the Yellow Pages. There are more ads for escorts in Washington D.C. than there are for lawyers.

THE COURT: I find that hard to believe.

MR. PLEDGE: Your Honor, this is just a boilerplate motion that all the CJA lawyers file. It's our position that the U.S. Attorney's Office can prosecute whomever we want. If a police officer witnesses a crime, he has a legal obligation to make an arrest. You can't dismiss this case just because we haven't arrested all of the prostitutes and escorts in town.

MR. MCNAUGHTON: Your Honor, that's a little simplistic. It's an equal protection question we're talking about. What's the rational basis for treating two different classes of prostitutes differently?

THE COURT: I've heard enough. I know about this motion. Judge Mendelsohn, I believe, denied it, and I adopt his ruling here. I deny it.

MR. PLEDGE: Thank you, Your Honor.

THE COURT: Ok, how many witnesses?

MR. PLEDGE: Just one witness, Your Honor.

THE COURT: What? OK, one witness. And you there, Mister –

MR. MCNAUGHTON: McNaughton.

THE COURT: Right. So how many witnesses, sir? Are we on the record? Madam Clerk, has this case been called?

[inaudible]

MR. MCNAUGHTON: Just one, Your Honor, maybe.

THE COURT: OK, I'm not sure we were on the record just there. This is the case of United States versus – I can't see this – oh, — Candy Anus. Mr. Pledge and defense counsel are present, the defendant is present.

MR. MCNAUGHTON: It's Ennist, Your Honor.

THE COURT: What?

MR. MCNAUGHTON: Candy Ennist. E-N-N-I-S-T. Ennist.

THE COURT: Let's move along, counsel, we don't have all day.

MR. PLEDGE: Were you talking to me, Your

Honor?

THE COURT: Yes, sir, call your first witness, please.

MR. PLEDGE: Ok, Your Honor, it's just, I thought you were talking to me.

THE COURT: I am talking to you, Mr. Pledge! Put on your first witness. It's almost time for the afternoon break.

MR. PLEDGE: Your Honor, I would like to give my opening first.

THE COURT: Mister – counsel, your client, Miss Anus, is she really going to testify? I mean, come on!

MR. MCNAUGHTON: I guess not, Your Honor. Miss Ennist has been through some pretty serious trauma over at the jail. Miss Ennist tells me that she lost her leg. An infection or something like that, Miss Ennist tells me.

THE DEFENDANT: Goddam niggers stole my leg, that's what happen!

THE COURT: We will have order in this courtroom! Madam, you will sit down this instant.

THE DEFENDANT: Hands off!

MR. MCNAUGHTON: Sorry.

[inaudible]

MR. MCNAUGHTON: — the Marshals. I think she's ok now.

THE COURT: Miss Anus! Miss Anus! You will sit down right now. That's OK, Marshal! No, that's not necessary. Madam, contain yourself! This case is not about your leg. I'm sure that if something bad happened to you at the jail your lawyer here can tell you what to do.

THE DEFENDANT: Ha!

MR. MCNAUGHTON: Your Honor, if I may?

THE COURT: That's enough from you. Now just sit down, or you'll sit in the dock. Is that understood? The choice is yours.

THE DEFENDANT: Oh, alright.

MR. PLEDGE: Your Honor, I don't know what to say. This is outrageous.

THE COURT: Then don't say anything. Put on your first witness. Let's go!

MR. PLEDGE: But my opening, Your Honor.

THE COURT: Mr. McNaughton, you waive your opening, right?

MR. MCNAUGHTON: I guess so. Ah, wait a second. Yeah, that's OK.

THE COURT: Mr. Pledge?

MR. PLEDGE: Your Honor, if I don't open, they can ask for a directed verdict.

THE COURT: That's not the way things happen in my courtroom.

MR. PLEDGE: Your Honor, I'll be brief. I promise.

THE COURT: Mr. Pledge, I hope that whole book is not your opening.

MR. PLEDGE: No, Your Honor. This is my trial notebook. This section is my opening. I have it all tabbed.

THE COURT: No, no, no, no, no. Alright, go ahead. Keep it brief, though, counsel.

MR. PLEDGE: Thank you, Your Honor. Your Honor, if this case had gone to trial, the government would have proved beyond a reasonable doubt –

THE COURT: Wait a second, I thought this was a trial. Did you all reach a plea agreement while I was gone?

MR. PLEDGE: No, sorry, Your Honor. Wrong section. Let me start again. Your Honor, December 24th, 1994, was a clear and cold day. Officer Benito Gilroy, who you will hear from today, was driving his unmarked police cruiser northbound on North Capitol past the intersection of Bryant Street Northwest, an area known as 'The Bins.'

Traffic was light, and there were no obstructions to Officer Gilroy's visibility. Officer Gilroy was assigned to the 4th District Vice Unit, and has been with MPD in that capacity for two years. Officer Gilroy was part of a team in an operation to address the many complaints of prostitution in and around the Bins. Prostitution, as this court is aware, is not a victimless crime. The neighborhood there, Your Honor, was the victim, with the increase in trash, noise, traffic, drugs and —

THE COURT: OK, that's it. Time's up. Officer, step up here. Government, this is your first and only witness?

MR. PLEDGE: But I wasn't finished, Your Honor. With my closing. I mean, my opening.

THE COURT: Yes, counsel, you were. Madam Clerk, swear in the witness.

[WHEREUPON THE WITNESS WAS SWORN IN]

Q: [BY MR. PLEDGE]: Your Honor, I'd like to proffer this to the Court.

THE COURT: What's that, Mr. Pledge?

Q: My opening statement.

THE COURT: Mr. Pledge, take your papers back to your table. Did we swear in the witness? OK, officer, tell me what happened.

A: Can I look at my report, Ma'am?

106

THE COURT: Will your report reflect your prior recollection?

A: Ma'am?

BY MCNAUGHTON: Objection, Your Honor!

THE COURT: Over-ruled. Mr. Pledge, give him his report. Show it to defense counsel first.

Q: Here it is, Your Honor. May I approach the witness?

BY MCNAUGHTON: Objection, Your Honor! This is not the proper way to reflect his refreshment, I mean, the refreshment of his recollection.

THE COURT: Counsel, come on. You know the rules. He can read the police report. OK, go ahead, Mr. Pledge, you may continue.

Q: So, does that document refresh your recollection, sir?

A: On December 27, 1994, the undersigned, I mean me, I was on routine patrol –

BY MCNAUGHTON: Objection!

THE COURT: Denied.

MR. MCNAUGHTON: But he's just reading the –

THE COURT: Sit down, sir. I've made my ruling.

Go ahead, officer.

A: At approximately fourteen thirty, I was northbound on North Capitol Street, that's headed towards Bryant Street, in an unmarked police cruiser, in an area that's known for high prostitution –

THE COURT: OK, you can skip all that part again. Just tell me, why'd you arrest this lady here for soliciting?

A: Ma'am, I arrested that lady there because she's a – I used to see her down on Logan Circle before she – she's always out there, is what I'm trying to say, and you know, she's a –

MR. MCNAUGHTON: Objection!

THE COURT: No sir, I mean, on this particular day, what was she doing that drew your attention to her.

MR. MCNAUGHTON: Move to strike!

THE COURT: Go ahead officer.

A: Oh, right. On that day, this report says, the undersigned noticed the suspect, later identified as Candy Ennist, white female, approximately five foot one inch and 115 pounds, standing on the corner of North Cap and Bryant. I pulled the car over, and rolled down my window.

Q: [BY MR. PLEDGE]: Ok, go on. Did the defendant say anything to you.

MR. MCNAUGHTON: Objection! Hearsay!

THE COURT: Go ahead, just tell me what you said and what the defendant said.

A: OK, the following conversation ensued. I asked the defendant, Miss Ennist, "What's up?" And then she said, "Nothing, what you lookin for?" So I asked, "How much for a blow job?" And she said, "Twenty-five dollars." So I said, "Twenty-five?" And she said, "Yeah." And I said, "Get in," and that was it.

Q: What happened next, Officer?

A: That was pretty much it.

Q: I mean, did you give a pre-arranged signal –

A: Oh yeah, right. When she got in I gave the pre-arranged –

MR. MCNAUGHTON: Objection! He's totally leading the witness.

A: – signal for the arrest team. I mean after she got in the car.

THE COURT: Sustained. Let's move on counsel, I get the picture.

Q: Yes, Your Honor. Thank you. Officer, do you see that woman here in court today? The woman who you say, well, who you spoke to on the afternoon of December 27th?

A: Yeah, that's her right there.

Q: Can you identify a piece of her clothing for the record, or state where she is sitting?

A: Oh yeah, she's right there next to her lawyer, there, and she's wearing a blue jumpsuit.

MR. PLEDGE: May the record reflect an in-court identification of the defendant.

THE COURT: What?

MR. PLEDGE: May the record reflect that Officer Gilroy identified the defendant?

THE COURT: Oh, yes. Go ahead.

Q: OK, finally, sir, Officer Gilroy, did the defendant make any statements to you after she was arrested?

MR. MCNAUGHTON: Objection!

THE COURT: Overruled.

A: Yeah, she said she was working to support her drug habit.

MR. MCNAUGHTON: Your Honor. I object. I ... they never ... in the discovery provided to me.

MR. PLEDGE: It's in the PD-79, Your Honor.

THE COURT: Sir, I already overruled your objection.

Q: That's all I have, Your Honor.

THE COURT: Alright, Officer Gilroy. Don't leave quite yet. Counsel, your witness.

Q: [BY MR. MCNAUGHTON]:   Officer, you didn't read Miss Ennist her rights, did you?

A: No.

MR. MCNAUGHTON: Your Honor, move to strike the statement. He didn't give her her Miranda rights.

A: My partner did. Officer Lewiski.

Q: Oh, your partner did?

A: Yeah, when she was –

THE DEFENDANT: Liar!

A: – in the station house.

THE DEFENDANT: God damn liar!

THE COURT: Order! Ma'am, you'll get your chance to testify, now just hold on.

MR. MCNAUGHTON: Miss Ennist, you have to sit.

THE DEFENDANT: I told you don't put your hand on me. You with them too!

[inaudible]

THE COURT: Madam! Madam. Sit down!

THE DEFENDANT: You all ain't real! You think you for real? This ain't nothing. You not no lawyers. This is just made up, a T.V. show for real!

THE COURT: My word!

THE DEFENDANT: That judge up there? She ain't real! You ain't real!

THE COURT: Alright, Marshals ... yes, step her back. No, no, not that! You're in contempt! Oh my word! The court will take a recess.

[Whereupon the proceedings recessed at 2:38 p.m.]
[Whereupon the proceedings resumed at 3:23 p.m.]

THE COURT: Alright, Mr. Pledge, defense counsel and the defendant are all present. What is that officer doing there?

[inaudible]

MR. PLEDGE: Your Honor?

THE COURT: Just a minute, counsel. Oh, yes, go

ahead sir.

MR. PLEDGE: Your Honor. I believe you were entering a finding of contempt against the defendant.

THE COURT: Contempt? What case is this?

[inaudible]

THE COURT: A plea? Not a plea. Oh yes, I remember, Miss Anus. How are you feeling, Ma'am?

THE DEFENDANT: Me?

THE COURT: Yes, I'm sorry the Marshals had to carry you out like that. I didn't mean for you to be disrobed.

THE DEFENDANT: These jumpsuits come awful loose. But I'm OK now.

THE COURT: Good, because I want you to know one thing. As you can see, I am real. Mr. Pledge is real. Your lawyer is real. You are on trial, ma'am, and I have a real job to do, and they have jobs to do. It's about being professional, see?

THE DEFENDANT: I am sorry, Your Honor. It's just –

THE COURT: That's OK. From now on, you just talk through your lawyer.

THE DEFENDANT: Yes ma'am. I will. I

understand all that you said about being a professional and all.

THE COURT: Alright, did the government finish with its closing?

MR. MCNAUGHTON: Your Honor, I believe it was my turn to cross-examine.

THE COURT: Cross examine? Who?

MR. MCNAUGHTON: Officer Gilroy.

THE COURT: Is that you, sir? OK, come on up. I thought you had finished.

MR. PLEDGE: Your Honor, before we continue. I want to raise the issue of defense counsel. I mean, his client pushed him away. She tried to hit him. I guess I just don't know. Can he continue?

THE COURT: Are you asking for a mistrial, sir?

MR. PLEDGE: Absolutely not. Just want to make sure this doesn't come up on appeal.

MR. MCNAUGHTON: Your Honor, I take offense here. Miss Ennist and I spoke during the break. There's nothing wrong here. We're in the middle of the trial.

THE COURT: So you're not asking for mistrial?

MR. MCNAUGHTON: Well, yes. Yes, I am.

THE COURT: Why?

MR. MCNAUGHTON: Well, because I just think in fairness to the defendant.

THE COURT: Fairness, huh? Well, that's not a reason. Let's move on. We are ending this today.

Q [BY MR. MCNAUGHTON]:   Court's indulgence. OK, Officer, you didn't see my client talking to anyone else before you arrested her, did you?

MR. PLEDGE: Objection!

A: No.

THE COURT: Overruled.

Q: And you said you offered her $25. Did you actually give her the $25?

MR. PLEDGE: Objection!

A: No.

THE COURT: Overruled.

A: No money is exchanged in these kinds of busts.

Q: So you did not.

A: Yes, I did not. As soon as she said the words, I gave the signal, and she was arrested. Then we processed her down at 4D, and when she said that she was working –

Q: Just answer the question, sir!

A: – trickin' to –

MR. MCNAUGHTON: Objection!

A: – to support her –

MR. MCNAUGHTON: Non-responsive! Move to strike!

A: – her habit.

MR. MCNAUGHTON: Your Honor! Please!

THE COURT: Officer, just answer the question.

A: Yes, ma'am.

Q: Ok, Officer, twenty-five dollars? That's not the usual price, the street price –

MR. PLEDGE: Relevance!

Q: – it's more like twenty, right?

THE COURT: Counsel, no. Officer, don't answer that. Move on. Sustained.

Q: Oh. OK, if I could have the court's indulgence?

THE COURT: Sure, take as much time as you like, counsel.

[inaudible]

THE COURT: OK, Mr. McNaughton. Sir. We'll have to move on now. The Chief Judge's courtroom just called. They want to you to return tomorrow morning. A bench warrant return, I think, is that right?

[inaudible]

THE COURT: On what matter? Madam Clerk? Stancil. OK. Got that, Mr. McNaughton?

MR. MCNAUGHTON: Yes, Your Honor. Thank you. May I proceed? I think I got it figured out.

THE COURT: Surely.

Q: Officer Gilroy. You said Miss Ennist offered, I mean .... strike that. You asked her how much a blow job costs, and she said twenty five dollars, correct?

A: Correct.

Q: OK, so let me ask you this. Do you read the newspaper in the morning?

MR. PLEDGE: Objection!

A: Sure.

THE COURT: What is this counsel?

MR. MCNAUGHTON: Please, Your Honor. I think you'll see after a couple more questions.

THE COURT: Proceed.

Q: Officer Gilroy, you say you read the paper. Which one, the Post or the Times?

A: That Moonie paper? Please. I read the Post. Sometimes.

MR. PLEDGE: But Your Honor! I object!

THE COURT: I said proceed.

Q: And do you know how much a Washington Post costs?

MR. PLEDGE: Objection!

Q: Go ahead, Officer.

A: Twenty-five cents.

Q: Officer, here's a quarter. If I may approach the witness, Your Honor?

MR. PLEDGE: Objection!

Q: Your Honor, let the record reflect I've given Officer Gilroy a quarter.

A: Yeah? So?

MR. PLEDGE: Objection! Relevance!

THE COURT: Counsel? Mr. McNau – ? Hold on a minute!

Q: So? Give me a Washington Post!

A: What?

Q: Give me today's Post!

MR. PLEDGE: Objection! Strenuously!

THE COURT: What?

Q: Sir, do you have a newspaper or don't you?

A: A newspaper? Nah, I ain't got no newspaper.

MR. PLEDGE: Objection! I object, Your Honor!

THE COURT: Sit down, Mr. Pledge. You too, sir. Get back behind defense table. What is this? What is this, counsel? You know the rules! What is this?

Q: Can't give me the morning paper even though you know how much it costs? How about that, Officer Gilroy?

A: I – you – no –

Q: No more questions!

MR. PLEDGE: Your Honor. He's leading the witness! It's ... it's very speculative, totally irrelevant, without foundation and beyond the scope!

THE COURT: Alright, everyone take a breath. I'm starting to get a headache. Counsel? Explain.

MR. MCNAUGHTON: It's simple, Your Honor. The only evidence in front of you is that my client told the officer the price of a blow job, that she knew the going rate, shall we say, for something. She never said she was offering that thing. She never said or did anything to indicate that she was taking the money in exchange for –

THE COURT: She got in the car, didn't she?

MR. MCNAUGHTON: Yes, but that's not soliciting. Officer Gilroy told her, "Get in." Maybe she didn't think she had a choice. Or maybe she thought he was offering her a ride. Maybe she was going to show him where he could get what he wanted. You know, hey, you can get a blow job over there for twenty-five. You can get a hand job over here for twenty, whatever.

THE COURT: Mmmm-hmmm.

MR. MCNAUGHTON: So all you really have are the words, and that's not enough.

THE COURT: Mr. Pledge?

MR. PLEDGE: Your Honor, I object. Who cares what newspaper Officer Gilroy reads. All the cases are like this.

THE COURT: But you see his point? Where's the solicitation?

MR. PLEDGE: She did. Your Honor, she did.

THE COURT: No, I don't think so. Not from what I've heard –

MR. MCNAUGHTON: So, then, Your Honor, I guess I move for dismissal.

MR. PLEDGE: No, Your Honor, I object.

THE COURT: Hold on, I got some questions. Officer? Where'd he go? Oh, there. Officer, tell me, when you drove up to the defendant, before you spoke to her, what was she doing?

A: What was she doing?

THE COURT: Yes, what was she doing? Was she just standing there minding her business? Or was she beckoning, you know, waving over to motorists?

MR. MCNAUGHTON: Your Honor! Come on!

A: Yeah, that's right. She was kind of making eye contact with passers-by.

THE COURT: And what was she wearing?

A: Just a t-shirt. A long white t-shirt. Had a big green marijuana leaf on it. But that's it.

MR. MCNAUGHTON: Your Honor! Move to strike! And I object to your questioning! I mean, if the government didn't ask –

THE COURT: The court will ask whatever questions the court wants. Alright, do either of you have any follow-up to my questions?

MR. MCNAUGHTON: Ah, gee, Your Honor. I guess not.

THE COURT: Any motions? Government, you rest?

MR. PLEDGE: No, Your Honor. I want to ask Officer Gilroy some follow-up.

THE COURT: Like what?

MR. PLEDGE: Like, like, like whether the Officer has ever had any dealings before with this defendant. Or what a blow job means to him.

THE COURT: I don't need to hear any of that. Mr. McNaughton. Closing?

MR. MCNAUGHTON: Just a minute, Your Honor. If I can just review my notes. And confer with my client. OK? No? Nothing? Your Honor, first I move for judgment of acquittal. The government didn't prove jurisdiction. They did not prove this event, whatever it   was, occurred in the District of Columbia.

THE COURT: Counsel, he testified that all of the events occurred in Washington.

MR. MCNAUGHTON: No, I don't believe he did.

MR. PLEDGE: He did, Your Honor. I distinctly remember asking him if this all occurred in the District of Columbia. The record will bear me out on this.

THE COURT: That motion is denied.

MR. MCNAUGHTON: Well, I just want to say, on behalf of Miss Ennist, that the government failed to prove its burden of beyond a reasonable doubt. They did not prove it. All they had was the words –

THE COURT: And the beckoning.

MR. MCNAUGHTON: Well, you should disregard the officer's testimony on that subject.

THE COURT: And her getting in the car.

MR. MCNAUGHTON: I still don't think that makes the case for solicitation.

THE COURT: Really? Come on, counsel.

MR. MCNAUGHTON: No. I think I made my

record. We just ask that if you find her guilty, you sentence her to time served. She's already been in around a hundred and fifty days, including the time in the halfway house.

THE COURT: All right, first, counsel, I find your client guilty of solicitation. I'm reading from the D.C. Code: "It shall not be lawful for any person to invite, entice, persuade, or address for the purpose of inviting, enticing, or persuading, any person or persons in the District of Columbia for the purpose of prostitution or any other immoral or lewd purpose." She spoke to the officer, wearing clothing that – she beckoned, using hand signals, and making eye contact. And she offered to perform a sex act for money, in response to the officer's questions. Though those words could have a different meaning in a different context, I don't find that here. Does your client have anything to say before I sentence her?

MR. MCNAUGHTON: You have to stand up.

THE DEFENDANT: Your Honor –

THE COURT: You can remain seated, madam.

THE DEFENDANT: Alright. Your Honor. I'm sorry for what I've done. I need a drug program or something like that. If you could give me a drug program. That's all.

THE COURT: Government?

MR. PLEDGE: We'll defer to the court. We just note that this is Miss Ennist's third solicitation conviction, in just, there's one in 1992, one in '94, and she has several other arrests, other cases, that appear to have been dismissed as part of a plea deal. Plus she has one conviction, a felony, for possession with intent to distribute heroin, back in 1989. And I see that there's a pending case, a new case, but I don't have that information. I think she should get, well, some time.

THE COURT: She's been in the halfway house for how long?

MR. PLEDGE: Actually, she escaped out of the halfway house, and I think she's being held without bond right now on that case.

THE COURT: Ah, well, there's no reflection of that here. Still, she's been in on this case for more than thirty days, it appears, so I will give her a period of one hundred twenty days, to run consecutive to any other sentence. So Miss Ennist, that means that whatever you are being held for now, if you are being held, I don't know. But you will have to do the four months on my case, minus whatever credit you get for the days you spent in the halfway house.

MR. MCNAUGHTON: What? Oh. My client says that was just three days in the halfway house, Your Honor.

THE COURT: Plus I must award costs, in the amount of $25. How long does your client need to pay that amount, Mr. McNaughton? Twenty-five dollars? Mr. McNaughton?

[a technical error in the tape ended the transcription]

V. Friday, June 16, 1995
Part One

Office of the Independent Counsel Press Release.

The following statement was issued by Independent Counsel Kenneth W. Starr from his office in Little Rock, Arkansas.

On June 16, 1995, United States District Judge George Howard, Jr., sentenced Robert W. Palmer to a term of three years probation, a $5,000 fine, and a $50 special assessment fee. The Judge placed a special condition on the first year of the three-year term of probation, by imposing home confinement, monitored by an electronic device.

On December 5, 1994, Robert W. Palmer, a resident of Little Rock, pleaded guilty in the United States District Court for the Eastern District of Arkansas to the felony offense of conspiracy. The plea was entered before United States District Judge G. Thomas Eisele and was the result of the Independent Counsel's ongoing investigation into matters concerning the operation of Madison Guaranty Savings & Loan, an insolvent federally insured institution taken over by federal regulators in March 1989. Mr. Palmer was a real estate appraiser who regularly appraised property for Madison Guaranty.

* * * * * * * * * *

126

~ Chapter Ten ~

"Nother Dewars."

"Sorry, pal. Last call is last call."

Liam stood up and tried to orient himself. The giant marble columns and towering ceiling resembled those in Union Station.

"Where do ya' think you're going?" a woman called out in a slight Irish brogue. "Don't ya remember me?"

He stared at the redhead and tried to work backwards: Union Station for cigarettes. Irish car bombs at the Dubliner. Nuggie, Mo, and the cab ride from the Grille. Hanging out with the Murder Lawyers. One drink, maybe three. The quarter and The Washington Post. Candy's pink stump.

"Memory's over-rated," he slurred.

"Come on now," the woman purred. "Show me that big car of yours. And maybe I'll show you my Delorean."

Liam looked at her again and staggered a bit. The woman was old, really old, maybe as old as his mother. How'd I wind up with her? he wondered.

Then, as she looped her boney arm around his, he had another thought: Car? Dude, you don't have a car!

§ § § § § § § § §

Nine hours earlier, Liam had gone straight to the National Grille, wanting to tell the Murder Lawyers about his first trial, especially the part about the quarter, but no one was there, so he started drinking, and by the time they arrived, he was well into his fourth scotch.

He repeatedly tried to recount his Perry Mason moment, but the Murder Lawyers ignored him – they were transfixed by the CNN news loop of O.J. Simpson trying to squeeze a black

THE HEYWARD SHEPHERD CONSPIRACY

glove on his hand.

"Acquittal," R.G. said with a huge smile. "Acquittal."

"Come on! He's guilty all the way," countered Liam, sore that no one wanted to hear his war story. "I mean, look at the DNA evidence!"

"O.J. has too much money," snapped Mo. "He has all the best lawyers. Whether he did it or not doesn't' matter."

"Whatever."

"This case was over the second Jesse Jackson got involved," Nuggie chimed in, drawing curious looks from everyone save R.G.

"Jesse Jackson?" Liam asked.

"Yeah. Remember, right after O.J. was arrested, when Jesse Jackson and his boys went to L.A. and convinced the District Attorney not to seek the death penalty? That told O.J. right from the beginning that he could beat the case."

Liam and Mo shook their heads in agreement, impressed with Nuggie's analysis.

"I mean, think about it: lying in wait, malice aforethought, a premeditated deliberate killing – and still no chance of getting the chair? If they go for the death penalty, O.J. would've pled, no doubt about it. No way he's gonna face down the electric chair, not with all that evidence against him. But with the death penalty off the table, why not roll the dice and try to beat it?"

"Wow, Nuggie, I never thought of it that way," Liam said.

"You make a good point," added Mo.

Nuggie suddenly looked embarrassed. "Well, at least that's what R.G. was saying last night."

"Six fifty-nine, fellas," Bobby Conti sighed. "And now our stories are getting syndicated. I'm outta here."

The lobbyists, Hill staffers, and agency muckety-mucks had begun to crowd the scene, signaling that it was time for the Murder Lawyers to prepare for departure. Red was poking through his shirt pocket when Liam tugged on his elbow.

"Hey, R.G., can I ask you something?"

"Go ahead, kid."

"I got this new case... it's in front of the Chief Judge. I godda go back tomorrow morning. It's a show cause. In a felony case. I'm not sure I can handle it."

"Sure you can, kid. Just make sure you get a voucher."

"See, the guy beat up his girlfriend couple of years ago. Kicked her, something like that. He's got eight years back-up time."

Liam waited for some reaction from R.G., but it took something really horrific to freak out a Murder Lawyer, so he pressed on.

"Anyway, now he's on probation – and he broke into a school or something. How do you defend that? I mean, either he was in the school or he wasn't, right?"

"Just make sure you get the voucher. Then investigate the shit out of the case. You never know, maybe he had a right to be there."

Nuggie stumbled by, validated parking ticket in hand. "Hasta la vista, baby."

"Drive safe, Sperminator," R.G. quipped.

"Hey Red, you promised you'd stop calling me that!"

"Apologies. Gentlemen, see you tomorrow."

"Need a ride, Nuggie?" Liam asked.

"Nah, I'm OK. Mo and I are going over to the Dubliner. Get us some Irish pussy."

"Irish pussy!" Mo called out from the coat check. "So Young Liam, the young lion, are you in, or are you out?"

§ § § § § § § § §

"In," Liam recalled saying. But that's about it. He searched his mind and remembered the red-haired Mrs. Robinson at their table, rubbing her foot along his leg and chain-smoking. Mo was matching her cigarette for cigarette and getting her goat by proclaiming Gerry Adams the Irish Mandela. Nuggie, meanwhile, had his head on the table, unconscious.

How Liam wound up here, alone with the redhead in her Nissan Sentra, was anybody's guess.

"Here you go," she said, pulling over to the curb. "That's your car there, I should say?"

Liam swiveled his head around. First he saw a river – the Potomac River. Then, on the other side of the road, the Lincoln Memorial.

"Not there, sonny. Over here!"

Drawing in his focus, Liam suddenly saw the familiar white Expedition – Nuggie's car.

"Oh, that! That's not my –"

Before he could finish, the woman shoved her tongue in his mouth, and though she tasted like cigarettes and recent dental work, Liam gave her an energetic response. He lifted up her shirt and began kissing the thin skin of her stomach, working his way up towards her flabby tits – when something came off her skin into his mouth.

"What's this?" he asked, spitting what looked like a Band-Aid into his hand.

The red-headed Mrs. Robinson took one look and laughed, "Oh, that's me patch. Me Nicotrol patch."

Liam turned the other way and began heaving out the window.

§ § § § § § § § §

Lying in the grass just a few yards from the road, he was jolted to a seated position by a fiery hiss, and through the billowing exhaust, he could see that a giant white tour bus had pulled up behind Nuggie's Expedition. The red head's Sentra was gone.

The door to the bus popped open and a horde of Japanese tourists began filing out, snapping flash photos of the Potomac River, the Lincoln Memorial, and the intoxicated American in repose. Liam stood up gingerly, something jabbing him in the leg. He reached into his pants pocket – the apparent source of the pain – and pulled out Nuggie's golf club key chain.

"How'd these get here?"

Ignoring the polite laughter and applause of the Japanese tourists, Liam climbed into the giant SUV, located the ignition key, and began to start the car. But he stopped half-crank when the big truck's head-lights popped on and illuminated a car parked inches in front of him. He looked behind him and saw that the tour bus was just about sitting on his back bumper. He was completely boxed in.

"Damn Nuggie," he said, "I thought you didn't know how to parallel park."

Figuring he was probably too drunk to drive anyway, Liam turned on the radio and waited for one of the two vehicles blocking him in to move. His patience lasted all of five minutes. Hungry, tired, and eager to get home, he began laying on the horn, to no avail, so he hopped out of the Expedition, looking for trouble.

The door to the idling bus was open, but it was pitch-black inside.

"Hey," Liam yelled. "What the fuck? Could you be any closer to my bumper?"

"Go on away from my door," a voice in the darkness commanded.

Feeling himself swaying backwards, Liam overcorrected and fell forward into the bus.

"Move your fucking bus, man!" he yelled, extricating himself from the doorway. "You got me blocked in!" Then he kicked the side of the bus for emphasis, hurting his foot more than anything.

A short black man in a starched blue jumpsuit came hurtling out of the darkness. "You kick my vehicle?"

"I didn't do nothing to your vee-he-kol," Liam said, backing up.

"I'ma call the police, that's what I'ma gonna do," the man said before marching back into his idling bus.

"Go right ahead! Call the po-lice! See if I care! I ain't afraid of no cops! I know my rights! I'm a lawyer – a trial lawyer!"

As he inhaled the diesel fumes, Liam suffered a sudden loss of bravado. He staggered away, found a soft spot in the grass, and passed out.

~ Chapter Eleven ~

A nasally voice woke Liam from his stupor.

"I figgered you for a trial lawyer," the man was saying, "and by god, if you didn't just plead guilty on all counts!"

When he saw that it was the ponytailed cop he'd seen outside Judge Malley's courtroom, Liam quickly tried to stand up, almost falling in the river.

"Whoa, Sailor," the man said, grabbing him by the arm. "You don't want to be swimming in D.C.'s feces."

"That bus driver is lying if he says I kicked his door," Liam protested, yanking his arm back. "Why don't you go give him a ticket for blocking me in?"

"A ticket? What are you talking about?"

"I know my rights! He blocked me in."

"You think I'm a cop?" the ponytailed man laughed. "You think I'd work for that crackhead Mayor of yours?"

"So, what? You're just touring the area? Checking out the sites?"

"Take it easy, fun guy. Lemme show you something." The man pointed to the beat-up car parked in front of Nuggie's Expedition. "We're in the same boat, you and me. I'm boxed in too."

Liam could see that a white box truck was parked immediately in front of the man's car, blocking his exit as well.

"That's ... your car?"

"Sure is," the man said proudly. "Like it?"

"I guess."

"Know what it is?"

Liam didn't know much about cars, so whenever he was put on the spot over a sixties-era muscle car he always guessed Thunderbird.

"Close! She's my '74 Toronado!"

"I really thought T-bird."

"An understandable mistake. Big difference: my Toronado's automatic." Ponytail held up his right hand and twisted it stiffly. "I got trouble handling a stick, you see."

"A Tornado, huh?"

"Tor-o-na-do. The kind of car Mannix drove. Remember Mannix?"

"I'm more of a McCloud guy."

"That's pretty good," Ponytail laughed, pulling a small wooden box from his shirt pocket and wedging it in between the rubbery fingers of his right hand – a hand Liam could now see was a prosthetic. "So, McCloud, you wanna smoke?"

"Umm, nah thanks."

"Well, don't mind if I do." The man plied the top off the box with his good hand and out popped what Liam instantly recognized as a metal pipe designed to look like a cigarette. The man then swung his ponytail behind his back, stuck the pipe between his lips, and lit up, using a Zippo he fished from his pants pocket.

Liam's nostrils flared at the smell of burning cannabis.

"Whoa! *That* kind of smoke."

"Want one now?" Ponytail asked, sucking in his breath.

"You know, if you're a cop, this is, like, totally entrapment."

"Do I really look that much like a cop?"

"Well, yeah," Liam shrugged.

"Well, I'm not," Ponytail said, exhaling.

"Sorry."

The man jammed the pipe in the wooden box a few times.

"No problemo," he said softly before handing the pipe to Liam. Then he hit the lighter again, and gave Liam the flame. "I mean, I used to be with the Marshal's Service. So I guess you could say I used to be a cop."

Liam reared back. "The Marshal's Service? The *U.S. Marshal's Service*?"

"'Used to,' I said. But if you don't want it –"

"Alright, alright." Liam stepped up to the flame, drew on the pipe, and began coughing hard.

"Careful. Comes out hot."

"This is some good shit," he said, holding his breath. "There's no way I'm driving now."

"I wouldn't worry about it. That Driving Miss Daisy motherfucker ain't going nowhere soon."

"Really? Why'd you say that?"

"Those little dinks of his probably just flew in to check out that new Korean War Memorial, and they're still on Far East time. It's lunch time for those yellow bastards."

"Oh."

"Fucking mockery," Ponytail said, hawking up a loogie and spitting it in the river.

Liam felt himself floating away, until two police cars suddenly screamed round the corner towards the Kennedy Center.

"You want another hit?" Ponytail asked, not bothering to hide the pipe.

Liam craned his neck to see where the police went. "Do I want another? Dude, you bet I do! You don't even want to know how long it's been since I last got high."

§ § § § § § § § §

As he settled in with that second hit, Liam couldn't help but think about that last time, those heady, humid days when he was still living with Julianne in her high rise apartment, and their New Mexican dope stash had ran out.

135

Julianne had suggested they buy some off the street, but Liam had thought better of the idea. But she was adamant. "Come on, Yum!" she said. "I know just the place!"

So off they went in her Miata, driving through the mean streets of Anacostia with the top down, Liam at the wheel, Julianne giving directions.

"These Rasta guys, I know they were selling dope," she said, scanning the sidewalks. "I swear they were just around the corner here. I saw them that day, that day I got my ....."

"Your birth control?" Liam asked, trying to finish her sentence. "So why don't we find that clinic you went to and go from there?"

"What are you talking about? We've driven past the damn clinic three times already!"

"We have?"

"Yeah, Yum. Right there." She pointed to a small concrete block building covered in muddy beige paint and fresh graffiti.

"You gotta be kidding me. That place? I thought you said it was Planned Parenthood."

"I said it was *like* Planned Parenthood. Who cares, anyway?"

"'Eunice's House of Healing and Prayer'? That's where you went to get your birth control pills – or whatever?"

Julianne had grown quiet. "Yeah, my whatever."

As they continued down the street in silence, the little clapboard houses gave way to rows of abandoned tenement buildings. Tall weeds and broken glass all but covered the crumbling sidewalks, and thickets of tall trees began to blot out the light.

"Maybe we ought to turn around," Liam suggested.

"Keep going. I think those dudes are at this intersection coming up. They were like standing off to the left, all to themselves."

Liam read the rusty street sign. "Green Street?"

"Ya mon!" Julianne responded, causing both of them to convulse with laughter.

But their mirth disappeared minutes later when they found themselves at a dead-end. The paved road they were on simply stopped; the dirt road that followed in its path traveled just few yards before tumbling headlong into a dense growth of vines and fallen trees.

Liam put the car in reverse, but when he turned to look over his shoulder, he saw five young black men in the middle of the street.

"Shit," he muttered under his breath.

"What is it?" Julianne asked. "Oh fuck. Where'd they come from?"

"Those aren't the Rastas we're looking for, are they?"

"No shit, Yum. Let's get the fuck outta here."

Liam painted a smile on his face. "Scuse me, guys, mind if we get by?"

The men laughed casually. One of them, dressed in fatigue shorts, was palming a half-deflated basketball. Meeting Liam's gaze, he slammed it on the ground, making a loud pop. Julianne jumped at the noise.

"Chill, baby, chill," a dark-skinned man said, suddenly appearing at Julianne's side. "You workin', sweet thang? Or y'all lookin for a little sumpin sumpin?"

"No, we're just a little bit ... lost," Julianne said, attempting to smile. "You know, trying to get back to –"

The deflated ball popped on the ground again, stopping Julianne mid-sentence.

"What the fuck, Derwin?" yelled the one next to Julianne. "I already toll you, nigga! Get ridda dat gotdamn ball!" The man leaned in closer, draping his arm over the windshield.

137

"These are some dumb-ass niggas right here, I tell you. So, you two? You together?"

Liam put his hand on Julianne's leg. "Just taking her home."

"That's cool. Jungle fever. I'm down with that."

Liam glanced in his rear view and saw that the other men were gone – now they were right next to him. Derwin – the one in the fatigue shorts – stiff-armed the deflated ball to within an inch of Liam's nose. "Fo' ya go home," he drawled, "y'all gon hafta pay atoll."

"A what?" Julianne asked, her voice rising.

"A toll."

"Shee, Derwin, quit fooling," the one next to Julianne said, smiling broadly.

Derwin pulled the ball back behind his head as if he was winding up for a pitch. "You think I'ma foolin, white boy?"

"Definitely not," Liam stammered. "How much?"

"He wanna know how much," Derwin laughed. The other men began laughing too.

"We don' want yo money," the one next to Julianne said, drawing his tongue over his gold-capped teeth.

"What – what do you –?" Julianne asked, the words sticking in her throat.

"Fust thing, we gon take yo' car," the man next to Julianne said matter-of-factly. "Then we each gonna take our toll. Now git out."

The men began rubbing their hands together, saying "Yeah, yeah, yeah" as they crowded in closer. Liam looked at Julianne; she stared back, gripped with fear. But when he reached for the ignition in order to turn the car off, her eyes turned wild.

"What the fuck are you doing, Yum?"

"J, they just want the car," he whispered back. "They're

just kids."

"Just kids?" Julianne suddenly stood up on the car seat. "You ghetto niggas can just back the fuck off! My father bought me this car!"

Liam mashed his foot on the accelerator and the car sprinted backwards. Julianne fell headlong over the windshield, but Liam was able to grab the back of her blue jean shorts with one hand while steering the car backwards with the other, and they drove that way down the block, dodging thrown bottles and bricks, Julianne yelling and cursing the whole way.

"My father is a lawyer! My brother is a doctor! You Bama niggas want a car? Get a fucking job!"

When they got to the top of Green Street, Liam slammed on the brakes, sending Julianne back into her seat. He then spun the car around and they drove back to Virginia in silence.

Back inside her Pentagon City apartment, Liam grabbed a bottle of vodka from the freezer and collapsed on the white leather sectional. Julianne, meanwhile, was frantically picking through the cigarette butts, ashes, and old wads of gum in every ashtray she could find. Five minutes later, she dropped a small pile of roaches on a magazine and placed it on his lap.

"Please, Yum, roll us a good one, OK?"

"Sure, baby, no problem. I'll take care of you."

With his hands still shaking, it took him several tries to get it right. Then they went out onto the balcony, where the sound of the air-conditioner units drowned out the highway traffic below. The autumn sun was setting behind the Washington Monument in the distance, and after a few puffs, Liam began to relax.

"Shit, J, you really blew me away out there," he finally said. "I didn't think you had it in you."

He saw her eyes welling up. "There's a lot you don't know about me, Yum."

139

He held out his arms and she jumped onto him, almost knocking the two of them over the railing. She wrapped her long legs around him, and he carried her back into the living room. He was kissing her face and her tears, and she was breathlessly saying, "I'm sorry, I'm so sorry. Those guys, that clinic ... I should have told you."

"It's O.K, J," he whispered back. "Whatever happened, happened. It's not anyone's fault."

~ Chapter Twelve ~

"Women troubling ye?"

Liam took a moment to remember where he was. "Scuse me?"

"Them's of the feminine persuasion, that's what's ailing ya, isn't it?"

Liam saw that it was the man in the Buffalo Sabres jersey, the one with the ponytail, the one he had seen in court. The one who talked like a pirate.

"Shame, too," he continued. "That redhead of yours looked like a nice piece of mature ass, the kind that makes you miss yer momma."

"Her? The red head?" The memories of Julianne vanished. "Nah. I was actually thinking about the last time I got high. With my girlfriend – my ex-girlfriend."

Liam gave Ponytail the quick run-down on his lunatic love affair with Julianne, explaining how he had pulled up stakes and traveled across the country for her, only to lose her months later.

"I can't believe you would move from New Mexico to this cesspool."

"You've been there? To New Mexico?"

"Sure. I told you I worked for the U.S. Marshal's, right?"

Liam shifted uncomfortably.

"'Used to,' counselor, remember? 'Used to.' Relax. Here, lemme pack you another bowl. Yessir, the Service sent me all over this god forsaken country of ours. Texas. Wisconsin. North Dakota. California. Federal prisons, federal courts. When they sent me out to New Mexico, I was just a rookie. I was on a team that was sent to monitor the sitch-ee-ation during the Santa Fe State Prison riot. You remember that, right?"

141

"Sorta. I musta been in junior high when it happened."

"Well, anyways, I used to go back there every couple of years, hook up with some of the people I met out there. Prison guards, state cops, that kind of thing. We'd go out there in the dessert, drink beer, shoot coyotes. But I haven't been back in years."

He held up his prosthetic hand again and gave it the familiar twist.

"Can't really shoot anymore, with my hand and all."

Why does he keep bringing up the hand, Liam wondered. Does he want me to ask about it? Should I just acknowledge it and move on?

"Nice view from here, huh?" he finally said, trying to change the subject.

"Like most things, depends on your perspective."

"I guess."

"You see, all of that land over there belonged to Robert E. Lee." Ponytail pointed across the river to the Arlington National Cemetery. "That is, until the Union confiscated it and started burying their dead in it."

"Hmmph. I didn't know that."

Ponytail studied Liam clinically. "You should know your Civil War history, being a lawyer and all. Fourteenth Amendment changed just about everything in this country."

"Well, of course –"

"That's why you got the Orientals and the women and the illegals all screaming discrimination these days. That's why you got these old eunuchs saying it's OK for women to kill their babies."

"Eunuchs?"

"You're shit in the middle of American history here, McCloud. Just about all of the War of Northern Aggression was fought between here and Richmond. Ever been to any battlefields?"

"Civil War battlefields?"

"If that's what you call 'em."

"Nah. I just moved here back in August."

"Well, shit! Been here almost a year and no battlefields? We'll just have to fix that. Nothing like being eye-level and boots-on-the-ground. Then you'll see that virtually everything your history teacher told you was 180 degrees backwards. Lemme give you a for instance. I'll bet you think you know what started the Civil War – as you call it."

Liam scrunched up his forehead. "Uh, Fort Sumter?"

"Good guess! Fine guess! You just earned yourself another bowl. But this is exactly what I'm talking about. You see, what they didn't teach you in history class was that the first shots of the war were fired two years earlier, with John Brown's raid on Harper's Ferry. October 16, 1859, to be exact."

"Oh, sure. I heard of that. John Brown, I mean."

"You gotta admire the man, thinking him and a handful of other fanatics could start a slave insurrection – a civil war – all by themselves. But you know the old saying, don't you? 'A well-organized minority can defeat an unorganized majority.'"

Liam shrugged his shoulders.

"Problem was, they were expecting the goddam slaves to rise up instead of sitting on their lazy asses and waiting for the usual handout. What a joke! And you wanna know the irony of the whole thing?"

"Shoot."

"The first guy killed by John Brown and his crew was a slave who had bought his freedom. Heyward Shepherd was his name. Ever heard of him?"

"No, I don't think so."

"You saying you never heard that name? Heyward Shepherd?"

143

"Name sounds kinda familiar, now that I think about it."

"They got a nice little monument up there for him in Harper's Ferry. Some think that he was killed by friendly fire – that he was actually a co-conspirator with John Brown and just got killed in the confusion of the initial assault. Others say he was a faithful servant for the B&O railroad, that he had run to alert the authorities after stumbling upon Brown's men out there on the tracks. But you say never heard of him, huh? Heyward Shepherd?"

Liam handed Ponytail back his pipe and lighter. "No. Sorry. Can't say that I have."

"Hmm. That's too bad," Ponytail said warily. "Well, anyways, like I was saying, you have to admire the man's determination, his vision. John Brown, that is. Heyward Shepherd, he's a mere footnote. See, the important thing is not that he happened to be killed, this Heyward Shepherd, it's that his death didn't cause John Brown and his men to give up their objective. I mean, think about it – you aim to free all the slaves, and yet the first guy you kill is a freed slave. But John Brown was a true leader of men. I imagine that he used the killing of Heyward Shepherd to enthuse his men, to fortify them in the belief that they were acting upon divine principle."

The air was thick and still, and when Ponytail finally stopped talking, Liam became aware of an eerie plop-plop-plop sound in the water.

"Hundred thirty sixth anniversary coming up this October," Ponytail said wistfully. "Sure would like to do something special to commemorate it."

"Say, I better get going," Liam replied. "You think I could have another hit for the road?"

"Sure, sure. Sorry for rambling on there."

As Ponytail slowly and deliberately packed the pipe, Liam congratulated himself on rightly picking him out as a cop. Not a regular cop, but a U.S. Marshal all the same. "So, do you mind if I ask, what were you doing in court when I saw you?"

"Looking for you, partner."

"Me? What for?"

"Man, you are a jumpy one," he laughed. "I gotta wrongful termination lawsuit going on and I just like to go to court and see who's trying cases."

"That makes sense," Liam said, still spooked.

"They canned me after I lost my hand, if you can believe that."

As Ponytail examined his prosthesis clinically, Liam noticed that the life-like plastic arm even had tattoos – a Confederate flag, a silhouette of a naked woman on her hands and knees, and a portrait of what looked like Jesus wearing a little Charlie Chaplin mustache.

Ponytail abruptly pulled down his sleeve. "You wanna know what happened to my hand?" he seethed. "You really want to know?"

"Sure, man, if you –"

Ponytail's eyes narrowed and his face went dark. "Matthew 5:30," he said in a voice not his own. "'If thy right hand offend thee, cut it off, and cast it from thee, for it is better than thy whole body should be cast into hell!'"

Liam scooted backwards on the grass several feet, thinking, One of us is having a bad trip, and I know it ain't me.

"What was that about?" Ponytail laughed, his voice returning to normal. "Oh well, nothing a dose of lithium can't erase. But seriously, you wanna know what happened? I'll tell you. I dropped a VW on my arm. Just a fucked up accident. Had it up on blocks, and it just fell on me. I was fucking pinned on a cold concrete floor for five hours before someone found me."

"Wow. That's fucked up."

"Yeah, I should have died from the blood loss, but thank god for cold Jamestown winters."

"What was this, when you were a kid?"

"No, no, just a few years ago. Right after Ruby Ridge. You know about –?"

"Sure," Liam said curtly, trying to cut off another history lecture. "I think I read about it after the Oklahoma City bombing. It's why McVeigh was all pissed off. Someone got shot, right? A kid or something?"

"No, not a kid. A man and his wife. Poor woman was holding her baby when the bullet blew her head off."

"Oh, right."

"Fucking FBI fucked the whole thing up. I mean, we had everything under control."

"'We'?"

"The Marshal's Service. OK, so a couple of our guys fucked up serving a warrant. Problem was they were led by some faggot San Francisco bureaucrat and they violated all the rules of engagement. They were pinned down all night, but it was nothing my extraction team couldn't handle. But when DOJ sent my unit to guard some fucking hospital in town, that's when I knew that the fix was in, that this was an ATF frame-up."

Liam tried to suppress a yawn. "Hey, d'ya keep hearing that noise out on the river?"

Ponytail ignored the question.

"Believe me, a couple of us thought about turning in our badges right then and there. Me, I just took some time off, went back home, worked on cars, tried to figure out what I was going to do in life. And then, boom, car falls on me, almost kills me. The Service eventually cans me on account of my hand, but the EEOC gave me my right-to-sue letter. That's where you come in."

146

"I'm not sure I'm following you."

"I need someone who goes to court and fights, not some goddam desk jockey. And don't worry about getting paid. My case is solid. I had sixteen years in, worked myself up to a senior level. Hell, I was just about running the Special Operations Group! I had staff, I had people working for me. That is, until that draft-dodging cocksucker Clinton came in. I swear, after he took over, every goddam black woman below me got promoted two bumps: one day I come into work and these women who used to be under me are now *my* supervisors. I can't understand it. I'd waited to get my GS-14 for three years, and these cunts leapfrog over me? See where I'm coming from?"

Liam stared at the trash-strewn surface of the river, avoiding eye contact.

"Anyways, after I got out of the hospital and off disability, on account of my arm, one of these two-fers decides to take me off the SOG and put me in charge of protecting abortion clinics. Fucking abortion clinics! Can you believe that? Listen, partner, let me tell you something. It was all part of their plan to get rid of me, but I just didn't go for it." Feigning a woman's voice, Ponytail said, "'Well, if you can't do your job, or if you won't do your job, we'll just have to terminate you.' So you know what I say? I say, 'Well, fuck you very much. I'm going back out on disability. And by the way, here's an EEO complaint. Go ahead and try to can me now! Then I'll nail your asses on a retaliation claim!' Fuck Janet Reno!"

With that, Liam stood up and pretended to stretch, hoping he might see the Japanese tourists returning to their bus.

"Listen, man, if I sound crazy, it's because I am."

"That's cool," Liam said nervously.

"Yeah, I got an actual diagnosis. That's part of my claim, too. ADA, you know. But I really do need your help. I really do want you to be my lawyer. You'd have no problem with those government lawyer assholes they assign to defend these cases. No problem at all."

"Well, wait a second. I should tell you, I've never done any employment discrimination cases. They can't be *that* easy."

"Don't worry about a thing. Man, you gotta understand, I've been living this case for three years. I've had a lot of time to work on it. All I need is a young aggressive lawyer, someone who can try a case."

"Well, that is what I do," Liam said, feeling flattered. "In fact, I just tried a great case today, man! Yesterday, whatever. It was just a prostitution case, but you should've seen it –"

"How about felonies?" Ponytail interrupted. "You know, big cases?"

"I mean, to be honest, most of my cases are misdemeanors." Seeing Ponytail's disappointment, he quickly added, "But I got some felonies. Some serious shit too."

"Really? Like what?"

"Domestic violence, mostly. I got this one guy, see, he kicked his wife or girlfriend or whatever, real bad, broke her ribs, I think it was." He waited to see Ponytail's reaction.

"Broken ribs? Oh, my! What kind of man hits a woman?"

Liam laughed. "Well, you know, he *allegedly* did it."

"Right. Allegedly." As both men laughed, something splashed hard against the surface of the river beneath them.

"What the fuck was that?"

"I dunno," Ponytail said. "Probably fish jumping. So lemme ask you something. How do you represent someone like that? Someone who's obviously guilty?"

"Well, it gets better. Believe it or not, now my guy's charged with an Unlawful Entry, so he's kinda got two cases going on. In fact, I gotta go back to court tomorrow – today, I guess – in front of the Chief Judge."

"The Chief Judge?"

"Yep, that's right."

"Breaking-and-entering, huh? What's that all about?"

"Just a misdemeanor. Unlawful Entry is what they call it. He broke into a school apparently."

"A school, you say?"

"Yeah, some Catholic school on North Capitol."

"I see. So how do you beat something like that? I mean, what's your guy saying? Did they catch him with anything? You're gonna plead him guilty, right?"

Liam instantly regretted bringing up his new case, thinking, *A real trial lawyer wouldn't brag about a client he'd never met.* He was trying to formulate a way to change the subject again when he saw something moving in the water below. "O.K. now! What the fuck was that?"

"Where?"

"There! Right there! Is that a fish?"

Both men stared at the oily blackness below, and after a moment, Ponytail began laughing. "I guess that depends on how much currency you give the theory of evolution."

A rat jumped out of the water, several inches in the air, the moonlight illuminating its red eyes as it dove back in. Then another rat followed a second later.

Liam recoiled. "Holy shit! Flying fucking rats!"

"Just eating the bugs, man. Cept maybe for that one over there."

Liam looked just over the edge of the river wall, where his feet had been dangling moments earlier. There, on the surface of the water, was a rat flicking its long pink tail as it rolled on its back, gnawing on what appeared to be the soggy remains of a seagull.

"I'd say that's an omen of where we're going with my

case," Ponytail exclaimed happily. "You? You're the rat. Janet Fucking Reno, she's the bird!"

§ § § § § § § § §

The eastern horizon was turning a fluorescent blue. Liam noticed that the bus had finally left.

"Shit, I better get going. I gotta go to court in, what, five hours? Thanks for the smoke, though."

"Pleasure's mine," Ponytail said. "Hey, gotta card?"

"Sure." Liam pulled his gold plated card holder from the interior pocket of his suit jacket. "Here ya go."

"Let me give you my number, OK? Call me if you want to check out some battlefields or whatever." Ponytail wrote his number on the back of Liam's card and then gave it back to him. "I mean it, call me for anything, OK?"

"Oh, O.K.," Liam said, trying to read the flowing cursive. "Here, I got another card, if you want *my* number –"

But it was too late. He had already hopped in his Toronado and was gunning the engine.

"As we used to say in the Service, catch you later!"

When Ponytail pulled off, Liam could see that he had left Nuggie's headlights on the whole night, and now they were at a low dim. He quickly got in, pumped the gas, and turned the key, but nothing happened.

A car revved its engine next to him. It was Ponytail, leaning over the passenger seat.

"Hey McCloud, what's up?"

"Battery's dead."

"Ain't that just the shit?"

"Yeah, the shit," Liam said dejectedly.

"Come on, I'll give you a ride. Where d'ya live?"

"Just up the way. On Capitol Hill."

150

Liam slid into Ponytail's car, and they sped up Independence Avenue, past the omnipresent federal government buildings and the shining dome of the U.S. Capitol.

"Turn here on Second. I'm just behind the Supreme Court."

"Hey, you're not too far from the old St. Martin's Church," Ponytail observed. "The one where that priest got defrocked for marrying that little Korean unit. You know who I'm talking about, right? The Reverend Clinton Augustus And-One? It was in the news about a year ago."

"Sorry," Liam answered. "But I haven't really been in D.C. that long."

"Right, right," Ponytail said as he pulled the car up to the curb alongside the back of the Supreme Court. "I keep forgetting that."

"Hey man, thanks for the ride. Thanks a lot."

"I'm from the government, and I'm here to help."

"You know, I've been in D.C. for almost a year now, and I don't know too many people who ... ah ... you know, I don't have too many friends that ... and it's nice to...."

Ponytail stared back impassively.

"What I'm trying to say is, it was cool hanging out like that, getting high and all. So if, you know, you want to talk about your case or whatever."

"You got it, counsel. Take it easy. And remember, call me for anything. Got it? Anything."

"Sure, you bet."

Liam stumbled out of the car and down the steps into the little alcove that lead to his apartment. But when he reached into his pocket for his keys, he found only Nuggie's long string of miniature golf clubs.

"What's wrong now?" Ponytail called out.

"I think I may have left my keys at the courthouse metal

detector this morning. Yesterday morning. Whatever."

"You locked out?"

"Nah, I got a spare." Liam leaned over and lifted up the mat beneath his door. "Got it!"

Ponytail laughed. "Last place anyone would expect." Then he gave Liam a quick salute with his plastic hand and sped away.

VI. Friday, June 16, 1995
Part Two

From the Washington Times, page C6.

MARYLAND NEWS

BRIEFLY

FAIRMONT HEIGHTS

A 17-year-old girl was charged yesterday with attempted murder of a newborn baby found abandoned in a trash can Sunday.

The girl, who was not identified because she is a juvenile, was rushed to Prince George's Hospital Center after calling to say she was having a miscarriage.

But doctors at the hospital soon realized the girl had already given birth.

The teen-ager's mother called authorities a short time later after finding the infant near her home in the 5100 block of Duel Place.

The newborn, who is healthy, is being held by the county's child protective services, police said.

* * * * * * * * * *

~ Chapter Thirteen ~

McCoy cruised up North Capitol, past the St. Nick's school, across the southernmost tip of Sursum Corda, and then up the hill to the Bins. He had timed the drive on numerous occasions and under differing traffic patterns, always reaching the somewhat obvious conclusion that the drive could easily be done in less than fifteen minutes.

What he really wanted to know was how long it would take on foot. He sometimes thought about trying it himself, but McCoy knew that even as a cop, it was just too dangerous a part of town to try.

Just past Channing Street, he pulled his squad car to the curb. What is it about the Bins that keeps drawing me back, he wondered. Is this the third point for my triangle?

Staring at the brick silos, McCoy tried to meditate, to focus on those first two points – Sursum Corda and the Fourth District Police Station – to recall precisely what had happened in the early-morning hours of April 19th.

He remembered that he had just finished the paperwork on the Malcolm X. Stancil arrest and was about to take him downtown when the radio run came in for gunshots inside a residence at 162B First Terrace N.W. He immediately dumped Stancil off on the desk sergeant and raced for his car, arriving at Sursum Corda minutes later.

At least three other units had responded ahead of McCoy, but none were willing to go inside the unit.

"What are we waiting for?" McCoy had demanded.

"*We* are gonna canvass for witnesses," one of the cops responded. "But, hey, Supercop, you want to go on ahead of the SWAT Team, well then, be our guest."

McCoy remembered checking the apartment's metal security gate and the heavy wooden door behind it. Both were unlocked, neither showing any sign of forced entry, so he tentatively stepped inside.

As he poked around in the dark entry way, a skinny black woman in her night clothes crashed through a curtain, wailing, "My gran-chile! She dead! And she dead too!"

McCoy had grabbed the woman by the shoulders. "Ma'am, is there anyone with a gun in the house?"

"The Devil was in my house this morning! Someone call the police!"

"Ma'am, I am the police!"

But the woman would not be consoled, so he shoved her outside into the arms of his fellow officers. Then he took a quick look behind the curtain – a large room containing nothing more than a small refrigerator, a stove, and a dirty mattress. McCoy drew back the curtain, checked his back, and pressed on.

There was another room at the bottom of the stairs, illuminated by the flickering light of a television set. McCoy peered around the door jamb and saw an old man with an oxygen mask watching the muted T.V. When the man's panicked eyes met McCoy's, he took the mask off his face and tried to talk.

McCoy rushed forward. "We got a call for gunshots in this apartment," he whispered. "You know anything about that?"

Gasping for air, the man tried to get up out of his seat, knocking over an aluminum folding table. A small glass pipe fell at McCoy's feet, cracking in two. McCoy pushed the man back into his seat and helped him put on his mask back on. When the man caught his breath, he opened his palm wide, showing McCoy two blue zip locks.

"That's not why I'm here, sir. You just put those away for now. Just nod yes if there's a back door out of here?"

155

The old man shook his head no.

"How about upstairs? Any fire escape or balcony I need to know about?"

The man again shook his head no.

"OK, last question. Anyone upstairs?"

A tear trickled down the man's cheek as he nodded yes.

McCoy unholstered his Glock and stepped up the dark stairway, quickly and quietly. This was the path the gunman had taken, McCoy concluded, right through the front door, past the two bedrooms, and straight up the stairs. If the gunman was still in the apartment, he would have to come back the same way to get out.

At the top of the stairs, McCoy could hear music coming from the adjoining room. He recognized it as "Waterfalls," a TLC song he often heard playing in the night clubs and bath houses on P Street.

"Metropolitan Police Department!" McCoy called out. "Identify yourself!"

Hearing no answer, he counted to three to steel himself, then kicked the door in. From a bed with yellow and pink Hello Kitty sheets, not five feet away, two teenage girls stared back at him, each shot point blank in the forehead.

McCoy fought the urge to vomit, then quickly searched through the tiny room. The girls' blood had just begun to pool under the bed. The killer was gone, but he hadn't missed him by much.

Back downstairs, he raced past the old man sitting just as he had found him, watching T.V. in his Sunday best. The hysterical grandma was still outside, held back by several officers.

"Hey, Supercop! What's up in there? Looks like you seen a ghost."

McCoy looked back at the room with the flickering

television light. "All clear," he had said. "Cancel SWAT and call the M.E."

Now, two months later, the case of the executed teenagers remained unsolved. Ballistics test determined that both girls were killed by the same gun – an SMC-380, a somewhat rare Hungarian-made weapon that was known as the poor man's Walther PPK. Beyond that, however, the killer left nothing behind that could identify him – no fingerprints, no hair, nothing.

The detectives assigned to the case learned that one of the girls, Constance Settles, had recently moved to Sursum Corda to live with her grandmother; the other victim, fifteen-year-old Empress Alsbrooks, evidently was spending the night. The grandmother called 911 after she heard the shots, but claimed she hadn't seen anyone come in or go out.

Junie – grandma's "ole man" – was even less helpful. A diabetic whose kidneys and lungs were failing him, he was mostly confined to his La-Z-Boy recliner. Though the killer would have had to walk past the room where he was, the old man told the detectives that the television was on so loud that he didn't hear the shots, much less the killer's footsteps.

The detectives began focusing on how the intruder would have got into the unit, which the grandma said she always locked tight. The only other person with keys to the security gate was the Resident Manager, a belligerent Muslim who refused to speak to the police. Such reticence naturally drew the focus of the detectives, who discovered that the Resident Manager had fathered a child with the mother of a small time drug dealer. That drug dealer went to the same school as Empress, and rumors were that the two were romantically linked.

"So we're looking at the angle that this was a crime of passion," the lead detective had explained to McCoy.

"According to kids in the neighborhood, this girl Empress had broken up with the drug dealer because she decided she was going to be gay. And these kids, they say that everyone knew that Constance was gay. So we got the Resident Manager opening the door for the killer."

"I just don't buy it," McCoy said. This had all the markings of a professional hit: no muss, no fuss, just two shots to the head when the girls were least suspecting it. "What's the drug dealing boyfriend saying?"

"Nuttin'," the detective chortled. "He was shot and killed two weeks earlier, end of March, beginning of April, something like that."

"Hard to see how he could have done it then. And if he's out of the picture, what's the Resident Manager's motive?"

The homicide detective just shrugged his shoulders in response. "Look, Supercop, that's all we have to go on right now. Why do you think we're coming to you?"

§ § § § § § § § §

Annie Fairbrother looked at the clock again. It was almost five a.m. – another night of no sleep.

She just couldn't get out of her mind Steve's offhand comment, upon her arrival home that evening after she'd kicked the shoes off her swollen feet: "Honey, there's a message from Dr. Bandy."

"There is?" she'd replied. "What'd she say?"

"I don't know. I didn't listen to the whole thing. I mean, it wasn't from Dr. Bandy herself, of course. It was from her office."

"You didn't listen to it?"

"No. I saved it for you. Something about scheduling another sonogram or amnio or something like that."

You selfish bastard, Annie now thought, looking at her sleeping husband. Maybe if you'd gone to just one of my doctor's appointments, you'd know the difference between an amino and a sonogram.

Annie wiped a tear from her eye. Being upset with her husband made it easier for her to not completely break down worrying over her babies. But the questions kept flooding back: Why would I need another amnio? Is there something wrong with my babies?

With two amniotic sacs – one holding her son, the other, her identical twin daughters – Annie required what amounted to two tests. And in the case of an amniocentesis, that meant two needle-sticks, doubling the not-insignificant risk of an inadvertent laceration that could kill or maim one of the children and cause Annie to bleed to death as well.

And now they want me to do it again?

Her thoughts were racing now. Maybe they just mixed up the results, maybe that's why they have to do it again. Or maybe the office just called the wrong number. Maybe they just left their message on the wrong machine.

"Honey, something wrong?" Steve asked groggily. "You've been tossing and turning all night."

"No. It's ... nothing."

"OK, look, I got that big meeting with the Director tomorrow? On that Saudi deal?"

"It's OK, Steve. I'll go sleep in the guest room."

"Thanks, babe," he said, digging his face in the pillow. "You're still the greatest."

§ § § § § § § § §

When the beginnings of daylight began streaming through the dirty window, De La snapped the heavy curtains shut.

"This job with the Captain got me all screwed up," he complained. "But what'd I expect bumping curbs?"

He grabbed the pitcher full of water and celery sticks and took a long draw.

"Ah, that's good! Minister say this tonic gon help me get rid of all these muthafuckin germs I's got. Fuck that AZT shit! Pills be expensive as a muth and still don't do nothing!"

De La wiped his mouth on his short, muscled arm.

"So anyway, yeah, I'm down with Minister And-One. He ah-ight. But that Captain? I'm telling you! First, it's git the nigga in the courthouse. Then it's like, don't git him cuz we gotta find out if he did what he 'sposed to do. Then it's back to square one, but first make sure to take his bag from him. What I wanna know is, who wants some homeless muthafucka's bag?"

De La took another long drink of the celery water.

"Look, I'm just a soldier, I know that. If Captain want me to go back to court today, I'll go back. If he want me to go back tomorrow, I'll do that too. But I ain't stupid. You can 'splain a little bit to me 'bout what's going on. It ain't my fault that Ko-rean done kicked it fo' telling me about this Greek Fire bidness. Who knew a man could be kilt by a Taser?"

A car alarm began sounding from outside. Standing on his tip-toes, he peered through the peep-hole.

"You know, I read," he said under his breath. "I study. I travel. Y'all think I ain't been outta D.C.? Shee, I been all across this country doing jobs. Texas, Cali, even been to Wyoming. So what the fuck you know? You stupid ass niggas probably never heard of no Wyoming!"

De La feigned a kick towards one of the two prostitutes who sat tied up together on his floor, but the woman did not flinch. The other woman followed him with terrified eyes.

"Wake up bitch! I don' pay you hoes to sleep!"

160

De La resumed his pacing.

"Now I want you all to listen closely, cause what I'm about to tell you is going to educate you in a way you dumb ass niggas never heard. Trifling niggas think they gonna get over on the Devil? Muthafuckas! Don you all know that we all just the Devil in disguise? He's right here, he's in the bowels. That's right. Mind you, I study, I read, I actually be listening to what Minister And-One gotta say. It just makes sense. If God made everything, then he had to have made the Devil too. That's why even little chilluns do bad things, see? But it's OK, because all the bad shit we do is balanced out by the good things we do. Or the good things we going to do. You know, in the future and shit. It's like a bank, see?"

De La noticed that the one whore was still eyeballing him.

"Oh, that's right, you dumb hoes don't know nothing about no banks. Well, let me break it down to you this way: see, it's like lay-away, or when you go halves on a dove and you – Bitch! What you squirming for? I'm trying to learn you some knowledge here."

He bent over and yanked the duct tape off the frightened prostitute's mouth.

"Please, Mr. De La. It's just that Shameika, she cold. I can feel it."

"Whuz that gotta do with me?"

"Well, I was just wondering, since she don seem to want it, if I could have hers?"

De La deliberated the request.

"Ah-igght," he finally said. "How you trickin' ho's split up yo money is yo bidness." He picked the pipe off the table and jammed it between the woman's cracked lips.

"Ain't you gon let me hold it, Mr. De La?" the woman managed to ask.

"No, bitch. You think I'm gonna untie your schemin' ass?

161

You want the pipe or not?"

"Yes, Mr. De La. Thank you, Mr. De La. Could you just light it for me then?"

He rolled his eyes as he lit the glass pipe for the woman and let her draw on it. She exhaled the sweet smoke and began to ask for more, but he slapped her mouth back shut with the duct tape.

"Now, as I was saying before I was interrupted, it's all about balance. See, what you poisonous bitches don understand is that by taking your little babies and killing them before they's born, you don messed up the whole thing. No balance, see? You don killed this little baby, but this little baby never don' nothing wrong to nobody. Now he's dead, and that bad thing done to him, he never gets a chance for sumpin good to happen so as to balance the whole thing out. Right? So it falls on you, see? It's all gotta fall on all you bitches."

A coughing fit suddenly overcame De La. He spit a mouthful of blood on the floor before resuming: "Point is, there's so many of them dead babies, all out of balance, that the whole of this here society needs to be – needs to have – oh what the Minister call it, a regurgitive? Re-spurkelative? Sumpin like that."

He took another long draw on the celery water.

"Mmm-mmm! It's like this here celery juice. Our society needs to have its shit cleared out, flushed, destroyed, just so's we can make it back to square one, see? Just so we can get back part of our balance. And I aims to do my little part, see?"

De La picked a small black case off the floor and placed it on the table. Then he pulled out the soldering iron and plugged it in.

"That Captain," he chuckled, "he sure do got the best toys."

The whore that had been eyeballing him began pulling

162

herself to the door, frantically dragging the dead one with her.

"Oh no, you don't," De La said calmly. "We got some more balancing to do here fust."

§ § § § § § § § §

McCoy started to pull off from the Bins when something caught his eye. On one of the nearby silos, he saw a spray-painted swastika – the counter-clockwise swastika he remembered seeing near the school where he had caught Stancil. The radio was quiet, so he decided to take a closer look.

As he crawled through a hole in the fence, he immediately detected the unmistakable odor of rotting flesh, and as he followed the trail of spray-painted swastikas, the odor became stronger. McCoy pulled out a handkerchief and held it to his nose as the graffiti ended at the arched entrance to one of the brick silos.

He took a deep breath and stepped in, scanning the interior walls with his flashlight. The silos were a lot bigger than they looked from the street. The place was filled with trash and discarded furniture; there were flies buzzing all over. And then he saw it – the decomposing body of a huge Rottweiler.

"Just another one of your wild goose chases," he exhaled.

Back in his car, he called the Fourth District Dispatcher. "This is Scout Car 16, over."

"Over 16."

"Can you put a call in to Animal Control? Report of dead animal. Have them check the McMillan Reservoir, just off of the corner of First and Channing Northwest. Follow the smell. Over."

"Roger that 16. Uh, 16 ... We got a memo here... The city's Animal Control Department has been ... uh, canceled."

"Canceled?"

"Affirmative, 16. Budget issues."

"We don't even have a dog catcher in this town anymore?"

"Uh, 16, all calls are being referred to the SPCA. Or I can call Department of Public Works, have them send a trash truck?"

"Negative on the trash truck. Send over the Humane Society or whatever. Looks like they're holding dog fights in the Bins again; probably something they should look into."

A gust of wind came rushing across the reservoir, and McCoy realized that his uniform now smelled like dead dog. That smell then touched off a memory – a memory of the strong smell coming from Malcolm X. Stancil's clothes on the night he had arrested him. McCoy had originally thought the smell was gasoline – but now he remembered that it was more subdued, like the odor of a strong glue or epoxy.

"Those weren't paint cans I caught him with," McCoy said to himself. "So why would he have a bunch of empty apoxy cans with him?"

It was a small detail, but an important one – if only because it had been omitted and overlooked, and the discovery of one overlooked detail would inevitably lead to some other omitted piece of evidence.

Like the blue zips old man Junie had offered him.

~ Chapter Fourteen ~

Not in the original design of the courthouse, the Lawyer's Lounge sits across from the cafeteria, carved from the space underneath the escalator wells. The blinds covering its windows are stained yellow with age, while its wooden entry door hangs on one hinge. A bubbling splatter of red escalator lubricant has seeped into the back wall, threatening the funeral notices, office-space advertisements, legal announcements, and out-of-date phone directories. The coat rack near the door sags under the weight of a variety of men's polyester suit jackets, shabby overcoats, and dozens of wire hangers, while several mismatched women's shoes are strewn about the floor, as are half-a-dozen broken mini-umbrellas, an empty plastic vodka bottle, and several moldy Styrofoam take-out containers. Overflowing ashtrays litter the room, even though smoking is not permitted in the courthouse. An old-style black rotary phone covered in dandruff sits atop a slightly off-center wooden table, along with a variety of take-out menus, packets of condiments, and weeks-old newspapers.

Despite its name, the Lawyer's Lounge is not inhabited by lawyers; rather, CJA investigators rule the roost. Mostly irascible old black men, the investigators work almost exclusively for the Fifth Streeters, helping them run their shoestring law practices by making phone calls, picking up and answering mail, monitoring court dates, feeding parking meters, even handling the completion and filing of the lawyers' CJA vouchers – just about anything short of actual investigation.

Nursing a wicked hang-over, Liam found himself in this very same Lawyer's Lounge, waiting behind just such a fellow. Liam had come to court early, hoping to use the CCS computer to gather some basic information about his new client, but unfortunately, no amount of throat clearing or audible sighing made the investigator type any faster.

"Excuse me, sir?" he finally said. "Are you gonna be much longer?"

"Won't be but a minute."

Liam stared at the clock on the wall. Ten to nine. "Lawyer's Lounge's supposed to be for lawyers," he said under his breath.

"Oh, sorry, counselor," the old man smirked. "Were you waiting? I's almost done."

Liam could see he'd irritated the man. "Sir, I've gotta go before the Chief Judge in, like, five minutes. And I'm kinda new around here."

"The Chief Judge? Why didn't you say so?"

When the man got up, Liam took his seat and began typing his client's name into the computer. "How does this thing work again?"

The old man sighed. "Stucky come to find out that I be helping a newbie? Sheee! Just press the F10 key."

Liam stared at the screen, unsure of what he was looking at.

"Jamal Stancil, D.O.B. 11/10/67," the man said, reading over Liam's shoulder. "See there? He's got a conviction for Attempt PWID in '87."

"Pwid?"

"Possession with Intent to Distribute. See the asterisk? That means a conviction. And that right there means that the judge put your man on probation for two years. Next case, see there? Another conviction, less than a year later. Distribution of Cocaine. And a few months after that, he pled guilty to a felony failure to appear. See that? Bail Reform Act?"

"Oh yeah."

"Young man got a rack of time. One-to-three on the Attempt PWID, one-to-three on the Distribution, and one-to-three on the BRA, all consecutive."

"Oh. What does that mean?"

"He could have been locked up for as many as nine or as few as three, all at the whims and fancies of the Parole Board. Scroll down a bit. See? Man can't stay out of trouble. See here? Look at all those '90 cases, probably right when he got out on parole. Simple assault. Simple assault. Both cases DWP'd."

"Dismissed for want of prosecution?"

"That's right. And here, he's got another three cases. Threats, Unlawful Entry, Destruction of Property. All three DWP'd. This gotta be a domestic case for real."

"How can you tell it's domestic?"

"I've only been doing this for ten years, see?"

"Oh. Sure."

"Now see this case in '92. See? All these charges got the same case number."

"Damn!" Liam became excited as he read the charges out loud. "Assault with a Deadly Weapon, Felony Threats, Burglary, Unlawful Entry, two counts of Aggravated Assault, three counts of Simple Assault, one count of Contempt."

"But only one conviction." The old man nodded at the screen.

"Agg Assault. That must be the one the judge was talking about. But three to ten for kickin' your girl in the ribs?"

"If that's what it says."

"I mean, I know it's serious to beat up your girlfriend or whatever. But ten years? What could the guy have done to get ten years?"

"Hey, it's all a crapshoot out here."

"So, is that it?"

"Whatchu mean?"

"Are these all his cases? Isn't there anymore?"

"That's it for this guy."

"No Unlawful Entry charge for this year? See, that's what triggered the show cause I've got."

"Doesn't look like it. But who knows? Maybe your man used an alias when he was arrested; or maybe his name done punched in wrong on the computer. You might wanna look at the court jacket for that '92 case. You're going to see stuff in there that you can't get from the computer. Better act quick, though; some other lawyer gonna get that CJA voucher."

"Well, thanks. Thanks a lot."

"No problem, counselor. Now, if you're through?"

"Oh, I'm sorry. Hey, I didn't get your name."

"Name's Handy. Handy Mann."

"Handyman?"

"That's right. If you ever need an investigator, give me a holler. This is where I be most the time."

"Didn't you say you work for Stucky?"

"Stucky, Stove, all them Fifth Streeters," the man said with obvious pride. "But it ain't no thang. Half those guys headed for retirement, half on their way to being disbarred. And then what am I gonna do? Go back to drivin' a cab and bumpin' curbs? At my age? I don't think so. Besides, I see you coming up the ranks with a case like that one 'ere."

Liam blushed. "Oh, come on."

"Oh yeah!" the man laughed. "You gonna make a lot of cake on that dude there."

§ § § § § § § § §

With time to spare and a certain weakness of the knees, Liam decided to risk the elevators, and as luck would have it, the doors to one of the four elevators opened just as he approached.

A single homeless guy stood inside, wiping fresh vomit off of his mouth with his sleeve. Liam recognized the man as "Hip Hop," the Capitol Hill vagrant who got his nickname from his peculiar two steps-forward one step-back hitch.

"Help the homeless?" Hip Hop asked. "Buy me a baloney sandwich?"

Liam shook his head no and stepped back from the elevator, and as he did, a young black woman with long blond hair ran past yelling, "Hold the door!" But it was too late – the elevator had already started its ascent.

"Can you believe that?" she said. "Trifling nigga can't even hold the door!" She was wearing black jogging tights and a man's long sleeve collared shirt, and with one button loose, Liam took note that she was not wearing a bra.

The woman pressed the up button several times and, after a moment, Liam stepped forward gave the button a push too.

"Solidarity," he said with a shake of his fist.

A moment later, the doors to the same elevator opened and the blond haired black woman sashayed in. Smiling at Liam, she pulled out a cigarette from her purse and lit it.

"Ain't you coming?" she asked.

"Ah, no, I'll wait for the next one." Though Hip Hop was no longer on the elevator, Liam could see that the remnants of his shelter breakfast were.

But as the elevator doors began to flutter to a close, the woman shot her arm out to stop them. "Whatchu mean, the next one?"

"I'm, ah, waiting for the – you know, the other one. I mean, I'm taking the stairs. Or the escalators."

"What's wrong?" the woman asked, blowing smoke rings. "You 'fraid to ride with me?"

Liam cleared his throat. "No, it's not that. It's, ah, that elevator, the floor, it's, like, covered in puke."

"Oooh, you right," she cackled, looking at the bottom of her high heeled shoes before darting out just as the doors closed behind her. "That elevator be stinkin' like a muth!"

"Told you."

The woman took a long look at Liam before asking, "You a lawyer?"

"Uh, yes."

"You any good? Cause you look like you a good lawyer."

Liam blushed. "Yeah, I'm O.K., I guess."

"Got a card?"

"Of course. And what's your name, young lady?"

"Brandy Carey," she purred. "For men who like their Brandy with a 'y', not an 'i'." For emphasis, she stuck her index finger in her mouth, wet it, and drew an imaginary 'y' in the air.

"Well, B-b-brandy with a 'y,'" Liam stuttered, "maybe I'll, uh, catch you later."

§ § § § § § § § §

"Mr. McNaughton, we're still waiting for government counsel," the Chief Judge said as Liam walked into the empty courtroom. "Your client is in the dock if you wish to speak to him."

"Thank you, Your Honor. I was hoping to take a look at the court jacket first, if I may."

"Madame Clerk, make it so."

Surprised to find the judge on the bench this early, Liam kept looking over his shoulder as he leafed backwards through the thick court file. He found the probable cause affidavit, and as he read the document silently, he realized this was no ordinary Agg Assault:

> *On November 23, 1992, at 1442 hrs. C-1 and C-2 reported to 7D to complain that C-1 had just been assaulted by her boyfriend S-1 Stancil, Jamal. C-1 complained of stomach pain where S-1 had stomped on her with his shod foot. C-1 is 8 - 9 mo. pregnant. C-2 is the mother of C-1.*
>
> *An ambulance transported C-1 from 7-D to D.C. General Hospital, where C-1 gave birth to a stillborn baby girl.*
>
> *The undersigned Det. Birru interviewed C-1 and C-2 at the hospital. C-1 states that when she came home to 1334 Stevens S.E., Unit 101, S-1 began yelling at her, and grabbed her throat to choke her. S-1 asked C-1 where had she been, was she up at Potomac Gardens again. S-1 said he had brought some diapers and shoes for the baby. S-1 threw C-1 on the bed and continued to choke her. C-1 told S-1 she had come home that day but left to go up to her moms to get some food. S-1 left outside, but came back an hour later and demanded that C-1 let him in. C-1 did let S-1 into the residence. S-1 turned the radio up loud and pulled down the blinds and told C-1 that she would wish the f– she hadn't open the door. S-1 grabbed C-1 by her hair and threatened he would kill her and C-2. S-1 threw C-1 on the floor and stomped on her stomach three times while wearing Air Jordan sneakers. Then S-1 demanded to have sex, but C-1 said her stomach hurt too much, and S-1 fled the scene.*
>
> *C-1 called C-2 to come take her to the police. C-2 says that C-1 has stayed with S-1 too long, and that S-1 has beat her before but C-1 never showed up in court so all the cases were dismissed.*

171

> *C-1 initially denied that S-1 stomped her, and said*
> *that she got elbowed by another girl at a basketball*
> *game. C-1 further stated that she cut S-1 with a box-*
> *cutter two times in the past and threatened to put him*
> *in the morgue. C-1 also stated she will never testify*
> *against S-1.*
>
> *On November 24 1993, S-1 was arrested at his job*
> *at the Anacostia Vet Clinic and charged with ADW -*
> *Shod Foot. On that same date, at 1334 Stevens S.E.,*
> *Unit 101, at 2115 hrs., taken from scene was one (1)*
> *pair Air Jordan sneakers found in kitchen trash can.*

Liam closed the file and pumped his fist, catching the eye of the Chief Judge.

"Counsel, are you quite finished?"

"Thank you, judge! I am. If I could just have a minute to meet with my client, that'd be great!"

The judge waved him on, and the two Marshals nodded in unison, so he proceeded into the dungeon, eager to see the monster.

§ § § § § § § § §

The orange-jumpsuits began the usual calls. *"You my lawyer?" "Got any cigarettes?" "Marlton Stove out there?"*

Liam ignored them, calling out his client's name in a serious voice.

One orange-clad man silently pushed his way forward.

"You Stancil?"

The man nodded sullenly.

"Great! My name is Liam McNaughton. The court appointed me to be your lawyer today. Actually, yesterday. I mean, I'm representing you today; I got appointed yesterday. But never mind that. What's that bandage on your head for?"

"Marshals stole me."

"*Stole* you? OK, whatever. We don't have a lot of time, and I'm not sure where to start. Your old lawyer, Bunning Goodwine? He's a judge now."

"He a judge?"

"Yes, *he's* a judge. In Maryland."

"He still be my lawyer?"

"Well, for a variety of reasons, no, he isn't." Liam tried to explain that a sitting judge isn't allowed to appear in court as a legal advocate, but his client interrupted him.

"What about that lady lawyer? Downstairs. Yesterday. When I walked in."

"You went through C-10 yesterday?"

"C-10? I guess so."

"Well, that's good news! I should be able to get the Chief Judge to quash the bench warrant he issued for you. You can't be in two places at once, right?"

"How many cases I got?"

"Two, I think. This one here is a show cause. You're on probation. Remember Judge DeMaglio?" The man stared at Liam blankly. "Well, anyway, he died. So now the Chief Judge has your case. He's going to determine whether you violated your probation like the government says you have."

"I didn't violate nothing. I ain't even supposed to be up in here."

"And that's what I'm going to help you prove, Mr. Stancil. I mean, unless you want that lady lawyer you had downstairs?"

"Nah, you ai-iight. I dinit think she all that anyhow. She won't let me talk or nuthin."

"Right. Well, I'd prefer that you don't talk either. Not yet." Liam motioned to all the other orange-clad brothers in the cage. "Not here," he whispered. "Too many people, no privacy."

"Oh, yeah. Privacy. I can dig it."

"Well, look, Mr. Stancil, like I said, I don't know what your new case is about. I thought I read that you were charged with Unlawful Entry –"

"At the school?"

"A school? Actually, I don't know where it happened. I mean, if it happened at all, if you catch my drift."

"I was out there doing the right thing, man! Working n'shit! Staying out of trouble!"

"I see. You were working at the school? Is that what you're saying?"

His client looked at him with suspicion, and Liam could tell that he wasn't getting through, so he tried to channel Red Green by saying, "You know, Mr. Stancil, it's your choice whether you go to trial or plead guilty. You're the boss, see? I work for you."

"Guilty? Whatchu talking 'bout guilty?"

"No, no! I'm not saying that. Today, right now, we're pleading *not* guilty, so I can try to get you out of here. OK?"

"I am not guilty."

"Right. And you can have a trial, if that's what you want. But let's find out what the police are saying first. Like I said, now is not really the time to discuss it."

"Privacy?"

"Exactly."

"Can I axe you a question then?" Leaning in closer, the man held his finger in the air for emphasis. "Jes one question."

"Sure."

"What's that unlawful entering? What is that? I done been charged with that before. I just never knew, you know, what that was."

"Unlawful Entry? That's when you go into some place – some building, let's say – and you're not supposed to be there.

Like trespassing."

"But I was supposed to be up in there! They let me in!"

"Who?" Liam asked a little too loudly. "Who let you in?"

The man took a look on either side of him, then pushed his face up against the bars. "Yo, you think I'm gonna get outta here today?"

"I'm certainly going to try," Liam said, taking a step back. "You do have some back-up time, though."

"Back-up time?"

"Yes. From your other case. The one you pled guilty to. Aggravated Assault. You got a ten year suspended sentence on that. But, look, if the judge steps you back today, the good news is you'll get credit against your sentence for every day you do."

"Whut!" The man pulled his face from between the bars and stepped back. "'Good news?' You say that like a nigga wanna stay locked up!"

"Well, I –"

"You ain't never been to no prison, have you?"

"Well, once," Liam said weakly. "Class trip, during law school."

A few of the orange-clads chuckled.

"Look, maybe we should start at the beginning," Liam said, trying to recover. "If I can just get some quick info about you. Your biographic report says you are NFA. You know, 'No Fixed Address'? But in the comments here it says you report living the last ninety days in something called 'The Bins'? Is there an address there where I can send you mail?"

"Look, man, I don't care about no mail. Damn! I knew I shoulda brought them lady-bug jumps wid me. Now they all dead fo' sure."

"Ladybugs? Mr. Stancil? I'm sorry, did you just say –?"

The man jammed his face back against the bars. "I gotta

THE HEYWARD SHEPHERD CONSPIRACY

get outta here!" he screamed. "I promised on my life to never kill nothin again! Them bugs gonna die on account of me, and then all them chiluns and babies gonna die too!"

Just then, the Marshals banged open the heavy iron door that separated the dungeon from the courtroom. One Marshal – a young muscular white guy – jingled the strand of chains he had draped over his arm; the other, an older black man in a three-piece suit, said in a smooth voice, "Judge called the case. Wait outside, will ya, Counsel?"

§ § § § § § § § §

Liam scampered into the courtroom, took up his position at the defense table, and scanned the nearly empty gallery. Several Fifth Streeters were in the front row, sizing him up no doubt. A mustachioed white cop sat in the last row, closest to the door; and right in front of the cop slumped a short, muscular black man in dark glasses.

To Liam's immediate left stood Dan Gerson, the buzz-cut prosecutor from the day before, joined this time by an obviously pregnant black woman.

Bringing out the big guns for me, Liam smirked to himself.

Gerson and the woman were staring back at him with obvious looks of disgust as Liam's client shuffled up next to him, hands and feet shackled, a Marshal on each arm.

The Chief Judge cleared his throat. "Mister McNaughton, we were expecting your client yesterday, as you know."

"Yes, Your Honor. I've spoken to Mr. Stancil, and it appears he *was* in court yesterday. Possibly even C-10. Just not this courtroom."

"The show cause notice directed him to appear here, sir, in my courtroom."

"Well, ah, yes, Your Honor. I haven't really asked him about that particular aspect of that, ah, situation. To be honest, I can't really say whether he - Mr. Stancil – even got that show cause notice because I really haven't had enough time to interview the defendant. I mean, my client. If we could just pass the matter –"

"Oh there'll be no passing of the matter, sir. I've called Miss Fairbrother away from a trial. A jury trial, isn't that right, Miss Fairbrother?"

The black woman prosecutor scowled at Liam. "Yes, Your Honor. That's right."

"So we will be dealing with this matter right now. Miss Fairbrother, what do you know about this man being in C-10 yesterday?"

"The government's file jacket indicates that the defendant was arraigned on a citation on June 15th. One count of Unlawful Entry."

"And is that what this probation violation is based upon?"

"It is, Your Honor."

"I see. Do we have the probation officer here to see how was doing otherwise?"

"No, Your Honor. Mr. Stancil was apparently on unsupervised probation."

"Unsupervised probation? Well, well, well, well, well. Miss Fairbrother, I certainly wish someone from the probation office was here right now, cause I would certainly let them know that that is totally unacceptable as far as this judicial officer is concerned!"

The courtroom was silent for a moment. Liam looked over to see his client staring back at him. "Aint you going to say nothin?" he asked plaintively.

Liam gave the thumbs up and whispered back, "I got this."

"And Miss Fairbrother," the Chief continued, "do you

know who that new case is going in front of?"

"Misdemeanor Calendar 2. Judge Malley, Your Honor. My notes here say it's set for trial on June 22nd."

"Next Thursday? Isn't that the ...?"

The courtroom clerk looked up. "Yes, Your Honor, Judicial Conference, June 22nd and 23rd."

"Thought so. Well, counsel, Judge Malley's chambers will have to figure that one out. Mr. McNaughton?"

"Yes, Your Honor?"

"You'll be representing Mr. Stancil in the new case?"

"Well, sure, Your Honor. I just don't know if, yesterday, he was assigned other counsel."

"I'm appointing you counsel right now. Draft an order and submit it to chambers. How long do you need?"

Liam asked for two days.

"You don't need two days to draft an order, counsel. Submit it to chambers no later than noon tomorrow. Now, to the business at hand."

The Chief Judge turned to face Liam's client directly.

"Mr. Stancil, one of the standard conditions of probation is to obey all laws and not get arrested on probable cause in any new case. Now there's been an allegation that you've been arrested for Unlawful Entry. That is a misdemeanor, sir, punishable by six months. Or, pardon me, up to 180 days. Same thing. So, Mr. McNaughton, will your client be submitting?"

"Submitting? Submitting to what?"

"Submitting to the fact that he was arrested on probable cause, sir, so we can proceed directly to sentencing."

Liam looked at his client and gave him a confident wink.

"Absolutely not, Your Honor! We insist that the show cause trail the resolution of the new case. My client is presumed innocent, of course, so I would ask that Mr. Stancil be released on his personal recognizance and that this matter be scheduled sometime after the trial before Judge Malley."

"Counsel, did you say you wanted me to reconsider his conditions of release?"

Liam looked over at his client, who was frantically mouthing the words, "Get me out!"

"Yes, Your Honor … that's right. I'm asking that my client be released. "

"Mr. – sir, your client, he's being held without bond in the case before Judge Malley. Now you know I can't change his bond status there – unless, of course, you want a hearing right now under Rule 32.1."

"Rule 32?"

"Rule 32.1, sir. The government would have to show probable cause right now. Are you ready to proceed on that, Miss Fairbrother?"

"The government *is* ready, Your Honor."

Liam had no idea what was going on, so he tried to buy himself some time.

"Your Honor? If I may be heard on that? I just don't think –"

"Just a second ago, Mr. McNaughton, you were insisting – insisting! – that my determination of whether your client violated his probation be put off until the matter before Judge Malley is resolved, whenever that may be. But at the same time, you ask that your client be released. So it appeared to me that maybe you were not aware of the procedures we follow in this court. But if you and the government are both in agreement, then we'll go ahead and do the probable cause determination right now."

"Uh, Your Honor?"

Liam was momentarily distracted by his client, who was dramatically craning his neck, looking around the courtroom.

179

"As I was saying, Your Honor, I just don't think that would be ... appropriate. You know, under the circumstances."

"And what circumstances would those be? Hmmm? Mr. McNaughton? Do tell. Please, enlighten the court."

Liam wondered what he had said or done to so piss off this judge. Whatever it was, he thought, it couldn't have been *that* bad. He just couldn't believe that any judge – much less the Chief Judge – would be so – so –

"Petty!" a voice called out from the audience. It was the blond-haired black woman – Brandy with a 'y.' She had made her way to the front row of the gallery, her shapely ass squarely in the leering faces of the seated Fifth Streeters.

"You petty nigga," she continued, seemingly directing her comments at Liam. "You just a dirty, crazy ol' fool, hiding out in some *reservoir*, stead of coming home like you know you should!"

The judge rapped his gavel frantically. "Madam, that will be enough from you! Who is – Marshals, remove that woman!"

"I'm going, I'm going," Brandy said, putting a cigarette in her mouth as she scampered out of the courtroom. "Y'all gotta chill!"

"I'm sorry, Your Honor," the prosecutor said. "That woman is the complainant, or, rather, was the ... she's the victim in this case. She and the defendant had a relationship, many years ago. I asked her –"

"I don't care who she is, Miss Fairbrother! I will not allow my courtroom to become a circus, with people screaming at each other! All right? Marshals, come back here! Never mind her!"

The judge's shoulders were heaving up and down.

"Now - here - is - what - we - are - going - to - do," he said slowly. "We're going to do the probable cause hearing right now, since Mr. McNaughton is insisting on it. Right now! And if I find probable cause, we will proceed directly to sentencing. Miss Fairbrother, do you have your witness?"

"Yes, Your Honor. Government calls Officer James McCoy to the stand!"

Liam sat down, butterflies dancing in his stomach. He pretended not to see his wide eyed client looking back at him.

"Your Honor, if I can have just a minute," the prosecutor said, somewhat sheepishly. "My officer must have stepped outside."

Liam began praying, *Please don't let there be a cop, please don't let there be a cop, please don't let there be a cop,* only looking up when he heard the judge say, "Miss Fairbrother, any news?"

The prosecutor had a packet of Rolaids in her fist and appeared to be eating one after another. "Uh, Your Honor," she said, swallowing hard, "my officer, he was right here a moment ago. If we could just pass the matter?"

"Well now, *Miss* Fairbrother," the Chief Judge seethed. "I just got done telling defense counsel over here that I wouldn't pass the case for him. I certainly can't do that for the government now, can I?"

"Your Honor, I do have to return to Judge Roundtree's courtroom for my trial. I'm sure I can be back here with my officer at noon. Or at one – whenever we take our lunch break."

"No, no, no. I'm not messing up my calendar on account of the U.S. Attorney's Office being unprepared. Your request for a continuance, Miss Fairbrother, is denied. Mr. McNaughton, this appears to be your lucky day. I'm not going to trail the matter on Judge Malley's calendar. No sir, I will not do that. We will simply set this case down for trial and see if the government can prove that your client violated his probation."

"You mean, a trial on the Unlawful Entry charge?" Liam

asked.

"Yes, sir, that's right," the judge said with a pronounced sigh. "I'm going to do that in about 30 to 45 days. You might want to take a look at Rule 32.1 before then, sir. You know how these trial matters get delayed, and I'm not going to wait for months and months while this case sits on the Misdemeanor Calendar waiting for trial. How is June 30th? Two weeks?"

Liam flipped open his empty calendar. "I'm sorry," he lied, "that day just won't work."

"OK, then, the following Monday. July 3rd."

"Your Honor, is the court really going to be open that day? I mean, that's the day before the Fourth of –"

"Miss Fairbrother? The 3rd?"

"Yes, Your Honor, that's fine."

"July 3rd it is then.   Unless there is anything else? Marshals, step him back."

Liam felt someone tugging on his jacket. It was his client. "Can't you get me in a half-way house or something?"

"Ah, yes. Your Honor, excuse me. What about my request regarding Mr. Stancil's release status? I mean, at least, in this case. Not Judge Malley's case, of course. My client did turn himself in on a citation yesterday, Your Honor, so I don't hardly think he's a flight risk."

"You want him released in this case?"

"Yes, Your Honor."

"Even though he's being held without bond in another case?"

"Uh, yes. I mean ... that's what he wants."

"We'll see about that. What's the government's position?"

"Your Honor," the prosecutor said, her voice rising, "the government vehemently opposes any release conditions for this defendant, in this or any other case. As Your Honor knows, this defendant pleaded guilty to a serious felony, Aggravated Assault, for stomping on his long-time girlfriend. And Your Honor saw how small that woman was, Brandy Carey, the defendant's ex-girlfriend, when she was in here earlier."

"She didn't look so small to me," the judge smirked. "Or all that intimidated by him either."

"But Your Honor, this man has a long history of violence towards his girlfriend, then-girlfriend, Miss Carey. Stalking her, destroying her property. He's destroyed the property of her mother. He's threatened the mother! There were something like sixteen counts in that indictment. Sixteen!"

"Fifteen of which were dismissed as part of the plea. Do I have that right, Miss Fairbrother?"

"Actually, Your Honor, yes. Our office was considering —"

"No, I don't want to hear what you were considering. What we're really left with here is this new case. Unlawful Entry. A misdemeanor, Miss Fairbrother."

"But at a school where Brandy Carey, the victim in this case, is employed. Or I should say, rather, where her mother — where her mother Bootsy Henson works."

"The victim's mother works at the school? Or the victim works there?"

The prosecutor seemed momentarily flustered. "The mother, Your Honor."

"Well, that's not enough for me."

"There's one more thing." The prosecutor took a deep breath before continuing. "Though he pled to the Agg Assault, Mr. Stancil was originally brought in on an arrest for an ADW-Shod Foot, for stomping and kicking Miss Carey. At the time, Your Honor, she was pregnant, nine months pregnant. That was indicted as an ADW Shod Foot and an Aggravated Assault. But, at the time, Your Honor, our office elected not to proceed with the murder charge against Mr. Stancil."

"Murder?"

"Yes, Your Honor. For the killing of his unborn child!"

"Miss Fairbrother?" the Chief Judge said, leaning forward. "Hasn't that ship already sailed?"

"No, Your Honor. There is no statute of limitations on murder. It wasn't dismissed as part of the plea offer. And I intend to re-indict!"

Liam gasped, his client began shaking his head no, and an audible cry came from the Fifth Streeters in the front row. "The rookie?" they stammered. "A murder case?"

"Order!" commanded the Chief Judge. "I will have order in the court! Miss Fairbrother, you're telling me that he kicked a pregnant woman and killed her pre-born?"

"Yes, Your Honor, that's right."

"Incredible," he said, shaking his head. "Just incredible. And you say that the defendant now has had some contact with the young woman's mother, who works for this school?"

"He was in the school, Your Honor! We have evidence that he was even in the particular location of where Miss Henson works, near the auditorium, near the dining room."

Liam noticed his client begin to tap his chained feet up and down. The two Marshals, noticing the same thing, stepped up close behind.

"Mr. Stancil. Mr. Stancil! Look up here, sir. I'm speaking to you now," the Chief said slowly and deliberately. "Let me tell you something, sir. Where I came up, in Detroit, we had a word for a man who beat up on his woman. You know what we called men like that? We called them punks. Punks! Are you a punk, Mr. Stancil? Are you?"

"I dinnit kill that baby! That's a lie! Miss Fairbrother knows —"

"Mr. Stancil, you will sit down!"

"This here is a frame-up! You know it! My lawyer know it!"

The Marshals jumped into action, pushing Liam aside and dragging his client back to the dungeon. "I dinnit do it!" he continued to yell. "I dinit kill that baby!"

"That's right, Marshals, remove the defendant," the Chief said. "He will be held without bond in this case as well."

~ Chapter Fifteen ~

Annie had to sit down. Her head was swimming and she felt like she was going to cry.

She had just gone way out on a limb by threatening to bring a murder indictment *the* U.S. Attorney had ordered her to bury three years earlier. Maybe it was her hormones, she thought, or maybe it was just the heat of the moment.

"Miss Fairbrother, you may be excused," the judge said. "Miss Macaby informs me that Judge Roundtree's courtroom has called up here several times. They've got a jury pool waiting. Feel free to let Judge Roundtree know that I personally ordered you to appear here this morning. I'm sure he'll understand."

"Thank you, Your Honor," Annie replied. "I'll do that."

She pushed herself out of her seat and waddled out of the courtroom, dragging her litigation box behind.

§ § § § § § § § §

De La Suggs held the courtroom door open for the lady prosecutor, checking out her ass as she passed by.

He wondered what it would be like to bend over a pregnant bitch.

"This fat little D.A. better hope I don't decide to find out," he said under his breath. "Give her *and* that baby this AIDS."

§ § § § § § § § §

McCoy pulled up to the liquor store, just a block off of Sursum Corda. Olsen was there, waving him down.

He had never driven so fast, making it from in front of the

courthouse to eight blocks away in less than three minutes. He felt bad leaving out on Miss Fairbrother like that, but it had looked like they were going to continue the case as usual.

Besides, this was his opportunity to catch a killer. Soon as he received Olsen's page, he had to move.

§ § § § § § § § §

Liam returned to the gallery and placed his briefcase in an empty seat next to the scowling Fifth Streeters. I can't leave things like this, he thought. I gotta go talk to this guy before they send him back to jail.

Inside the little dungeon, his client was pacing back and forth in the crowded cell, constantly running into the other prisoners.

"Hey Stancil!" Liam called out. "Mr. Stancil!"

"Why dinnit you get me out!"

"Look, man, you just gotta calm down."

"Yeah, nigga, you best calm down!" several voices called out.

"I'm gonna help you, Mr. Stancil, I promise," Liam said, beckoning his client near. "I'm gonna try to get you out of here. Don't worry."

"Why was she there?" he asked, on the verge of tears.

"Who? The prosecutor? Miss Fairbrother?"

"No! Brandy!"

"Oh, her?" Liam shifted uncomfortably. "I don't know."

"She look kinda skinny to me," he sniffled. "Like she still on the pipe. What you think?"

"Uh, I didn't notice."

"Man, I gotta get out of this joint. Right now!"

"Mr. Stancil, let me try to explain what's going on, OK?

187

I don't know much about your case yet 'cause the government hasn't given me shit. But we're gonna beat this thing. It just might take some time. You know, let me get all the paperwork in order."

"How much time?"

"I - I don't know. Not much. Look, the judge said you've got to go before another judge, Judge Malley, in two weeks. I know Judge Malley. I'm, like, in front of him all the time. I'll file a bond review motion before him –"

"Ain't gonna last two weeks in 'ere."

"– and then after that, I'll file the same motion in this case and – What? What d'you mean you ain't gonna last? It's just two weeks."

Liam stared into his client's eyes and, for the first time, saw the monster he was hoping for. *Dark pools of shimmering wet hate, a certain lackadaisical lowering of the eyelids, a distance beckoning from inside trying to negotiate the terms of surrender.*

"Two weeks?" his client said in a half-laugh, half-cry. "Gonna be dead in two minutes. That's all the time I need. You just wait and see."

Then he resumed his pacing.

Liam didn't know what to do or say. The other men in the cell began yelling at him to get the Marshals, so he ran back into the courtroom.

"Um, excuse me," he said, crouching next to the young white Marshal. "I gotta problem. My client, he's, like, going berserk back there."

"Ask the clerk for the form."

"What form?"

"The medical alert form."

Conscious that the Chief Judge was eyeballing him again, Liam approached in as servile a posture as possible.

"Excuse me, Ma'am," he whispered to the clerk. "Do you have some kind of form, like a medical alert form?"

"Of course, dear," she whispered. "What's the problem?"

"I think my client is –"

Liam stopped short. It seemed wrong to share something so personal about his client with a stranger and he wondered if he was violating some sort of client confidence.

"Well, dear, what is it?"

"I think my client is trying to hurt himself."

"Oh! You have to tell one of the Marshals to put him on suicide-watch right away! Go on! Do it!"

So back to the Marshal he went, telling him that he thought his client might be suicidal. The young tough looked at him indifferently. "Yeah, yeah. We'll take care of it."

So, without anything more to do, Liam retrieved his briefcase and stalked out of the courtroom.

§ § § § § § § § §

McCoy drove up next to Olsen, drivers-side to drivers-side in their department issue Chevrolets. "So he went in?"

"Just like you said he would."

"How long ago?"

"When I first paged you," Olsen said, "he and Junie were just sitting in the car for a while. Maybe ten, fifteen minutes. They went in, I'd say, no more than two minutes before you pulled up."

"How'd Junie look?"

"Like the junkie scum-bag that he is."

The two cops exited their cars and stood at the edge of the alley. McCoy noticed that the shirt Olsen was wearing had a huge Confederate flag on it and said in bold letters, *YOU'VE GOT YOUR 'X', I'VE GOT MINE.*

"All right," McCoy sighed. "When they come back out, Junie's supposed to pull his handkerchief from his pocket and blow his nose. That's the sign, that's when we pull our badges, that's when we take him down."

"That's when I go for the gun!"

"Hey, Dennis, we do this right, and no one should have to pull a gun."

McCoy had gone back to Sursum Corda earlier that morning to ask Junie about the blue zips he'd shown him on the night of the shooting. The old man said he'd been wondering when the police were going to figure things out and come back and get him. Sure, he confessed, he knew a man was coming to kill Empress. But he never would have unlocked the doors like he did if he knew that the assassin was also going to kill his old lady's grandbaby.

Junie told McCoy he was sorry, real sorry, for the killings, but he was sick, he was an addict, he needed a program. "Please don' tell my ole lady bout that," he begged. "That'll just kill her. Tell her I'ma gone to jail over the drugs you caught me with."

"No can do," McCoy answered. "You aided and abetted a murder."

He *Mirandized* Junie, and told him that if he wanted a lawyer, he could get one from the CJA Office in a couple of hours. But Junie said he didn't need no lawyer, he knew what he done was wrong.

"I'm old and sick," he wheezed. "It don't really matter what they do to me. But y'all oughta get the dudes that did this thing, for real!"

McCoy's jaw dropped. "You know who killed the girls?"

"Sho' I do. His street name Devil. He not from roun' here. But the one that puts him up to it, I know him too. It was Ali done the ordering. It was one of Ali's boys that done gave me them little zips for payment."

At this point, McCoy took out his mini recorder and re-*Mirandized* Junie on tape. Then he asked, "So why did Ali hire Devil to kill the girls?"

"Kids shooting dice, that's all," he answered, leaning in close towards the tape-recorder. "See, Empress done seen one boy shoot another – that little yella kid she used to go with, I don' really know his name. Empress wasn't working with the cops, she knew better. But your detectives kept pressing her anyway, going in and out her momma's house. What you think them drug boys gonna think? Homicide going in and out of yo' house? Sheet, if them young'uns gonna go down on one murder beef, they might as well go down on two."

"Or in this case, three," McCoy quipped.

Junie volunteered to help McCoy catch the killers, just so long as the homicide detectives weren't involved.

"They's just as guilty for them girls' dying as me," he said bitterly. And lest Junie change his simple mind, McCoy put him into play that very morning.

The plan was simple. Junie was to put the word out that he wanted an additional payment from Ali since the killing of Connie wasn't part of the original deal. And to lend an air of credibility to the set-up, McCoy had made sure Junie would come cheap. "All's I wants is another couple of rocks," the old man told Ali's messenger boy. "Jes like last time."

McCoy gave Junie his pager number, telling him he had 24 hours to arrange the meeting with Ali, Devil, or both; after that, he was turning him over to Homicide. Though he figured the killers would move on Junie quickly to prevent the old crackhead from bartering what he knew elsewhere, McCoy was startled to receive Junie's page just two hours later. He knew he couldn't do this alone, and since he was scheduled to partner with Olsen that afternoon, he reluctantly decided to bring him in, calling him at home that morning.

McCoy had assured him that he would share in the credit for breaking the case, something that would surely get Olsen off his quasi-suspension.

"Come to work two hours early for that?" Olsen replied. "I don't think so."

Then McCoy told him that he'd get to wear civies and drive his own department issue car, and Olsen replied, "Now that's what I'm talking 'bout! Where we meetin'?"

Now, nestled behind a dumpster, McCoy and Olsen had a clear view of the liquor store. They didn't have to wait long. Junie came out of the store, wheeling his little portable oxygen tank and carrying a 40 oz. bottle wrapped in a brown paper bag. A tall skinny man with corn-rows, sharply angled eye-brows, and a pointed beard came out after him.

"That's Devil," Olsen said. "I know it. Just look at him!"

"Didn't you tell Junie to walk two yards ahead of him?" McCoy asked. "He's too close. We gotta back off."

"Fuck that! It's go time!" Olsen suddenly charged forward, his weapon drawn. "Get on the ground, motherfucker!"

Using Junie as a shield, the man with the corn-rows calmly pulled out his big silver semi-automatic and, holding the gun sideways, started squeezing out a flurry of shots.

A bullet glanced off Olsen's shoulder blade, and he fell to the ground screaming.

McCoy had no choice now. With his Glock drawn, he walked directly at the man, arm straight out, taking aim. He felt the bullets whizz by him, but he plodded on and took his shots, wild-west style – blam! blam! and then splat! McCoy's third shot spiraling past Junie's ear and through the other man's forehead. The corn-rowed man stood straight up for a moment, cross-eyed, then crumpled backwards, pulling Junie to the ground with him.

McCoy ran to Olsen, who was rolling on the ground in pain.

"You OK?"

"No I'm not OK! But, I'm alive. Damn, McCoy! I wish I could shoot like that!"

"Spend more time at the range, less at the gym," McCoy said over his shoulder as he pulled out his walkie-talkie and called out 10-53 with shots fired and his location. Then he went to attend to Junie.

He pushed the other man's body off of him and, holding Junie's purple face in his hands, asked, "This is Devil, right? He's the one who shot the girls, right?"

Blinking rapidly, Junie managed to make this dying declaration: "That Ali. That other boy, De La ... he got that brand on his neck, you know? He said, he said, he couldn't make it, other business to attend –"

§§§§§§§§§

Liam sat down in a brown Formica chair and tried to catch his breath. Out of the corner of his eye, he saw a flash of blond hair.

"So what kind of lawyer are you?" Brandy Carey asked. "Just stand there and don't say nothing?"

"Well, Miss," Liam fired back, "if you hadn't of run out of the courtroom, you might have seen that I kept your boyfriend from being sent back to jail for a long, long time."

"Scuse me! He ain't my boyfriend, number one. And number two, if you so good, where he now?"

With Brandy getting up in his face like that, Liam saw her that the man's button-down shirt she wore was frayed around the collar and stained yellow around the pits. Both of her ear lobes had been ripped clear through and her fingers were covered with red oozing burns. When she caught Liam staring, she drew her hands behind her back self-consciously.

"I ain't on the pipe, if that's what Mal toll you."

"Mal? You mean Jamal? Jamal Stancil?"

"Jamal? Please! His name Mal. After Mali. That country in Africa or wherever. That the name his mother gave to him."

A long yawn came over Liam. "So, Miss Carey, what exactly are you doing here?"

"The lady D.A., Miss Fairbrother, she the one that called my ma," Brandy said, lighting up a cigarette. "She toll my ma that Mal was up to his old tricks. Sneaking up in where my mom works and all that. I think the D.A. want us to go to the grand jury later today. So I'm jes waiting here so I can get my witness fee voucher."

"Your mom works at the school? What – is she a teacher or something?"

"No, she ain't a teacher! And she ain't the janitor neither! She may not be all educated and shit, but she run the whole gotdamn cafeteria. Five hundred girls a day eats in there. She makes good money, too."

Brandy blew a puff of smoke in Liam's direction. "Coulda got me a job there too, 'cept I don' get along with no Mexicans."

"I can't imagine why not."

"Thank you," she said cheerily. "You know, maybe if *you* gave me a witness fee voucher, we could jes go ahead and roll outta here together."

Liam shook his head, the fatigue setting in. "I don't think so, Miss Carey. I gotta get going. You got my card if you wanna talk about the case or whatever. And you know, you're not really supposed to be smoking in the courthouse."

Brandy rolled her eyes as she put the cigarette out against

the chair. "Don't you wanna see the pictures 'fore you go?"

"Pictures? Of what?"

"The baby. The one he kilt."

Liam's eyes opened wide.

"I got them right here," she said, pulling two Polaroids from her purse. "Here, lookit."

Liam examined the photos. The first one was dark and blurry. "What's this?"

"That's me," Brandy said proudly. "That's my stomach." She pointed to a particularly dark spot on the photograph. "Right here's where Mal stompted me. See the bruises? They shaped like his foot."

Liam nodded his head and said, "Oh." On the reverse side of the Polaroid he saw a yellow Exhibit sticker with the hand-written words *U.S. v. Jamal Stancil, Government Exhibit 3A.*

"How'd you get these?" he demanded.

"Them's the D.A.'s. But after Mal copped, she said I could keep 'em."

"I see."

"Ain't you gonna look at the other one?"

"Sure. Why not?"

The second photo showed Brandy proudly displaying a baby in what appeared to be an over-sized Baptismal gown and white bonnet. A woman stood over Brandy's shoulder, looking off-camera. "That's my mom standing there," Brandy said, pointing to the woman. "She talking to the detective or sumpin. And that there is my little girl."

Liam squinted, focusing on the little shriveled face inside the bonnet. He recoiled when he realized he was looking at a still-born baby.

"The people in the hospital let me hold her a while," Brandy explained. "I named her Mallory, after Mal. She was going to be such a good baby, too. So quiet and peaceful...."

Liam handed Brandy back the photos.

"You got any kids?" she asked.

"No. Not that I know of."

Brandy turned her head sideways, as if she didn't understand.

"It's a joke," he mumbled. "No, I don't have no kids."

"Well, I've had two – three if you including little Mallory. And let me tell you sumpin. These little babies be kickin' like a muth, all moving around inside of you and shit, specially near the end fore they come out. But not Mallory. Mmm-mm. She just lie there quiet, dinnit bother me the least bit. Not at all, not for weeks. That's what make a good chile good."

Liam thought he saw Brandy's eyes well up.

"Mal done kilt a good chile," she said softly.

The door to the Chief Judge's courtroom suddenly swung open.

"Hey you," the well-dressed black Marshal called out. "Yeah, you! That Stancil, he's yours right?"

"Yessir," Liam said, standing up. "Why?"

"You with Law Students in Court or something?"

"No sir. I'm a lawyer. An actual member of the bar."

The Marshal smiled broadly and clapped his hand on Liam's shoulder. "Well then, that was a good call, counselor. A good call indeed!"

"Uh, what was?"

"Putting your man on suicide watch like that. By the time we got in there, he was half-way to a tweener."

"A what?"

"An in-betweener."

Liam shrugged his shoulders.

"The inmate, see, he jams his head up between the bars, wedge it in there real good like, then he jump in the air. Twist your neck like that, you kill yourself quick."

196

"Glad I could help."

"What happened?" Brandy asked. "What'd Mal do?"

Liam felt like he was going to faint.

"He just tried to kill himself. But don't worry, the Marshal says he's OK."

"Worried?" Brandy cackled. "Damn, fool, I ain't worried. I can't wait to tell my moms that stupid nigga trying to kill his-old-self again!"

~ Chapter Sixteen ~

The phone in the Administrative Office started ringing again, and when he could take it no longer, Minister And-One got off his knees to answer it.

"Ah, how I long for the days of an organized staff," he lamented, directing his comments towards the portrait of Sun Yung Moon that hung on his wall.

Just as he picked up the phone, however, the church's answering machine took control, his own tape recorded voice saying, "Praise God and Salutations! You've reached the most revered St. Gerard Majella's New Moon Temple, Incorporated, Minister Clinton Augustus And-One, Pastor. I'm so humbly sorry I can't be here to take your call. Please leave your name and number, and with God's grace, someone will get back to you."

The caller began speaking in frantic Korean, so Minister And-One quietly put the receiver down, letting the machine continue the conversation.

He tried to return to his prayers, but was distracted by the same second guessing that had plagued him since he first broke free from the Vatican's yoke some three years earlier. His decision to start an independent congregation seemed like the right thing to do at the time: the Minister would get to keep all the money in the collection plate, he could embrace the Afro-centricities his congregation was demanding, and he didn't have to answer to Rome (or anyone else for that matter) if he decided to take a wife.

The Catholic Church struck back quickly, of course, immediately excommunicating the Reverend Clinton Anderson – as he was then known. Worse, the Washington Diocese's civil action to recover their real assets churned slowly and expensively against the Minister in the local court.

Though his sermons would become far more charismatic, it turned out that his long time parishioners didn't much care for his Pan-African Catholic-lite with a Unification twist, and consequently the church coffers began to dry up. Even the Korean wife he was given didn't turn out as expected. Sure, she doted on him like a servant and submitted to him willingly, but she didn't speak English, and all those pickled vegetables she served for dinner made him terribly gassy.

So, perhaps it was entirely predictable that just nine months after breaking away from the Catholic Church, Minister Clinton Augustus And-One – as he came to be known – decided to abandon the gothic church building that was St. Martin's and move his laughable little flock to a strip mall in Suitland. But just as he was prepared to throw in the towel, God sent him a blessing in disguise: the long-haired white man who showed up one day at the church flashing a smile and a U.S. Marshal's badge.

He said he was there to serve one Reverend Clinton Anderson with a "pad-locking" order to prevent the building's continued use as a place of worship. For emphasis, the man rattled the chains he had draped over his arm.

Minister And-One had protested vehemently – *"How come my lawyers haven't seen this?"* *"This violates my freedom of speech!"* *"And besides, you can't serve me with that – I've legally changed my name!"* – and to his surprise, the white man relented.

The Captain – as he liked to be called – said he'd read the newspaper articles about the Vatican's high-handed legal maneuvers and, as a man who had himself accepted Jesus Christ as his savior, he decided he *just* had to help. The Captain claimed that he was close to a local judge who was a dark horse contender for the job of Chief Judge. Though mostly a ceremonial position, the Chief Judge nonetheless had the power to rotate judicial assignments and control the court's calendar. If the Minister could just help him win enough votes from his fellow judges – and in particular, the white judges – the Captain promised that *Chief* Judge Armstrong Cummings would be in a position to "take care" of his pending litigation with Rome.

And all the Captain wanted in return for brokering the deal was for the Minister to look the other way while he ran his prison ministry out of the basement of the disputed church building itself. "All I need is a phone line so I can log on to the internet," the man had said.

At first, Minister And-One thought he was being flimflammed. "What you talking 'bout, the 'internets'? And what kinda ministry you run? I know I ain't never seen you down at Lorton. Besides, what kind of pull do you think I have with those Caucasian judges?"

"It's not so much *your* pull," the Captain had replied. "It's your people's newspaper. What do you think all of them Gingrich revolutionaries are reading up there on the Hill? The Washington Post? If you can get your people to write a few articles about the election for Chief Judge, a few favorable editorials here and there, you just watch what happens next. Trust me, if their new overseers in Congress decide Armstrong Cummings is the man, those white judges will follow suit."

The Minister did as he was told, and it turned out Reverend Moon's newspaper editors were all too happy to intervene on behalf of the law-and-order tough-on-crime candidate (and it certainly didn't hurt that the judge was married to a Korean). And sure enough, Armstrong Cummings was elected by his peers to the Chief Judge post, unexpectedly garnering the majority of his votes from the court's white judicial officers.

But here, six months later, as the archdiocese's lawsuit against Minister And-One continued to drag on, and with his church practically becoming a homeless shelter for every manner of shady character claiming allegiance to the Captain, the Minister began to wonder if he had made a deal with the Devil.

The phone in the administrative office rang again, breaking Minister And-One's concentration. He got to the phone quickly this time. "Hello? Saint Gerard Majella's New Moon Temple."

"Hey partner. How's it swinging?"

Minister And-One immediately recognized the nasally mid-western voice of the Captain.

"My Norse brother! I was just thinking about you. I've so been meaning to speak to you. Matters of grave importance, I'm afraid."

"Wanna hear the good news first?"

The Minister involuntarily sucked in his breath. "Am I on the podium?"

"Like the sound of that, huh? Oh yeah, imagine the headlines: 'Minister And-One Shares Million Man March Podium with Farrakhan!' Boy, you'll have that temple of yours filled to the rafters after that."

"Praise Jesus!"

"Just one catch, partner. You really gotta wow them with your speech. I mean really knock 'em dead. This is going to be your moment in the sun. I mean, who else is talking about abortion in the black community?"

"You're right, you're so right."

"Is Jesse talking about abortion? Is Farrakhan for that matter?"

"Nope."

"Johnny Cochran?"

"No, not him."

"No Augustus, you are. You're the only one."

"Yes, yes, I am. I am the only one."

"Just you knock that speech down at St. Nicks' and it's all but in the bag that you'll be on the podium."

"And you really think a single speaking engagement will get the Roman Pope off my back? I mean, I'm still spending an awful lot of money on them lawyers. That's what I wanted to talk to you about –"

"Come on, partner, think about it! The leading African-American pro-life advocate in the nation? You think the Catholic church is going to mess with you then?"

"So when is it, Captain? I've almost got the whole speech committed to memory, and I have some edits I'd like to discuss."

"It's all set up for Monday, October 16th, round noon. And, ah, no edits."

"October 16th? Why that's the day of the March, isn't it?"

"It is now. Unless Farrakhan changes it again."

"My, oh my! How am I going to know if I'm on the podium if I'm giving the speech that same day? Is someone from Farrakhan's group going to be there? Does the diocese know I'll be speaking at the school? They're not going to be too happy when I show up there, you know?"

"Hey, hey, hey! Too many questions! Come on now, Augustus. What are you worried about?"

"Well, come on now indeed! That's a lot of pressure, coming down there and all, not sure if I'm gonna make it on the podium."

"Listen, that's just the way things work in Washington – no one wants to put it down in writing. You're going to have a huge crowd in there – five hundred seats plus. That speech of yours will absolutely light a fire underneath them. And please, tell me you haven't you forgotten our little contrivance?"

"The ladybugs?"

"That's right! What was that term you used? Oh yeah!

'Curtain of Life!'"

"Yes, well –"

"'Curtain of Life!' Say it with me, Augustus!"

"Curtain of Life. Yes, yes. It's just that it will be so ... unusual."

"Exactly. That's the point. Look, the Olympics release doves, the Vatican sends smoke signals. You think colored balloons dropping from the ceiling is going to get you on CNN? We're talking about creating a whole new paradigm here. Your presentation has to be moving on a number of levels."

"But those bugs ... are they really gonna hatch or whatever when I need them to?"

"What did I tell you? Everything has been worked out. Except for maybe one thing. We may have a problem with that guy you got for me."

"Malcolm?"

"Yeah, that one."

"Why, I haven't seen Malcolm since that day your mob tore after him. What, two, three months ago? What happened? Didn't he do what he was supposed to do?"

"Yeah, he did what he was supposed to do. But we're concerned, really concerned, that he might have gone *back* into the school and messed things up."

"Messed things up?"

"With the ladybugs."

"Oh, that. Can't we just go back in? Check and see if the boxes are where they're supposed to be? What about the plumber? Mr. Kim? Isn't he still at the school?"

"Mr. Kim... he's gone. That job ended."

"Why not just send one of them hoodlums you got holed away in my church? Have one of them go in there and, you know, check. It ain't like they doing anything else worthwhile."

"Look, Augustus, there's a lot of heat on that school now, especially after Malcolm got himself arrested. You wanna try sneaking back in that school? You wanna try looking on the bottom of five hundred seats to try to find twenty five boxes of bugs?"

"Well, no. Like I said, I'm not actually sure the school will even let me in there for my speech. I'm excommunicated, remember? St. Nick's is still a diocesan school."

The Captain sighed. "How many times do I have to tell you, things have been taken care of. But if you want out, I'm sure I can find some other life crusader who will be honored to take your place."

"No, no," the Minister said quickly. "Just tell me what you want me to do."

"Two things, Augustus. The first thing, I want you to go down to the jail and speak to your man Malcolm X. Find out if he went back in that school, maybe ask him where he was staying before he got locked-up. And his bag – we're interested in his bag, the yellow one we gave him. But don't come right out and ask him about it, OK? The less he knows about the plan, the better."

"Oh, don't worry about that. I can do nuance."

"And the other thing: find out if he's been talking to his lawyer. Our friend the Chief messed up and assigned some wet-behind-the-ears rookie to the case. I just want to make sure everything turns out all right for Malcolm."

"O.K. But I ain't talking to no lawyers."

"Leave that to me, Augustus. Leave that to me. Now, just one last thing: I'm sending over two more of my boys to St. Martin's."

"St. Gerard Majella's," the Minister corrected.

"Right, you're right. Sorry. Anyways, these guys just got out, they'll need the usual. You know, a cot, regular meals, one of those Raider football jerseys. They'll be coming by tonight."

"Now look here, Captain. I appreciate everything you're doing for me. I really do. But I already got half-a-dozen of these ex-cons staying here. I don't know if I got room for no more."

"Augustus, you got the room. If there is anything you got over here, it's room."

"But look, these guys you're sending over, I don't know, they bad."

"You'd be bad too if you just got outta the joint. Minister to them, Augustus, make them one of your moon warriors. I really don't care. They just need a place to hide out for a bit."

"But –"

"One kid's called Dione, something like that. The other one is Ali. You know the deal. They're hot. Don't let no one know they're there. No one, understand? And next time I'm in the neighborhood, I'll try to bring you another donation for the poor box."

"Just so long you don't send that Devil back here! Don be making him yo' little messenger boy over here no mo!"

"Devil? You mean De La?"

"De La, Devil, whatever the man call his-self. I don't like him one bit. No sir. That's where I have to draw the line. Do you know I found him in Koko's bathroom?"

"So?"

"She was taking a bath! The man was – abusing himself! Right in front of her!"

"You don't say," the Captain laughed.

"It's not funny, sir! Not funny at all! You know, she's thinking about going back to Korea over this!"

"All right, partner, calm down. You're right, I shouldn't joke when it comes to your wife."

"That's right! Thank you."

205

"Look, these young guys, they got some problems, we both know it. But when the apocalypse comes – and it is coming, Augustus, it's coming soon – these are the kind of soldiers you want around you, soldiers in the army of God. Just do your part. The rest will take care of itself."

§ § § § § § § § §

When the Captain didn't immediately respond to his page, De La decided to take the initiative.

He went back to the Chief Judge's courtroom to see who was there and upon his arrival he found the young white lawyer and Mal's little skeezer talking to one of the courthouse security guards. When they all split up, he decided to follow the lawyer.

The white man walked fast up Constitution Avenue, and De La began lagging behind just past the big government building – the one he thought looked like a big white titty – but he was close enough to see when the lawyer ducked down some stairs mid-block, right in front of another big white government building.

"Place crawling with pigs," De La remarked.

Trying to remain inconspicuous, he walked up on a little booth full of uniformed policemen and asked them what the big marble building was.

"Uh, the United States Supreme Court, sir."

"The Supreme Court?" De La aped. "Man, you must have to do something really bad to get caught up in that jump?"

Since the cops in the booth didn't seem to be paying him any mind, De La crossed the street, stopped in front of the lawyer's apartment building, and bent down on one knee to tighten up the laces of his Timberlands.

Stooped down like that, he could see right inside the

lawyer's apartment, and he watched with a bit of excitement as the white man took off his clothes and lay down naked on top of his bed.

A group of Japanese tourists suddenly approached De La, holding out their cameras, asking him in broken English to take their pictures. De La waved them off furiously before taking one last look at the lawyer.

"Sweet dreams, nigga," he said between his teeth. "Better hope you don't see me in any of 'em."

§ § § § § § § § §

Liam looked up at the polished walnut dresser where his father kept his black socks, V-neck undershirts, boxers and briefs. His father's face stared back at him from within the laboratory identification card that hung from the knob of the dresser door.

The dresser began to grow bigger and bigger, threatening to topple over him as if pushed from behind. He held his arms over his head to brace for impact, but popped out the back side of the dresser instead.

It was dark and cold there. He took one tentative step, then another, then fell off a ledge into space. He tried to scream, but could make no sound. With nothing below him or above him, he did not stop, but he did not hit bottom either.

He was in space.

Floating.

At peace.

Then he looked at his hands. They were the hands of a toddler, maybe an infant, covered in soap bubbles. He saw that he was in an antique bathtub, the water level rising quickly. His head felt heavy, his neck weak, and the water began to overtop him.

He ducked down into the soapy water and frantically pawed the bottom of the tub for the drain stopper. He was just out of air when his chubby, child-like hands found the chain. He pulled it free with his last effort and the water began to recede just as quickly as it had filled up.

He could breathe again. He felt such joy, he began crying tears of happiness.

Then a black shadow came over him. A huge Nike sneaker pushed him back under the water and began to stomp him until his chest caved in.

VII. Summer/Fall 1995

Some say the blacker the berry, the sweeter the juice
I say the darker the flesh then the deeper the roots
I give a holler to my sisters on welfare
Tupac cares, and don't nobody else care
And uhh, I know they like to beat ya down a lot
When you come around the block brothas clown a lot
But please don't cry, dry your eyes, never let up
Forgive but don't forget, girl keep your head up
And when he tells you ain't nuttin don't believe him
And if he can't learn to love you should leave him
Cause sista you don't need him
And I ain't tryin to gas ya up, I just call em how I see em
You know it makes me unhappy (what's that)
When brothas make babies, and leave a young mother to be a pappy
And since we all came from a woman
Got our name from a woman and our game from a woman
I wonder why we take from our women
Why we rape our women, do we hate our women?
I think it's time to kill for our women
Time to heal our women, be real to our women
And if we don't we'll have a race of babies
That will hate the ladies, that make the babies
And since a man can't make one
He has no right to tell a woman when and where to create one
So will the real men get up
I know you're fed up ladies, but keep your head up

2Pac, Keep Ya Head Up (1993)

~ **Chapter Seventeen** ~

Thursday, June 22, 1995
Dear Dad:
I sent you a Father's Day card a couple of weeks back, but it came back "undeliverable." I'll try sending this letter to your work address – I'm sure it'll find you there. Anyway, happy belated Father's Day.

I'm writing this letter to you from the District of Columbia Jail. Relax! Your first-born son is not a criminal. Rather, I am a criminal defense lawyer.

I'm here to speak to a client of mine who is locked up pending his trial. He's got some pretty serious charges, and may even be prosecuted for killing a baby! I know it may sound a little heinous; but my job is to give zealous representation to my clients, no matter what they are charged with. The system would fall apart if there were not defense lawyers willing to do what I'm doing.

Actually, this is my first time here, and I've just learned the hard way that the jail does something called the "count" at three o'clock every day. Once they start the count – where they literally count every head to make sure that no one has escaped – they stop moving the prisoners. So that means no legal visits until the count is over. I got here around 2 o'clock, but it took about 45 minutes to get through all the security procedures they have here.

(I don't know what's harder to do – breaking out of jail or getting in!)

Anyway, by the time I reached this clump of dirty glass cubicles the lawyers use for legal visits, it was five minutes to three – evidently not enough time to get my client from the bowels of the jail to the visiting area before the count started.

So I'm here waiting with two other attorneys, relative

newcomers like me. They think the count will stop soon, and say that this kind of delay is not unusual. So I figured I'd use my time wisely and try to catch up with dear old dad.

I moved to Washington D.C. last summer, after I took the bar exam. I live in an apartment that's right across the street from the Supreme Court. Really! You can see the roof of my apartment building in some of the postcards of the Capitol – I'll send you one! I've met a lot of people here, and have a lot of great friends. Money is a little tight right now, but I think I did the right thing moving out here.

Do you remember that trip we took to Washington when we were kids? I think I must have been eight, Owen was probably four or five. Remember how we were driving around all frantic, looking for parking near the monuments? Well, guess what? I now realize where we were. We were over by the Lincoln Monument, where Rock Creek Parkway begins. The roads really get confusing over there, and I think you must have accidently turned onto the highway entrance just past the volleyball courts. Once you do that, you can't do anything but drive to Virginia, which is exactly what we did. Next stop Williamsburg!

You know, if you want to visit Washington again, you could stay with me at my apartment. I've got a couch that folds out into a bed and my place is really convenient to all the sights. I don't think I've seen you since you visited us in New Mexico. That was what? Christmas, fifteen years ago? I must have been twelve years old. Remember the sled you brought us all the way from New York? The one with the blades? Funny how these memories are coming back. I think Owen and I used that sled once, on one of the irrigation ditches we had in our neighborhood. It may have been that winter, when you visited, it may have been the year after. Anyway, one morning we woke up and there was just enough snow to shoot down about six feet of irrigation ditch into an alfalfa patch. By mid-day, the snow was melted and our little hill had turned to mud.

We did OK, me, Owen, Mom. I don't mean to say we didn't miss you – at least Owen and I. It would've been great if you moved out there with us. Or if we moved back.

Well, I got to go. A guard's coming around, checking our credentials.

. . . .

Dad, you'll never believe this! The guards won't let us out! There's several prisoners missing on the count and they've locked down the jail. Not only are all the legal visits cancelled, they won't let any of us leave because they don't have any spare guards to "escort" us out.

Oh, and wait. It gets better. The client I came here to see – the one who stomped his baby (that's a story for another day) – the guard tells me he's not even at the jail today because he's across the street at D.C. General Hospital. I was just now informed that he slashed open his wrists last night. Can you believe that? I got the judge to put him on suicide watch, and somehow he gets hold of a razor? What kind of place is this?

Anyway, I got to go again. The other lawyers are arguing with the guard, and it looks like they're winning, so maybe I'll get out some time this evening.

Your Son, Liam

§ § § § § § § § §

Monday, July 3, 1995.

Whoops! Sorry Dad. My bad! I'm sitting in court right now, waiting for that same client's case to be called (the client I was waiting to visit in jail), and I just now came across this legal pad with the letter I wrote you, still in the file. I promise I'll send this out if I ever get out of this courtroom today.

I'm finding that being a lawyer means lots of waiting around. I don't quite know why, but even routine matters seem to take forever. Some judges, like the one I'm in front of now, think they can hurry the cases along by being gruff and denigrating to the lawyers, but that just starts arguments and bickering back and forth, and before you know it, the routine scheduling matter takes twenty minutes. And it's not just rookie lawyers like me – the judge I'm in front of now, he's the Chief Judge, and he picks fights with everyone!

Take my case, for example. My client, he calls himself Mal, he's been arrested for breaking into a school, and the case is in front of a judge named Malley (a good Irish Catholic, he takes Mass every day at noon, just like you, Dad – Not!). The case was originally set for trial on June 22nd, but on that day there was a "judicial conference" – whatever that is – and the whole courthouse was shut down. So my guy's trial was automatically re-set for another day, all the way to October 16th, which is kind of a good thing since I hadn't really spoken to my client about his case and wasn't really prepared for any kind of trial. Unfortunately, that meant that my client would have to stay locked up for a while longer, so I figured I had better tell him in person – that's what I was doing down at the jail the last time I wrote you.

Well, since then, I've gone back again and again. You could say I'm a regular at the D.C. Jail now. And with what

213

I've come to learn, I can say that my client has some serious problems, not all of them related to his current incarceration.

See, a couple of years ago, the cops arrested my guy after his nine-month pregnant girlfriend showed up at the police station with foot prints all over her stomach. She claimed Mal had beaten her, just like before. This time, however, the cops and the prosecutors really went after him. As I understand it, in order to avoid a trial on the charge of killing the baby, Mal pled guilty to kicking her, or stomping her, or whatever. Anyway, for this Aggravated Assault, the judge gave my guy a "split sentence": two years of incarceration followed by four years of probation.

So fast forward to April of this year. Mal gets arrested for breaking into this school, which in turn triggers a hearing on whether his probation should be revoked in the first case. Ordinarily the judge with the probation case simply "trails" the resolution of the new charge: in other words, the trial of the new charge always goes first. If the defendant is found guilty in his new case, then his probation can be automatically revoked by the "show cause" judge, and the defendant is returned to prison to serve the rest of his sentence. But if the guy beats the charges – you know, found not guilty – then the "show cause" hearing is dismissed and the guy continues on probation.

So here's where it gets weird. The Baby Stomper case – that's what I call the underlying probation case – was set for hearing this morning, and we've already been up before the Chief Judge. I made the rather routine request that my client's "show cause" hearing be continued past October 16th – the day of his Unlawful Entry trial. But the judge denied it! The prosecutor (everyone calls her Miss Fairbrother, even though I'm pretty sure she's married), she told the judge that she really doesn't object to trailing the new case, since she just learned that the principal police witness in that case had recently been suspended for a shooting he was involved in.

The judge still said no.

Well, when the judge said that, the prosecutor began to look like she was going to throw up, which kind of surprised me because I've heard that Miss Fairbrother is a pretty experienced prosecutor. According to these guys I hang out with (I call them the Murder Lawyers), she was the lead prosecutor on a lot of really gruesome cases, cases that were in the papers and stuff.

So after an awkward silence, Miss Fairbrother tells the Chief Judge that she'd like to advise the court about some medical issues she's dealing with, and the judge says go ahead. She asks if she may approach the bench (you know, so that the whole courtroom doesn't hear what she has to say), but the judge says no.

And I swear, I saw the prosecutor begin to cry. She pulled herself together pretty quick, though, telling the judge that she's been scheduled to undergo some tests later on today. But the judge just twisted his face up like he'd tasted a lemon, and said, "So?"

Miss Fairbrother, who is pretty obviously pregnant, said something about how she was expecting triplets, two girls and a boy, but something had come up or whatever and she and her husband had some important decisions to make that afternoon. By the time she finished, tears were just streaming down her face, and she had this pathetic whistle coming from her nose. I've never seen anything like that.

So the judge – the prick – he says, "Miss Fairbrother, please compose yourself. You are a representative of the U.S. government, and I expect you to comport yourself in that manner. I'll pass your case for a moment so I can decide what weight to give you and defense counsel's joint request for a

215

continuance."

So now we're just sitting here waiting for the judge to decide whether to go forward or not, even though both sides want to come back another day. It seems like the Chief Judge is determined to make us try this case twice – once in front of him, and then again in front of Judge Malley – and I can't afford to lose either case.

(I mean, my client can't afford to lose either case. Me, I expect to go over the $1,250 limit on both vouchers easy! And trust me, I really need the money.)

I mean, it's pretty simple. Either my client was in the school or he wasn't. He seems like a nice enough guy, which seems strange given some of the things he's done in the past. Problem is, every time I start asking him about this case, the Unlawful Entry case, he breaks down and tells me he took an oath on his life never to kill again. When I ask him what he means, he starts talking about how if we can't kill babies, we have to stop killing the ladybugs.

Frankly, I have no idea what he is talking about – maybe he's a Buddhist or something. Apparently, the court did a forensic examination of my client back in April and found him sane. But he definitely has a thing for these ladybugs he keeps talking about.

Anyway, back to today. It's like this judge wants to make us sweat a little bit, Miss Fairbrother more than me, I guess. I don't want to say that this is typical, cause there other judges who seem to run their courtroom in a far more efficient manner. But on the other hand, it's not atypical. I guess I just expected that the Chief Judge would run things in a more professional way. Making that poor woman have to explain her medical condition in front of a crowded courtroom.

I feel very bad for her.

. . . .

Well Dad, you're privileged to be one of the first to hear about yet another rookie move by yours truly. I felt so bad about Miss Fairbrother's treatment by the Chief Judge, I went over to her and just sort of put my hand on her shoulder, to comfort her, you know?

And she snarled at me! Really! Snarled! And she looked at me, I don't know, like I was the stupidest person in the world.

I was just trying to help....

. . . .

OK. So the judge just called our case. He said: "I've decided to grant the parties' joint request for a continuance. I'm not going to trail the matter. I'm not going to wait for the trial to go before Judge Malley – not on the Misdemeanor Two calendar. No sir, no way. I've already told you both that I will not do that. Miss Fairbrother, I want you to put word out in your office that I expect these kinds of cases to be moved forward with the utmost urgency. It's not my job to be putting your feet to the fire; you and I both know what's going on here. This man, the defendant" – and at this point the judge sort of dismissively waved towards my client – "I remember him from the last time he was in front of me. So I don't need to repeat my assessment of him, a man who beats a pregnant woman.... I don't know, I don't know.... There are bigger things at stake here, Miss Fairbrother. Justice delayed is justice denied."

Blah blah blah!

Judge Cummings then asked his clerk for the next available date – and guess what – it's October 16th – the same day my client is scheduled to go to trial before Judge Malley. And that's the date he picked! What a jerk! I mean, how am I going to try the same case at the same time in two different courtrooms!

~ Chapter Eighteen ~

"Hello?"

"Hey my brother! What's up?"

"Liam?"

"Yeah, bro! Happy Birthday!"

"Dude ... that was last month."

"I thought August 25th –"

"Uh, try July."

"July?"

"Yeah."

"Oh. Sorry, Owen. Anyway, what's going on out there in the land of fire and cactus?"

"I was asleep."

"Asleep? What time is it there, eight thirty?"

"Seven thirty."

"Ah, shit, I'm sorry. Shouldn't you be awake anyway?"

"It's Tuesday, dude. I'm in college. So what's up?"

"Not much. Just got back from court. Had a little plea bargain go down today. Nothing much, just some possession of 'heron' case. That's how they say heroin in D.C. – 'heron.'"

"Mmm-hmm."

"And let's see, what else? Yeah, I've been starting to get some cases now. I think they're starting to notice me down at court. Been doing a lot of writing, you know, in my journal and shit. I plan to write a book about all this one day. You just wait. Let's see, what else …. Oh, I been working out in this great gym I found. It's called Finley's. 'Too Sharp' Johnson works out there. You heard of him, right? Hey, you still there?"

"Yep."

"So, tell me, how hot is it there today? Huh? Hundred and ten?"

"I dunno."

"Dude, you think Arizona is hot? You wouldn't believe how nasty it gets here! The heat and the humidity and the bad air! I swear, dude, two or three weeks ago I played a couple games of beach volleyball down by the Mall on a Code Red day, and, I'm still hawking out purple loogies."

"Nasty."

"Yeah, right. Hey, hear anything from dad?"

"Nope. And don't care to either."

"Oh."

"Ah fuck. So what's up with you? What ever happened to that girl you were dating? The black girl?"

"I dunno. One day, I thought we were gonna get married and have a baby and shit; the next day, we break up. I think something happened between the time we met in New Mexico and the time I caught up with her in D.C. Maybe it's the whole black-white thing.... I don't really understand it. See, in D.C., everyone is black. The mayor, the city council, half of the judges – everyone! Whenever I call Grandpa Irv and I tell him about my business and being a lawyer and all, and I tell him about this client or that client, he always asks, 'Is he colored?' You know Grandpa, with his New York accent: 'Colored?'"

"Yeah."

"So I told him, 'Grandpa, whenever I tell you anything about my life here in Washington, just assume that everyone is black. Black is the default position.'"

"'Colored.' That's funny."

"Yeah, 'Colored.' Oh man, listen! I almost forgot! One of my cases was in the papers out here!"

"Really?"

"Yeah! These two teenage girls were shot and killed and –"

"Don't tell me you represent the guy that did it?"

"No, not that. I, ah, represented one of the girls. Before

she was killed, of course. I didn't notice it the first time, back when she first got shot. But it just hit the news again when the dude that did it – the guy that shot the girls?"

"Uh huh."

"– he just got totally blown away by the cops."

"Oh."

"Yeah, I'll bet the reporters are going to be on my case any day now. I mean, this girl's story was just horrendous. What was her name? Connie, Constance... I don't even remember her last name. I was picking up juvenile cases for the first time, maybe the week before Christmas. You know, I get fifty bucks an hour for these cases –"

"I know."

"Anyway, so right around four o'clock, they call my name, tell me that a case has been assigned to me: a fourteen-year-old girl charged with assault with intent to kill. We call that 'AWIK.' The arrest report says that this girl pulled a knife on her stepfather and cut him up around his armpit, and he bled so bad, he almost died in the hospital. But just before I go into the holding cell to talk to the girl, the city prosecutor catches up to me and says they're going to dismiss the whole case because after talking to other family members and looking at the angle of the wound, they determined that she had stabbed her stepfather – who was a paroled sex offender – to get him off of her. So when I hear that, now I'm really pissed –"

"Pissed? Didn't you win the case?"

"Well, yeah. But you only get vouchers for cases that are 'papered.' And if I don't get a voucher, I don't get paid. Worse yet, when they appoint you to a juvenile case, you have to represent the child through their release – even if the charges are dropped – and the court won't release them until one of the parents comes to pick them up. So there I was, almost the entire day down at court with no billables to show for it, and now I'm gonna be late for the Christmas party Dorsey – you know, my former boss – was throwing – "

"A Christmas party?"

"Exactly! So you can see why I'm a little torqued off when I go to visit this girl, you know, to tell her the news. She's in this little holding area that looks more like an office. On one side, near the door, you've got a desk. On the other side, you've got these stalls, you know, like a dressing room, but without the doors. And there's the girl, fourteen years old, standing there naked."

"Naked?"

"Yeah. The guard with me yelled at her to get her clothes on, and she did. It was like a hospital robe, made out of paper or something. But I got a good look at her."

"You did?"

"But, you know, she was just a kid. So anyway, I told her that I was her lawyer and that the charges were being dropped and all that, and that I needed to contact her mother so that she could come down to court to take her home. And she just laughed at that. She said, 'My mom's aint gonna git me. I stuck her man real good this time *and* I got him locked up!' Of course, I told her that just because the charges against her were dropped didn't necessarily mean that her stepfather was going to be arrested."

"So they didn't arrest the guy?"

"Uh, I dunno. I don't think so. That's not the point. See, she was gonna get released as soon as I found some suitable adult who would come and get her. And she says to me, 'Why can't I go home with you?' And I was like –"

"Yeah?"

"Heh heh. But I could see she was totally playing me. So I pulled out my legal pad, that's what I do when I get nervous, and I got her name and address, date of birth, that kind of thing.

221

She gave me the names and phone numbers of maybe half a dozen people – relatives, friends, anyone she thought would come to re-claim her. And dude, check this out: her mother's name wasn't even on the list. None of the phone numbers worked anyway, except for her 'grand ma-ma,' who told me, 'Connie ain't nothing but trouble and Sursum Corda ain't no place for a chile like that.' Sursum Corda is this reprehensible housing project. I mean, I've never been there personally, I've just heard about it that way. Anyway, she – the grandmother – told me to call Connie's father – another name, not on the list."

"Hmmph."

"So I finally get ahold of the guy, and he's decent-sounding. He hadn't seen his daughter in years, but he said he'd take her in even though it would cause him big trouble with his wife. They lived off in Prince George's County somewhere. You know, Maryland? He said he'd do it for a week, you know, let things cool down over at her mom's. But after that, she'd have to work things out with her mother or move in with 'grand ma-ma' and her ol'man. So I ran back into the juvi cell-block and when I told her her father was coming to get her, she was blinking, almost like she wasn't sure if she was awake, so that put me in a better mood. But then I asked her, wasn't that great that she'll get to spend Christmas Day with her father, and she said, 'Christmas Day?' and I said, 'Yeah, Christmas Day.' And then she says to me, 'Christmas is a day?' You know, like she's asking a question. And I'm like, 'Of course it's a day. It's next Tuesday (or whatever it was).' But it was like she still didn't believe me. She kept saying, 'We don' go to school for Christmas, and that's for more than one day.' So I told her I would show her my calendar as soon as we got into the courtroom, but she just shrugged her shoulders and said 'What's a calendar?'"

"Come on! She didn't know what –?"

"Yeah, I know. And even though her dad came to pick her up and there was all these hugs and kisses and good feelings, I walked out of court that night feeling ... I dunno, lost, I guess. Like, what kind of people am I dealing with here? Who doesn't know about Christmas? Don't know what a frickin' calendar is? Well, I was so messed up over this, that I went home – I had just moved into my own apartment behind –"

"I know, behind the Supreme Court."

"– right, and I totally forgot about my Christmas party. Julianne was supposed to have met me there, and of course, when I didn't show, she got mighty pissed off. Around three a.m., she called me all drunk as shit and we had this huge blow up on the phone. I tried telling her how I helped this young girl and she basically said why was it that I was helping out all these other people and not her. And –"

"Hey, Liam, look, I gotta go. Nature calls."

"Oh. O.K. Sorry for rambling on there. That girl's still got me messed up."

"The girl in the newspaper?"

"Nah, Julianne. Well, yeah, her too, I guess."

"Man, I don't know why you don't just bail out of there."

"Where?"

"Washington. It sounds like shit to me."

"Yeah, well, I guess it's my shit now."

"Whatever."

"Alright, bro. Sorry to wake you up. Maybe I'll catch you later."

223

§ § § § § § § § § §

Budget Analysis: 1st and 2nd Quarter, 1995
Law Office of Liam McNaughton
Washington, D.C.

	A.	Avg. Monthly Costs:
Rent		$595
Phone		$69
Grocery		$160
Rx		$33
Dry Clean		$25
Student Loan		(forbearance)
Visa		$61
MasterCard		$70
Filenes B'mnt		$25
Macy's		$20
Discover		$86

TOTAL $ 1144 ⇒ I have never had a monthly expenditure this low ∴ must be spending close to $1000 - 1500 in CASH on misc/entertainment, for which zero (0) was unrealistically budgeted in original projections.

Until cash flow improves considerably, must stop these cash expenditures. NO MORE DRINKING WITH THE MURDER LAWYERS!

In order to meet monthly expenditures of $1144, need to bill a minimum of 5.72 hours of CJA per week! More realistically, to meet actual expenses, need to bill 10 hours/week = $500/week or $2000/month. Based on a 6 day work week, that's just 1.6 hours a day. If I could bill 4 hours CJA per day, 6 day work week ⇒ that's $1200 per week or $4800 per month or $57,600 per year.

[I could definitely live with that!]

B. <u>Assets</u>:

Signet checking account	$ 710
Riggs savings acct.	$3300
Outstanding CJA vouchers	<u>$3393.68</u>*
TOTAL	$7403.68

* Per CJA Office, payment is imminent.

C. <u>Conclusion</u>:

Fixed Monthly Expenses	$1144
Allowable Cash Expenditure	<u>$ 400 ($100 per week)</u>
	$1544

∴ if I can maintain spending at $1544 per month, and I get my vouchers paid, I can last another four to five months, Christmas-time at best.

(Hang in there, bro).

D. <u>Potential Budget Busters</u>:

TAXES [1994] DC	($400?) [due August 15!]
TAXES [1994] US	($850?) [Note: find out what "quarterly tax" means]
Bar dues (DC)	$125
Bar dues (NM)	$75
Overdue phone bill	$100
Overdue rent	June/July
Health concerns:	asthma Rx [Call mom on this!]
Plane ticket home	?

~ Chapter Nineteen ~

Thursday, October 12, 1995
Julianne,

Been thinking about you, thinking about the day we met.

I've been holed up in my apartment for almost a week, sick with some type of wicked summertime cold that's stayed with me through the fall. With the blinds drawn, I can't tell if it is day or night. I don't know what's wrong with me, but I swear, I'm coughing out chunks of lung.

(I know, too much information!)

Probably caught whatever it is at the jail. I can't tell you how much time I've spent there over the last three months. It's such a nasty place, but I've been working on a case.

My client's case.

Mal's case.

I guess I never told you about him. His trial is Monday.

It's pretty sad. My client was reportedly abandoned by his mother when he was six years old and grew up in various foster homes, including with his paternal aunt Lovey Green (who – believe it or not – is a correctional officer at D.C. Jail).

((Lovey is not a pleasant lady, I have to say. Every time I go to the jail, she gives me a hard time, telling me that I don't have enough experience for a case like this, saying it's my fault (!) that Mal keeps trying to kill "his-self." She claims her family is pooling their money together to replace me with a "paid" lawyer.))

(((Mal just laughed when I told him that. He says that Aunt Lovey never spent none of that foster care money on him growing up if it meant her boys Ronel and Le'Nor going without, so he doubted she'd pony up any cash for his sorry ass now. I told him we were stuck with each other, and that made him laugh.)))

One time, I stupidly asked this guy Mal if I was the only white person he'd ever got to know, and he kind of snorted a laugh. "White people been in and out my life since day one," he said. "Most tried to do good by me. But they just temporary, dig? You ain't the first, but you probably gonna be the last."

I can't really tell you the details of my client's case – that would violate attorney-client privilege – but needless to say, he's looking at a lot of time. He's having a real difficult time being locked up, and I can't blame him. All concrete and metal, stale air and florescent light, the squawk of walkie-talkies – I get a little weird in the head if I'm in the jail for more than a couple of hours.

I don't think I got much of a good shot. To win my client's case, I mean. But check this out – my client's ex-girlfriend isn't the little victim I originally thought she was. I've seen the scars on my client's arms and hands where she caught him with a box-cutter. He's also got a permanent lump on his noggin where she got him with a metal pipe. He claims that all his problems with Brandy stem from her mother. He says that after he got out on parole and got back together with Brandy, her mother would actively support her drug habit, giving her money for crack, giving her rides out to the corners, covering for her when Mal came looking.

It's not really relevant to Mal's new case, and I don't really know if I should believe it. I'm not even sure how I'd use this at trial – maybe for impeachment.

(I know, I know, you hate when I start sounding like a lawyer).

I've spoken to Brandy's mother on the telephone – her name is Bootsy Henson – and she seems OK. Except when it comes to my client, who for some reason she refers to as her son-in-law. She told me flat out that if she ever got the chance to kill Mal, she would, and if it weren't for her having to be at the school where she works twelve hours a day, she'd probably have already done it by now. She even bragged that she's told my client on several occasions that he could come over on her job anytime day or night and just try to beat on her like he done to Brandy, and she'd stab out his black fucking heart!

My client, for his part, generally denies ever laying a hand on Brandy, and as proof, points to all the cases against him that were dismissed by the U.S. Atty's office. When I point out to client that he pled guilty to an aggravated assault on Brandy, he protests that his CJA lawyer sold him out and that he never "stomped" her. Beyond that, he won't really give me his side of the story – of what happened to Brandy, of what happened to the baby. Bunning Goodwine – my predecessor – sent me his entire file (two boxes worth!) on the underlying probation case, and I've sent little Mallory's autopsy report to an expert witness in ABQ to look over.

Who is Mallory, you're probably wondering. On second thought, maybe I don't need to tell you about <u>all</u> my cases.

As for the school case, my client insists that he was working when he got arrested but the phone number for the Korean guy he claims was training him as a plumber's apprentice just rings and rings. I can't bring up the possibility of entering a plea without my client going off the deep end and threatening to kill himself (threats I unfortunately have to take seriously).

The prosecutor in the case has been on some type of extended leave, I think she's having a baby, so my strategy for legal victory is to pray that her replacement will just drop this silly case.

At this point, I guess you could say I'm preparing for Mal's sentencing before he's even convicted. I mean, I haven't filed so much as one motion – no seized evidence, no statements to suppress – and my client won't help me. The best thing I can do now is collect letters in support of his character, mostly from those temporary white people he was talking about – school teachers, social workers, Mormon missionaries.

So far, I've totally struck out in this regard. The last person on my list is the Imam at the Fruit of Peace (I'm guessing he's not white). The Murder Lawyers told me about the Imam – they said he'll write a letter requesting leniency for anyone, even people he's never met!

I'm thinking of going out after the Great Imam as soon as I'm finished with this status hearing I've got tomorrow morning. The Fruit of Peace is located over by Potomac Gardens – kind of a scary area, I've heard.

(Though it certainly can't be any worse than our experience on Green Street. Yeah mon!)

I investigate all my own cases now. It really helps bump up my vouchers. I've got to go to all sorts of really nasty neighborhoods. My trick is to go early in the morning before the bad guys all wake up.

What I really ought to do is just call in sick on Monday, like I've seen other CJA lawyers do when they don't want to go to trial. But I worry it will be too easy. You know, if you throw in the towel once, how hard will it be to throw in the towel twice?

It seems I've had a life of giving up and being given up on – so much so that sometimes I can't tell the difference.

J, I fell in love the moment you called me Yum. Why can't you tell me what happened to us?

Liam.

229

VIII.Friday, October 13, 1995

During the late '80s, Americans shook their heads in disgust at reports that poor black mothers were sacrificing the little ones resting in their wombs for the pleasures of crack cocaine, callously dooming a new generation to "a life of certain suffering, of probable deviance, of permanent inferiority," to quote columnist Charles Krauthammer.

Seizing on early studies that raised alarm over fetal damage from cocaine, scientists cited the same inconclusive data again and again. Local news organs spun their own versions of the crack-baby story, taking for granted the accuracy of the premise. Social workers, foster parents, doctors, teachers, and journalists put forward unsettling anecdotes about the "crack babies" they had seen, all participating in a sleight of hand so elegant in its simplicity that they fooled even themselves. They talked of babies shrieking like cats and refusing to bond, of children unable to focus on a task – and then they slipped in the part they should have tested, attributing these problems to prenatal cocaine use. Reporters went into hospital nurseries and special schools and borrowed the images of premature babies or bawling African-American preschoolers to illustrate their crack-baby stories. By 1991, John Silber, president of Boston University, went so far as to lament the expenditure of so many health care dollars on "crack babies who won't ever achieve the intellectual development to have consciousness of God."

Katherine Greider, "Crackpot Ideas," Mother Jones (July/August 1995).

~ Chapter Twenty ~

Annie rifled through her purse for the bottle of anti-depressants and popped three of the little pills into her mouth. She grabbed for her water bottle, but it was empty, so she dragged herself down the hall to the break room and quickly poured herself a cup of water.

"'Scuse me, ma'am," a male voice called out from behind her. "Aren't you Annie Fairbrother?"

Annie swallowed hard as the pills stuck in her throat. "Yes?"

"I'm don't mean to bother you none," the man continued. "It's just that I inherited one of your cases. The Jamal Stancil case. Trial is Monday. So I was kind of hoping to ask you a couple of questions. You know, how the case is sorta ... messed up."

"Messed up?" Annie was surprised by the energy in her voice. "How so?"

"Well, he – the defendant – he's been held without bond for almost four months. He can't get more than six months for unlawful entry, so, I guess... what I'm trying to say is –"

"Did you review the underlying felony case? Do you know what this guy did?"

"I'm not saying this guy is any kind of angel or whatever. I know he's got a lot of back-up time."

"Eight years."

"Yeah, eight years. But other than this re-arrest, he's had no problems on probation. He never tested positive for drugs. He stayed away from his ex-girlfriend. He even told Pretrial Services that he was employed."

"I'm sorry, tell me your name again."

The young prosecutor introduced himself as Jayson Pledge. "Howard U., Georgetown Law," he smiled. "Just like

231

you."

"Been checking up on me, Mr. Pledge?"

"Oh sure! I mean, no! I wasn't, like, checking up on you. It's just that, you know, we were all really thrilled when we heard that you were coming back to the office. I saw you in action, you know? A couple of years ago, when I was interning for the U.S. Attorney, and I got to watch a few days of trial. It was that one case, you know? It was in all the papers?"

Annie shrugged.

"You know, the guy with the pit bulls? Oh, what was the guy's name? You guys were calling it the Doggy Style Rapist case."

The name came to her through a fog of emotion. "Johnson," she said softly. "Marcelus Johnson. That's his ... his Christian name." For years, Annie had thought nothing of the blithe little nick-names the prosecutors and cops and coroners had used to describe her cases, her defendants, her victims. *Doggy Style Rapist. Keisha the Crackhead's Kiddy Camp. I've-Dropped-My-Arms-And-Can't-Get-Up. Baby Stomper.* But three months ago, when her OB-GYN's use of the term "Mo Mo" twins elicited a loud guffaw from her husband, Annie felt what it was to be on the receiving end of a nickname.

"Mo Mo twins," the doctor explained, "means that the girls are mono-amniotic mono-chorionic. They share the same sac and the same placenta. It's a condition that often results in the children being grafted to one another."

"Mo Mo twins," her husband repeated, trying to sound more serious.

"Yes, something that should have been picked up much sooner," the doctor continued. "Unfortunately, I can't personally look at *every* sonogram my patients get. Surely, you understand?"

"Are we, like, talking about Siamese twins," Steve asked.

"That would be correct. The good news, Annie, is that the fraternal twin – your son – is perfectly fine. I'm just concerned that the girls' condition might cause a miscarriage. You can take this to term. I'm just afraid that unless something drastic is done, the risks of spontaneously aborting all three goes way up."

Annie didn't remember much after that, except that her husband, who had earlier recused himself from the birthing process, now took over like a man on a mission, lording over the decision to move forward with the procedure known as a *reduction*: the termination of her grafted daughters in order to save the life of her unborn son.

Six weeks later, when her son was ripped from her stomach and placed in an incubator, Annie felt no particular joy, and no particular sadness. All she wanted was to be left alone.

Thus started the fatigue. She tried to nurse her son after he was released from the hospital, but she was just too tired. She missed her follow-up doctors' appointments; she had her husband take Elijah – her son – back for his. She refused the calls and cards of well-wishers. All she wanted to do was sleep. Steve, knowing her better than anyone, finally figured out how pull her out of her horrible lethargy. "Maybe you should just go back to work early," he said one day. "Maybe that will bring back the old fighter."

Annie grabbed another glass of water and sat down. "Will you excuse me for a moment, Mr. Pledge? Today's my first day back, and I'm not sure I'm gonna make it."

"Oh, that's OK."

"Why don't you sit down too?"

"Oh, sure."

"So, you've been assigned the Stancil case.

Congratulations. The case is yours now. If you're thinking of dismissing the case, that's your call. Me? I always liked to try cases."

"I'm not saying I'm afraid to try the case. It's just that ... you know this case so well, and maybe...?"

"Sure, Mr. Pledge." Annie realized she was smiling, perhaps for the first time in weeks. "I'd be happy to help you out. Why don't you go get the file and meet me in my office?"

§ § § § § § § § §

"You say the judge is expecting you, Mister ....?"

"Minister. Minister Clinton Augustus And-One."

"And-One?" Miss Macaby repeated. "Minister And-One?"

"That's right. Tell ol' Armstrong to come on out here and show a brother some love!"

Miss Macaby was instantly suspicious of the man, doubting that the judge had ever heard him. And yet, moments later, the Chief came bounding from his inner sanctum.

"Right this way," he said gruffly, grabbing the man roughly. "Jacky, don't let anyone in. I don't want to be disturbed."

"My brother, my brother!" the Minister said, breaking free of the judge's grip. "Just take a look at you! Chief Judge! My, my, my!"

Miss Macaby cleared her throat.

"Ah, I'm sorry," the Chief said. "Jacqueline Macaby, meet Clinton Anderson."

"And-One," the Minister corrected. "I thought they told you. About my name change and all."

"Right. Sorry. Clinton And-One. And this is Jacqueline Macaby. She's been with me for what, nine, ten years?"

234

"Fifteen. Thank you, judge."

"Hold my calls, please, Jacky. We won't be but a minute."

Once the heavy oak door closed behind them, the Chief asked in a hushed scream, "What the hell you doin' here?"

"Hey, Armstrong! Chill baby! You know I ain't gonna be talking 'bout our friend over no telephone."

"What friend?"

"The Captain! He's got me real messed up. My place is all full'a these hard-assed niggas, like he's got a little army stowed away there, just waiting for the command. He calls them his 'Raiders.'"

"Yeah, well, I've got my complaints too. That kid the Captain has working for him – Devil, De La, whatever his name is – his name's got a trail of bodies on it. His name come up in at least two different grand jury investigations."

"Whatchu mean bodies?"

"That shooting of those teenagers down Sursum Corda. And your Korean handyman, the one they found in the old reservoir. There's a detective, some new guy, who's all over that."

"Oh, Lord Jesus! What's his name?"

"The detective? I don't remember. Caucasian guy, mustache."

"That's McCoy!" the Minister cried. "Detective McCoy! He's been over my church, asking bout swastikas, asking 'bout my connection to Mr. Kim. I sent Koko out to speak to him on account she don't speak no English, so he jes left his card, said he'd be back."

"Now what the fuck did you go and put that Nazi symbol on your church for anyway?" the Chief muttered. "That's something I never could quite figure out."

"It ain't no Nazi sign, Armstrong. It's an Ashanti fylfot, symbol of our African forefathers. I can't do nothing about

235

taking it down now no how, at least not as long as that restraining order is still in place. You still working on that, right?"

"Think you can come in here and shake me down, do ya?" For all those jokes about how he had to sit on top of a stack of Yellow Pages to see over the bench, Armstrong Cummings was still a five-foot three, hundred and eighty five pound spark-plug of a man and he had no problem striding up to the Minister and grabbing him by his collar. "Well, let me tell you something. I don't need your people's support no more, and I'm done turning my head to their little cloak and dagger tricks."

"So you think you got that much juice now, huh?" the Minister managed to say. "Now that you Chief Judge?"

The judge strode to the far end of the study, pulling the Minister behind him. "See these here paintings, my brutha? This one here is Frederick Douglass. He was the Recorder of Deeds, in 1881 to be exact – not more than thirty years after being a runaway slave."

"Yeah, so?"

"See, back then, the Recorder of Deeds was a position the City of Washington traditionally gave to the Negro. Now see here?" The Chief swung the Minister to the next painting. "This here white man, he took away the job. And the next three paintings? Those are the next three Recorder of Deeds, all white men. Don't you know that there was a time when this town was run by an arm of the KKK?"

"Ok, ok! Now let a'loose!"

"But things change, don't they, Mr. Anderson? That Frederick Douglass painting is priceless. These white men? I could have maintenance come in here right now and toss them in the cafeteria dumpster and no one would care. See, I'm in charge here now, Augustus. I am! So, yes, I do have the juice!"

Minister And-One broke away from the judge's grip.

"Now don't forget who helped you get there, Armstrong," he sputtered. "Don't you forget! You didn't become no Chief on account of twenty-five black votes. Or did you think them white judges voted for you on account of your stellar judicial platform?"

"I am no one's slave!" the judge said through clenched teeth.

"That's why I'm here, Armstrong! That's why I had to come! You gotta call the Captain, call this thing off."

"You want me to tell the Captain to cancel your speech? Why me?"

"Armstrong, you the one who turned me onto him. He's your boy!"

"My boy? He's your boy! From the newspaper! You brought him to me."

"No, sir. He came to me saying he been knowings you!"

Both men stood there, startled and confused, realizing they'd been played. Finally, the Chief spoke.

"We ain't going to do nothing, Augustus. Nothing. Look, after the March, after Farrakhan, the world's going to change for us."

"You really think Farrakhan gonna get a million brothers out there?"

"Negro, please. Won't be any different than any other march. Abortion. No Nukes. AIDS blankets. The number of people ain't the point. It's the number of cameras that matters. My boy, your boy, it don't really matter. After Monday, we won't be needing this white Captain no more."

"I do hope you right, Armstrong, cause I'm strugglin' now."

The Chief looked out the window pensively. "Strugglin' time is over, my brother. After the March, we'll be like Jesse or Kwesi or Ronnie – untouchable."

237

"Untouchable. I like that."

"The white man has always enjoyed all the perks of his office, hasn't he?"

"Yes, he has."

"I mean, just read the papers! You got Congressman stealing postage stamps, taking bribes from the Arabs."

"True, true!"

"You got the President of the United States flimflamming some backwater savings and loan, for god-sakes!"

"That's right! You said it!"

"Almost a million of our African brothers were killed last year in Rwanda in the space of a month. A month!"

"Mercy, mercy!"

"And what did our benevolent white overlords do to stop it?"

"Uh, I dunno."

"Nothing! That's what!"

"Oh, Jesus. That's right. Nothing."

"Damn straight. So who's gonna condemn us – who's gonna condemn our people – for doing what we gotta do to get over?"

"Not me, my brother!"

"We're trying to uplift our community here, aren't we, Augustus?"

"Well!"

"We're trying to stop the genocide!"

"Well well!"

"We're not just trying to get out of the fields so we can get a job in the house! No, sir, we're coming to take over the house!"

"Well well well!"

"We're coming for what's ours! And we'll burn down the mother fucking house if we have to!"

The Minister suddenly let out a high pitched scream, "Hal - eee - lie – yah!   Hal - eee - lie – yah!   Hal - eeeeee - lie – yah!"

The door to the study suddenly opened. "Chief, everything OK in here?" Miss Macaby asked.

"Oh! Miss Macaby! Yes, yes, everything is –"

"It's almost one o'clock," she continued. "You've got the grand jury re-convening."

"Sure, Jacky, sure," the Chief said. He grabbed the Minister by the shoulder and ushered him out.   "Well, Reverend, I'm sorry I can't help you."

The two men then gave a firm if not self-conscious white man hand shake.

"I'm sure you can find your way out," the judge said, pushing the Minister through the chamber's door. "And good luck with the speech! I'm sure it'll be a real barn burner!"

§ § § § § § § § §

"United States versus Vernon Bogash," the courtroom clerk called out between a yawn. "Docket number M 33415-04."

Liam eyed his watch as the jovial Nigerian lawyer strode up to counsel table, his bedraggled client trailing behind him as if walking through quicksand. The whole day had felt like that for Liam – walking through quicksand.

"Good morning, Your Honor!" the Nigerian chimed in his English school-boy accent. "My name is Kumibala Bengalla Kiyotoo! For the defendant Vernon Bogash! He is present here, Your Honor!"

"What are we here for again?" the judge asked no one in particular.

239

"Sentencing!" the lawyer with great relish. "Your Honor will recall that Mr. Bogash pleaded guilty! To attempted possession! With intent to distribute! Marijuana!"

The old black judge lifted his chin in such a way that it appeared he was looking at the prosecutor. "That right?"

"Uh, yes, Your Honor. Mr. Jones, I mean, Mr. Bogash, yes, I have his file right here. The government does not object to probation, which is the recommendation of the Presentence Report writer."

"There's a Presentence Report?" the judge asked to the groans of the audience.

The courtroom clerk handed the file up to the judge. "Right 'ere, You Honor," she said.

"Oh, thank you."

"And for Your Honor's learned consideration! Let the record reflect! I am passing forward! The Defendant's Memorandum in Aid of Sentencing!"

"This is your memorandum? One page?"

"Yes, Your Honor! It's from the Peace of Fruit!"

A spurt of laughter broke out in the gallery, and Liam, who was falling asleep, suddenly came to attention.

The Nigerian lawyer laughed heartily at his mistake. "Correction, Your Honor! The Fruit of Peace! The most exalted! The most revered! His Excellency Brother Khan has written about my client's reputation in the community! For non-violence! And honesty!"

"Yeah, yeah, I've seen that letter before. Alright, give me a moment."

Liam looked again at his watch. Case after case it went on like this, the judge, prosecutor, and defense lawyer repeating their mantras, the outcomes of virtually every case pre-ordained: plea, probation, bench warrant, *nolle*, continuance.

When his case was finally called, he stood up quickly.

"Liam McNaughton for the defendant Bernard Grant. I've not seen Mr. Grant today. With no other representations, Your Honor, may I be excused?"

~ Chapter Twenty One ~

Annie went right to work, spreading the multi-tiered Stancil file out on two small tables.

Jayson mainly deferred, saying more than once, "Your office sure is nice and clean, Miss Fairbrother."

Ordinarily, Annie's office overflowed with boxes of files, boxes of evidence, and boxes of boxes; her desk, side tables, and windowsill all covered by papers, folders, manila envelopes, computer diskettes, videotapes, audio tapes, packages of photographs.

Today, however, the office was virtually empty.

Before taking leave, Annie had spent sixteen straight hours neatening her office and, more importantly, distributing her open cases. She wrote transfer memos for each new prosecutor and left detailed voicemails for each detective, expert witness, cooperator, and victim, explaining that until early next year she'd be on medical leave, and identifying the name of the prosecutor who'd be replacing her.

When the dust had finally settled, there was just a handful of case files left: bench warranted cases, cases up on appeal, cases that for one reason or another had remained at the bottom of her pile. These were the ones that Annie dumped on the Chief Felony Assistant's desk to distribute as he saw fit.

Jamal Stancil's case was in that pile.

Annie had physically, mentally, and emotionally removed herself from the case after breaking down in court back in July. She could count on one hand the number of criminal prosecutions she'd walked away from in her ten years as a prosecutor, but this one had gotten too personal for her on so many levels. Since it was a simple two-witness case – the arresting officer and an official from the school – she figured she'd let another prosecutor take a crack at it.

242

And just let go.

Still, she was surprised to see an unsupervised rookie inherit the Baby Stomper – or rather – the Jamal Stancil cases. So after they had settled in, she decided to let her young protégé do all the talking so she could measure just how green he really was.

"Alright, Jayson, it's your case. Where do you want to start?"

"Here's the Misdemeanor case file," Jayson was saying rapidly. "Here's the whole Felony folder. I got some photos of the school, right here, the drain pipe where the defendant climbed up. Those are the files from his old drug cases –"

Annie stopped him mid-sentence. She knew how the file was organized. She was the one that put it together. "What I want to know, Mr. Pledge, is what evidence can you point to that indicates that he was going up?"

"Well, that's in the picture of the pipe," he answered, frantically searching through the photos. "Uh, what's the question again?"

"*Up*, Mr. Pledge! You said this is the pipe he was climbing *up*! Officer McCoy's report doesn't indicate that he caught the defendant climbing *up* the pipe, does it?"

"I guess I just assumed that's how he got in."

Annie puffed herself up in the assuming position of a judge. "Counsel, did I just hear you say assumed?"

"Uh, yes. Assumed."

"'When you assume, counsel, you just make an ass out of you and me,'" Annie said in a booming male voice. Giving Jayson's arm a playful squeeze, she continued in her own voice, "But seriously, Jayson, why should we care whether he was in or out? So what if he was going up or going down?"

"I'm not sure I follow... Your Honor."

Annie laughed. "We're prosecutors, Jayson, not

explainers-of-all-things. We don't have to prove he was *in* the school, we don't have to prove how he got there. We just have to prove he was there *at* the school! Coming or going, on the wall or on the roof, it doesn't matter. He was *there*, he wasn't supposed to be *there* – that's the evidence. Keep it simple. All you need is an official from the school, and the arresting officer – Officer McCoy, I think it was – and you're gonna get your conviction."

"I thought the arresting officer was Dennis Olsen."

"Olsen? God no!" Annie examined the officer's name on the signature block of the probable cause affidavit. "Hmmm. You're right. Dennis Olsen. Now I remember. I think Officer Olsen technically is the one to have narrated P.C. even though McCoy was the one who actually caught him and wrote up the report."

"That means we need McCoy to make the case," Jayson said sullenly, "and I only got Olsen under subpoena."

"Don't worry about Officer McCoy," Annie said reassuringly. "I've got Supercop's pager number … somewhere around here."

"Uh, Miss Fairbrother, I mean, Annie. You know he's Detective McCoy now?"

"*Detective* McCoy? I can't believe it. I knew that he was going to take the detective's exam or something. But wasn't he suspended over that shooting of the Sursum Corda killer?"

"I don't really know. I met him in grand jury."

"Really? So you've got other cases with him?"

"He had a couple of things going on. Mostly hate crimes, things like that."

"Hate crimes?"

"Well, really it could be two murders," Jayson said, growing animated. "I'm hoping he'll bring me in on it. See, Animal Control found the body of this Korean man at the

Reservoir.   You know, the Bins?   The ME's Office says it looked like the man had been tortured, and later on, Crime Scene found some graffiti in the area of the body. And the outlines looked like swastikas. You know, like the Nazis."

"I think I know what a swastika is."

"Oh, yeah. Right."

Annie looked down at her empty desktop calendar and tried to suppress a yawn. "So what you're telling me, Jayson, is that now our office is treating some graffiti near a dead body as a hate crime?"

"Well, yeah. We got orders to do that now, like, specially identify any cases that can be prosecuted as possible hate crime."

"Hmmm. Sounds like DOJ grant money talking, if you know what I mean." By the look on his face, she could tell he didn't. "Anyway, did McCoy ever mention to you that he saw some swastikas or something like that in this case? The Stancil case?"

"Oh wow. No. I never really talked to him about *this* case. I don't remember seeing anything like that in the paperwork though."

"I don't think it's in any of the police reports. It's just something he mentioned to me at one point. I got his pager number right here. Let's give him a call, see what he thinks."

As she dialed the number, she turned to Jayson. "So? Tell me about the other murder."

"Oh, the other one. An unidentified female body, down at the morgue. She's got a burn mark on her forehead. Also a swastika."

"She Korean?"

"No," he said. "She black."

Momentarily taken aback by Jayson's matter-of-fact tone, Annie realized just how out of practice she was. Every big city prosecutor eventually comes to terms with the fact that virtually all of the carnage being wrought on the streets is black-on-black. Worse yet, far too many victims of this internecine warfare are hardly what you would call innocent bystanders – as often as not, they too have long and violent criminal histories. For an African-American woman like Annie to succeed as a career prosecutor, she could never allow herself to identify with the perpetrators of these heinous crimes in any way, shape or form – they had to be seen as an alien species, foreign and dangerous, deserving of her contempt and the severe and sometimes arbitrary punishments meted out by the justice system. As for their imperfect victims, their flaws had to be ignored, just as their skin color was assumed.

The job was just easier that way.

But the way Jayson said, "She black," made Annie have a sudden realization: *I'm different now. Something has happened to change things. I just can't do it that way anymore.*

§ § § § § § § §

By the time Liam got home from court, it was already a quarter to three. He took off his worsted wool suit and put on his "investigator clothes" – blue jeans, hooded sweatshirt, and running shoes. The bad guys will definitely be up by now, he thought as he headed back out the door.

The Murder Lawyers had plenty of tales of Potomac Gardens – heroin on Twelfth Street, crack on Thirteenth, gun violence in between – but as Liam walked across Pennsylvania Avenue and through the happy hubbub of the House Office Buildings, he wondered, how bad could it really be just ten blocks from the U.S. Capitol?

Two blocks later, as he trekked across a large park full of dead trees, brown grass, and hypodermic needles, he got his answer as he gave a wide berth to the various couples having sex on the picnic tables and playground equipment. As he proceeded up G Street, he found himself in the he shadows of several turn-of-the-century school buildings, shuttered and vandalized, and he wondered where had all the children gone.

The late afternoon sky had turned a New Jersey license plate yellow. Dust and debris blew through the close-in row homes lining the street, their "For Sale" signs clanging and banging like so many wind chimes. Metal bars covered every window and door, and the further Liam went, the fewer "For Sale" signs appeared.

After passing through a small commercial area of barber shops, liquor stores, and Chinese take-outs, he continued eastward, passing rows of boarded-up row homes – empty shells, many showing signs of fire damage. The sidewalks were laden with broken glass, car batteries, condoms, and chicken bones. Plastic garbage bags were stacked unceremoniously in the gutters – banana peels and cigarette butts and jagged metal soup cans spilling forth, flashes of movement suggesting the presence of maggots, rats, and feral kittens. Dust devils swept up newspaper inserts, take-out menus, and potato-chip bags – a twirling ballet of litter.

The smell of urine pervaded the air; the noise was becoming oppressive: the menacing bass of a stereo boom box, the insufferable whine of car alarms, the faraway laughter of children, the unseen hollers of "Hey nigga!"

The rusted remains of a car that had crashed into a retaining wall blocked the side-walk, so Liam crossed the street in front of a group of teenage girls.

"Hope you ain't alone," one of the girls said under her breath, causing the other girls to shriek with nervous laughter. "You in the Gardens now!"

And there, in front of him, he finally saw it. Potomac

Gardens – the group of high-rise brick buildings surrounded by a scattering of low-rise concrete block apartments, all of it hemmed in by a seven-foot-high spiked iron fence.

Liam pulled out the little pad he had tucked away inside his sweatshirt and found the address he had copied from the White Pages. *F of P*, he had written, *801 12ᵗʰ Place S.E.* Potomac Gardens appeared to occupy the entire 700 block of 12ᵗʰ Street. "Shouldn't be too hard to find," Liam assured himself.

Continuing onto the next block, however, he found that the little ramshackle houses all had street addresses in the 900's. Worse, 12ᵗʰ Street dead-ended at what appeared to be a wholly separate public housing complex that was seemingly constructed for the sole purpose of holding up the highway overpass.

Liam remembered the Murder Lawyers talking about how in hot drug neighborhoods the local dealers would mess with the street signs so as to confuse the cops. But, he wondered, could the bad guys really make an entire block disappear?

§ § § § § § § § §

McCoy glanced at his pager. He didn't recognize the last four digits, but the first three were 514 – a call from the U.S. Attorney's Office.

A few seconds later, the same page.

McCoy discretely turned off his pager and returned to attention. DuVall Washington, the Acting Chief of Police, was in the process of inducting McCoy and the two others on stage to the rank of detective. Everyone was in full dress uniform and the cameras were rolling.

"Whereas Officer James McCoy has been a faithful,

upstanding and decorated officer of the Metropolitan Police Department since 1982;

Whereas Officer McCoy showed great resolve in tackling and solving one of this city's most heinous crimes, the execution-style slayings of two minor girls at the Sursum Corda housing projects; and

Whereas Officer McCoy is a man of upstanding moral virtue and character, he is hereby sworn into the ranks of Detective ...."

Moral virtue. Character. The words echoed inside McCoy's head. As he stared up into the klieg lights, his knees grew weak, and he wondered: How did I get here?

Officially, he had been awarded his detective's shield on August 17th – the last day of his suspension. The city had received a "Notice of Intent To Sue" letter from some ambulance chaser looking to fleece the District of Columbia out of a few bucks for McCoy's killing of Ali Satterwhite – the man implicated for the Sursum Corda double homicide. So at that point, the department decided it had no choice but to take McCoy off suspension and promote him to detective.

McCoy learned of the decision after being summoned to headquarters to sit for the detective's character examination. Part lie detector, part multiple choice, what was jokingly called the "dick exam" wasn't much different from the test he took to get into the police academy. The big difference was the question about whether the examinee was "a practicing homosexual, polygamist, or practitioner of some other sexually deviant behavior."

When McCoy paused before answering the question with a firm "No, sir," he thought he saw the examiner wince. But at the conclusion of the test, First Lieutenant Rory McNulty barreled into the room, giving handshakes all around.

"Well, son, you're in!" he had cheered, putting his meaty

paw on McCoy's shoulder. "Now you play it straight with that lawyer the city's got representing you, alright? The union's backing you on this too, so if you need to speak to your own lawyer, we got 'em on retainer."

"Thank you, sir. I don't know what to say."

The old cop got misty-eyed. "Look James, I knew your dad. We all did. Back when he ran those liquor stores, I was a beat cop then. Your dad was good to us cops. He was good to me personally, you know what I mean? The day he died ... ah, I wanted to burn the city down."

"Thank you, sir. That means a –"

"We take care of our own," the Lieutenant winked, "that's all I'll say." Then he crouched low and whispered in McCoy's ear, "Don't make us regret our support. What you do on your own time is your business. Just don't embarrass us, Jimmy."

The next morning, McCoy reported for duty at the detective squad and found a stack of cold cases waiting for him. Scanning through the files, McCoy found that he already had a personal connection to two of them.

The first was the Sursum Corda double murder, still an open investigation despite MPD's pronouncements that the case had been "closed as solved" with the death of Ali Satterwhite. McCoy knew, as did the MPD brass, that the actual trigger-man, a shadowy figure known only as "Devil," was still at large and wholly unknown to law enforcement.

The second case was the unsolved murder of Sammy Kim, the Korean building contractor whose moldering body McCoy inadvertently discovered back in June. Animal Control had found Kim's body underneath the Rottweiler McCoy had seen in the Bins. Rumor had it that the medical examiner found the private parts of the dog deep in the dead man's throat.

The Kim case, McCoy learned to his chagrin, was a two-fer, on account of the fact that another unsolved "hate crime homicide" came with it: the body of a Jane Doe prostitute found nude behind a dumpster, a swastika burned into her forehead.

After giving cursory review to the remaining files, McCoy decided to take a trip downstairs to Police Archives. He had yet another murder to investigate – the juvenile case In re. De La S., his father's killer.

Over the years, any number of detectives and prosecutors had offered to do the same for him, but he had always demurred. No sense in frightening up those old ghosts, he had thought. His promotion to detective, however, gave McCoy a newfound sense of responsibility – an obligation to keep score.

Looking at the case had turned out to be somewhat of a let-down, however. Most of the microfiche had been damaged, so that the scans of the long since discarded paper file were for the most part irreparably lost. The only image clear enough to retrieve was an unlabeled fingerprint blotter. McCoy realized that the way the records were disorganized and mis-filed, it was far from certain that they were the actual fingerprints of the juvenile who had killed his father. But he printed a copy anyway, slipped it in with his other requests, and brought them to the Fingerprint Analysis Division.

There, McCoy was in for further disappointment. The fingerprint technician told him that it would be a couple of weeks if not months before he would get to McCoy's request.

"Funding priorities," the technician explained. "Remember last summer when those two rapists waltzed outta Lorton by switching their 'face sheets' with low-level prisoners who were scheduled for release? I guess Congress got tired of hearing about that, cause now we got an earmark to create a fingerprint database for the local prison population, and now we're swamped, fingerprinting every prisoner in the system – pretrial and post-conviction. Check back mid-October, maybe we'll have something for you then."

~ Chapter Twenty Two ~

While he re-traced his footsteps along 12th Street, Liam noticed a gang of young men gathering on the corner.

"This is why you do your investigations in the morning," he told himself.

When the inevitable catcalls and snickering began, he quickly retreated into the shabby foyer of a corner store. An old Korean woman sat on a stool behind the bullet-proof glass, eyeing him suspiciously.

"Uh, hi there. I'm, ah, looking for the Fruit of Peace?"

"One dolla," the woman said, holding up a twenty five cent pack of Juicy Fruit.

"No, ma'am. Not that. The Fruit of Peace." Liam repeated it loudly and slowly. "FRUIT OF PEACE."

"Fruit? No fruit! Try Safe-a-way."

"No, it's a church, or a community center type thing. It's on Twelfth Place Southeast, I've got the address right here –."

As he reached into his pocket, Liam was interrupted by an eye-burning smell. A nappy-headed black man wearing several heavy coats had staggered into the foyer.

"Wine," he said, holding himself steady against the bullet-proof glass.

"No touchy glass!" the old lady yelled. "I call police!"

"Din't touch no gotdam glass, Mamma-San!" The man turned briefly to look at Liam, taking one step forward then one step back. "Whatchu lookin at?"

For a moment, Liam thought about asking the man if *he* knew where the Fruit of Peace was, but then thought the better of it as the Korean lady re-appeared with a bottle of wine wrapped in a brown paper bag.

"Six dolla!" she commanded.

The man emptied his pockets onto the Lazy Susan, and the

old lady spun the coins, crumpled bills, and pieces of lint through the bullet-proof glass, the man's purchase coming back the same way. The man licked his chapped lips before twisting the top off the bottle and taking a long draw.

"No drinky in here!" the old lady shouted. When the man did not stop, she began to bang on the glass with a metal key ring, and like a dog in a thunder storm, the man dashed out of the store covering his ears, only to trip over the transom, falling face first into the pavement outside.

Liam rushed over. "You OK, Sir?"

The man pushed himself to his knees and grabbed his shattered purchase. "Don't step no further," he growled. He quickly separated the brown bag from the remains of the bottle and began dabbing the pieces of paper on the ground, periodically sucking the wine from his make-shift sponge.

"Look at that nigga, y'all!" a kid's voice called out.

Liam turned to see the gang on the corner crossing the street.

"Hip Hop done dropped his bottle!"

Liam looked down on the man and suddenly recognized that it was Hip Hop, his deterioration almost complete.

"Go on, nigga," the kids laughed, "get your drink on!"

And just like that, Liam found himself surrounded.

"Uh, hey guys," he said, "anyone been to the Fruit of Peace lately?"

"Fruit of Peace? Dude wanna know 'bout the Fruit of Peace!"

Liam felt a hand going for his wallet, so he started backpedaling into the corner store, just as a young Korean man wearing a Virginia Tech sweatshirt came barreling out.

"You kids get outta here before I call the cops," he said in surprisingly accent-free English. "Come on, Hip Hop. You're gonna cut your mouth if you keep that up."

"Excuse me, sir," Liam asked, "I was wondering if *you* could tell me where the Fruit of Peace is? 801 Twelfth Place?"

"You want directions? You gotta be kidding! You guys never come round here when we call, and now you want directions?"

"Uh ... I don't understand –"

"You cops are just too much. First, you –"

"Oh, I'm not a cop." Liam said quickly, following the man back into the store. "I'm a lawyer. I do CJA. You know, like a public defender?"

"Oh that's even better. You're probably here on behalf of that fucker who stole my mom's car and shit all over the dashboard. Or maybe you represent that little psychopath who keeps trying to stick the place up?"

"No, no, that's not my guy at all. My case is nothing serious, he just broke into a school, you know, allegedly, and he –"

"A school?"

"Yeah. It's not even around here. It's on North Capitol, I think, St. Nick's."

"You mean, you're the lawyer?" The man quickly leaned into the Lazy Susan and called out to his mother. Though he was speaking in hurried Korean, Liam thought he recognized the words "Captain-san" and "Wild Irish Rose" – and moments later, the old lady spun another bottle through the thick glass divider. Then she rushed off to the telephone.

The man with the Virginia Tech sweat-shirt picked up the bottle. "Well, I'm sorry, sir, there's no Fruit of Peace around here. Maybe try Northeast."

"No, it's definitely Southeast," Liam protested, following him back outside. "Over here, near Potomac Gardens."

"Sir," the man said, "those are the Hopkins projects." Pointing up the street the other direction, he continued, "Those there are Potomac Gardens. You better learn which is which, quick, fast, and in a hurry."

"Really? I thought —"

The man handed Hip Hop the new bottle, then quickly disappeared around the corner of the store, and Liam suddenly found himself in the midst of the kids again. He didn't think he could simply turn his back on the gang and walk away without incurring some abuse, so he puffed out his chest and went straight up to the biggest kid in the group.

"Say there, big man. I know that you know where the Fruit of Peace is."

The man smiled, but said nothing, his eyes glazed over.

Liam began to repeat himself when a one of the smaller kids strode forward and pushed the glazed-over man aside.

"You gonna axe any questions 'roun here, you best be talkin' to me!"

Dressed like an MTV gangsta – designer jeans hanging off his ass, wife-beater tee, thick gold chain around his neck – the kid couldn't have been more than ten years old. Stepping on his tip-toes, he tried to get in Liam's face.

"So, you down with Hopkins? Or you with the Garden crew?"

"No, you don't understand, I'm a lawyer. You know, a CJA lawyer?"

Nervous laughter erupted from the group.

"You back talking me? I axed if you was down with the Garden crew."

"No. I'm not."

"Ah-iight," the kid said, taking a step back. "Cause we don quarter no Garden niggas roun here."

"Triflin' motherfuckers," one of the other kids chimed in. "Hopkins for life!"

Liam tried to join in on their laughter without being too

obvious.

"So, you Mal's lawyer?" the ten-year-old gangsta asked, and suddenly all the laughing stopped.

"Yeah. How'd you know?"

The kid pointed over his shoulder with his chin to a guy in a wheelchair across the street. "That Mal's brother," the ten-year-old said. "He know you from the court building."

"Ronel?"

"No. Ronel kilt. He Le'Nor."

"That's Le'Nor? No way!"

Liam started across the street, but the little gangster stepped in front of him.

"Don be going over deh, man. Bring too much tension on us."

Liam looked down on the kid and thought, Why am I listening to this little brat? If I want to talk to my client's brother, I'm going to talk to my client's brother.

Then the kid pulled up his wife-beater and exposed the pearl handled pistol in his underwear. "Stop playing," he said, "n' follow me."

§ § § § § § § § §

McCoy sat in the sauna, one towel wrapped around his waist, another over his head. His mind was spinning, but every time he tried to stand, his knees went weak. He reached for his water bottle but knocked it down.

"I got it!" a chubby queen below him said. "Here you go, beautiful."

McCoy had always played it straight when he went to the gym, but today he found himself feeling more adventuresome, more daring. He had made it through the formal induction ceremony and now he felt like rewarding himself.

The old queen unwrapped his towel and began to stroke himself. "You scratch my back and I'll get yours?"

McCoy stared awhile, then abruptly walked out.   He dressed quickly and left the gym.

The late-afternoon air was cold and damp, and as he let the engine of his Jeep warm up, he decided to read the report he'd received from the Fingerprint Division that finally arrived on his desk earlier that day.

The results were startling, even by McCoy's standards. According to the report, the latent fingerprints taken off a can of spray paint discovered near the body of Sammy Kim matched those taken off the glass pipe found shoved deep into the young Jane Doe's rectum.   These matching prints had no hits in the national database; there were, however, two *partial* matches.

The first was from the Department of Corrections' new fingerprint database: the analysts found six matching points with the recently acquired fingerprints of a sixty-two-year-old inmate named Bennie Grimes.

The second partial match was from the fingerprint scan McCoy had obtained from the microfiche file of the juvenile who had killed his father.

Here was the problem with partials, McCoy lamented. Here's why the FBI looks for at least seven points to claim a match.   The juvenile who killed his father couldn't be more than forty five years old; this Bennie Grimes fellow, however, was in his sixties. Clearly they could not be the same person. Still, the hypothetical connection between the Swastika cases and the killer of McCoy's father left him shaken.

"Ah, Hell," McCoy said as he jammed the report back in the envelope. "It's Friday, work's over. Time to celebrate."

§ § § § § § § § §

As they walked, the ten-year-old gangsta introduced himself to Liam as Lil' Predator.

"I ain't no Muslin," he explained, "but I used to play a lot of basketball over there in that Fruit of Peace jump, you know, when I was a kid."

"When you were a kid?"

"Yeah. You think that's funny?"

"No, no, sorry," Liam said, regretting he had said anything. "You were saying, the Fruit of Peace...."

Lil' Predator stopped in front of a pile of stuffed animals at the corner of the fence that surrounded Potomac Gardens. Liam could see that the toys constituted some sort of shrine, complete with fizzled candles, deflated balloons, dried flowers, and empty bottles of Remy Martin. A rain-soaked sign on the fence read, *"RIP 'Big Pred', 12/20/1994."*

"That's Garden territory," Lil' Predator said, "and I ain't going no further. But you just go down that alley there, see? On the other side of the street? That Twelfth Place back there."

Liam took a few hesitant steps across the street. He didn't want to turn his back on the kid.

"That's right! Down the alley! Jes bang on the green door real hard, the one with that tiny moon on it. Sumun cumun git yeh."

When he turned the corner, Liam's trot turned into a run. Twenty feet in, the alley dog-legged into a cobblestone path, surrounded on both sides by high brick walls. Liam tripped forward in the darkness, crashing over a rusted mattress frame, and landing against a stack of wooden pallets.

As he dusted himself off, he heard voices coming from behind him. The path in front of him dog-legged again and as he scampered forward, motion detector lights kept popping on.

Now he was sure the voices were closing in on him.

He saw the green door with the crescent moon and rushed forward to open it. When the door knob began to jostle from the other side, Liam suddenly realized that he'd been set up, so he threw his shoulder against the door and charged forward. He felt the other person go down, so he slid inside and slammed the door behind him.

The room was dark and steamy and smelled of burnt marshmallows and body odor. He could hear the static of a transistor radio broadcasting what sounded like a baseball game. Behind him, he heard a groan. An old black man in a maroon sweater was picking himself off the floor.

Liam got in a fighting stance. "I ain't got no money, man! And my credit cards – they're all maxed out!"

"Money?" the man said in heavily accented English. "You don't need money here."

As his eyes adjusted to the dim light, Liam could see that the man was not black, but a dark-skinned Pakistani.

"Oh shit! I'm really sorry I barged in like that. I, uh, thought I was getting robbed or something."

"Quite alright."

"No, really. If you're not hurt, I can just go back the way I came."

"No, please, not that way! I keep telling the people that that's our fire door. Emergency Exit Only. Regulations, you know? Let me show you to the front."

The man gently guided him into what he now saw was a kitchen.

"You like baseball?" the old Pakistani asked, giving a self-conscious glance at Liam's still-clenched fists. "Playoffs. Mariners are leading the Indians three to two, fifth inning."

"Could I maybe just get a drink of water?" Liam asked, burying his hands in his pockets.

"Of course," the man laughed. "Right here, sit down, please."

He directed Liam to a bar stool next to a six-burner stove; then he shuffled away in plastic sandals two sizes too big.

"You drink this," he said, returning with a Styrofoam cup in one hand and a plastic bottle of water in the other. "Ever since they closed McMillan reservoir," he said with a wink, "the city water is just no good."

Liam gulped down the water, and before he knew it, the man filled his cup again.

"Thanks, thanks a lot. But, I mean, I can pour it myself, I don't want to trouble you or anything. And again, I'm, uh, sorry I knocked you down back there. Saw my first gun today, and I was just a little freaked out, if you know what I mean, so that's why I barged in like that."

"A gun, you say?" the Pakistani chuckled. "I thought maybe you could not resist the smell of my food!"

"Well, it does smell good. What are you cookin'?"

"This," the man said, pointing to one of the roiling pots, "this is dal. This over here is alu gobi. And this, this is yellow curry. You've heard of curry before, yes?"

"Sure, like, Indian food?"

The man smiled wanly. "So I take it you are not Muslim?"

"Ah, no." Liam wondered if he had said something insulting. "But I'm always open to new things."

"Well then, please, you try a little?" The man quickly pulled out some charcoaled flat bread from what looked to be a pizza oven and placed it on a paper plate in front of Liam. Then he spooned out large splotches of red, yellow, and orange onto another plate.

"Oh no, I couldn't," Liam demurred. "The reason I'm here, I was looking for the Fruit of Peace, and I think I got kind of lost."

"You're not lost," the man said, placing a spork and a napkin next to Liam's plate. "This is the Fruit of Peace!"

"Really? I'm here?"

"Yes. You are indeed here!"

"Hmmph. In that case...." He intended on taking a polite bite of the food before getting onto the business of finding Brother Khan, but the man kept dropping some new kind of treat on his plate: dates and other dried fruit, a piece of fluorescent orange deep-fried dough, a dense and spicy burger patty. Liam could barely keep up with him.

"I don't mean to be rude or anything," he said with his mouth full, "but I'm looking for someone called Brother Khan. I guess he's the Imam or whatever, you know? I need to get one of those letters."

"Of course, of course. If you can just wait one more minute. As you can see, I'm in the middle of cooking, and I have many mouths to feed."

"Yeah, sure, many mouths to feed."

"Yes. Today is the last day of Ramadan, soon as the sun goes down, you see."

Thinking about having to walk back home in the dark gave Liam a momentary fright.

"Shit, it is getting dark! Oh, I'm sorry about my language. But you're right. I really ought to get going, especially with – I can see that your, ah, little celebration is about to start. If you could just point me to Brother Khan? I mean, if he's even here. Or if not him, you know, his secretary? So I can maybe schedule an appointment with him."

"An appointment?"

"Like I said, I wanted to get one of those character reference letters of his. Not for me, of course. I'm a lawyer. You know, for a client?"

"Of course, of course. Write down your fax number and I'll make sure you get the letter."

Liam looked at his watch: it was almost six thirty.

"I'm sorry, sir, I don't have a fax machine, and I really need the letter, like, today. If you're too busy to take me to Brother Khan right now, then just point me the way – I'm sure I can find him myself."

The man wiped his hands on his apron, took Liam's empty plates and dropped them into a large garbage can. "Quite right. Come this way, please."

Liam followed him through a curtained door into a small indoor basketball court. Diagonally lain carpets covered the floor except for half a dozen card tables at the periphery, where several taxi driver types were chatting.

"Wait here," the man said, pulling out a chair for Liam. "Like your Arnold Schwarzenegger says, 'I'll be back.'"

Liam looked at his watch again as he sat down next to a heavy, olive skinned man who was speaking with a heavy, almost asthmatic accent. "I can't do it," he sputtered. "I can't wait any longer. Abdul, what time is it?"

"Again you ask me, Bassiri?" The men at the table all laughed. "You can see with your own eyes that the sun is still up!"

"I know, I know," the big man muttered, holding his head in his hands. Then he turned to Liam and said, almost as an aside, "For me? Booze, no problem. Women, ah... you know women. But cigarettes? This is killing me! It's my jihad!"

Liam smiled and nodded profusely until the cook returned holding a manila folder.

"Brother Khan, salaam alaikum!" the big-faced man said excitedly. "Surely a powerful Imam like yourself can make the sun set faster?"

"Don't be foolish," the cook – Brother Khan – answered,

smiling at Liam. "May I introduce you to my friend here, Mister ....?"

"McNaughton," he said, feeling very stupid. "Liam McNaughton."

"This young man is an attorney! A CJA attorney, is that correct? And he's come for one of my famous letters, he says."

The men all nodded and said "Ah ha!" as if they had been expecting him.

"Now then," Brother Khan continued, "what did you say your client's name is?"

"Jamal Stancil. Or just Mal. Whichever one is easier."

Brother Khan's face froze. After a few moments, he cleared his throat.

"Allah be praised! My friends, I believe this young man has been sent here on a mission! A mission to help our brother – Ishmal Stancil-El!"

~ Chapter Twenty Three ~

With the last of the Stancil file packed away, Jayson held up his hand for a high five and exclaimed, "Monday's gonna be a total slam dunk!"

Annie didn't reciprocate. Though she didn't disagree with her colleague's assessment, she couldn't get her arms around what was giving her such a funny feeling about the case. She'd had the same feeling before in her career, mostly when she caught a snitch or a cop lying to her, so she wondered if it was on account of McCoy. Something was odd about him, for sure – but no, it wasn't him. How about Olsen then? His reputation as a case wrecker was well earned, but his contact with the Stancil matter was minimal enough for Annie to have crossed him off the list. The thing with the Chief Judge back in July maybe? Annie thought. No, I've got thicker skin than that.

Come on, girl, let's face it – it's Stancil himself. The Baby Stomper? Hello! Annie ended her internal debate with a sigh. *No, he means nothing to me. Not anymore. This is just me doing my job.*

"Alright, Miss Fairbrother," Jayson called out. "Have a great weekend. See ya' Monday morning."

Morning! That's what had been bothering her – the call that morning alerting her to Stancil's arrest.

"Jayson, wait!" As soon as he turned around, Annie reconsidered her plan of action. This was something she would have to figure out on her own. "I, ah, just wanted to tell you...."

"Yes, ma'am?"

"Jayson, you gotta watch these DV cases. They've got high blow-up-in-your-face potential."

"I've done my tour on the Misdemeanor Calendar, Miss Fairbrother, I mean Annie, so I've done my share of Domestic

265

Violence. I know that sometimes your complaining witness turns against you, or worse, she doesn't show up."

"Right. Or they just blow the case because the jury finds them to be totally unlikeable."

"Well, I haven't done a jury trial – yet. So, yeah, I can't say."

Annie felt bad; she hadn't meant to embarrass her young peer. "Fortunately we don't have to worry about that here, do we, Jayson?"

"You mean, trying the case to a jury?"

"Well, yeah. It's a bench trial, duh!"

Jayson gasped.

"It's a misdemeanor," she continued. "180 day misdemeanor, right? There's no jury trial for Unlawful Entry."

Jayson looked deflated. "Actually, Miss Fairbrother, it's a six month misdemeanor."

"Right, 180 days, six months, same thing."

"Actually, no."

Annie's heart sank.

"The Court of Appeals issued an opinion just last month," Jayson explained, "Turner v. Bayly I think it's called – reversing a Misdemeanor Threats case on account of the defendant being denied a jury trial. Remember how the City Council dropped the penalties to 180 days on all those one year misdemeanors so we wouldn't have to deal with all those jury trials? Well, there were a couple of crimes that had always carried six months, and the Council never changed 'em. Everyone thought 180 days was the same as six months, but they're not – apparently you can count it out on a calendar. The law says defendants get a jury trial if they face more than 180 days, and there will always be more than 180 days in any six month period, so now the six month offenses get juries: Threats cases, Unlawful Entry, and one other one. What was it?"

"Jayson, why didn't you say something?"

"I thought you knew. I thought that's why we were looking at the Jury Instructions."

Annie felt like she was going to throw up. She had been eager to get back in the game, but wanted to take baby-steps at first.

"Jayson, I always check the Jury Instructions, even in misdemeanor cases. You gotta know what you've gotta prove, don't you?"

"I guess so."

"Now, there's a lot more to a jury trial than looking at jury instructions. The lead prosecutor on a case like this will typically have to work through the weekend to be adequately prepared for a Monday-morning jury trial. I'm certainly not staying here all weekend – I've got an infant child at home to take care of."

Jayson looked at her blankly.

"So I guess what I'm saying is, you're going to get your first opportunity to first chair a jury trial."

"You mean –?"

"That's right – this jury trial. Now let me tell you what you need to do this weekend. First, you got to think about *voir dire* and figuring out who you want on your jury. And of course, there's your opening argument. Then –"

Annie stopped when she felt something wet on her blouse. She was lactating.

"Oh my god!" she cried, covering her swollen breasts with her hands. "Jayson, would you excuse me please?"

"I don't understand," he said hesitantly. "Should I take the file with me?"

"Yes, just take it and go!" As she kicked the door closed behind him, she cried out pathetically, "OK, see you on Monday."

She pulled the new electric breast pump from her Chanel diaper bag and began tearing the plastic packing materials off with her teeth. She tried putting the pieces together, but nothing seemed to fit right. Her blouse was soaked, and she started to cry.

She finally pulled herself together enough to call her husband.

"I'll be downstairs in fifteen minutes, babe," he said over the telephone. "Try to keep your head up."

§ § § § § § § § §

Liam thought he might have struck gold with Brother Khan, but after talking to him for a few minutes, he realized his fortune was bit of a mixed bag.

The Imam had first met Jamal Stancil in D.C. Jail several years earlier. Mal had been detained there after his arrest for stomping Brandy, and because word had gotten out that he had killed his own unborn child, he was kept in solitary confinement for his own protection. For years, the jail guards had been allowing Brother Khan to read the Koran to the men in solitary, and Mal really took to him.

But shortly after pleading guilty in the case, Mal had been transferred to Lorton Prison to serve out the rest of his term, and it was there, Brother Khan later learned, that Mal began receiving pastoral counseling from the Reverend Clinton Anderson – an ex-communicated Catholic priest and rumored adherent to Sun Yun Moon's Unification Church.

As Brother Khan explained all this, Liam sniggered. "So I guess Mal wasn't all that good a Muslim, huh?"

The Imam shot him a scolding look.

"In Islam, there is no good Muslim and bad Muslim. If you wish to know Allah, you are a Muslim. Ishmal, I believe, had come to know Allah. Was there also room in his heart for Jesus Christ? Was there also room for Reverend Moon? I think your client has a bigger heart than you know."

Liam rolled his eyes. "So it sounds like you really haven't seen him since round about '92 or '93?"

"No, not true. Brother Ishmal's path crossed mine several times since then."

"Well, do you know what he was doing on the rooftop of St. Nick's in the early morning hours of April 19th?"

"I understood him to have had some sort of job at that particular school. A plumber's apprentice, if I can recall."

"Hmmm. I'd like to believe that too. But I've struck out with trying to prove it. I mean, none of the phone numbers he gave me worked. Every piece of mail I sent came back as 'undeliverable' or 'no such address.'" Liam looked away from the Imam. "I don't know," he said softly, "maybe I'm just not cut out for this."

"Don't you worry yourself, young man. The truth will guide you to justice."

The Imam signed the form letter attesting to Mal's reputation in the community for honesty and non-violence. "Allah be praised, I'll do whatever I can to help."

Liam took the letter, put it in his back pocket, and got up to leave. "Well, thanks, I guess. And thanks for the food. And sorry, again, about knocking you –"

The Imam suddenly jumped out of his seat.

"God is good! I almost forgot! Come, come, follow me! I have something that might really be of help to you!" The Imam plucked a bright red duffle bag from an overflowing closet and handed it to Liam. "Please, you take this. It belongs to Ishmal. He said he had to go to court and that he would be back for it the next day, but he never returned."

"When? When'd you see him last?"

269

"Oh, this had to be the end of May, maybe June, if I'm not mistaken."

"So, what's in there?"

The Imam smiled. "I couldn't tell you. The last time Ishmal left a bag here, he asked me to give it the upmost care because he said it contained ladybugs. Ladybugs! Imagine that! After he came and got that bag, he showed up with this red one just a couple of weeks later. Only Allah knows what he put in his bag this time."

Liam reluctantly took the bag, then politely declined Brother Khan's invitations to stay for the Ramadan celebration. Exiting through the building's front door, he found himself on 11th Street. Looking up the block towards 12th Street, he saw the corner store where the pee-wee gang was still milling about. Only now, Le'Nor had joined them.

Feeling slightly disoriented and not wanting another run-in with Lil' Pred, Liam slung the bag over his shoulder and began walking in the opposite direction. Bag's got some weight to it, he thought. Wonder what Mal's got in here? A gun? A knife?

He was about to look in the bag when an old model American car sped by, its bright yellow bumper sticker saying in bold letters, "FREE PAUL HILL." When the car screeched to a halt in front of Le'Nor and his crew, the kids all ran off in different directions bellowing, "Yo, yo, yo! Five-O!"

The car then pulled off just as quickly as it had stopped, taking a hard left turn at the corner, and speeding down 12th Street towards Potomac Gardens.

Liam caught a glimpse of the driver – it was his old friend Ponytail!

"So this is where he scores that good weed," Liam laughed. He considered racing around the block to see if he could catch up with Ponytail, maybe hang out and get high and yak about Civil War trivia again, but Le'Nor – Mal's brother – was wheeling himself full-speed straight at him.

"Oh, hey Le'Nor," Liam said jumping out of the way, "I'm Mal's –"

Le'Nor put his finger to his mouth and scowled; then he backed himself into a cut in the grove of weed trees. "Don jes stand there, fool," he commanded. "Get in 'ere!"

Liam followed him and tried asking what was going on.

"It's hot as a muth down in here!" he replied. "Now keep quiet for second, will ya?"

A few moments later, a long whistle came back from one of the upper-floor windows of the Hopkins building.

"Ah-igght," Le'Nor said assuredly. "He gone. That nigga crazy if he think *I'm* gonna serve him."

Liam laughed. "You think that dude was a cop, don't you?"

"Course he a cop."

"Just because he's white, huh?" Liam immediately regretted how smug he sounded.

"Nigga, please. Y'all need to be getting' over this O.J. thing quick. You think we don' serve white folks over here? Course we do. Who do you think drive all dem cars with dem Maryland and Virginia plates? We just know who's hot and who's not, that's all. You don't *all* look alike to me."

Liam jumped when someone walked up behind him.

"Hey, Lil' Pred," Le'Nor said. "Whassup?"

"Nothing, L. I got yo back." Eyeing Liam, the ten year-old sneered, "So, bitch? Did I hook you up or what?"

"Uh, yes, Little Predator, you did. Thank you."

A few more kids squeezed into the little space between the trees, gathering around Le'Nor. "So my man Lil' Pred tells me you be gettin' one of those Brother Khan letters for Mal."

"Yes, that's right," Liam said, proud of the

271

accomplishment. "I got it right here. I got Mal's bag too."

The glazed over man Liam had originally thought was the pack's leader suddenly stumbled forward. "Yo man, you really a lawyer?"

"Course he is, nigga!" Little Predator sneered. "He be Le'Nor's god-brother's lawyer n'shit!"

"You do all kine a cases?" the glazed over man asked, ignoring the admonishment. "Cause I gotta question: You gotta pay chile support for a chile that ain't yours?"

Liam laughed, instantly recalling the most useful thing he ever learned at law school. "It depends," he answered.

Drawing more information from the man and making the group laugh with his somewhat professorial explanations, he began to feel more relaxed. Soon, every other member of Le'Nor's crew lined up to ask their own legal question – *Can they bug one dem cellular phones? It true they ain't no mo' mandatory minimums? You think $4,000 is a good settlement ona accident case? You be knowings Johnnie Cochran?*

There must have been eight or nine of them all huddled together, with Liam holding court. When someone lit a joint and began passing it around, Liam made a grab for it as the man next to him tried to pass it around him.

"Don't mind if I do."

The man with the joint looked at Le'Nor for guidance, but Le'Nor just shrugged his shoulders. "My bad," the man said. "Here you go."

Liam then took a long, hard hit. The smoke had a foul smell, almost like gasoline, but he tried to keep it in as long as he could. "So, you all going to the Million Man March on Monday?" he asked, sucking in his breath.

"Who wanna go see a million niggas?" someone said. "All my niggas right here."

When Liam tried to take a quick second draw, Le'Nor

reached out and grabbed his wrist like a vice. "So, lawyer-man, you gonna get my brother off, right?"

"Shit, man," he coughed. "I dunno. I'm trying, man, I really am. But, you know, Mal won't really talk to me, tell me what's up."

Le'Nor released his arm. "That nigga just be quiet like that sometimes. But me? You know what I think? I think that bitch Brandy set him up."

Liam's eyes had narrowed to slits and he felt something roiling in his stomach. "Shit, man, what kind of weed was that?" he said to no one in particular.

The boys all started laughing hysterically.

"Dude, you gonna ride the Love Boat!" one of them said.

"You on the Buck Nekid!" said another.

Then Lil' Predator walked up to Liam and tugged on his shirt in almost child-like fashion. "Mister, you really ain't never done no dippa?"

Liam's head was swimming now and he had a hard time hearing anyone over the sound of the blood rushing to his brain. He saw that Le'Nor was still talking to him, so he tried to focus on his words.

"– that they put a hit out on him last time, you know, time he was locked up over there in D.C. Jail after he stomp-ted Brandy. Ten thousand dollas they put on his head. Brandy's people, they's just some public assistance muthafuckas! Mal had him a good job at that school, and them P.A. people just hate to see that."

Liam tried to shake his head clear. "I'll have to write all this down," he said, pawing at his sweatshirt. "If I can just find my note-pad."

"Jes let the man put his bugs in the seats or whateva. I mean, he jes doing his job." Le'Nor shook his head ruefully. "You don' have to put 5-O on him for that!"

273

"Bugs?" Liam said. "You mean bugs, like in Watergate?"

"Watergate? Whatchu talking 'bout Watergate? Mal be out there trying to save some lives, dig?"

One of the boys on the periphery suddenly called out, "Shit, who dat?"

Another voice, that of the glazed over man, rang out with alarm, "Dem Garden boyz on our corner?"

The crew suddenly disappeared in unison, leaving Le'Nor and Liam alone in the thicket.

"That not Garden crew," Le'Nor said, sounding scared. "Those niggas be grown men and shit."

Curious, Liam poked his head out of the thicket and saw a group of black men getting out of a white box truck that had stopped in front of the corner store. The men were all dressed in Los Angeles Raiders football jerseys, and appeared to be spreading out across the block.

"Is it the cops?"

"Maybe," Le'Nor said cautiously. "But they's definitely looking for somebody. Let's go."

Oddly engrossed with the steam coming out of the mouths of the black men who were sprinting towards them, Liam didn't hear Le'Nor's command.

"Indirect evidence that it's cold outside," he laughed to himself. "So why do I feel so hot?"

Taking a few tentative steps backwards, Liam tore off his sweat shirt and the undershirt he had beneath it and dropped them to the ground, but he still felt like his blood was boiling. He was about to take off his pants when the box truck he had seen on the corner came crashing over the curb into the thicket of weed trees. The rear doors swung open and two more black men jumped out, each holding a corner of what appeared to be a thick painter's tarp.

Liam finally realized it was *him* they were after.

§ § § § § § § § §

As Steve fuddled in the garage, Annie rushed inside with a mixture of fatigue and curiosity. She had barely reached the kitchen when Leonie, their newly hired Filipina nanny, appeared holding a baby.

Her baby. Her son. Elijah.

The tiny woman, whose skin was darker than Annie's, thrust him forward. "He sweet baby, Miss Annie," the woman said. "Mama? Go to mama?"

Annie stood as still as a statue, unable to reach out for her own child. She felt like she was having a nightmare, where she was trying to move forward, to grab her child, to protect him, but she was frozen, unable to lift her arms from her side.

Finally, the nanny stepped forward and placed the child in Annie's arms.

"Thank you," Annie said, beginning to cry.

The tiny woman came close to Annie, stroking the small child's head as he nestled into Annie's breast. "Bye bye, Elijah! You with Mommy now. See you Monday, Miss Annie!"

Annie took off her soaked blouse, sat down in the rocker, and began to nurse her hungry son. As she swayed back and forth, she began humming a tune, and after a while, she realized that it was the lullaby her great-grandmother used to sing to her.

The words came to Annie from a deep place, and she began to sing:

> *Who dat tappin' at de window?*
> *Who dat tappin' at de door?*
> *Mammy tappin' at de window*
> *Pappy tappin' at de door.*

~ Chapter Twenty Four ~

Shirtless and holding his client's red duffel bag, Liam sprinted down the middle of the street towards the highway, the men wearing the Raiders jerseys close behind. The box truck spun its wheels reversing out of the thicket, then sped by all of them, skidding to a halt at the far end of the overpass.

Liam could see that he was trapped, so he hopped over the guardrail without thinking and began sliding down a steep embankment until he reached the railroad tracks below.

He was at the mouth of a tunnel. The air coming from inside was cool and damp, so he stumbled forward into the oily blackness. He turned to look back when he heard the voices and could see the silhouettes of half a dozen men at the tunnel entry.

"Man, I ain't going go up in there!"

"Can't see a gotdam thing!"

"Shit nigga, get offa me!"

"Dione, go n'git da flashlights! Resta you niggas git in there afta him, dammit!"

Liam ran further into the tunnel, feeling his way along the jagged wall. He found it was easier to navigate the contours of the tunnel if he closed his eyes, and he could hear that he was out-distancing the pursuing voices.

Then Liam tripped and fell to the ground, losing his grip on the bag.

Getting to his hands and knees, he could tell that he was in the middle of the tracks, away from the walls. The voices of his pursuers seemed very faint, and because of the echo, he couldn't tell from which way they were coming. The smell of rotting flesh was all around him, and he realized for the first time that he might not ever get out of there.

"I gotta get that bag," he said aloud. "Gotta do this for

Mal."

As he flailed away in the darkness, Liam became aware of the rather unusual absence of any fear. He knew he was high, but he truly felt something transformational was going on. He recognized that he had spent much of his life afraid –morally ambivalent, distant and suspicious, afraid of being judged, afraid of finding fault. *Maybe that's why I became a lawyer,* he thought. *It's much easier to fight other people's battles.*

"But this is my battle now," he said to himself sternly. "And I won't be afraid!"

He began crawling down the tracks in the direction he assumed he had come, hoping to stumble over Mal's bag. But he stopped and sat up when he noticed a pin-hole of light. Like a lightning bug flying just out of reach, it disappeared every time he tried to grab it.

The pin-hole was growing steadily, slowly illuminating the tracks ahead of him. The tunnel walls looked as if they were awakening, and in the weak light, Liam could see the dead dog that he had evidently tripped over.

He stared at the dog.

The dog stared at him.

Liam laughed, seeing his own reflection in the dead dog's eyes. "Trippy, dude."

"Think that's trippy?" the dog said. "Here comes the train!"

A piercing train whistle brought Liam's hands instinctively to his ears. In the distant glare, he could see that one of the Raiders was just ahead of him. When the train whistle stopped, Liam could hear the voices coming from behind.

"Hey Shorty, you walked right by him! There he is! He's right behind you!"

Then Liam saw it – Mal's bag – it was right there next to

277

the mangled dog corpse. He grabbed ahold of it, but it didn't move – one of the Raiders had his foot on the other end.

The tunnel was fully illuminated now, and Liam watched in horror as the man drew a pistol from under his waistband and leveled at him.

"Second time today!" Liam lamented.

The earth beneath them began to shake violently – the locomotive was upon them, along with another ear piercing whistle. Liam pulled hard on the bag, rolling his body back over the track. He saw the flash of the gun and felt a hard, wet slap across the side of his head, and just as quickly as the tunnel had become illuminated, it was now growing dark as the long line of train cars stampeded by.

He picked up his client's bag and ran in the direction of where the train had come, his heart racing, his ears ringing, stumbling out of the tunnel mouth just as the last train cars rumbled in. Standing there bathed in the misty yellow light, he could see that he was just behind the park of dead trees and copulating prostitutes where he had started his journey earlier that day – only a high-barbed wire fence separated him from his road home.

Then, through ringing in his ears, he heard the voices coming from inside the tunnel. *"There he is!" "There's the muthafucka!"*

He had to go the other way, over a short stone wall and through a pasture of horses that grazed under the highway. Liam was sure he was hallucinating – who ever heard of horses in D.C.? – but kept running just the same.

When he thought he had lost his pursuers, he paused to scrape the horse manure from his feet.

Then he resumed the running, with shadows and car doors slamming and far away voices giving chase, and soon he found himself in a maze of warehouses. Rounding corner after corner, never knowing if he was going to come face to face with the Raiders, he suddenly ran into two skinny black dudes. The men were smoking perfumed cigarettes and, like Liam, both were shirtless.

"Oh my god! What happened to you?" one of them asked in a very fey voice. "Did someone, like, rob you or something?"

"Don't look now," the other one said, "but here the muthafuckas come!"

"Go back inside," the first one said, pushing Liam into the building. "Hurry up, girl! Safety in numbers!"

§ § § § § § § § §

When the pulsating beat of Donna Summer's "In Love" broke through the mix, McCoy tossed back the last of his drink, took off his shirt, and began swimming through the sea of half-naked men.

Trax was hopping tonight, the usual anonymity doubly so with all the beautiful black men in town for the Million Man March. McCoy smiled as he wedged himself between two muscular black dudes with dreadlocks. But he broke it off when he recognized a lawyer from the courthouse coming right at him.

Shit, he thought, anonymity blown.

He immediately moved in the opposite direction, making his way alongside the outer edge of the club. There he found more trouble.

"*Fucking sodomites!*" a hard voice called out. "*Y'all sicken me.*"

Three black men in black football jerseys were pushing through the crowd, daring anyone to stop them. McCoy knew that if something serious went down – a shooting, a knifing, a large melee – the police would come down on Trax like a ton of bricks: Vice Squad would cordon off the club, check I.D.'s, and photograph every person on the way out. No way he was going to get caught up in that. What would be his excuse for being there – undercover investigation?

McCoy quickly put his shirt on and made his way towards the coat check, where he couldn't resist slipping a fiver down the pants of the hottie who took his ticket. As McCoy slipped on his leather jacket, the coat check boy reciprocated, sliding his soft, slender hand into McCoy's pants.

"Meet me in the men's room in five minutes," the coat check boy said with a smile, "and I'll finish you off there."

§ § § § § § § § §

Liam curled up on the dirty toilet seat. Two or more men were having sex in the stall to his left, someone was snorting lines to his right. He raised his feet up to avoid the layer of muck that covered the bathroom floor, but people kept pushing and banging on the door thinking the stall was empty, so he reluctantly returned his feet to the floor.

He stared at the canvas duffel bag on his lap, wondering what he'd been risking his life for. Emptying the contents of his client's bag on his lap, he found a box cutter and several small hand tools, a large box of matches, a cassette tape entitled "GO GO MUSIC," and random magazine clippings. Digging deeper, he found an empty can of epoxy, a half-filled container of turpentine, a sweat shirt, several degraded packets of condoms, and a pair of rubber gloves.

A piece of paper was stuck to the side of the can of epoxy, so Liam gently pulled it off. On one side was a hand-drawn grid, letters and numbers delineating rows and columns, while dozens of red-inked "x's" filled random squares. On the other side – what Liam assumed were his client's amateur rap lyrics, written in flowery cursive. He read it aloud:

Ladybird
Ladybird
Fly away home.
Your house is on fire,
Your children will burn.

Better than the usual bitches and ho's, Liam thought. But sorry, pal, Tupac you ain't.

Then he noticed that the magazine clippings were not at all random. Every one of them contained close-up images of what Liam thought were tadpoles. Looking closer, he recoiled. These were pictures of fetuses – bloody, aborted human fetuses, each with distinct fingers and toes and adult-like expressions of horror frozen on their glossy little faces.

"Inventory complete," Liam said, stuffing the flotsam and jetsam back in the bag.

In his haste, he dropped the matchbox into the muck below. He leaned over and snatched it up before it floated away.

Upon closer inspection, he saw that the box was marked with the words, "Caution: Frozen Specimen – Do Not Refreeze," and it had a small hole bored in it, like something had drilled its way out. Curious, Liam turned the box over, and the contents poured out through the hole and into his hand. He stared in amazement at the dusty pieces of insect parts – the legs, heads, and tails of what were unmistakably dried-up praying mantises.

Focusing on one relatively intact mantis body, Liam became consumed by a childhood memory. His father, who was spraying the lawn with some chemicals, told him to come over quick with his sand pail. There, on the sodden edge of the lawn, underneath the hedges, his dad had discovered a colony of mantises. One had crawled onto the back of his father's hand, looking for a fight.

"You know why these insects are like humans?" his father asked, picking a second mantis off a leaf with his other hand. "They'll eat each other if they have to."

Brushing both mantises into the plastic sand pail, his dad gave it back to him. "Go ahead, sonny boy, watch for yourself."

A loud knock on the stall door broke Liam from his trance.

"Done flipping out in there, cutie?" a voice called out.

"Fucking white boys can't handle their ex!" another voice complained.

Liam tossed the box of mantises on the floor, wrapped the duffel bag's drawstring around his arm, and walked out of the stall. Pushing his way through the crowd to the long shelf of sinks, he looked at his dilated pupils in the mirror.

"Fuck, dude," he said. "You. Are. So. High."

A man dressed as a woman tried to squeeze into Liam's mirror space.

"Scuze you!" the queen griped. "But do you need to hog *all* the mirror?" Then he jumped back in horror. "Oh lawd ha'mercy! What's that on your face?"

Adjusting his frame of reference away from his own eyes, Liam saw that he had streaks of blood dripping down his forehead. He instinctively reached for the back of his head and felt a wet matted area. As he pulled off a long piece of bloody scalp, he thought, I've got to be hallucinating. Could I have been shot and not even felt it?

"We got a head wound here!" someone called out. "Anyone a doctor? A nurse?"

A mustachioed white man emerged from one of the toilet stalls, pulling his pants up and muscling his way forward as if it was his business to figure out what was going on. "What happened here?" he demanded, inspecting Liam's head. "Did a car hit you or something?"

Liam stared at the piece of scalp in his hands. It wasn't his own curly hair; rather, it was the kind of tightly knitted cornrows that a black man might have – just like the man in the tunnel holding the gun.

"Not a car," Liam answered. "A train."

The mustachioed man leaned in close. "Look, I know who you are," he whispered. "I promise not to tell anyone that you were here. But you need to see a doctor quick. I'm gonna have someone call you an ambulance."

Liam looked at the man, really for the first time, and said, "Hey! I know you! You're a cop!"

The restroom went quiet and several dudes began stepping out the door.

"So, what, are you after me too?" Liam demanded.

"After you? You must be delirious." The man grabbed a stack of paper towels and quickly wetted them. "Keep this on your head for now. You've probably got a concussion. And here, take this, you've got to stay warm, otherwise you can go into shock."

As the man draped his leather jacket over his shoulders, Liam saw in the mirror that the three Raiders had entered the restroom.

§ § § § § § § § §

"You niggas look inside those stalls. White boy probably hiding in there. N'make sure you get da' bag!"

As the men started forward, they were immediately confronted by the transvestite, his big eyelashes batting. "You can't just barge in here like you own the place, Mister!" he said before the Raiders shoved him skidding face first into the urinals.

McCoy noticed that the lawyer had his face hidden under the faucet and was trying to conceal a duffel bag under his jacket. So it's you they're after, he thought.

When the men in the Raiders jerseys passed by, McCoy suddenly pulled the lawyer from underneath the sink and began to push him out the door.

"There he go!" the Raiders called out. "Get his ass!"

McCoy turned to face the men, allowing the lawyer to disappear into the crowd. "Hey guys," he said in his best queen voice. "You wanna go with me?"

"Fuck you, cocksucker," the one in charge said as he moved to sweep him by. But McCoy sidestepped him, grabbing the man's outstretched arm and breaking it with a snap. The man's howling brought the other two into the fray. McCoy got a good body shot into the first one, but the second guy was able to tackle him to the floor. The dude felled by the body shot then rushed over and mashed his boot into McCoy's face. Then the other man – the one with the broken arm – he joined in, and soon, everything went black.

§ § § § § § § § §

Hopefully that dumb-ass cop bought me some time, Liam thought as he bolted out of the club. He had seen the men come into the restroom – that's why he hid his face under the faucet. He'd hoped to have slipped away without notice, but now, thanks to the meddling cop, he couldn't be sure that he had lost his tail.

After a third pass by his apartment, he decided to give it a try.

His security gate and front door were unlocked, but he didn't think much of it – he was just happy to be home. He went straight to the fridge, crouched down, and stared at its empty shelves. If I can just get my head together, he thought, I'll be able to figure out what's going on here.

A loud pop brought him to standing and for a second he felt something stinging him from the back of McCoy's jacket. As he tried to reach around to pull whatever it was out, he saw the shadow of a man in the middle of his apartment. The man was holding the other end of the strings – the strings that were attached to the back of his jacket.

Liam was suddenly lifted off his feet and slammed to the ground. Barely conscious, he heard the man yell, "Damn nigga! He walked right up on me! S'posed to be watching the door, fool! What da fuck you doing back there?"

A second, much bigger man came running out of the bathroom, pulling his pants up. "Damn, Dione, his eyes still open! You got him good, dog!"

The first man laughed. "Yeah! And where the wires stuck him, jumps caught on fire and shit!"

"No! Where?"

"Right there, on his coat."

Liam could feel one of the men digging through his pockets, eventually pulling out his wallet, and then tossing it in the corner next to Mal's bag.

"Nigga broke as a muth! Whoever heard of no broke lawyer?"

Liam was starting to feel the tips of his fingers again, and the tingling continued down his arms.

"Look, Dione! He starting to move! Hit him wit da Taser again!"

"Nah, man."

"Then give me a go!"

"Nah man! You only get one shot with this thing."

"Bullshit. I seen them on T.V. Them's like fishin' poles.

Let me see it."

The big man, still holding his pants up, stepped across Liam.

"Nigga, you trippin? Captain gave this to *me!*"

"What the fuck you care, Dione? Lemme have a go!"

Now they both had their backs to him, so Liam hopped up stiffly. He grabbed an iron that was sitting on the stack of moving boxes that served as his filing cabinet and walloped the big man behind his ear. Then, without thinking, he ran to the back of his apartment and locked himself in the bathroom.

"Open up muthafucka!" Dione called out from the other side of the door.

"Yo, man, yo," came the voice of the big one, already up. "Don't be screaming like that. Sumun call the police."

"Yo, dude, yo head's as big as a watermelon!"

"Shut up, nigga, and start pushin."

The flimsy door began to bulge towards him and Liam could see that the door hinges were about to pop off, so he put his own weight against the door, countering the move.

"You guys better get out of here now!" Liam called out. "I'm gonna call the police. I've – I've got a cell phone right here."

The apartment went silent and Liam wondered if his ploy had worked.

"Fuck that," the big man wheezed. "He's lying. Broke ass lawyer ain't got no cell phone. Go on, nigga, pull on that shit whiles I sits down for a minute and rests."

When the door began to bulge outward, Liam grabbed the door knob and pulled back. "Just take what you want and get the fuck out of here," he cried. "All I gotta do is yell and someone will hear me."

"Man, you just don't get it, do you," Dione said. "We scouted you out, muthfucka. Ain't nobody upstairs but an empty mail room. And down here, you got the laundry on one side and an empty apartment on the other."

"Yeah, so you all alone in there, bitch," the other man said through a cough-laden laugh. "All alone 'cept yo' sticky dicky magazine."

Liam looked to the floor next the toilet, and there it was – the Victoria's Secret catalogue he had recently purloined from the mail room.

"Thought you had that shit hid, dinit you!"

Liam was aghast. Holding the flimsy doorknob with one hand, he snatched the catalogue off the floor and tried to return it to its usual hiding place under the sink. When he opened the cabinet door, the small plastic trash can that held his toilet cleaning brush fell out, along with a half-empty bottle of bleach and a yellowed roll of toilet paper.

Liam picked up the toilet brush and gave it a couple of swings to see if it could be used as a weapon. How pathetic, he thought, seeing his reflection in the bathroom mirror.

"Look," he whined. "What the fuck do you guys want with me?"

"Likes you don't know." It was Dione's voice now. The other man was wheezing loudly. "You think we don't know what you up to? You think we don't know what you and dem muthafuckin' snitches down at the jail be conspir-i-sizing to do?"

"I ain't no snitch! None of my clients are snitches!"

"Man, you think all us niggas is just stupid, don't you, jes cause we felons and shit. You trying to set us *all* up! And you crazy if you think I'ma going back to prison. Cap'n done explained it clear – da' fucking CJA lawyers is in on all of it."

"What are you talking about? I've never even been to a debriefing. You can check my files!"

"Fuck all this talking," said the big man. "I ain't got much longa. Lookit all this blood – here, nigga, use dis iron. Smash on through that piece of shit."

At the first stroke of the iron, the flimsy door began to splinter, and Liam could see that they'd be in in seconds. There was no escape – he'd have to fight them with his bare hands. He tossed his ridiculous little toilet brush back in the garbage pail, and girded for battle.

Then, he had an idea.

He quickly twisted the top off the bleach and began pouring it into the plastic garbage pail. Then he reached under the sink and started dumping in everything else he could get his hands on – Liquid Plumber, Mr. Clean, Dr. Bronner's soap – but it wasn't until he poured in the half bottle of Windex that a truly noxious cloud began to rise up from the garbage pail, causing Liam to choke.

Just then Dione poked his face through the hole he had hammered through the door. "Here's Johnny!" he cackled.

Liam gave the heave-ho and sent the roiling concoction squarely into the man's face. As Dione started shrieking uncontrollably, Liam put his shoulder into the cheap bathroom door and popped it out of its frame. Using the door like a bulldozer to push the two men aside, he scampered out of his apartment, back out onto the streets.

IX. Saturday, October 14, 1995

CNN Correspondent John Holliman reporting from Washington:

How do you handle a million men crammed into a 23-block area between the U.S. Capitol and the Lincoln Memorial? The answer, it appears, is that nobody knows.

"Washington knows how to handle large crowds," said Mayor Marion Barry. "There are more buses and cars coming in. We're ready for that."

Privately the mayor says he can't worry about logistics, that Monday's march will take care of itself. But the city's government has been frustrated by the lack of organization by Million Man March planners, and by the fact that it has never had to deal with this many people in Washington on a work day.

Organizers must find places to park for 11,000 buses, which would stretch for 100 miles if parked end to end. Washington's RFK Stadium can hold only 2,500 buses, and the Pentagon has told organizers the buses can't park in its huge lots.

Authorities say they will need 3,000 port-a-johns lined up along the mall, and so far they've only been able to find 1,000. Do the math – that translates to one for every 300 people.

Major streets around the Capitol will be closed during the march, and police will be stationed on every street corner for 20 blocks. Officers won't go into the crowd unless they're needed. The Nation of Islam promises 10,000 marshals to work inside the crowd.

Many of the 400,000 federal workers here are expected to come in to work, but they're not happy about it. "What about the rights of businessmen in the city to sell products?" said Bert Croushorn. "What about our rights?" And bus driver Ben Ladd summed up many Washingtonians' feelings about Monday. "I think the city is going to be a mess," he said.

~ Chapter Twenty Five ~

"Cellie, you up?"

"Nah, man. I 'sleep."

"Come on, yo," Mal called down from his bunk. "I gotta come down to piss."

"Why muthafucking Corrections be getting us up this early?"

"Even on Saturdays, yo," Mal said, "They just try to keep us tired and dis-orientated. You get used to it."

"Disoriented, nigga," the man huffed. "The word is disoriented." The man then kicked his feet off the bunk, walked over to the toilet, dropped his jail-issued drawers, and pissed standing up. "Yo, Malcolm X. That was real good of you to give up the bottom bunk."

"Ain't no thang," Mal said, staring at the ceiling. "I been in here for a minute. You just got here, so, you know, it's cool. They done kept me in solitary all this time so I just happy to be outta the hole, ya dig?"

The man finished peeing, shook, and jammed it back in. "So I'm guessing you in here for some hardcore stuff, huh?"

"Nah, man," Mal sighed, "I'm too old for that kind of running around. Just in the wrong place in the wrong time, that's all."

"'Wrong place, wrong time.' All dem young niggas say that!" The man stood in front of the cell's tiny sink, admiring himself in the hazy mirror. "Man, you ain't gonna beat no charges on that."

Mal jumped out of bed. "Yeah, yeah, you right."

"Maybe you can claim self-defense or some shit like that. Or use one of them alibis. Alibis are good."

"Ah, man, I don't wanna get into it or nothing. I mean, my lawyer, he said not to be talkin' 'bout it and shit."

"Your lawyer?" The man gave Mal a hostile look. "Fuck your lawyer. I know you're in here on a little trespassing beef."

"O.K., I ain't gonna lie. I toll you I ain't no hard-core thug."

"True that."

"Well how 'bout you, Bennie?"

"What?"

"What you in for?"

"Uh, heroin. Distribution or some shit like that."

Mal looked at the short, stocky man. He seemed far too healthy to be a heroin addict. "So you really be slinging out there, dude? Cause you don' look like no heron user I never seen."

The man gave Mal an aggravated look. "Well, shit, nigga. Looks *can* be deceiving."

"For real, for real." Mal tried to slide by his cellmate in order to get to the toilet but the man stood firm.

"So nigga, when you go back to court then?"

"Monday." Mal's full bladder was causing him to grimace.

"Same as me!" The men were standing toe to toe now. "Who yo judge?"

"The Chief Judge, I think."

"Cummings? Armstrong Cummings? That's who I got too! The boss of all da judges. The worstest of the worstest, that's what I be hearing."

"Well now that we got all these here co-inky-dinks out the way," Mal said angrily, "I'd like to use the ba'froom!"

For a moment, the man didn't move. Then he smiled and stepped aside. "Oh, am I in yo' way? My bad."

"Thank you." Mal dropped his drawers, and peed quickly.

"You must have pissed someone off real bad to be down here on some trifling trespassing shit, Mr. Malcolm X.. But you know, you don' wanna talk about it with me, that's cool."

"Nah, man, it's not that .... It ain't no big deal, that's all."

The man dropped to the floor and began doing push-ups. "I mean ... it's not like ... we've known each other ... for more than ... a couple of hours."

"Well, you know the ole saying, 'If you can't trust yo cellie, who can you trust?'"

Mal chuckled at the old prison joke, but the other man kept on with his push-ups.

"I just be real down about the whole thing," Mal continued cautiously. "Don't really like to talk on it ... on account ... I think it was a set-up."

The man stopped his push-ups. "A set up, you say?"

"Yeah, man. They had the cops just waiting for me."

"Who did it? Who set you up? We gonna get 'em, right?"

"Na, man, it wasn't nothing like that." Mal's voice went real low and soft, almost as if he was talking to himself. "I mean, I took care of everything, see? The killing just gotta end. The babies, everything, all God's children."

"Go on," the man hissed. "Go on."

"I mean, even bugs, man. I can't kill no bugs."

"Bugs? Nigga, I ain't hearing about no bugs. We talking bout did you do yo job or not. That's all I want to be hearing bout!"

Mal looked over his cell-mate. "You sho' do axe a lot of question. And you act like you ain't never been in no prison. But by that tat you got on yo neck, I'ma guessing you're one Minister And-One's boys."

"This?" the man said of the swastika branded on his muscled neck. "Nah. This just means I'm a bad ass. I could burn you one too, muthfucka. Balance you out."

Just then, the skinny guard everyone called Bones came walking down the hall, banging and clanging his key ring against the bars of the cells. "Get up, ladies! Breakfast time. 'Cept for you Stancil! You got a legal visit."

"Legal visit again?" Mal asked, slipping on his prison-issue Keds. "Oh well. Must be important."

"Little early in the morning for a legal visit," his cell-mate said, directing the complaint at Bones.

"Legal visits are 24/7, shit bird," the guard said. "That's what the court says we gotta do, so we do it."

"Well we busy right now, nigga," the short stocky man seethed. "Can't you see we talking here?"

"You better get that bass out yo' voice, boy! You ain't been here too long to know, Mr. Bennie Grimes, but you better axe somebody. Bones don't play."

"Fucking nigga, you lucky we ain't on the outside, cause then we'd see how you play."

"Heels to the wall, Grimes," the guard said plainly, pulling something off his belt. "You two ladies can get back to doing the nasty when I brings him back."

"Hey, Bennie, chill," Mal said, eager to get out of the cell. "Bones be lethal."

But his cellmate wasn't having any of that. "Fuck that heels to the wall bullshit, muthafucka!" he said as he charged the bars.

With one swift move, Bones sprayed the man in the face with the pepper spray, causing him fall to his knees shrieking. Then the guard opened the door to the cell and kicked the man squarely in the chin.

"Let's go, Stancil," he said. "I ain't asking again."

§ § § § § § § § §

Liam sat by himself in the back of the Number 32 Metrobus. Over and over, he asked himself the same two

293

questions – *Can I go home? Should I call the police?* – but the answer remained the same for both: no.

The Metropolitan Police Department, U.S. Capitol Police, Park Police, Uniformed Secret Service, Federal Protective Service, Library of Congress Police, and the Supreme Court Police all regularly patrolled the area in front of his apartment, and look what good that did him. Sure, he could file a police report claiming that a gang of black men in Raiders jerseys tried to rob him; but what would he say about his smoking PCP and running half-naked through a train tunnel? In reporting the invasion of his home, would he have to reveal that he might have killed a man with an iron, or that he probably maimed and blinded one of the intruders with a chemical facial?

Sitting there in the back of the bus, Liam felt so anonymous and insignificant, so utterly foreign to this place, he simply could not believe that anyone would take him seriously.

When the bus pulled up to L'Enfant Plaza, he figured he'd had enough of the 32 Line, so he hopped off in front of the massive Mitch Snyder homeless shelter, just down the street from the Superior Court. He began rooting through the bags of clothes that had been left outside and eventually found a shirt that fit – an ugly maroon shirt decorated with three beer-bellied men in pig-snouts saying, "Go Hogs!" The shirt smelled like someone had urinated on it, but he couldn't find anything better, so he put it on.

Then he noticed a top hat. It looked way too nice to have been left for the homeless, and it fit him to a T, so he decided to keep it, and headed off towards the rising sun.

Just past Union Station, another discovery: a roll of quarters in the pocket of the leather jacket he had taken from the cop the night before.

On impulse, Liam commandeered a pay phone and dialed Julianne's number.

The answering machine picked up, playing Lauryn Hill's "To Zion," a song she used to listen to over and over when they were still together:

> *Unsure of what the balance held*
> *I touched my belly overwhelmed*
> *By what I had been chosen to perform*
> *But then an angel came one day*
> *Told me to kneel down and pray*
> *For unto me a man child would be born*
> *Woe this crazy circumstance*
> *I knew his life deserved a chance*
> *But everybody told me to be smart*
> *Look at your career they said*
> *"Lauryn, baby, use your head"*
> *But instead I chose to use my heart*

Finally, Julianne's unusually sullen voice came on, saying, "Sorry I'm not in. You know what to do."

"J, it's me," Liam said after the beep. "If you're there, pick up, OK? Please, I need to speak to you. I miss you and I really —"

He hadn't meant to say that, so he hung up. Then he dropped in another quarter and called back. He waited for the Lauryn Hill song to end, and then left another message:

"Hey, Julianne, it's me again. I just need to speak to you, it's kind of an emergency. It's been a while, I know, and, well, I'm in a real jam right now. I can't really say exactly what, not over the phone at least. But I need some help, and really, you're the only person I know here."

He paused for a couple of seconds, waiting, hoping that Julianne would pick up.

"Well, I guess you're not there. Or you're still asleep. I know it's early. I hope everything is OK with you. You know, that you're safe and everything. Alright, well, I guess I'll call back later. Bye."

Liam put the phone back in the receiver. Feeling like a dupe for being concerned about Julianne's well-being, he deposited another quarter, and suffered through another dose of Lauryn Hill.

"Hey, J, it's me. Again. Look, don't call me at home, OK? I'm not there anymore, I can't go back. I've got nowhere to go. Where are you anyway? I mean, it's fucking Saturday morning! Pick up, goddamn it!"

He didn't waste another quarter calling back. Instead, he called the only other number he could pull from his damaged memory bank.

"Hallo," came the familiar voice. "Red Green here."

"Hey, R.G., it's Liam McNaughton."

"Hey, what's happening, kid? Haven't seen you at the Grille for a while. You still picking up CJA?"

"Yeah, yeah, I'm trying Red. But, you know, it's hard. I'm just not getting that many cases."

"Well, hang in there kid. Things will pick up eventually."

"Hey, Red, are you in the office right now? I kinda need to talk to you, and I'm not too far from the courthouse, so I could come up and –"

"Ah, no. Not in the office."

"Shit, I didn't call you at home, did I? I'm real sorry. I coulda sworn I dialed your office number."

"No, it's OK. I got my office number forwarding my after-hours calls to my cellular phone. I'm telling you, these little doo-hickeys are great. You really ought to get one."

"Well, maybe.... Look, Red, I could use some help right now. So if you've got a second, maybe I could meet you somewhere?"

"No can do, kiddo. To tell you the truth, I'm over in the drunk tank. Got me a *dewey*."

"A what?"

"DUI. Fairfax Sheriff pinched me last night. I almost made it home, too. One of these days, I'm gonna give up the Grille and head straight home like a good boy should."

"You're in prison?"

"Jail, kid, jail. You oughta know the difference by now."

"Yeah, you're right," Liam said dejectedly. "Well then, can I ask you something real quick?"

"Sure."

"It's about that case, you know, the Baby Stomper."

"You still got that case hanging around?"

"Well, trial is Monday. I'm not even sure I'm gonna make it, to tell the truth. But here's the problem – my client's not helping. You know, he won't talk about the case."

"So?"

"So, what should I tell the judge?"

"Tell the judge? Nothing! Nothing at all!"

"Nothing? Why?"

"Come one, kid. That's what got Nuggie kicked outta CJA. He's half-way to being disbarred."

"For talking to a judge about a client?"

"Exactly. The judges *are* the government. Why would you ever want to tell them anything?"

Before Liam could respond, he heard some men's voices laughing in the background.

"R.G., do the cops know you're in there with a phone?"

"Sure," he laughed. "Police out here in the Commonwealth are much more civilized. Even let me keep my belt and shoelaces. Anyway, look kid, I gotta get going. This place is turning into a gold mine for me. I've already got twelve of these guys signed up for clients. Maybe I can steer some of the work your way."

"Uh, thanks," Liam despaired. "But I'm not licensed in

Virginia."

"You're not? Really? I thought you were. Oh well. You ought to get on that, son, you can't really make a living just doing those CJA cases, you know."

"Yeah, I'm figuring that out."

"Great kid. Roger and out."

~ Chapter Twenty Six ~

Walking out of the hospital, McCoy could see the rising sun reflecting off the dark oblong windows of the neighboring D.C. Jail.

He knew that soon as he set foot in the detective squad, questions would be raised about his bruised and battered face. The Lieutenant's warning to him echoed in his head: "Just don't embarrass us, Jimmy. Don't make us regret our support."

Maybe solving the Swastika homicides will keep the heat off, McCoy thought, at least for a little while. Why not take a long shot and follow up on that partial print while I'm down here?

McCoy used his badge to rap on the thick hazy glass that separated the guard station from the Jail's public entrance, and eventually, the sleeping guard woke up.

"What you want?"

McCoy pressed the badge up against the glass. "MPD. Here to do an administrative interview."

"Right now?"

"Yeah, right now."

The guard gave McCoy a look over. Then he swung his feet down off the counter and pulled out a thick sheaf of computer paper.

"Get the name of the truck that hit ya?" the guard sniggered.

"What?"

"Never mind. O.K , Detective, what's your man's name?"

"Grimes. Bennie Grimes."

"You got a PDID or DCDC number?"

"No, just the name. Bennie Grimes."

The guard did not hide his look of disgust as he thumbed through the sheaf of paper. Drawing his finger down the page, the man read out the names: "Gates, Gill, Giron, Glanville, Gonzalez, Grady. Two Grady's. Granados. Gray. Gulliver. Gutman." The guard tossed the sheaf of papers back on the shelf. "Sorry. No Grimes here."

"Come on, officer," McCoy implored. "Check again. He's in here, I know it. I just got his print from here."

"His what?"

"His fingerprint record. It's just a couple of days old. You know, everyone going in and out of Corrections gets fingerprinted now."

"Sorry, Dick," the guard said, yawning. "He ain't here. His name's not on my list, and I do know how to read, OK? Could be he's over at CTF. They got their own list over there."

The neighboring Central Treatment Facility housed only two kinds of detainees – the ones with poor health (mostly AIDS patients, diabetics, and drug addicts) and the ones that were snitching – and for that reason, there was not a lot of movement between the two. McCoy pulled the fingerprint report out of the envelope and confirmed that Bennie Grimes' fingerprint had been taken just two days earlier at the jail.

"I'll try CTF," McCoy said to the guard, "but I'll probably be back in a few minutes."

But to his surprise, CTF quickly confirmed that Bennie Grimes was in their system, and twenty minutes later, McCoy was escorted to the Assistant Warden's Office where they had a broken-down man in a blue jump-suit waiting for him. He was slumped over the table, his hands on his knees, his eyes open but his gaze a thousand yards away.

"Bennie Grimes?" McCoy asked.

"Yes."

"My name is Detective McCoy. I'm with MPD."

"What happened yo' face?"

"Nothing. Fell down some stairs." McCoy nervously

300

motioned for the jail guards to leave the room. "Now look here, Mr. Grimes. I'm here to ask you some questions about a case I'm working on."

"Am's I under arrest?"

"No. Did you do something I should know about?"

"I got caught with some dope, that's all. But y'all got me on that already. Violate my probation. Petty shit."

"That's not why I'm here, Mr. Grimes. Of course, if you want your lawyer, we can try to get him down here...."

"Nah, that's OK. My lawyer ain't no good anyhow. Court gave me a blind man, if you can believe that. Gotdam CJA."

"Great. Then let me start by asking you about a symbol." Eyeing the man intently, McCoy drew out the clockwise-oriented swastika, but the old man just sat there, licking his bottom lip every few seconds. McCoy tried again, asking Bennie if he had ever known a Korean man named Kim, even showing him the dead man's driver's license photo, but Bennie didn't budge. McCoy saved the best for last, the crime scene photos of the dead prostitute sprawled out by a garbage bin in alley off of Dix Street Northeast, a swastika burned into her forehead.

"How about her, Bennie?" McCoy demanded. "Ever seen her before?"

Bennie bent forward and looked closely at the picture. "I ain't got my reading glasses, but that nekid girl, she dead?"

"Yeah, Bennie, she's dead. And your fingerprints were found on the crack pipe you shoved up her ass!"

Bennie's eyes opened wide. "I ain't got nothing to do with that!" he stuttered. "No sir, not me! I don' smoke no crack!"

"Don't try to play me, Bennie." McCoy held up the envelope the Fingerprint Division had given him the day before. "I got your prints! I got them right here!"

"You say you got my prints in there? *My* finger-prints?"

"Yep, taken just a couple of days ago at the jail."

"But I ain't been over to the jail. I'm over here, you know, at CTF. I'm HIV."

"It doesn't matter, Bennie!" McCoy yanked the anonymous fingerprint blotter from out of the envelope and slammed it flat on the table. "Coming in and going out, we take prints from all the prisoners now. Doesn't matter if it's CTF or D.C. Jail or Lorton Prison. You're in our database, and I know you were with this girl before she was killed. So why don't you just tell me what the swastikas are all about."

Bennie stared at the fingerprint blotter, moving his eyes from one print the next. "But ... but those can't be my fingerprints."

"Oh really? You're a fingerprint expert?"

Bennie smiled a toothy grin as he held up his cuffed wrists and spread his fingers wide. McCoy could see that the man had no thumbs.

"Pusherman done took 'em. Owed him ninety dollas. Bout ten year ago."

McCoy immediately called for the guards. "That'll be all," he told them, running for the door.

Bennie's taunts trailed after him. "I do be a thumb print expert, cocksucker! Ain't gonna pin no homicide on me!"

§ § § § § § § § §

"Hey Dorsey, it's me, Liam McNaughton."

"McNaughton," Dorsey said in his low husky voice. "Why you calling me on a Saturday morning? You gonna come by and bring me some money on those slip-and-falls I let you keep?"

"Wish I could, Dorsey, but I got some big problems right now."

"IRS?"

"No -"

"Bar Counsel?"

"No, not that. See, I was over at Potomac Gardens, or was it Hopkins projects? Anyway, these guys, these black guys, it's like now they're after me, and they got my client's bag, and I can't go home."

"Man, I told you not to do that CJA. Fifty-dollar-an-hour? Shoot, you don't see me hanging out round the projects for no fifty dollars, now do you? I keep telling you, man, personal injury is the way to go. In fact, soon as you come back to work for me, I'm putting you in charge of my Auto Neg practice, 'cause I tell you, this Med Mal thing I got is just taking off. I got five bad baby cases right now, and I'm up to my eyeballs in work."

"Bad baby?"

"Yeah, you know, obstetrical malpractice. Cases where the baby is born with some kind of defect or whatever, stuck with a needle during the amnio, mixing up blood tests, that kind of thing."

"Well, Dorsey, you know me. I'll always be grateful for the opportunity you gave me. I just really wanted to get into the courtroom, you know, try cases."

"Sure, whatever. Now look man, I gotta go. Remember Yolanda Basquat?"

"The Allstate adjuster? The one we called 'Low-balla'?"

"Yeah, that's right." Dorsey was whispering now. "You ought to see her in person, man. Forget that voice of hers, she's dynamite."

"You've seen her?"

"Yeah, man, she's right here. I'm 'bout to make us up some breakfast."

"You the man, Dorsey!" Liam began to really pile it on,

hoping that maybe his former boss would be more sympathetic to his plight. "Those female adjusters are just putty in your hands!"

"Yeah, well, I mean, she ain't *all* that. But let's just say I ain't gonna have to worry about her giving me three-times-the-meds no more."

Liam and Dorsey both laughed at that.

"Now, look," Dorsey continued, "I'm going to do you a favor and tell you what you need to do, and then I'm gone. This all started with you working up a case, right? So go see your client straight away, ask him what's up. He'll break it down for you."

"That's it? That's your advice?"

"Come on, Liam, think about it. You were out there on his case, a white boy walking around the projects, probably floating his name. Maybe he's with the Potomac Garden crew, and he's got some beef with Hopkins. Or maybe it's the other way around. Bottom line is they weren't after you, they were after that bag of his. At least, that's what you're telling me."

"But ... I don't have the bag anymore."

"Well, like I said before, what's this all got to do with me?"

"Come on, Dorsey! I've got nowhere else to turn."

"What about that black girl from the Christmas party?" he snickered. "The one you chased out here from Arizona."

Liam sighed. "It's New Mexico, Dorsey. Besides, I already tried her. I guess you could say she's not taking my calls."

"Well, that figgers."

Liam's face became flushed with anger. "What do you mean by that?"

"Come on man, you leave a girl like that by herself at *my* Christmas party? She's gonna spill some beans out the skeleton closet."

"What are you talking about?"

"Ah, don't fret about that girl, man. I mean, for all you know, she could've been stepping out on you anyway. So who knows, may not have even been yours. Look on the bright side – at least she didn't make you pay for it."

"Pay for it? For what?"

"Look, man, you ain't the first and you ain't gonna be the last. Just remember them jimmy caps ain't just to keep you from getting that AID's."

And just like that, Dorsey hung up.

~ Chapter Twenty Seven ~

Minister And-One clutched the pages of the type-written speech in his hands. The Million Man March was less than two days away. He'd been practicing for weeks, but he still felt uneasy giving the speech without the papers in front of him.

"An opportunity of a lifetime," he assured himself, putting the papers back in his pocket. "My best chance for redemption." He took up a position behind the lectern, an empty room before him. "And, if there's one thing I know how to do, it's preach."

So he cleared his throat and began:

Brothers, my African-American brothers! Welcome to Washington D.C.! Welcome to the Million Man March! How many? That's right! A million!

Now I'd like to say that it certainly is no coincidence that this historic event has taken place right here in the nation's capital. For it is here, my brothers, right here in Washington, D.C., that most of the injustices and transgressions that have taken place against our people have been hatched. It is here, my brothers, where most of the schemes to disenfranchise us, dis-empower us, and divide us have been born. Hatched in the minds of Southern bigots and Northern money lenders. A conspiracy against the black people, a conspiracy that brought together two natural enemies – the money lenders of Jew York City and the plantation owners of the Old Confederacy. A conspiracy against our people driven by a hatred of our people. What people? The first people! The African people. Praise be to God!

So welcome, one and all. Welcome to St. Nicholas' School for Girls, just blocks away from the U.S. Capitol, the gilded marble palace where so much of this chicanery

306

I speak of was originated and perhaps inspired by. Well, as Brother Malcolm once said, "It's time for the chickens to come home to roost!" Just as our enemies past and present gather in this place to plot for our destruction, so shall we – a million man strong – so shall we meet here to begin our resurrection! Our Salvation! Praise be to God! Thank you Brother Farrakhan!

But brothers, hear me! I mean to be quick! There are other messengers, far more eloquent than I, who are even now taking up the call for emancipation, taking up the call for reparations, taking up the call for equality and justice for the black man. The call for jobs and education; the end of these racially motivated sentencing guidelines; the end of police brutality! And hear them! Hear them loud and clear, I say, for they speak the truth! Praise be to God!

But brothers, there is another truth out there, a truth I want to share with you, my brothers. It's a truth that we don't usually want to talk about. A truth the black man don't usually want to hear about. But it is a truth, my brothers, my African brothers, that we must all face up to, right here, right now! Because the truth is the truth!

And that truth is this: that abortion is genocide for the black peoples!

There, you see, I said it, and some of you brothers just shook your head, as if to say, 'What Minister And-One talking 'bout?' Brothers! Brothers! Pay attention here! We must remember, that where the flesh is willing, the mind is weak. Everyone in this room knows what I'm talking about. You all know where I'm coming from, right? That's God's gift, y'all! There ain't nothing wrong with a man loving a woman! I can surely attest to that, praise be to God!

So brothers, hear me! Just give me minute more. The promiscuity that Minister Farrakhan talks about – Let me say it again! The promiscuity my brother Louis talks about, the unfaithfulness in marriage, the man who fathers children by three, four, five, six – yes six different women! It's all out there, my brothers, we can't hide it. We can change it, yes, but we can't hide it. The Lord sees all, the Lord knows all. Do you really think you can destroy the evidence of life? The evidence of love? No, my brothers, no! The Lord sees all, the Lord knows all, even in that most private of moments! Brothers, you must not kill that unborn child, that innocent black child. We must not! We cannot! God commands it!

Abortion is genocide for the black peoples! I'll say it again, my brothers! Let me break it down like this: Abortion is just another one of the white man's tools of genocide against our people – the African people. Think about it! Think about what it means to our people. You all remember 1808, don't you? No? I'm talking about the year on the calendar. 1808. That's when the United States of America – the Congress and the President – outlawed the importation of slaves from Africa. That's right, ended the African slave trade. Sound like good news, brothers? No, not really. Not for the slaves. You see, by ending the importation of slaves, there was born a huge demand for new slaves, domestically produced. You see, my brothers, them slave plantations didn't just grow cotton – some of 'em grew slaves!

Hear me now, my brothers, hear me, for this is crucial. Difficult to hear, painful to say, but crucial to know. See, that plantation master is a master of abortion, on account of his study of animal husbandry. Animal husbandry! You all know what I'm talking about here? Animal husbandry *is the breeding of livestock. The breeding of horses. The breeding of sheep. And when you get yourself a randy bull and a flock of cows, well, there's a certain lack of control by the plantation master over the breeding process. So he has to be a master of the abortion, skilled with the curette. Your randy bull just planted his seed in some tired old milk cow? Kill that baby; it ain't gonna be no good. Just another mouth to feed. Some old work-horse snuck into the barn and mounted your prize mare? Massa ain't gonna allow his prize mare's breeding value to diminish! Kill that baby without a moment's thought. And do you think that old milk cow or that prize mare gonna care one way or another? Other than having that metal poker – the curette – stuck up in her, after it's all said and done, she don't care one way or another. And the plantation master's dilemma, it's solved, just like that.*

And you don't think that animal husbandry ends there, do you, my brothers? You think this stops with the chicken and the livestock? No, my brothers, no. Massah ain't gonna allow the sheep and the pigs to decide when and where they going to have their offspring, and you can bet he gonna take the same approach, the same view, towards his slaves, his human bondage. Pregnant slave ain't no different than a pregnant sow or a pregnant bitch – that child is born property, property that the Massah can dispose of as he wish! If Massah don't want it, he can end that child's life in utero. God have mercy! He may even use the same tool!

The same tool he uses on his pregnant milk cow or sow or mare – will he use it on his slave woman? A black woman, my brothers! Held down by her brother and sister slaves, the wicked slave master doing his wicked doing? No, I say! That is wicked! We cannot let this stand! We will not let this stand!

Now, my brothers, allow me to conclude with what I have to say. Let me say it one more time, Abortion is genocide for the black peoples! Not 'was.' Is! Today, right now! Go to the abortion clinics in our ghettos, in our neighborhoods, in our public hospitals, and who you gonna see? White doctors, Jewish doctors. I tell you, it's the truth! Why? Ask yourself, why? Why do these rich white doctors set up their little house of horrors, their little strip mall laboratories in our ghettos? Why? Well, that question begs an answer. To suppress the black race, of course.

We are a virile people, my brothers, there's no doubting that. And the white man can count! Yes sir, if there is one thing the white man excels at, it's counting numbers. And the white man looks at our numbers, my brothers, and he is scared. Powerless to enslave us, the white man now resorts to trickery and deceit. And murder! Yes, my brothers, murder! Cause when you kill that unborn child, you are committing murder! Make no mistake about that. That white man is murdering thousands, thousands and thousands of black children every year, killing them when they are helpless to defend themselves, killing them with the tacit cooperation of the black woman! The black mother!

It saddens me, my brothers, it really, truly saddens me. But our sisters have been co-opted in this regard. So it's up to us. It's up to us. Yes, my brothers, the time has come for us to stand up to this practice, this practice of eugenics, this practice of abortion! We, the black men of America, we will stand up for those thousands and thousands of innocent lives, innocent black lives, that are being snuffed out every day! Every day! We can stop it, we must stop it, and we will stop it!

Today, my brothers, we stand a million strong. But nationwide, we are even stronger. Ten years from now, my brothers, twenty years from now, imagine, if we can put a stop to this sick vestige of the plantation master's animal husbandry, if we close down the abortion clinics, if we chase off the Jewish doctors from our neighborhoods. Imagine how many more of us there will be. There won't be no Million Man March ten years from now; we'll have us a Billion Man March. Numbers, my brothers, as the white man knows, don't lie.

So tomorrow, and the day after tomorrow, and the days and weeks and months after that, as you go forth from here with the message of equality and justice and jobs and reparations, remember that inside the womb of every black woman is the key to our future. The real key! The key to controlling our destiny. The key to life. And the question you must answer for yourselves, my brothers, is:

Who do you want to be holding those keys?

Let us bow our heads, and praise Him. Lord, help us to get those keys. Guide us in this regard. Hallelujah, Hallelujah! Praise the Lord.

Minister And-One stepped back from the lectern and mopped his brow with a handkerchief. Then he checked his watch – seven minutes on the dot. He tried to imagine what it would look like when there, right at the speech's conclusion, the swarms of ladybugs suddenly rose up from beneath the audience – a gimmick he no longer considered necessary.

Minister And-One turned off the lights and closed the door to the chantry. But if that's the way the Captain wants it done, he thought, that's the way I'll do it. After all, he did write me this speech.

311

~ Chapter Twenty Eight ~

Liam cut to the head of the line of young black women waiting to go through the jail's metal detectors for their Saturday morning social visits.

"Attorney McNaughton," he proclaimed. "Here for a legal!"

It was a bluff, really. After all, his wallet – along with his driver's license and bar card – had been liberated from him the night before. Plus, with his baggy eyes, top hat, Village People leather jacket, and "Go Hogs!" T-shirt, he hardly looked the part of a lawyer.

Surprisingly, the jail guard waved him through, and after a moment, the big metal door noisily slid open for him. Curious to see how far he could go, Liam quickly grabbed a "Request for Legal Visit" form and sat down, but before he could finish filling it out, a Correctional Officer strode up to him and snatched the paper from his hands. It was Lovey Green.

"You ain't be needin that," she said. "Mali's upstairs waiting for you."

"Don't I have to sign in?"

"I said, come on. It's not an invitation." As Lovey turned and began walking away, she pulled out her walkie-talkie and looked up at the camera fixed to the ceiling. "I got this escort."

Then they proceeded up the stairs at a fast clip.

The visiting rooms on the second and third floors were riotously full with the usual contingent of women, toddlers, and infants competing for floor space with the gaggle of lawyers waiting their turn for one of the attorney conference rooms. Liam had never been past the third floor of the jail, so he grew a little bit excited as Lovey pressed on to the fourth floor, where the visiting area was empty save a single lawyer talking to an orange-clad inmate.

Taking a second look, Liam saw that the inmate was Mal Stancil – his client. He hadn't immediately recognized him as he had evidently shaved his scalp clean of the tiny dread-locks he had been growing over the summer.

"Wait right here," Lovey commanded, directing him to one of the stools where the babies and their mommas usually sat down to conduct their visits. "He'll see you when he done talkin' to his *paid* lawyer."

And then, as if on cue, the mechanical steel doors separating the general public's visiting area from the attorney conference rooms rattled open like an iron curtain, and out popped the portly bearded lawyer in his tell-tale baby blue suit – the Fifth Streeter, Robert E.L. Stucky.

Liam raced over, trying to get through the mechanical doors before they began closing, but Stucky stepped in front of him. "Where do you think you're going, counselor? You've been retained out."

"I've got my entry of appearance in his case! You can't stop me from seeing my client!"

As the mechanical doors rattled to a close in front of him, Liam could see another guard approaching Mal, and Liam read the guard's lips to say, "Let's go."

As they did the slow walk by, Liam ran to the window along the general public's visiting area and picked up one of the phones that allowed communication between inmate and loved one.

"Mal, pick up!" Liam screamed. He continued to follow Mal across the visiting room, picking up each phone along the way. "Come on Mal! Pick it up! Let me talk to you!"

Finally, Mal made eye contact. Then he raised his shackled fists and made a gesture across his throat as if he was holding a knife.

"Don't start that shit, Mal!" Liam screamed. "You've got

313

my attention! O.K.?"

Mal shrugged off the guard and picked up the phone. The guard looked through the thick glass to Lovey, who nodded and mouthed the words "O.K."

Liam sat down across from Mal, who was holding the phone away from his ear.

"Come on, man, talk to me!"

Mal held up one finger.

"One?" Liam asked. "One what? One question?"

Mal nodded.

"O.K., O.K. Let me have it."

Mal put the receiver to his ear, and spoke slowly into the mouthpiece. His eyes were piercing through the thick, hazy glass that separated them.

"Can you write me up one of those last-wilson-testaments?"

"Last what? Last will and testament? Jesus, no! What the fuck is wrong with you, man?"

"You say you want to help me."

"I'm not helping you kill yourself. I'm not. I'm doing what I can to get you out of here!"

Mal gave Liam an exasperated look. "Why? Why you wanna help me?"

Liam thought about the question for a second. "It's ... it's my job. It's what I do."

"It's yo job? It's what you do? That's it?"

"Yeah, that's it."

The two men stared at each other, until Mal asked, "Where your clothes at, dude? You usually be lookin' a bit sharper than this."

Liam grimaced. "Look, it's a long story. I'm not sure I should even tell you –"

"O.K., O.K., then. You say you wanna help me, right?

Remember when we first met, when you said you was my lawyer?"

"Yeah?"

"You said that it was up to me if I was to have to plead guilty. You said I was the boss."

"That's right."

"O.K. then. You my lawyer, and I want my trial. For that school case."

"The Unlawful Entry case?"

"Yeah, I want a trial on that. I ain't pleading guilty to *that*."

"Great, let's go to trial! But help me out! Trial is Monday. You've gotta tell me what you were doing up there at that school. Your brother Le'Nor, he said you were doing something with bugs."

Mal recoiled. "You know about that? Le'Nor told you? So, what? You gonna go tell the police on me now?"

"The police? No! Why would I –?"

Liam stopped short and turned around. Stucky was standing right behind him, trying to listen in.

"Counsel, maybe I didn't make myself clear," Stucky said with a wry smile. "You've been retained out. That's effective immediately. I understand that Jamal's hearing is set for Monday, before Chief Judge Cummings. I'll need his file, right now."

"Back off, you fat fuck!" Liam said, and Stucky, appearing a bit rattled, did just that.

"Mal, why are you talking to this asshole?" Liam whispered, cupping his hand around the mouthpiece. "Did you really hire him?"

"Jes on that one case. I done my time on that one anyway."

"The probation violation case? You're hiring him to do

that?"

"Yeah, that one. He gonna do that one." Mal's voice trailed off. "The one where they say I kilt my baby ..."

"You still got eight years back-up time on that, Mal! How many times do I have to tell you? All Stucky's gonna do for you is plead you guilty!"

"Well, that's ah-ight." Mal looked away, barely holding the phone to his ear. "I am guilty."

Liam dropped his phone, but struggled to get it back into position.

"Look," Mal was saying, "sumpin bad gonna happen on Monday, sumpin real bad, so you might as well know the truth and you might as well hear it from me. I did stomp on Brandy. I – I told her I wasn't gonna be bringing no more crack babies into this world."

It took a second for Liam to regain his composure. "Mal, look. That's not really what this case is about. That's all in the past."

"You been real nice to me, coming to visit me in jail and all. So jes listen to me, ah-ight?"

Liam nodded.

"I had caught her up in some alley off Stanton Terrace, on accident, I wasn't trying to be following her or nothing. Stalking her, like they say I was. I was jes dumping the dog shit and other trash from the animal clinic – everyone dump in that alley – and I saw her in this tow truck. I could see the driver, some old G about to hit the pipe. And Brandy, she be sitting next to him, cigarette hanging from her lips, her eyes be all up in back of her head. No shirt, no bra, jes the old man's stuff dripping down between her titties. They was kind of big and floppy back then, like stretched out, and it was all pooled up like on top of her stomach. You know, the part that be sticking out."

Mal's eyes began to well up, and he scrunched his face in hard.

"She was real pregnant then, you know, she was big. We was gonna have the baby in a week, maybe."

"Mal, come on. You don't have to –"

"I didn't do nothing there in the alley. I left out, went back home and waited for her. When she came in, I locked the door behind her, drew down the blinds, turned the television real loud. Then I told her, 'You're gonna wish you never come home.'"

Mal suddenly hung up the phone and stood up.

"Mal? Wait! Talk to me! What do you mean something bad is going to happen Monday? Is something gonna happen to you? Or is something gonna happen to someone else?"

The guard, having snapped to, began crowding Mal, letting him know it was time to move on.

"Come on, Mal! Help me!" Liam screamed so loud that both the guard and Mal turned their heads. "Help me help you!"

Mal bucked the guard and put the phone up to his mouth. "I went back to the school and took care of everything!" he said quickly. "But I don' think I could save them lady bugs. I afraid they gonna die in the Bins. You really wanna help me? Go deh and git them and let them out 'fo they die!"

Two additional guards appeared out of nowhere and tackled Mal to the floor. Then the beating started.

"Now look what you've done," Lovey said, grabbing Liam roughly by the arm. "Your legal visit is over."

"Don't feel so bad," Stucky laughed. "Jamal just needs to get into a program, help him resolve his issues. Once you get a little experience, rookie, you'll learn to pick your battles. Look on the bright side. Now you'll get to turn in your voucher."

317

§ § § § § § § § §

Walking back the way he came, Liam arrived at the same bank of pay phones in front of Union Station. He dumped a pocketful of quarters in one of the phones and dialed long distance.

"Hey, mom, it's me."

"Oh my god! Liam! We haven't heard from you in such a long time! How you doing? How's your asthma? Are you remembering your sun block?"

"Mom, I'm O.K., I'm alright. Look, I'm in a bit of a hurry right now. Can't talk for long."

"Oh, I'm just so glad you called! My son, the lawyer...."

"Mom, I'm thinking about coming home."

"Oh, that'd be great! Your brother's gonna be here for Thanksgiving too! It'll be just like old times. I'll ask Uncle Charlie to come over."

"No, mom, I'm not talking about Thanksgiving."

"Christmas then? Maybe there'll even be some snow and you can go skiing."

"No, mom, I'm talking about now."

"There's no snow now."

"Mom –"

"Wait just one second, Liam, I want to get you something before I forget. Hold on ...."

"Mom?"

"One second –"

"Mom, look, I'm over here at Union Station. You know, the Amtrak station. Could you buy me a train ticket home? Like right now? I want to come home."

"OK, here it is ... let me put on my glasses.... O.K. Here it is. This is an article Dr. Carhart found for me."

"Mom, have you been listening to what I've been saying?"

"Are your allergies bothering you, Liam? I can always get you a prescription written, you know?"

"Oh Ma!"

"I always tell him about my son the lawyer. A lawyer in Washington, D.C.! I really want you to meet him."

"Who, mom? Who?"

"Dr. Carhart."

"I thought you said you'd never work for a male doctor."

"Well, Dr. Carhart's different. He's really on our side. But never mind that. This is important. He gave me this article to give you."

Liam could hear his mother softly reading the article to herself.

"It says in here that the risk of late term miscarriage or still birth is very high for mothers who smoke, and here they're talking about tobacco, nicotine. Rates much higher than a mother who uses alcohol, or even cocaine."

Liam wondered why she was telling him this. "Mom, what did he say about the autopsy report that I sent you?"

"Oh, yes, that. He said he didn't see anything in there that would help you. The mother's drug abuse and smoking wasn't listed as possible cause of fetal demise. He said you would've expected to see that, especially in light of the mother's history."

"The history? What are you talking about?"

"Medical history, what the patient tells the doctor. Didn't you tell me that you talked to the woman herself?"

"Yeah, but we didn't ...."

"Well, maybe it was in the autopsy report, I don't know. I just thought you told me that the mother was a heavy smoker."

"Yeah?"

"And that the baby wasn't kicking or moving inside of her several days before that horrible man you represent beat her up.

319

Liam, you still there?"

"Yeah, mom. I'm still here. So, is that all?"

"Well, Dr. Carhart says it sounds like the baby was dead inside of her already. Before she was kicked or stomped or whatever you call it. That most certainly caused that poor girl go into labor. But kill the fetus? I don't know. "

"Mom, when were you going to tell me about this?"

"Well, Liam, your phone hasn't been working for a couple of days, so I –"

"Look Ma, I gotta go. I gotta go home, back to my office. Right now. I'll call you back later about coming to visit."

"Alright, my love, please be careful out there."

§ § § § § § § § §

Liam approached his apartment cautiously. When he was sure no one was waiting for him inside, he tiptoed down the steps and quickly opened the door. The odor of bleach immediately overpowered him, and as he staggered inside, he followed a trail of blood to the corner where he had earliert tossed Mal's bag.

The bag was gone, but they had left his wallet. But only his wallet. His money, receipts, credit cards, Metropass tickets, all of his I.D.'s – bar card, driver's license, library badge – all gone. Everything except a single business card.

Liam pulled it out and inspected it. It was one of his own – the one Ponytail had written his number on.

"Call me if you need *anything*," he remembered the man saying.

"Well, I could use a little something, something," Liam chuckled to himself.

The phone company had cut service to his apartment several weeks earlier, so he would have to head back for the pay phones. But first, he decided to take a quick look around, maybe change clothes or even take a quick shower. As he searched through his tiny apartment, however, he found that all of his personal property had been removed. The furniture was still there, the filing cabinets too, but everything that had been inside – his entire legal practice – was gone. No towels in the bathroom, no soap or shampoo either. No clothes to change into, not even his own dirty laundry. Disconcerting, to say the least.

So, Liam left as he had come in, crossing the street under the wary eye of the cops manning the Supreme Court police hut. Back at the payphones, he held up his card to the streetlight. Ponytail's number was written in such strange, flowery cursive, Liam wasn't sure he had the right number. But this was his last quarter. There was no turning back.

The phone rang many, many times before someone finally picked up. "Prison Ministries."

"Yes, hi. My name is Liam. I'm, ah, looking for ...?"

"Liam McNaughton? Is that you?"

Liam recognized Ponytail's nasally voice.

"Right. From down by the –"

"'Down by the river!'" Ponytail sang, imitating Neil Young. "'I shot my baby!' Sure, sure. I remember you. How you been? You ever hook back up with the old red head?"

Liam laughed. "Nah. But look, I'm sorry I didn't call back sooner, you know, just to see how things were going on. You know, with your case."

"My case?"

"Yeah, you know, your employment discrimination case. With the Marshal's Service?"

"Oh yeah, that! With the Marshal's Service! How could I forget? You were gonna help me with that, right?"

"Yeah, sure. In fact, if you weren't too busy now, I might

be available."

"Right now?"

"Yeah. You see, I'm in a bit of a jam right now. I can't even begin to tell you – all I can say is, it will all work out for me on Monday. See, I'm, ah, going to trial, man. A trial! To tell you the truth, it'll really only be my second one. Ever. I'm sorry if I made it seem like I was some kind expert or whatever, you know, at the river."

"No problemo. No problemo at all. But slow down, O.K., you sound like your mind is going a hundred miles per hour."

"Sure, slow down. Right. The truth will set you free, and all that, huh? Anyway, until then, until Monday, that is, I kinda need someplace to stay, chill out, you know. Just for a couple days."

"Shoot, I'm over at St. Martin's Church right now, just a couple of blocks from you."

"You're at a church?"

"Yeah! I even got the keys! The place is closed now, some legal dispute between the IRS, the Vatican, and some local church. The Marshal's Service is keeping it locked up, making sure there's no activity going on inside, making sure the heat is on and the water's still running, things like that."

"Really?"

"Sure. In fact, I got a couple of my boys over here with me as we speak. I mean, we try to be pretty discreet about it. I certainly wouldn't want the Marshal's Service to know about it. But shit, there's a lot of stuff I don't want them to know about, eh counselor?"

"I thought you said the Marshal's Service fired you. For your hand and all."

"Oh yeah. We'll I'm, uh, back. Temporarily."

"So it's not a problem? It's mellow?"

"Mellow? Sure, man, it's mellow. Shit, dude, come on

over! One of my boys will be waiting by the door, over on the Maryland Avenue side. Come on in that way. Try not to let anyone see you, though."

"Be there in five minutes."

"Great. See you then."

"Hey, wait, you still there?"

"Yeah, what is it?"

"I really hate to ask this, but ... I forgot your name."

"Don't sweat it. Happens all the time. Name's Shubel Morgan. My friends call me Captain."

~ Chapter Twenty Nine ~

Liam winced when he opened his eyes. He was seated in a circular room, with walls made of large blocks, almost like a turret in a castle. Across the room he saw a poster of a man and woman holding hands, the sun setting behind them, the words "ABSTINENCE NOW!" across the top in bold letters.

A small stream of blood tickled past Liam's ear, but when he reached for it, his hand came up short – his arms were handcuffed around the back of the chair.

The last thing he could remember was walking into St. Martin's and seeing the oozing and blistered face of the man who had hit him with the Taser the day before. After that, everything went black.

Now, coming to, the only face he could see was that of Ponytail.

"Now hold on!" he was saying. "Don't go out on me again!"

"Where am I?"

"We're locked in a tower!" he cried in a female voice. "No seriously. We're up in the belfry of St. Martin's. You gotta check out the view from up here, dude. It's awesome."

"I – what –?"

"No? Don't want to check out the accommodations?" Ponytail made his way back to the table. "Tied up right now, are you? Well, another time maybe. Now, back to business."

He placed a small wooden box on the table, then slid its top off, placing it back-end on the table, its mirrored surface sparkling clean. Then, he pulled a razor blade from the box and wedged it in between the fingers of his plastic hand.

"Wouldn't think that you could do much damage with a razor. But send a man to prison, he learns to make do. Cut a man around his eyes, you can pretty much make him do

324

whatever you want."

Liam struggled to get out of the chair as Ponytail stood up.

"I'm really sorry you had to be dragged into this thing," he said ruefully. "I really am. I can't tell you the problems those amateur assholes in Oklahoma City caused me. Oh yeah, everyone wants to be a hero, but to really pull off something big, for it to be meaningful, you've gotta have the follow through."

He calmly walked behind Liam and then clamped his good arm around his neck.

"I wanna let you go. I really do. And I will. Just as soon as you tell me what's going on."

"Tell *you* what's going on?" Liam gasped. "What the hell are you talking about? Why are you doing this to me?"

"Don't play coy with me. You know what I want."

"I have no idea what you want!"

"Your man Stancil. Malcolm X. Stancil."

"Mal? What does he have to do with anything?"

"The bag, the bag your guy had?"

Liam paused before answering, "I don't know what you're talking about."

Then Ponytail nicked him under the eye with the razor.

"Whoa now, look at that! I told you to stay still!"

As Liam squirmed in pain, Ponytail returned to his side of the table.

"Look counselor, don't be stupid. We have the bag."

"So you got what you want!" Liam yelled. "Now what do you want from me?"

"Well, I'm guessing that since you had the bag, you must have seen the chart."

Liam shook his head.

"Oh, you don't know about that either?" Ponytail unfolded the graph paper with the little red 'x' marks on one side and held it in front of Liam's face. "The seating chart? Never heard of it, huh? Look, kid, here's all I want to know. Did your client go back into that school or not?"

"How would I know that?"

"Because it's the kind of thing he would have told you. And it's the kind of stupid thing he would have done."

Liam thought about what Mal had told him earlier that morning. "That's attorney-client privilege, man."

"Fucking lawyers! You don't even try to bluff!" Ponytail sat down across from Liam. "All right, since it looks like we're gonna be here for a while...."

Liam watched as Ponytail poured a vial of white powder on the mirrored box-top and then chopping up two long lines with the razor blade.

"Uh oh," Liam sniffed. "Looks like you got your chocolate in my peanut butter."

Ponytail stopped chopping, and smiled as if he couldn't wait to hear the punch-line.

"You're getting my blood in your coke, dumbass."

"Think this is coke? Shit. Coke's for niggers. This is meth, stupid. Maybe a little bit of Prozac, little bit of Lithium mixed in to take the edge off."

Ponytail ran the blade against his tongue, licking its edge.

"Ah yes, and some of your blood too. 'Chocolate in my peanut butter!' That was a good one, McCloud!"

Ponytail bent down and snorted both lines in one move. "I like it!" he shrieked.

Even though he still felt only half conscious, Liam realized that his relatively clear thinking might give him a momentary advantage over his drug addled captor, so he spoke quickly, not exactly sure where he was going with it.

"Look, man. I know about the whole thing. About the bugs, I mean."

"Really?" Ponytail answered, kicking his booted feet up on the table. "Do tell."

"I didn't really believe him, you know, my client at first, until I saw the – until I saw him, I mean, Mal, this morning. But now I know the truth. I know what he was doing in that school."

"But he told you everything was O.K., did he?"

"Yep, that's right. He told me everything was O.K."

"Everything okey dokey. Right?"

"Right. Don't need to worry about a thing. Everything's fine."

Ponytail stared at Liam.

"Well, time will tell if you're lying to me or not. The thing I have to decide is what to do with you now." He slowly laid out two more lines, snorting up just one this time. "Want one?"

"No thanks," Liam whimpered. "I really do have to be going now."

"Wise guy, eh? Well, stay a little longer, why don't you? Clean you up a bit, get you dressed and ready for court. I mean, really, you do look like shit right now."

Ponytail walked over to a small closet near the door and came back holding a suit – one that Liam immediately recognized as his own. "Jones New York! This will set you straight. I even got one of your shirts dry-cleaned medium starch, just like you like it. Tie, belt. Socks and shoes are over there."

He hung the clothes on the back of his chair, then sat down and snorted the remaining line.

"I was even able to save that stupid hat of yours," he said, blinking his eyes rapidly. "Dione wanted to keep it as a trophy, but I told him it must have some special significance to you."

"I'm a big Guns N' Roses fan."

Ponytail laughed. "You know, the original plan was to

327

just dump you in the river. But I like you, so I'm considering letting you live. You might just serve a greater purpose by bearing witness."

"Bearing witness? To what?"

"To how the war began."

"O.K., play time is over. Come on and let me loose."

"The days of killing abortionists and bombing clinics are over, my friend. A war is about to begin. A civil war. Total war. Our Final Days are upon us. You can feel it in the air, can't you? Armageddon, Liam. Maybe you've heard of it?"

"Oh, so you want me to bear witness to the Apocalypse. O.K., sure, no problem. I'll keep my eye out for the Four Horsemen."

Ponytail gave him a hard look. "You better change your attitude about the whole thing quick, my friend. Cause it doesn't get any better for you. See, you're not exactly the linchpin to this whole thing. But when the spark that ignites this war is lit, you'll be the only one to know how it really happened."

"Well you better tell me now, cause I have no frickin' idea what you're talking about!"

"Liam, they're all gonna believe it was your client who did it – that dumb ass Malcolm X. Stancil. The evidence will be irrefutable."

Ponytail was speaking slowly and deliberately now, enunciating each word through an ear-to-ear smile.

"All those scorched corpses, the handiwork of this one simple nigger. The plan was to have him killed right there in the courthouse back in April, see, just to tie up loose ends, gain a bit of notoriety, which will be helpful nine months later when the school goes up in smoke. Same goes for getting that shrill bitch of a prosecutor involved. But either way, after the fire, when the cops remember that your man was the one who broke into that school – that breaking and entering he's gonna go down on Monday – that's the spark that's gonna ignite the real conflagration. Oh yes, my friend! A greater fire will be struck."

Ponytail moved his chair next to Liam's and whispered, "Chrissakes! What do you think will be the reaction when they learn that this man has already murdered his own pre-born! Now he's gone and killed two hundred more of our babies? Those little children of God?"

"Mal didn't kill his baby," Liam protested. "That baby was already dead inside of her!"

But Ponytail wasn't listening. He hadn't even stopped talking.

"– and when the feminists and the queers try to stand-up and protect the abortionists, when the Jew media is exposed for what it is – that's when the people of this country will take up arms – against their own government if need be. It will be a grim task, no doubt about it. State against State, brother against brother. It's all right there in the Bible. 'Whoso sheddeth man's blood by man shall his blood be shed, for in the image of God made he man."

Liam hung his head in resignation.

"Don't get so down, partner! We're going to put a stop to these modern day Herods, I tell you! And this is where you come in. The word just has to get out that it was *our* people who started the conflagration."

"So Mal doesn't start the fire?"

"Course not! That stupid nigger couldn't start a can opener."

"And this is all supposed to go down on Monday, huh? The day of the Million Man March? You want me to let me go so I can tell the whole world that it was you who killed a bunch of black men? Is that it?"

Ponytail pounced on Liam, jamming the razor blade back near his eye. "Fucking race traitor! You don't even know the meaning of sacrifice! A million dead niggers? Shit, a million blackies were slaughtered last summer in Rwanda – you think anyone really cared? Meaningless! Sacrifice requires white blood! See this hand? See this arm? I don't know how I can make myself any clearer. 'If thy right hand offend thee, cut it off, and cast it from thee!' Remember? I told you, 'For it is better than thy whole body should be cast into hell!'"

"You... cut off your own hand?"

"Yes! Now you see! Like those before us, like those after us, maybe even you – *we* are the ones behind this, Liam. Look around – you don't think I'm the only one? Oh, our enemy is powerful, we are under no illusions of that. We will be the insurgency, no doubt. But we will be the first to strike, and that strike will be a mortal one, for when the truth of what's been done is acknowledged, it shall strike fear into the hearts of our enemies: we have given unto the Lord our own children – our own innocents – triggering His righteous wrath."

Ponytail slowly pulled his chair back to the other side of the table.

"I mean what I said about it only getting worse for you, my friend," he said, rocking on his heels. "You'll be a pariah – the kooky conspiracy theorist no one dares believe, but from whom no one can turn away. But you're a pretty persuasive fellow. I'm sure by the time the battle lines are drawn, *some* of them will believe. Some of them will come to know that they face an enemy whose love of life runs so deep, whose love of life runs so true, that we're willing to die for it, we're willing to kill for it, we're willing to sacrifice for it. In a fight-to-the-death battle between *life* and *choice*, who do you think's gonna win?"

"So I'm gonna leave here and tell everyone that you

started a war? That's what you want?"

"Like I said, it wasn't supposed to happen this way. But necessity is the mother of invention. And, as you know, there's only so much you can do on a shoe string budget."

"Then you're really just gonna let me go?"

Ponytail stared at Liam for a long time without saying anything.

"Well, Cassandra," he finally said, "maybe you do need to go in the river –"

Removing a bundled rag from his pocket, Ponytail ran forward and pressed it against Liam's face.

"Court's in recess."

Postmortem.
Monday, January 22, 1996

Now, why have you come today? You came not at the call of Louis Farrakhan, but you have gathered here at the call of God, for it is only the call of Almighty God, no matter through whom that call came, that could generate this kind of outpouring. God called us here to this place, at this time, for a very specific reason. And now, I want to say my brothers, this is a very pregnant moment, pregnant with the possibility of tremendous change in our status in America and in the world. And although the call was made through me, many have tried to distance the beauty of this idea from the person through whom the idea and the call was made. Some have done it mistakenly, and others have done it in a malicious and vicious manner.

Brothers and sisters, there is no human being through whom God brings an idea that history doesn't marry the idea with that human being, no matter what defect was in that human being's character. You can't separate Newton from the law that Newton discovered. It would be silly to try to separate Moses from the Torah, or Jesus from the Gospel, or Mohammed from the Koran. "Well," you say, "Farrakhan, you ain't no Moses, you ain't no Jesus, and you're not no Mohammed, you have a defect in your character." Well, that certainly may be so; however, according to the way the Bible reads, there is no prophet of God written of in the Bible that did not have a defect in its character.

So today, whether you like it or not, God brought the idea through me, and he didn't bring it through me because my heart was dark with hatred and anti-Semitism. He didn't bring it through me because my heart was dark and I'm filled with hatred for white people and for the human family of the planet. If my heart were that dark, how is the message so bright, the message so clear, the response so magnificent?

Minister Louis Farrakhan, Monday, October 16, 1995.

~ Chapter Twenty Nine ~

LIAM McNAUGHTON:

The funny thing about going to court that day, that Monday, was that all I could think about was that shit Dorsey was talking about Julianne. You know, how she and I broke it off so quick, so sudden.

When I first met her, in Albuquerque, her being black and me being white didn't seem to come with so much, I don't know, baggage. Here, in the Chocolate City, things were different. For both of us. I tried to give her all the room she needed. After all, this was a new city for her too. I had even put off going out on my own for some time since I knew she was against it. She suspected that if I ever got out of Dorsey's basement I would meet other women.

Which was true, in some respects. I expected to meet women, men, everybody. I mean, I moved out here with my eyes wide open. I sacrificed a lot just to get some experience. I mean, let's face it, law school basically teaches you to use the law library; it doesn't teach you much about how to be a lawyer.

And sitting in Dorsey's basement wasn't either.

Which is why I got so pissed off at Julianne, at the end there, after Christmas last year. Not last year, I mean '94. My first year in practice.

Back then, R.G. and some of the other Murder Lawyers used to invite me to second chair their jury trials. And while most of the time – heck, all of the time – the chance of doing a real jury trial evaporated – the client would cop a plea, there'd be a continuance, maybe once the government dismissed the case – you know, I still took each and every one of them seriously. Usually they'd let me cross examine a cop or whatever, nothing too serious. Still, I'd always get all geared up the night before these kinds of things, and maybe Julianne could sense that and get jealous or whatever.

I mean, we'd be sitting down after dinner, watching T.V., like a real couple, you know? That's when she would just start in on me. "Who'd you have lunch with today?" "Meet anybody down at court today?" And then she'd be off to the races. Julianne has a wonderful ability to find my deepest seeded inadequacies and just yank them to the surface.

So, anyway, on one of these nights, late December, maybe early January, Julianne really started laying in on me, claiming I had my eye on the girl down the hall or some shit. Then I was fucking the prostitute client I told her about. Blah blah blah. All night and all morning.

The difference was that morning, something *was* going to happen. R.G. and I had picked a jury out of the fourth panel rejects the afternoon before, so there was no doubt in my mind that I was about to do my first jury trial. R.G. was even going to let me give the opening, so, you know, I was really geared up and all.

So we're on Blue Line, and she's still going at it. I mean, it's embarrassing doing all that in front of people. Anyway, at L'Enfant Plaza, I stepped off, as I always did, to transfer to the Green Line, and at that moment, she finally stopped.

It was like she tossed me the hot potato: *O.K., go ahead, you say something now that the goddam train doors are closing. Now's your chance.*

And, of course, I took the bait. I just stepped up to the space inside the door frame and said, "We're through." Truth be told, I said it with more snivel than sneer, but the bottom line was: I had had it.

The Metro doors began fluttering to a close, you know, with that robot voice yelling, "Please stand clear of the doors!" so I stepped back, but she grabbed my shirt and pulled me towards her, like she was trying to kiss me, and she whispered in my ear, "If you only knew the sacrifices I've made for you."

We never saw each other again. Talked on the phone maybe once after that, and even that was like months later. Maybe that's what bugged me about my talk with Dorsey, something that still bugs me today. There was never a post-mortem between me and Julianne. I still don't know exactly what happened between us.

So, anyway, that's kind of what I was thinking about when I first spotted Ponytail in front of the courthouse that morning – the morning of the Million Man March. I knew by this time, of course, that he had allowed me to escape from the church tower – when I came to, you know, woke up and all, the cuffs were off and the door was unlocked, so I just grabbed my hat and my clothes – my suit and shirt nicely dry-cleaned, I should say – and then I took off, happy I wasn't sleeping in the Potomac River with its three-eyed fishes, if you know what I mean.

So anyway, there I was, with Ponytail in the opposite line from me, the shorter line, Officer Greezy's line. You know, that one guard, "Follow me easy, don't carry me greezy!" Anyway, Ponytail must have felt my eyes on the back of his head, 'cause he just turned and saw me looking at him.

He had one of those buffet-style take out containers, you know, wrapped in a yellow plastic bag, hanging from his prosthetic. When he saw me looking at him, he kind of hid the bag behind him while he held his real hand aloft like he was giving me the Sieg Heil.

But then he turned his thumb out and down, real Roman Emperor-style, like he was pronouncing a death sentence. Whose, I don't know.

Anyway, I just stared right back at him, raised *my* arm up, and flipped the sonofabitch off. Initially, he just sloughed it off. He may have even smiled.

But when I tipped my hat to him – you know, my lucky top hat – his smile disappeared. He freaked out, literally stumbling into the vestibule, Officer Greezy territory, you know, and that's where I think he lost his lunch. All on account of my haircut, I guess.

My haircut? Oh yeah, I guess I forgot to mention that. About my head being shaved and all, I mean. See, after escaping from that church, I headed straight back to the jail, figuring I needed to talk to Mal one last time, try to get to the bottom of all this craziness before the trial.

At least tell him what I learned about the baby being dead and all.

And that's when I saw them. The buses. An endless caravan of buses creeping east towards RFK Stadium. For a Redskins game, I guessed. The stadium is no more than a couple of hundred yards from the D.C. Jail, so I figured I'd at least see what all the commotion was about. But as I got closer, I could see this was no Redskins game. There were lines of buses on Independence Avenue, lines of buses on Massachusetts Avenue. There were buses on East Capitol and on all of the smaller side streets.

And there, in the stadium's parking lot, was a scene straight out of a Grateful Dead concert. Except that everybody was black and there were no women.

But a festive scene was erupting nonetheless. There were fires, music, African drums, chanting. Bow-tied brothers hawking bean pies. Smoke flowing out of these little ramshackle huts selling charbroiled chicken.

Oh, and the buses. The parking lot was jammed packed with 'em.

There were also a few church vans, and bunch of R.V.'s. I passed this one RV where the dudes had a television set up outside, and they were watching themselves being interviewed

336

on WJLA. You know, the local station.

I mean, up to that point, I hadn't really figured out that this was the beginnings of the Million Man March; but after watching the news interviews, it kinda clicked for me. It's kinda funny to think back on it. There I was, just a'strolling through RFK's parking lot, crazed-looking white boy in a nice suit and top hat. I probably looked like some kind of crazy Haitian zombie – no sleep for three days, major five o'clock shadow, bloodshot eyes. Still, no one cast me more than a second glance.

And I mean, it – there wasn't another white boy around. Just masses of black dudes.

Then, in the light of dawn, the whole crowd started moving, and I mean, I never seen anything like it – just a crush of men walking down East Capitol towards the Mall. It was truly amazing. I mean, shoulder to shoulder. Incredible.

Anyway, up around Eighth Street, I saw one of my clients, Bernard Grant, the dude who ditched court on the day all this crazy shit began, if you can believe that. Anyway, I called out to him, and when he recognized me, he ran over and gave me a big hug. I thought about telling him about the bench warrant the judge had just issued, but I kept my mouth shut. Bernard had on one of the most satisfied smiles. All the men around me had that same kind of ecstatic look on their face. Again, like I said, I've never seen anything quite like it.

Anyway, Bernard said he was going on down the road to the It-Pays-To-Look-Well barber shop and he suggested I do the same. And I thought, well, I probably do need a shave. Well, we literally pushed our way through the throngs of black men, down 8th Street, over by the Marine Barracks, and even over there, all the way down to the Navy Yard, the black men were absolutely crushing – just everywhere, totally law-abiding I should note, solid along the sidewalks, but not a soul walking in the deserted street.

But the barber shop – It Pays To Look Well – was empty, totally empty. Three old dudes were sitting in their own barber chairs, holding rolled-up magazines in their hands.

Bernard hollered, "Hey," asking where so-and-so was, and how come this guy or that guy wasn't around. Then he moved off to the back of the shop saying he needed to use the baf'room.

I was admiring the old boxing posters on the wall when one of the barbers asked me if I needed a cut n'shave and I said, "Sure."

I mean, I told him I didn't even have a dollar on me, but he said fine, and so I just sat down in his chair and he dusted me off and spent a long time fixing my collar and adjusting my apron and messing with his tools and all that.

And he asks me if I want it Taxi Driver style. "Like them Marine boys do it." I said, "No, take it all off." And then he says, "To the skin?" And I answered, "Yeah. To the skin."

So I sat there, almost in a trance, with that soft hum of the clipper going back and forth over my head and I must have gone to sleep cause I woke up when the guy started rubbing some kind of alcohol on my head.

And I swear, I saw a different person looking back at me from the mirror.

Maybe that same face is what startled Ponytail, Captain, whatever you want to call him. I really do think it jarred him a bit, because he got caught in the middle of some sort of commotion around the metal detectors. I could see the whole thing.

There were these two court employees, one a pretty black girl who kind of reminded me of — well, whatever, and the other was that lanky dude that works as a file clerk. You know? Misdemeanor Division? Anyway, they had both pushed their way to the head of the line, just in back of Ponytail. The file clerk dude was carrying his lunch take-out container in a yellow plastic bag – just like the one Ponytail had – and he was really aping it up for the woman, really goofing in front of her, carrying on about his sandwich – "a muthufuckin' Reuben!" Except he keeps drawing out the word "Reuben," saying, like, "I got me a big ass Rooooo-biiin, dog! Ain't never had no muthafuckin Rooooo-bin before!" And the girl, she just kept giggling every time he said it.

I guess Ponytail got distracted for a second when he saw my bald head – I don't know, maybe he thought I was a skin head, that he had mis-judged me or something – and when he stopped for that half-second, all kind of befuddled, that's when the Roooo-bin guy cuts in front of him.

When the woman tried to do the same, Ponytail wouldn't let her pass, you know, he kind of asserted himself by placing his lunch container on the table next to the x-ray machine, right next to the file clerk's bag. The file clerk had flashed his Court I.D. badge to Officer Greezy, so he kind of just sashayed through the metal detectors and picked up one of the yellow plastic bags. Then he was off, still carrying on about his Reuben. "Damn! Dis jump's heavy. I'ma be eatin this mutha-fuckin Rooooo-biiin to next week!" Shit like that.

I was just going through the metal detectors myself right about then, and the last I saw of Ponytail, he was picking up the other yellow plastic bag and heading off in the direction of the Chief Judge's courtroom.

Me? I headed downstairs for trial in Judge Malley's courtroom. I intended to beat this case, by any means necessary.

339

§ § § § § § § § §

ANNIE FAIRBROTHER:

Did I know that the Million Man March was going to be such an issue for the city? No, not really. I hadn't heard much about it. I hadn't really been following the news at the time. Mr. Pledge, a co-worker of mine, may have mentioned it to me. That Monday was just my second day back to work, mind you.

So, yes, I was caught totally by surprise. I think the sheer numbers just caught everyone off-guard.

I really don't know whether there actually were a million people out there or not. The reports vary. What impressed me was the total lack of problems. I mean, no arrests, nothing. Maybe that had something to do with the extra police presence, but I'd rather think that Mr. Farrakhan was right – that a gathering of a million black men from across the country will not necessarily bring with it a proportionate increase in the kind of crime we see here in the City of Washington on a daily basis.

I was really struck by one sign I saw a young man carrying near the courthouse. He had shackles on his feet and a crown of thorns – a little overdone, I'll admit – but his sign asked "HOW DIFFICULT IS IT TO BE A BLACK MAN IN AMERICA?"

That got me thinking about my son Elijah, and how he's gonna grow up to be a boy, and then a man, and I'm embarrassed to say, I think I began crying. We had had such a lovely weekend together. It had been so very difficult leaving that morning, that Monday, putting him in the nanny's arms. It's still very hard leaving him.

Excuse me. I'm sorry. Could we go off the record for just a minute....

O.K. Thank you.

So, yes, you could say I was distracted that morning when

I saw Mr. McNaughton coming through the security line at the courthouse. At least I thought it was him. At first, I wasn't entirely sure – he appeared to have shaved his head, and his face was sort of puffy. He was about to head downstairs – down the escalator, to be precise – so I stopped him and said, "Counsel, don't we have Mr. Stancil's matter together? You know the Chief Judge starts at nine sharp."

He took a second before answering, as if he was unsure of who I was. Then he said he had been fired from that case and that some other lawyer was taking over. And then he headed off, saying he was late for a trial before Judge Malley.

(Judge Malley is another one of those who starts at nine o'clock sharp).

Anyway, to this day, I can't remember if Mr. McNaughton said "a" trial or "the" trial. I'm pretty sure he said "a" trial, so of course I didn't pay it any mind and proceeded to the Chief Judge's courtroom. Had Mr. McNaughton said "the" trial, meaning "Jamal Stancil's trial," I might have proceeded differently. I had simply forgotten that Mr. Stancil's trial matter was before another judge; or to be more precise, I had presumed that the Chief Judge had consolidated the two matters – merits trial and show cause.

As it turned out, the Chief Judge inherited only the show cause matter after Judge DeMaglio passed away; the trial matter – the underlying case – was assigned to Judge Malley. So the mistake was mine. I clearly should have checked in with Judge Malley's courtroom first because under the court's administrative rules, trials always have precedence. But since Mr. McNaughton said "a" and not "the," I continued on to the Chief Judge's courtroom.

When I arrived, the courtroom was pretty much empty, except for the Chief Judge himself. Even the courtroom clerk hadn't arrived. Apparently, Judge Cummings had taken the bench at 8:45 a.m. and had been browbeating everyone who showed up at the appointed time of nine. Fortunately, Jayson Pledge, my co-counsel, had been there when the doors were unlocked, so the United States Attorney's Office was not in the Chief Judge's cross-hairs.

Until I came in, that is. Then, all of a sudden, it was *my* fault that Mr. Stancil had not been brought up to his courtroom.

Yes, of course, it was not *my* fault. And you bet I told the judge right there and then that the transporting of prisoners was not the job of the U.S. Attorney's Office. I know, it may have sounded a bit snide, maybe even disrespectful. But really, what did I have to do with the Marshal's failure to bring the defendant up from the jail? I understood that the courthouse was unevenly staffed that day, since many of the Marshals had been deputized by MPD to help with the March. The Million Man March, I mean. But what did that have to do with me?

I mean, by the looks of the replacement Marshal in the Chief Judge's courtroom, it was clear to me why there might be some mix-ups. This guy – who I'd never seen before – looked totally unprepared, totally unprofessional. Really, I thought the Marshal's service had a dress code! But this one looked like a member of a motorcycle gang, with his long dirty ponytail and visible tattoos. Hmmph!

Anyway, back to the Chief Judge. He told me that the Marshal's service was not the problem. The problem, he said, was that Mr. Stancil was downstairs in the dock behind Judge Malley's courtroom, probably conferring at that very moment with his lawyer, Mr. McNaughton.

§ § § § § § § § §

MALI STANCIL:
I dinit originally plan on telling Mister McNaughton about

all that shit I done with Brandy. You know, at the jail, when Aunt Lovey done got me that other lawyer. I don't know why I said what I said. Maybe cause I dinit think I'd be seeing him again. Or anyone, ya dig? I figured I'd be putting myself in the morgue for good this time. Nigga like me can't stay behind no bars.

But whatever, whatever. I dinit do nothing about it. Took my beating, and went on.

And so, when my lawyer first showed up outside my cell, you know, in the courthouse, on that day of my trial, I dinit expect him to go looking all happy and shit like he did. Yeah, he done cut his hair. His face look kinda busted up, too. Kinda lookin like me.

I had no problem with that. See, most of the lawyers I've had dealings with always be putting on that fake sad face, like some white man gonna be sad about a nigga pleading guilty and doing time. But Mr. McNaughton, he was happy most the time. What you call that? Enthusiastical?

And that morning, first thing he say is he gonna get me a jury for my trial, and that's what was making him so happy. That's what I liked about my lawyer. He promised me at the very start of this thing that I could have my trial. Everyone knows da' CJA lawyers be getting paid extra when they clients cop, so that was pretty generous of him to do that for me. And I gotta give the man his props. He did spend an awful lot of time coming down to the jail to visit me and all, you know, wanting to hear how that game plays out on the street, asking those silly white boy questions. Makes me laugh, even now.

Anyway, I know he dinnit have to do that for me. Let me tell you, when you incarcerated, you pray for a visit, don't matter who from. Truthfully! N'fact, that's how I got hooked up with da' Minister. Minister And-One. And before that, Brother Khan. Shee, down in Lorton, I even be talking to those

343

white boy Mormons if it get me outta my cell.

So, like I was saying, since I already told Mr. McNaughton bout Brandy, you know, what I done did to her, I figgered I'd let him know 'bout the Curtain of Life. I mean, I know it was supposed to be a secret and all. But I dunno, on account of him already knowing 'bout them boxes, the bugs, or whatever Le'Nor toll him? And then, later, he toll me he done seen the seating chart. So, I be trying to help-him-help-me, like he says.

And, mainly, cause it was all on the legit side, too, dog! I did be working in that school, I really did. Poppa-san could have told you. I still don't know why my lawyer didn't get no evidence on that. But anyways, on that Monday, the morning of my trial and all, I suddenly remembered 'nother witness, you know, a dude who could come to court and prove I done worked with Poppa-san at that school. It was the prison ministry dude, Mr. Shubel, the one they's call the Cap'n.

So I starts telling Mr. McNaughton all about it. How a bit of a minute ago, I was over by that school working for Poppa-san and I was cleaning that trap in the kitchen, not too far from Bootsy's office, if you can believe that, and I got bit by a spider. It's true. Kinda funny, huh? I'm over near Brandy's moms and I get bit by a spider. Figgers.

Anyway, my hand be swelling up real good, so I head back to the truck, see if I could find me a first aid kit or a box-cutter, something to help the swelling. And that's when I saw the dude who run the Prison Ministry, that one they do on the, uh, computer. What's that called? The internets?

Yeah, it was that dude Cap'n Shubel. He had jes gotten out of that old car of his – that Tornado, that what we call it – outside the loading dock to the school. See, I don' really be knowings Cap'n Shubel, but I been knowing Minister And-One for a real minute. *He* the one that hooked me up with Captain's Prison Ministry – what they called the Odin– or On-line Prison

Ministry, sumpin like that – and *they's* the one who put me in touch with Poppa-san. I mean, Mr. Kim.

See, Mr. Kim, he don taught me some mad skills. Plumbing. Fire sprinkler systems. So I wanted to go and thank Cap'n Shubel, you know, for helping me get a job and all that. But he was talking to Mr. Kim, and I dinnit want to be bothering them none, so I jes watched and waited and stayed real quiet like I do.

Cap'n Shubel had these jumps in the back of da' car, like a can – what they call that? – a canister. Like one them things you put in a barbeque, a gas barbeque. Poppa-san was stacking bout six or seven of these jumps onto a dolly, and he had a cigarette in his mouth, and he's just kind of nodding his head, asking Mr. Shubel in that way he speak, the way, I guess all Chinese people speak, saying, "Hooky this up? Me hooky this up to sprink-a-ler?"

And Mr. Shubel? Cap'n? I remember him just slapping that cigarette out Poppa-san mouth. I mean, he stole him good! And then – I remember this part like it was yesterday – he said, "That's Greek Fire, you stupid dink! No smoke-ee!" And he poked him the chest with that wooden arm of his.

After that, I decided maybe it wasn't no good time to be talking to Mr. Shubel, so I left out, but I guess that spider bite done made me dizzy or whatever, 'cause I kinda stepped on this pallet and knocked over these cans that hold the foam, you know, that goes into the fire sprinklers? Retardant, it's called.

And Shubel must have sighted me then, cause he start asking Poppa-san bout me right away after that. So I knows he could come to court and help me out. You know, be a witness on my side.

Well, when I told my lawyer Mister McNaughton all this, he got real excited, says he has to tell the police 'bout what I just toll him. Tell the police? Well, I just 'bout lost it there. "I thought you was for me, on my side!" I toll him. He tried 'splaining something bout attorney-client ... pledge, sumpin like that. But there was some rule, some 'ception, and he said that he thought a lot of lives gonna be lost and that he had to stop it.

I tried telling my lawyer about how I fixed it, how the Curtain of Life gonna work even better then befo', how the Minister's speech was gonna change things in this world, how we was gonna stop da' killing of dem little babies, how I was finally gonna make things right....

But he wasn't really listening to me. He start talking real fast now, telling me about some dude he called Ponytail but who was really the Cap'n, this Mr. Shubel, I mean. My lawyer say the Cap'n was trying to set me up or something, how he'd seen some chart, how that was the secret to the whole thing.

So, like I say, that's when I told him. You know, help him help me. Sure, that's the chart, I told him, the seating chart. For the school. But before I could finish telling him all I had to say, the Marshals came in and took me out into the courtroom.

346

~ Chapter Thirty ~

DENNIS OLSEN:

I remember that day, the day of that black parade. The Million Man March or whatever. Sure, I remember it real good. It was my first day back in Washington after that jig – scuze me, after that black *citizen* shot me. Back in June.

Getting shot hurts, let me tell you. And the District just don't pay enough to be getting shot by some Y.O. drug dealer or whatever.

Y.O.? You know, "yo." Like, "Yo, man, why you got them cuffs so tight?"

So anyways, see, soon as I was released from the hospital, after getting shot, I mean, I gave MPD my walking papers, and took a job with the Charles County Sheriff's Office. See, in Charles County, things are just a lot more, I don't know, *normal*, you might say. Sure, we got our drug dealers and gang bangers and all that. But in Charles County, we got judges who don't just let these guys back out on the street. We don't get sued when some – some douche-bag pulls a gun on you and you gotta take him down. I mean, with the Sheriff, I get my own car, my hours are a lot easier, I'm not getting pulled in to do overtime every time there's a march or protest or whatever. And, of course, I'm close to home now. I'm from Waldorf, you know?

So, yeah, I guess you could say I wasn't too happy about being subpoenaed down to Superior Court for some case I had nothing to do with. U.S. versus Malcolm X. Stancil? I mean, Jesus Christ, just take a look at the paperwork! I wasn't the arresting officer; McCoy was. All I did was walk the guy down to court for booking.

As I recall, that didn't even happen, cause the court closed or whatever.

On account of that McVeigh thing.

Well, yes, and the andro I accidentally left there at the Police Officer entrance. The union backed me up on that one, just so you know.

Anyway, so, yeah, I'm pissed I gotta drive back into the city. And then, when I saw all those – black guys, that's when I got really P.O.'d. They were just everywhere. Crossing the street against the light, blocking traffic in all these huge groups. A lot of attitude, is what I'm saying. Not too much respect for, you know, the streets and traffic and shit like that.

So then, it takes forever to find parking. And when I finally walk into Judge Malley's courtroom, the trial had already started. The jury was there, and the lawyers were up talking to the judge, and it was only like nine thirty, ten. Usually these kind of trials don't get started till after lunch.

I didn't see McCoy nowhere, so I just sat in the front row, kinda waving the subpoena, waiting for one of the prosecutors to notice me. Maybe cause I was in my civies, they didn't really acknowledge me. Finally, this young black guy thinking he was all that comes up to me and says real sharp, "Can't you see we're busy? What do you want?"

Well, trust me, I wanted to tell him where to go and what to do with it. But I kept my trap shut. I showed him the subpoena, and then he turned all polite. He asked that I wait outside the courtroom, and so that's what I did.

Yeah, tell me about it. Sit around and wait – pretty typical. "Stuperior Court," that's what we used to call it. They got these little rooms outside the court, these witness rooms, for us police. Some of 'em might have a little couch or a bench or something, you know, somewhere to catch some z's while you wait your turn to be called. So I checked out this one room but there was this pissed-off black lady wearing some kind of uniform, like a nurse or a cleaning lady or something. Maybe a cafeteria worker, like.

And she gave me a really shitty look, so I decided, fuck this, I'll just wait in the hall.

And that's where I was when I first saw McCoy.

He came running down the hall, all out of breath. He ran right by me to that print-out they have taped on the door, the one with the names of all the cases on it. I guess he didn't recognize me, so I, you know, I just said "Hey."

See, I used to be into weight lifting. Power lifting, really. Body building, body sculpting, all that. But after I got shot, I kind of got off my routine, my regimen. Still haven't really gotten back into it. I was able to pass the Sheriff's physical exam – shit, my grandmother could have passed that test. So, maybe I'm, let's say, twenty-five, thirty pounds off my target weight. Maybe a little bit more back then, whatever day that was.

October 16th, yeah. That sounds about right.

I could tell McCoy was trying to get someplace else. I mean, he was in his civies too. So I walked up to him and told him not to worry, that the trial had just started, so he wasn't late or nothing. But he said he wasn't there for a trial. He said he was looking for someone. And I remember this exactly. When I asked who, he said, "The Bennie Grimes who is not really Bennie Grimes."

See, that's the kind of thing that makes other police not feel right about McCoy. I mean, I told him right there and then, I said, "Look, man, this is your case – the Stancil case – and I want to get the Hell outta here! If you go bounding off somewhere else, the prosecutor's not gonna be able to call you to the stand, and then we'll have to come back tomorrow!"

So I guess it was about then that he remembered who I was. So, he was polite, asked how I was doing and all that, you know, with me being shot and all. And I told him about my new job, or at least I started to, when he goes on to tell me about his hunch.

And after just a few minutes of listening to that, I began to remember what a drag it was partnering with this guy, how we were always driving around chasing down his hunches, while the city was basically taken over by these drug dealers and car thieves and homeless motherfuckers. Granted, McCoy's hunch may have broke open that Sursum Corda killing. I will give him credit for that. But, truthfully, I believe he was just lucky that time. Crimes just aren't solved on hunches.

So anyways, as far as I recall, his hunch was this: he had a report that said this guy Bennie Grimes or whatever, his fingerprints matched up with the prints taken from several homicides, but that the real Bennie Grimes was an old junkie without any thumbs, so there must have been a mix-up at the jail, or someone in the jail using the old man's identity.

So I told McCoy, "Why don't you just go back to the jail and pick up your guy there?"

And he said, "Cause the court's computer says that this guy Bennie Grimes was supposed to be in court right then.

Today. Right now. Right here. That's what he said.

That's when that black prosecutor came out – the young dude – and told McCoy to come in. Me? I slipped back into the witness room. I saw that the pissed-off black lady was gone, and I had the place to myself pretty much after that.

In fact, I don't think I woke up until much later. You know, when the court was being evacuated.

§ § § § § § § § §

ANNIE FAIRBROTHER:
Naturally, I was quite upset about the Chief Judge's outburst at me. Really now, that was the second time he's tried

to embarrass me – to question my professionalism – in open court. As I said, it certainly was not my fault that Mr. Stancil was brought to Judge Malley's courtroom. In fact, it was I who was in the wrong courtroom, not him. Trials always go first. According to the rules, I should have proceeded to Judge Malley's courtroom for the trial call.

But none of this assuaged the Chief Judge, who continued to just huff and puff away at me, finally saying, "Well, I'm sending the Marshal for him!" Then he stormed off the bench, that scruffy Marshal I told you about right behind him.

Jayson and I immediately picked up our belongings and headed out for Judge Malley's courtroom, with that awful Mr. Stucky following close behind. He was evidently Mr. Stancil's new attorney, and he was trying to tell me that this was all Mr. McNaughton's fault, calling him a 23-110. You know, the code cite for ineffective assistance of counsel claims?

Anyway, as I was saying, I ignored him, Mr. Stucky, and fortunately, he eventually disappeared somewhere near the men's room.

I avoided the elevators, of course – you never know when they're going to break down mid-floor – and headed for the stairwell. That's when Jayson stopped me.

"You can't go down there," he said, almost laughing. I asked why not, and he said, "Haven't you heard?"

Well, of course I hadn't heard. I had been on maternity leave. Suffice to say, he told me that someone had been – how shall I say this – defecating? Yes, defecating in the stairwell. The stairwell of the court building. Virtually every day. Sometimes twice a day. Even now, I can hardly speak of it.

Jayson had warned me that the smell had made the stairway impassible, but I ignored him. I guess I just didn't believe him – besides, you gotta have a pretty strong stomach for this job. But when I pulled open the door, I was overcome by the stench – that barnyard stench.

I asked Jayson why the custodial staff didn't just clean it up.

"They did at first," he said, "But after several weeks of this, our office – the U.S. Attorney's Office – took over the case, identifying it as a hate crime."

Jayson said that now the, ah, evidence, has to be taped off, photographs have to be taken, samples for DNA testing, that kind of thing. I was totally aghast. And I still am!

Needless to say, after that, we took the escalator down to Judge Malley's courtroom. When we walked in, it was little past ten o'clock, and you'll never believe this – Judge Malley had already started the trial. The Stancil trial. The jury already picked and sitting in their seats!

To add insult to injury, the judge was calling us forward to brow-beat us for being late. Judge Malley had picked, sworn, and instructed the jury, all in the absence of government counsel of record, and now *we* were about to be sanctioned for being late.

That's when I told Jayson that I was planning on letting him to try the case.

"First chair?" he asked.

"You go, boy," I told him as I pushed him forward towards the judge.

This was going to be his first jury trial, and he was obviously excited. I know I shouldn't have dumped the responsibility on him, but he certainly deserves the experience. I've tried so many cases, I can practically do them half-asleep.

Which is how I began feeling as the trial began. This fatigue, this tiredness I'd been getting at that time. I would begin to feel very cold, and ... alone. Well, I don't mean alone. Zoned out, I guess you could say. There have been days since the birth of my son that I felt like this, when I couldn't really do anything but crawl up in a little ball and lie in bed. For days at a time, I'm ashamed to say. Thank God for my auntie and my younger sister, who came down from New York those first few weeks. And after they left, the nannie was a great help.

Not the first nanny, mind you. Oh no, she was ghastly. I mean the second one. The little Philippine woman. Even as out of it as I was, I could tell that first one wasn't working out at all. A mother knows.

Anyway, like I was saying, Jayson's opening argument.... I don't want to say that his opening was long, but – Anyway, I woke up when Mr. Stancil's lawyer – that's Mr. McNaughton – he told the judge he would save his opening for the defense case. A terrible mistake, by the way. But when he did it, Jayson quickly called Bootsy Henson as his first witness, before McNaughton could change his mind. Good move, Jayson!

During Ms. Henson' testimony, however, I found myself drifting off again. Bootsy is Brandy Carey's mother, she worked at that school – I think you already know that. Anyway, something about Jayson's questioning style – he had a difficult time asking non-leading questions, and after a while, with Mr. McNaughton's constant objections, I don't know, I just kind of tuned out.

I can remember very clearly that I was focusing on a small spot on the wall, just past where the Marshal was standing, right behind the defendant, and then I realized that what I was looking at was not the wall but rather Mr. McNaughton's shiny white head.

That caught me off-guard for some reason. Mr. McNaughton and his client were doing a lot of whispering back and forth during Bootsy's testimony, and the contrast of their bald heads couldn't have been clearer. Mr. McNaughton had a bandage under his eye, I think, and a large bruise on the side of his head. It might have even been a birth mark, for all I know. But truthfully, I've seen hundreds if not thousands of photographs of hematomas, so I'm pretty sure that's what it was there on Mr. McNaughton's head.

But nothing to compare to his African-American client, whose head was marked with several long keloid scars, countless small zipper marks where stiches had been taken out, and at least one significant indentation.

And I became ... startled, I guess you could say, because here I was looking at Mr. Stancil for what was really the first time.

Of course, I've been acquainted with the man for a long time now. Since 1992, in fact. That's when I prosecuted him for beating his girlfriend and killing her unborn child – the infamous "Baby Stomper" case. And that's what I used to see in him – "The Baby Stomper."

I didn't see Jamal Stancil, or Malcolm X. Stancil, or whatever he was calling himself back in those days. I didn't see him as a person, as an individual. I saw him playing a role. He was that day's defendant, charged with that week's outrageous crime. I was there playing the role of the aggrieved and angry prosecutor. Brandy Carey was cast, I guess you could say, to play the part of the victim, while her mother's cry for Old Testament style vengeance – an eye for an eye – had the potential to bring the audience – the jury – to its feet. It didn't really matter what the crime was – breaking into a school, killing a child – it was a performance, one that I had starred in for many, many years.

And that's when it really hit me how de-humanizing the whole thing was. Of course, the law – the criminal justice system – has to be impersonal. Justice is blind for good reason. But what I realized at that moment, as I stared at Mr. Stancil's and Mr. McNaughton's heads, was that the job – my job – had taken some of that human-ness from me.

And I thought to myself, right then, at that moment, maybe that's what makes me such a horrible mother.

§ § § § § § § §

LIAM McNAUGHTON:

When Miss Fairbrother started to cry right after Bootsy Henson's last answer, right before I'm about to get up there and cross examine her, I just thought, "Oh no, this can't get any worse."

This all-white jury, hand-picked by the judge, had just heard Miss Henson testify that she was the Executive Director of Food Services at St. Nick's and was appearing on behalf of the school pursuant to a government subpoena; that she was familiar with the records of the school generally and with the "barring order" that had been issued against Mr. Stancil particularly. Her recollection was personal as well as professional, as that barring order had been requested by none other than Bootsy Henson herself, several years earlier, when her daughter Brandy was still messin' with Mal.

Miss Henson also testified that on April 19, 1995, no one from the school had authorized Mr. Stancil to be on the premises. And then this surprise, at least to me: Boosty testified that she had personally responded to the school at approximately four o'clock in the morning after getting a call from security, or someone she thought was security, about a "breaking and entering" on the premises.

(My hearsay objection denied by the judge).

When she got to St. Nick's, she saw Mal in police custody and identified him by name.

(My objection to strike the "show up" identification as suggestive and unreliable denied by Judge Malley).

Finally, Mr. Pledge – the prosecutor – asked her how she felt seeing Mr. Stancil there in the school, in the early morning hours, having been caught climbing on the downspout, and Bootsy, to her credit, hit her line like a pro.

"I feared for my personal safety," she said, "and the safety of the school's property ... on account of Mali's – excuse me, Mr. Stancil's having *stomped* my Brandy and *kilt* that baby!"

(I objected again, but the judge overruled me, just like he had done again and again in this case).

So then, as if things couldn't get any worse, just as I'm about to begin my cross, Miss Fairbrother stands up, looking like she is going to faint, and she just starts crying! I'm talking, aloud! That kind of suppressed weeping, you know, the kind you see at funerals.

If she was acting, then I have to applaud her, cause she really took me to school. I watched as the whole courtroom's focus turned from Bootsy to Miss Fairbrother to me and finally to my client. Ouch.

Once the damage was done, Miss Fairbrother asked to be excused for a moment to compose herself.

"Of course, Mrs. Fairbrother," Judge Malley told her, all Irish-Catholic sweet. "Take as long as you like."

For my part, I approached the bench and demanded a mistrial. The judge denied it curtly. "Legitimate area of inquiry, Mr. McNaughton," he said, "and the jury is entitled to hear the witness' answer."

"What about Miss Fairbrother's crying!" I protested.

And the judge said: "That poor woman jest had a baby, Mr. McNaughton. Have ye no sense of decency in ye?"

Oh, that was rich! I knew Judge Malley had it in for me. He was obviously still sore about me demanding a jury trial. That had to be it. See, the moment I arrived in the courtroom that morning, the clerk told me that the judge had wanted my client's jury trial waiver form executed right away so that we could get the trial started.

I was caught totally off guard by that, I admit it. Truthfully, I didn't know that my client had a jury trial to waive.

See, judges convict at a much higher rate than juries. That's just a fact. Everyone knows that. And what happened, see, was that a year or so before I got to town, the U.S. Attorney's Office got together with a committee of Superior Court judges (led by none other than *Associate* Judge Armstrong Cummings, by the way) and they convinced the City Council into *reducing* the maximum jail time for virtually every misdemeanor, so that now, virtually all of the misdemeanors in the D.C. Code are punishable by up to 180 days. Prior to that change, most of these misdemeanor offenses were punishable by up to one year imprisonment. So why'd they do it? Why would prosecutors lobby for a reduction in criminal penalties? Seems counter-intuitive until you consider their motive.

You see, they claimed, and the courts pretty much bought into it, that the reduction of time to 180 days made all these misdemeanor offenses "petty crimes," which according to *their* reading of <u>Blanton</u> – this Supreme Court case – makes those offenses non-jury triable.   Never mind that the U.S. Constitution guarantees the right to jury trial in all criminal prosecutions! The Framers of the Constitution even put the right to jury trial in there *twice* – Article III and the Sixth Amendment. But a lot of good that did. The D.C. Court of Appeals predictably upheld this little coup in a series of cases. After all, what other branch of the government wants average citizens poking around where they work, making daily trouble for them?

By that summer, most of us had stopped filing our jury

357

trial demands – this boiler plate motion you could pick up in the Lawyer's Lounge – because the Court of Appeals, like I said, had upheld the denial of jury trials for these 180 day offenses. That's why I pretty much assumed that Mal's trial was going to be a bench trial.

But give credit to the CJA lawyers – a couple of jury trial die-hards kept appealing the issue and then – boom! – along comes the case of Turner v. Bayly. It's a great case – you gotta read it. Evidently, the City Council and everyone else involved in this sordid little power play assumed that the two misdemeanors in the D.C. Code that were already punishable by only "six months" – Unlawful Entry and Misdemeanor Threats – didn't need to be amended down to 180 days because six months was the same as 180 days.

But guess what? Six months will *always* consist of more than 180 days, and the Court of Appeals basically said in Turner v. Bayly, "You're right." The Supreme Court's Blanton case says you get a jury trial if the crime is punishable by more than 180 days. Accordingly, Unlawful Entry and Threats are the only misdemeanors where defendants in the District of Columbia are entitled to a jury trial.

Did I know all this before that Monday? No, I admit I did not. Look, it's hard working solo. The decision had come down earlier that summer, and I didn't have many cases in court then, I spent most of my time down at the jail, so there was really no way for me to find out.

Of course, as a result of the Turner v. Bayly decision, the judges began arm-twisting defendants to waive their jury trials in these kinds of cases. But me? I told the courtroom clerk, "We're not waiving nothing!"

Then I went into the lock-up behind the court to see Mal, to tell him the good news, and to see if he would finally explain to me what was really going on that day at the school. And that's when he told me this eye-popping story that made me think that something really bad was about to go down.

But before I could get Mal to give me the straight story and stop pussy-footing around, the Marshals came in for him, literally pushing the two of us back out into the courtroom. And not only was Judge Malley on the bench, he had the jury panel waiting for us.

And what a surprise! The whole room, full of white people. I guess all the black people had taken the day off from jury duty, what with the Million Man March and all. Judge Malley had called my bluff. Then he showed me why the house always wins.

"Do you have your proposed *voir dire*, Mr. McNaughton?" he asked. Of course I didn't have my proposed *voir dire*. I hadn't even known it was going to be a jury trial til that morning!

So he says, "I can't help it, Mr. McNaughton, if you have not read my Courtroom Memorandum on Jury Trials. This is how I select a jury. Now if you please? Yes, you there sir, Juror seated in seat one. Yes, come on up."

The judge then brought the juror in the first seat up to the bench, read off his basic juror bio to confirm he had the right person – "Juror Number 422. Age: 48. Occupation: Engineer. Lives in: Northwest." Then he asks, "Know any of these lawyers? No? And let the record reflect that we've proceeded without the assigned prosecutor on account of her tardiness."

(And truthfully, that's the first time I really noticed that there wasn't a prosecutor!)

Anyway, so the judge is saying, "Now, back to you, sir. Know the defendant? No again?" Then the judge took out the Gerstein affidavit. "How about a police officer named McCoy, or an officer named Olsen? Hmmm? You've indicated 'no.' Know how to be fair and impartial? Yes? Well then,

359

congratulations sir, you're on the jury. You may return to your seat."

Boom, boom, boom, boom – the seats fill up with the first fourteen jurors, twelve whites, two Hispanics (both of them the alternates). This, in a city that is something like 80% black.

But I figured that once we started, we would have to win – after all, there wasn't anyone there to present the government's case. But wouldn't you know it? Just as the jury is sworn in and instructed, Miss Fairbrother and another prosecutor I know, Jayson Pledge, come barreling into the room. We all go up to Judge Malley, he scolds Miss Fairbrother and Mr. Pledge for being late, and that was that. Let the trial begin. What a bummer!

Why'd I waive my opening statement? Well, first of all, I didn't technically *waive* it. I mean, I would have been able to give an opening at the end of the prosecution's case, if we even got that far. I know, I know. The Murder Lawyers say you never waive your opening argument. But in this case, I really didn't know what to say. I was beginning to have some idea why Mal was in that school. He was being set up by Ponytail – that much was clear. But for what? And how?

All through Bootsy Henson's testimony, I was talking to Mal, whispering really, trying to convince him to let me tell the cops about the seating chart. That was key. Mal had put something under those seats, and I was pretty sure that it was something that would disrupt the Million Man March – how, I don't know. But Mal definitely wasn't going for that.

This was just like a law school exam, where the question centers on the exception rather than the rule. Of course, Mal had attorney-client privilege; I understood that very well. There are exceptions, however, at least as far as I can recall from the Ethics class I took, what, my first year of law school. The class didn't seem so important at the time, but now I wished I had paid a little closer attention.

I knew that I would be relieved of the attorney client privilege if I gained information that my client was going to do some significant harm, like killing someone or wounding them badly. But what if I believed someone else had set my unwitting client up to do that harm – was I bound by the pledge of confidentiality then?

~ Chapter Thirty One ~

STANLEY HORVATH:

Juror Number 422? Yeah, that was me. Sitting in the first seat, the one closest to the judge. Closest to the witness box, too.

I for one thought the defendant – whatever his name was – was guilty. First second I saw him. Just my opinion, that's all I'm saying. The way his lawyer and he were whispering the whole time, like they were up to something. Trying to come up with some trick to fool the jury, I guess.

But that wasn't gonna happen. I for one wasn't gonna fall for any tricks. I've got friends that are lawyers. Neighbors, really. I know a little bit about the law myself. The point I'm trying to make is that no one's gonna pull the wool over my eyes. That's what I'm saying.

Like those instructions the judge gave us at the beginning there? Reasonable doubt? I mean, come on! What does that mean? Either the guy did it or he didn't do it. The prosecutor, he told us what the guy did right there – in his opening, I think it's called. The defense lawyer, when it was his turn, he didn't even say anything. So he's guilty, right? Nothing unreasonable about that.

I liked the prosecutor, Mr. Pledge, I think his name was. I wish there were more like him in this city, I really do. For mentoring, being a role model, that kind of thing.

Well, anyways, I wasn't thrilled to get picked for this jury, let me tell you. I know it's my civic duty and all that, but come on! I mean, it was Monday, I was missing work, the whole Metro system was filled with these black protestors or whatever, for the Million Man March. A guy breaks into a church or a school or whatever – I gotta miss work for that? *The cops caught him red-handed!* The cop that did it, that guy

McCoy, well, he's even been promoted to detective. That's pretty impressive. That suggests that he knew what he was doing.

And then, the defense lawyer's questioning of Detective McCoy? That really solidified it for me, that his client was guilty, you know? I mean, first of all, he was real aggressive about it, no respect for authority, you know? And pointless! My God, the questions were pointless.

"Did you investigate inside the auditorium, Detective McCoy?"

"Did you look under any seats, Detective McCoy?"

"Would anybody have something to gain by having Mr. Stancil get caught breaking into that school?"

Oh, and this: "Did you examine the contents of the bag my client was carrying?"

What kind of questions were those? The judge sustained – is that the right word? – sustained all of the prosecutor's objections. So, clearly, the defense lawyer was out of line.

I guess he felt kind of full of himself after questioning that black lady, I don't remember her name. From the cafeteria. Yeah, she was some kind of supervisor at that school, something like that. So the defense lawyer got that lady – I thought her name was Betsy but he kept calling her Bootsy – he got her to admit that she had dared the defendant to come down there to the school anytime for a fight or whatever. Well so what? I don't see how that gives him permission to break into the school like he did.

So, like I said, I had this guy pegged for guilty all the way. But after the detective's testimony, the judge told us to go back into a little room behind the court. The jury room, he called it. Just a little room with a long table, bunch of chairs. Not bad. It was clean, had a little bathroom. We all just kind of stood around, saying hello, that kind of thing. The judge had told us not to talk about the case, but after about ten minutes of just sitting around, what else is there to do? So, yeah, eventually all of us kind of sat down and talked the case out.

This one smart guy – he said he was a lawyer for some government agency – he volunteered to be the foreperson. That kind of peeved me a bit. Like, oh, just because you're a lawyer, we all need you to be our boss or whatever. I mean, I was in Seat Number 1. I was the first one chosen. That's all I'm saying, you know?

I guess another thing we did that the judge told us not to do was to listen to what was going on outside the door. In the courtroom, I mean. See, this jury room, it was directly behind where the judge sits. And believe it or not, there's nothing but thin particle board between us and the judge. So we pretty much heard everything that was going on in the courtroom. I mean, we could hear the judge talking to the prosecutor, talking to the two defense lawyers.

That's right, two defense lawyers. The public defender guy – the one with the bald head – and then another one, one who we hadn't seen during the trial. Stucky, he said his name was.

He must have come in after we were sent to the jury room. He claimed that *he* was the defendant's real lawyer, not the other guy. McNaughton, right, that's his name. Anyway, this new guy, Stucky, he was real loud. He kinda sounded like an angry Matlock. You know, from T.V.?

But that whole little interaction happened *after* the prosecutor started arguing with the judge about the evidence. We heard all that too. But the prosecutor doing the arguing, see, it wasn't the male one. It was the lady, the one who had started to cry earlier in the trial. I definitely recognized her voice telling the judge, "You have to let this case go the jury."

She didn't sound all that convincing, to tell the truth. She sounded like she really didn't believe in what she was saying, like she really just wanted to get out of there.

You and me both, that's what I was thinking!

Anyway, it was in the middle of all that, *that's* when the other guy – this Stucky fellow – showed up, yelling about how dare that other lawyer steal his client. It sounded like there was some kind of scuffle, I don't know between who, and the judge called in a Marshal or something like that.

Then things got really crazy. The defense lawyer began screaming like he had lost his mind or something. The bald headed guy. He was saying to the judge that the Marshal wasn't a Marshal, that he wasn't real, that he couldn't let the Marshal take his client in the back. A couple of us jurors looked at each other and shrugged, like, Why would they bring the defendant back here with us?

Then the judge raised his voice. We could tell that he was walking off the bench, cause he was close to the door that lead back to where we were. He screamed, "The Chief Judge of this court ordered Mr. Stancil to appear before him forthwith, and I will abide him!"

Abide him. Forthwith. I remember him saying that distinctly. You don't hear those kinds of words very often.

Anyways, that's when the fire alarm started ringing. Or maybe it started to ring before the judge began yelling. I can't remember. But we could hear it from a distance, like it was coming from somewhere above us, maybe on the main level where the entrance is. We didn't hear any alarms go off in our courtroom – Judge Malley's courtroom – and since no one came to get us, we just stayed where we were.

The alarm stopped a couple minutes later, and then, it was like totally silent. We just waited and waited for someone to come get us, to finish the trial or whatever. That's when we began talking about the case, like I said. I mean, what else was there to do?

So, anyway, after about a half an hour of just sitting there gabbing, that fat guy – he claimed he was a Maryland cop – he came in and got us, told us to go ahead and leave. So that's what we did.

§ § § § § § § § §

JAMES McCOY:

Bit eerie hearing the fire alarm go off upstairs but not on the JM level where we were. In all my years, I'd never heard that happen before. It was almost like we'd been forgotten.

I was sitting in the first row, behind the prosecutors, when it happened. Judge Malley told his clerk to find out if this was a real emergency, which I thought was the correct call. Alarms go off in court all the time. A mom starts screaming when her son is sent away for life, courtroom clerk gets panicky and calls court security. Fire in the bathroom from a tossed cigarette. Things like that. Happens all the time down here.

But evacuations are rare, and usually a little less haphazard. I guess after Oklahoma City, you got the Million Man March basically surrounding the courthouse, I can see how the powers-that-be might be on edge.

We learned later that the matter really was quite serious. A court security found a hand-gun in a trash can in the secure corridor behind the file clerk's lounge. On the third floor. Just down the hall from the Chief Judge's chambers.

They found the gun sticking out of a Styrofoam lunch container. At first they thought it was a toy, on account of how small it was. But it wasn't a toy – it was a semi-automatic double action pistol. SMC-380. Made in Hungary. Known as the poor man's Walther PPK. Next to a sawed off shotgun, it's probably the best weapon you'd want in a real tight crowd.

366

Small enough to fit in your palm, the SMC-380 feels like a pair of brass knuckles.

But, as I was saying, as we sat there in Judge Malley's courtroom, we had no idea what the alarm was for. Also, for the record, I did not immediately tie it in with what happened next.

See, at the time, with the alarm going off, I was just hoping to get out of there – out of the courtroom. The guy I was looking for, this Bennie Grimes imposter, I knew he was somewhere in that courthouse. I just had a feeling. But Miss Fairbrother, the prosecutor, she had directed me to wait in case the judge re-opened the case or whatever. For more evidence, I remember her saying.

Miss Fairbrother hadn't really been involved in the case, which kind of surprised me, given her experience. She let the other guy do the case. Jayson Pledge, I think his name is. Until the end there, that is, when the defendant's lawyer – McNaughton – asked for a directed verdict. Since the government couldn't prove that Mr. Stancil didn't have a right to be in that school.

See, the first witness, Miss Henson, Bootsy Henson, she was the only witness who could say that Mr. Stancil didn't have a right to be there. She was a supervisor or a manager or whatever at that school. She was empowered to speak on behalf of the St. Nicholas' institution. In cross-exam, McNaughton got her to admit that she had personally told Mr. Stancil – the defendant – that he could go there anytime. To fight her, I guess. So there just wasn't any evidence to prove that he – Mr. Stancil – had *unlawfully* entered the building.

I'm not a lawyer, mind you, I'm only a cop. A detective. This is just how the lawyers explained it to me.

So, yeah, that's what I remember about Miss Fairbrother. She had sort of took over the case from Mr. Pledge at that

367

point, saying she wanted to put me back up on the stand, that the judge had to let the case go to the jury. That kind of thing. The judge didn't look like he was buying any of it, said something about making a ruling after lunch.

That's when the other lawyer, Mr. Stucky, came barging in. Claimed McNaughton had stolen his client. Good thing I was there because it took both me and Mr. Pledge to separate the two of them. The lawyers, that is.

And then came the alarm. Or did the Marshal come in first? Now that I think about it, the alarm went off just *before* the Marshal came into the courtroom. Yeah, that's right. The judge told his clerk to call court security, find out what was going on. Then *she* handed the phone to him, to Judge Malley, saying, "I'm sorry, Your Honor. It's the Chief Judge. He says he needs to speak to you."

That's when the Marshal came in for Mr. Stancil.

No, I didn't notice anything unusual about the Marshal. I mean, other than the fact that he wasn't the one who was there earlier. Obviously, Mr. McNaughton had some issue with him. The two men looked like they knew each other.

But I really didn't know what all that was about. Like I said, I didn't really notice him, the Marshal. At least not at first.

It was the prisoner he was escorting. That's who I was focused on.

Black male, about five foot two. Stocky guy. Hand-cuffed only at the wrists. *That* was the first thing that told me something was wrong: when these guys are brought before a judge, they're supposed to be manacled at the ankles *and* wrists. And their hands are supposed to be hand-cuffed behind their backs, not in front like this guy.

Another thing that bothered me: I'd never seen a Marshal escort one defendant into the courtroom in order to retrieve a

THE HEYWARD SHEPHERD CONSPIRACY

second. Another violation of the rules, no doubt. One Marshal cannot be counted on to handle two defendants.

So, in retrospect, maybe I should have suspected the Marshal was behind all this. But, no, at that time, you have to understand, I was only focused on the man he had brought in. The short little stubby man with the swastika branded on his neck. The man I recognized as the kid who killed my father.

It hit me like a ton of bricks. I was staring at the man who killed my father, and he was staring back at me. Do you know how long I'd waited to be in that position? But I tell you, when this Marshal we were just talking about lead Mr. Stancil and the other prisoner – the man who killed my father – back behind the dock, I was frozen. I wanted to follow them, but I couldn't move my legs. I looked up at the judge, as if he could somehow read my mind and tell me what to do, but he was on the phone again.

It was Miss Fairbrother who snapped me out of my fog. She said, "Looks like you've just seen a ghost." And I told her I had. And she said, "If you're thinking *that's* gonna get you released as my witness, don't bet on it."

I like Miss Fairbrother, I really do. I don't mean to make her sound so, you know, bitchy. She's just all business, and I can respect that.

Anyway, she started badgering me about how I ran out on her last time, about how she wanted to write me up for leaving out of my police report the spray-painted Swastikas I told her I had seen near the school.

That's when the dots connected for me. The Swastika homicides. The partial matches of fingerprints. Bennie Grimes. The man who killed my father. The brand on his neck. I don't believe in coincidences. It all had some connection with this case. The Stancil case.

It was something bigger than me, bigger than what I was

looking for. Whatever it was, it was coming all together in that courtroom, right then, right there.

Those weird questions McNaughton was asking me on cross.... Had I ever looked under the seats of the school auditorium? Did I have any opinion on whether someone might have put Mr. Stancil up to it? Lawyers never ask those kinds of questions.

And the worst one – Had I looked in the bag?

Of course, I looked in the bag. The bag Stancil had with him on the night I arrested him. A few empty cans of what I now believe was epoxy or glue. A few brushes. Magazine clippings.

I think I told Miss Fairbrother about all that. I'm sure I also mentioned that little box, the one wrapped in gauze. The one with the crude drawing of a ladybug on it.

When I first found the box, I naturally suspected it might be a package of drugs or some other contraband. So I opened it. But it was nothing more than a box of matches. I dumped them all out to make sure there wasn't anything else hidden inside – the guys do that sometimes – but the only thing other than matches was, like, a Timex clock face. You know, a wrist watch without the band? Digital, too, if I recall.

I didn't think much about it then, the watch that is. Guys hide strange personal stuff all over. As for the box of matches, I now look back and realize that something like that could start a small fire. If it was ignited, I mean. Nothing a good soaking from a fire-sprinkler couldn't handle, but a potentially dangerous little fire nonetheless.

So, as I'm sitting there, frozen, wanting to go after the man who killed my father, I began to wonder if that's what McNaughton was getting at – that his client had been trying to burn the place down. I mean, I had no evidence to suggest that this guy was an arsonist or whatever. And I don't see how a single box of matches could do much damage.

But like I said, something big was going on, I could feel it in my bones. So I immediately asked Miss Fairbrother if I could take a look at the bag. I mean, I checked it into evidence, so surely she had it with her. But she had just picked up the phone, and it looked like she was getting bad news.

I'll never forget this, it still gives me goose bumps: the judge and Miss Fairbrother each put down their respective phones and said, simultaneously, "There's been a gun brought into the building! Everyone must evacuate immediately!"

As everyone rushed about, gathering their belongings, I heard the clerk ask the judge what she should do about Mr. McNaughton – he had evidently snuck into the lock-up while the judge was on the phone. The judge looked right at me, I guess cause there wasn't a Marshal anymore, and he asked *me* to retrieve Mr. McNaughton.

It was the excuse I was looking for. I was back there in a second.

As soon as I got in, I saw the other Marshal – the real Marshal – cuffed to one of the cells, his head all bashed in.

But no McNaughton, no Stancil.

And that ponytailed Marshal and his prisoner – my suspect, the man who killed my father – they were gone too.

§ § § § § § § § §

MALI STANCIL:
Nah, I dinit think much of being tookin away like that. That's how they do it in court. You beat the case, you still gotta go back with the Marshals, so they can check for warrants and that kinda shit.

But when I sees Mr. Shubel, I shoulda known he was up

to no good. See, I knew he was no Marshal. And also, he had Bennie with him. You know, that lil'snitch they set me up with back at the jail?

But I still thought I was getting out, going home, ya dig? The judge done said there wasn't 'nuff evidence, and he was cancelling the jury or some shit like that. But when we went into the lock-up, I could see that the other Marshal, the one who done brought me into the court that morning, he was out cold and locked in *my* cell.

That definitely wasn't right.

Then Shubel be pushing me into that dark stairwell, axing me about the bugs. You know, saying like, "Did you put them where we told you?"

Well, Mr. Shubel, he dinit show me where to put them boxes; Minister And-One did. Being it was s'posed to be a big surprise and all. And since Shubel was kinda pressing me, I only told him half the truth.

"Yes," I toll him, "I done put them little boxes under the seats, jes like I was toll to." After all, he dinnit say whether he meant dem ladybugs or dem other jumps – dem praying things.

So then, he gets right up in my face and says, "Don't shit me nigger!"

That's right, he call me a nigger! To my face!

And he says, "We've been back in that school," and he holds up that map, that seating chart the Minister gave me, and he says, "and they're not under the seats we marked out for you."

Well, I told him that map wasn't no good for me, on account of the letters. And that's the truth, too. The numbers, I could handle, but the letters ... see, the letters go up and down these rows, and there's a lot of lil' rows, some of them even got two letters. There's something wrong with me, with my eyes; when I try to look at them letters, they get all twisted around, so they look different each time I looks at them.

I mean, I can read, jes a little bit. Dem doctors say I got dis dyslexia thing, but I do know how to read. I can't write all that, I'm just being honest, but I can read a little bit.

So I toll Mr. Shubel again that I put dem lady bug underneath the chairs, just not where he had dem on da map. Instead, I bunched them all together, like, in rows M, A, L, and I.

Maybe I left just one out, I toll him, on account of getting kinda dis-orientated on account of the fumes, them epoxy fumes, but I still got twenty four out of twenty five of them jumps in place.

And that is the truth - same as I did for them praying jumps. Twenty four out of twenty five.

Seeing that Mr. Shubel wasn't up to no good, I toll him I was the only one who knew where dem boxes be, and I'd be *sho enuff* happy to show him where they were just as soon as I cleared it with Minister And-One. You know, I was shucking and jivin' a bit, jes trying to buy time or whatever. See, I wanted to get outta there, alive, ya dig? Get back to the Bins, ya dig, so's I can finds out whether them ladybugs died or not, even though I pretty much knew they was dead already.

But Mr. Shubel, he wasn't playing. He jes smiled and said to Bennie, "Do this last job, then I'll give the Devil his due."

§ § § § § § § § §

LIAM McNAUGHTON:

When I came rounding the corner, I saw the little black dude standing over my client, choking him with the chain of his cuffs.

My man Ponytail was also present, just standing there with an amused look on his face, still holding that Styrofoam container I had seen him with earlier.

When I yelled for the dude to get off of Mal, Ponytail reached into the container, you know, made a reaching motion for what I could only imagine would be a gun – I don't know why I thought that, maybe it was just that look he had on his face – but what he pulled out and pointed at me was a corn-beef sandwich.

Yeah, that's right – a motherfucking Reuben!

Well, when I saw that, I rushed him, but the other guy – the short stocky dude, the one Ponytail brought into the courtroom – he dove down at my legs and tripped me up. At least I got him off Mal, but now the little stocky guy was on me. He had his hand-cuffs looped around my throat, and was kind of getting me to the ground.

I was fighting with him, doing the best I could, expecting Ponytail would start double teaming me, but I saw that he had run away up the stairs.

So I was basically blacking-out when that cop – McCoy – came into my view. I guess the dude who was choking me bailed when McCoy showed up.

Anyway, McCoy asked me, "What the heck is going on here?" or something like that, and I shot back, "You tell me what's going on!"

And he asks me, "The man choking you –he's the one you were trying to alert me to when you were questioning me, right?"

"No, not him," I said. "The white dude with the ponytail! I told you all and none of you would listen! He's not a real Marshal! He's just some nut case trying to start a race war or something!"

Then some doughy white dude named Olsen walked in on us. Apparently, he's former MPD, and he knew McCoy. He was kinda huffing and puffing from being out of breath. He was telling us that he had been all alone in the witness room, but eventually came back into the courtroom and found the jurors kind of wandering around, asking, "Where'd everyone go?"

And then this guy, Olsen, he stops what he was saying and yells, "Holy shit! What happened to him?"

He was talking about my client. It fucking looked like Mal had been opened up with a sword. Olsen was standing over him, trying to avoid the pool of blood that was forming around his mid-section. Mal's eyes had already gone back in his head.

I remember thinking at the time that, yep, Mr. Mali Stancil had finally succeeded in killing himself, though I had no idea how he did it.

So what happened next? McCoy told Olsen to take his radio and call for a medic. And then he tore off, directing Olsen to tell them that he was pursuing an escaped prisoner "through the C level security corridor."

Me, I tore off, too, but in the opposite direction. I felt bad leaving the fat white guy to administer last rites to Mal. I never did get to tell him that he didn't kill that baby. But I suspect that he had known that all along.

And besides, I had something to settle with Ponytail.

He wasn't too hard to find, lumbering up the frozen escalators. In fact, he was calling after me, goading me, "Your man had to die! It's October 16th! Heyward Shepard has to die!"

I didn't exactly know what he was talking about at that point, but I distinctly remember what he was saying. He kept saying, like, "You might've beat the charges, but everyone will still know that he's the one who did it. He'll be blamed for starting the fire! He will start the war! History won't forget him this time!"

I charged up after him, not really knowing what I was

375

going to do, and I was right on his heels at the third floor landing, but he left the escalator and jumped into the stairwell. I followed him but I must have slipped on something cause I just came crashing to the floor, just as the door to stairwell closed behind me.

And lying there on the ground, I became aware of the smell of shit. It was overwhelming, and I was disoriented for a second or two. When I regained my footing and my senses, I could hear the heavy foot-steps going up up up, towards the top of the courthouse, so I followed after him, and rounding the Fourth Floor, I saw the source of the shit smell.

It was Robert E.L. Stucky. He was squatting down and holding his ass up with one hand, jerking off with the other, and there was a fresh load of steaming watery shit right underneath him.

Ponytail must have run right by him.

Stucky's eyes were closed tight, so I tried to just step past, but he grabbed my leg and shouted, "You little pissant! You ever steal another case from me, I'll kill your ass!"

I don't know what it was, maybe the adrenalin, but I drilled Stucky square in the cheek, and I'm pretty sure I knocked him out. I'd like to have seen how he explained to court security what he was doing there with his pants around his ankles. The case of the courthouse shitter solved.

But I had bigger fish to fry. I wanted Ponytail. And I caught up with him, like, seconds later. The door leading to the Fifth Floor was still closing when I caught it, jumping through. He was right in front of me now and I kind of used my momentum to knock into him, and both of us fell over the guard-rail. Oh shit, I thought, we were both going to be dead!

What was I thinking? I mean, it's more than a five floor drop right there where atrium opens up. Actually, it's closer to a seven floor drop if you were to make it all the way to the C-level.

Anyway, thank god, that didn't happen. You know that little concrete out-cropping? The one lined with plants? Dude, we both landed on it! This little planter box couldn't have been more than two or three feet wide, but we made it!

Ponytail got up first and crocked me with an elbow. Then he took off running, tip-toeing really, across this narrow ledge, crushing and mashing the plants as he went. I got up and chased after him, but I was scared shitless. I mean, it was still a long way down, and you couldn't quite reach up to the guardrail, so there really wasn't anywhere else to go other than to chase after him.

So when Ponytail reached the end of the ledge, where it meets the wall, I had him cornered, and I asked him, "Why'd you pick me? How far does this go? Is Nuggie in on this? Julianne?"

"Fate picked you," he said. Then he held up his prosthetic hand, flipped a switch, and a long blade popped out.

It still had blood on it.

Mal's blood.

Now it was my turn to run! When I got to the other end of the ledge, over by the windows in the front of the building, I didn't have anywhere else to go, and he was right behind me, so I jumped up to the scaffolding that holds up those skylights, you know, the ones that line the atrium's ceiling, and I thought I could swing myself over to the next outcropping of plants.

But you know how those windows on the ceiling are always steamed-up? Well, that should've told me this was a bad idea. The scaffolding was wet with dew or whatever and I could feel myself slipping as soon as I got hold of the bar. Worse, my momentum was swinging me back towards my launching pad, where Ponytail was waiting for me. He pulled that sword or whatever back behind him like he was winding up for a big swing, but he whiffed – he must have slipped on those mashed-up plants, I guess.

Me, I just let myself go – I didn't have much choice, really – and as I was going down, I grabbed for his arm, the one with the blade. I landed on the side of my head, and just like that, Ponytail tumbled over the ledge, and there I was, holding him by his plastic arm – just like something out of the movies!

I yelled to him, "Come on, man, give me your hand! I'll pull you up!"

And when he turned to look at me, he smiled. "Be patient," he told me. "It takes nine months to bring a child into this world, so on the appointed day, three hours after sunrise, our sacrifice will reveal itself to you."

Then he reached up and clicked something in his prosthetic.

"And you *will* bear witness," he sneered.

Then I saw him getting smaller and smaller. He had disengaged himself from his hand. I watched him fall for what seemed like forever, until he ca-thunked on the floor of the C level, probably no more than five feet from the cork bulletin board where they tack up the nine o'clock list.

~ Chapter Thirty Two ~

DE LA SUGGS:

So there I was, breaking outta jail after sneakin' in, cops right on my heels, chasing me through da' courthouse.

Ah, the jobs I won't do. Bumpin' curbs, bumpin' curbs.....

What's that? Bumpin' curbs? Oh, that jes be what the old time cabbies call it roun here when they pick up their fares from being flagged down. Not like those Ay-rab muthfuckas who just tool roun the airport 'n front of hotels. No, I'm talking 'bout the old timers roun'ere.

But that's another story. Back to that Monday.

So, like I say, I'm racing out the back doors, ready to die, ready to get that cop's bullet in my back. I'm not afraid of it. I welcome it. God knows I'm all out of balance.

But soon as I get outside in the sunshine, that's when I heard the drums, the African chanting, and I smell the smell of meat on a spit, and I'm thinking maybe the pigs already put that bullet in my back, and I'm on my homecoming journey, wherever that may be!

But when I see the parade of brothers, not twenty feet outside the court building, I realize I'm still alive. So dig it: I'm hand-cuffed, and the pig with that mustache be chasin me, and one of dem bow-tied bean-pie muthafuckas starts hollering, "Slave catcha! Stop the slave catcha!"

I still laugh when I think about it. Niggas all stupid like that, like they was 'specting some kind of movie scene n'shit. You know, dem niggas all wanna be part of some publicity stunt, by Farrakhan's crew, I guess. So sure enough, my niggas close in on that slave catcher, and I got away.

Made my way through a most decent crowd of niggas and eventually found me a machine shop off South Capitol, right there by the railroad tracks. Had them to cut the cuffs off me.

What's that? You wanna know how? How I make him?

Let's just say it's my way of looking at a man. Maybe it be the way I look *through* the man. See, I don't need no weapon, I just need a plan. I needs to form the intent. Intent to kill, like they say in the law. And once I form my intent, I'm gonna find some way, any way, to act on it. Weapon or not, I'm gonna kill you.

See, I don't really give a fuck about people. They no different than a dog or a snake or a rat to me. But just as I ain't killing *every* stray dog or cat that I comes across, most people ain't gonna have no problem with me. Jes the ones who piss me off, dig? Whores, dudes disrespecting me, that kind of thing. I hate people when they're not polite.

What my man Bushwick Bill say? "You bitches gotta stop killing little babies!" Them, especially.

If you ahead of me in the shopping mall, if you sit next to me on the bus, you ain't have nothing to worry over. Just don't cross me, that's all. Cause I got plenty of that *intent*. I fucking ooze the shit, if you know what I mean.

I'ma let you know right off – I am the Devil, the Devil his-self.

And everyone know you can deal with the Devil. See, I'm also a soldier, you dig? I get paid. Simple contract. That's my only relationship to this whole Heyward Shepherd thing – a contract I got with the Captain, a contract I now feel he has breached.

See I met the Captain out round Clay Terrace. He was sitting there in that old car of his. I had him figured for a cop right away. FBI been on my tail for years now, so I creep up on this white muthafucka, see if I can sweat him a bit, find out how close they were to me. But I sees that he be looking right at me in the side view mirror. I sees him smile.

Then he jes drop his arm out the window. Palm out, real

slow, so I can see. Dems prison tats, y'all. They tell d'own story. This man wasn't no fed. This was a job.

See, that's how they come. I ain't in the Yellow Pages, I ain't got no storefront address. Out there on the street, you just recognize me for who I am – a killer, a contract killer. Recognize who ya'll dealing with, then maybe we do some business. Some jobs big, some jobs small. I really don't discriminate. Bumping curbs is what I do.

Now, my contract with the Captain, it wasn't to be no easy job, mind you. First, he want me to hit this nigga right *in* the courthouse, just as he come outta C-10, but the courthouse closed down 'fore I could ace him. So then Captain send me out on the street to do it, but I ain't no godtam bounty hunter, I don' know where the fuck he at. So, then, roun' October, Captain say he gonna send me to jail to do it.

That one, I toll him, gonna cost you big. See, I been to prison once and only once. I had jes turned sixteen, they sent me up to D.C. Jail on account of them saying I had jes capped some old white muthfucka in a liquor store. But I had me a real good woman lawyer. First, she got my case back down to juvi court – that move saved me fifteen to twenty years easy. Plead guilty and do a couple of years at Oak Hill? Shee, that's like going to summer camp. N'better yet, a few years later, I gets a letter from my lawyer telling me that the *whole* case been done thrown out on account of that old detective hadn't read me my rights before he done beat me with the soap-sock.

I'm telling you this so that you appreciate what it was for me to go back to jail. See, when they let me outta Oak Hill, I was already 18 anyway, so they jes let me go. And then I was gone. Vanished out the system. I could be whoever I wanted to be, use whateva' name I wanted to. Totally underground. And trust me, that makes a big difference in my profession.

So you see, it wasn't no minor thing to gotdam incarcerate

myself. But every nigga got a price, see? I ain't no different. Learned that long time ago. I was even willing to let d'Captain lead me around down there in court, like some little bitch, like some pack animal.

But Captain, see, he relish the role of jailor a little bit too much, you dig? Like, he get off on calling me niggers and boys n'shit. So when we back there, behind the courtroom, after we picked up that nigga Stancil I been chasin' for the last seven months, piece of shit, I'm like, "Let's cap this nigga before the cops come!"

But instead of stickin with the plan, Captain say he want me to choke the man to death. Shee, takes a minute or two to kill a man like that! Trust me, I know! If you got that little gun there, let's use that.

Unless you saving that bullet for me! Ah ha! Didn't think I had that figgered out, did you, Captain? When I finish up strangling the muthafucka you gonna shoot me wit that gun I done smuggled in for you! Now ain't that the shit!

No, no sir. No amount of money gon fix this. Y'all gotta pay. I mean, I'ma patient man. I'm gonna git Captain, da Minister, and da rest of that crew, all in due time. Balance things out.

§ § § § § § § § §

Rev. CLINTON AUGUSTUS AND-ONE:
I think it is a gross mischaracterization to say that I knew anything about this so-called conspiracy. I'm just a simple preacher. A man of God, a messenger of God. Praise Jesus!

Who's that?
Jesus!
What's that?
Jesus!

He's coming! Be here any minute now! And let me tell you, He's coming home to share his message of forgiveness. Are you ready for that message? Are you open to God's word?

Forgiveness of all! Yes, Praise Jesus! He will forgive you and, God willing, He will forgive me.

And we ask, in Jesus' name, that He forgive these poor young girls – alone, scared, and full of life – tempted by the evil whisperings of the Devil. These girls are weak, oh Lord, so we also ask, in Jesus' name, for the power and authority to help them, to guide them, to tear them from Lucifer's clutches. Give us the keys, oh Lord, and let us show them the way.

That's what I prayed for on that Monday, the Monday of the Million Man March. Oh yes, I am not ashamed to say, I prayed all morning. I knew I would need God's help in getting on that podium. Yes indeed!

Did I think it was unusual to have this speech – this workshop – take place at St. Nicholas'? No sir! No indeed! Sure, it's a bit of a stroll from downtown, you know, the area where the March was going on. But you can't beat the facilities at St. Nick's. Why, when I was running the diocese, we used that school for every manner of workshop and bible study and prayer breakfast. Every January we'd open our doors for the hundreds of youngsters who come to Washington for the March for Life, and throughout the year we'd host speakers of national prominence.

Pat Buchanan spoke there once, I'll have you know.

But as I was saying, St. Nicholas' has a beautiful auditorium, and a cafeteria facility that can seat and feed over five hundred. So, no, it's not unreasonable to think that St. Nick's would offer its auditorium for Brother Farrakhan and his message of peace, freedom, justice, and – if I could help it – Life.

What I'm trying to say, my brothers and sisters, is that on

that day, on that morning, that Monday back in October, I really didn't think anything was ... amiss, shall we say?

At least not until I reached the doors of the auditorium itself. The St. Nick's auditorium, of course. For it was there that I saw all the children. The white children. There might have been an oriental in there somewhere, but pretty much all of them were Caucasian. After some questioning, I discovered that they were the national organizing committee for the Abstinence Now! Youth Corps.

Tremendous children, these youngsters. Tremendous. A very lively bunch, too, but not exactly the crowd I'd been expecting. But the Captain never did say who I'd be lecturing to, so I went ahead and gave it my best shot.

With these children, that is.

Now of course, I had prepared my delivery – my pauses, my cries, my inflections – for a slightly different audience. A darker audience, shall we say. So with these forty or so youths and their adult chaperones, my timing was just a bit off. The speech ran fast, definitely less than the seven minutes I was given, and I'm afraid I might have started early.

I simply didn't see any reason to drag it out the full seven minutes, despite the Captain's orders. The organizing committee had finished their business for the morning and a bus was coming to take them to the airport. Moreover, some of the children had become distracted by some insects that had evidently flown into the building – praying mantises, I believe they were.

Who knew praying mantises could fly?

Anyhow, I still say I held up my end. A backstage pass, that's what the Captain had promised me. That's all, nothing else. If something improper was afoot, I was as much a victim of this scheme as anyone else.

Did I know that John Brown's attack on Harper's Ferry

occurred on October 16[th?]   What you say – one hundred and thirty six years ago?

You kidding me? John Brown? Who's John Brown? As far as I'm concerned, October 16th will go down in history as the day of the Million Man March.

Which is exactly where I went after giving my speech to the white youngsters. Down at the National Mall, that is. The Million Man March.

What a sight! What a sight it was.

So, let me finish. I walked straight up to the podium, right in the shadow of the U.S. Capitol, but they would not let me in. The Nation of Islam guards removed me, quite roughly, in fact. So, like I said, I was a victim as much as anybody.

Maybe if – for that speech – maybe if I had just waited for the appointed time, for them ladybugs, you know, the Curtain of Life, things would've been different....

I don't know.

§ § § § § § § § §

LIAM McNAUGHTON:

You have to go back to that day, Monday, October 16th, to fully appreciate what was going through my head. As I raced out the courthouse doors, the main doors in the front, the lawyers, judges, cops, court reporters, civilians – everyone who had just evacuated the building – they came storming in.

I was still holding Ponytail's prosthetic arm. It's blade was still unsheathed, and it was dripping blood, but no one seemed to notice me.

All I knew was that I had to get to that school – St. Nick's – and warn them to get out before it was too late.

Running down K Street as fast as I could, you bet I had every intention of yelling bloody murder, screaming "Fire!"

into the crowded theater. Talk to the cops? Are you kidding? They wouldn't have believed me anyway. And I would've had to tell them about what Mal told me. I would have had to reveal a client confidence.

I would've done it, yes it's true. I honestly believed that St. Nick's was about to go up in flames. Besides, the attorney-client privilege ends with the death of the client.

Doesn't it?

But like I said, who'd believe me? And besides, by the time I'd finish explaining everything to the cops, it'd be too late.

As if was, I got to St. Nick's in about ten but there was no one there, no one to protect. The doors were locked, everything was shut down, the place was empty. No flames, no fire. No bombs went off that day, not at St. Nicholas', not at the courthouse, not at the Million Man March. Not anywhere.

Trust me, I felt pretty stupid standing there, my suit soaked in sweat, holding a man's weaponized prosthetic. I had thought about the previous four days or whatever of my life and wondered if it was all a dream. A hallucination.

But the day was not a total loss. As you know, my client Malcolm X. Stancil was acquitted of the charges. Or rather, he won on a directed verdict. I may have Judge Malley's order dismissing in my briefcase, if you want to see it.

I knew we had beaten the case, but it was still kinda cool to get the order in the mail. I was happy for Mal. I really was. I wish I had had a chance to tell him myself personally.

But wouldn't you know it? Chief Judge Cummings didn't dismiss the show cause hearing, even after I sent him a copy of Judge Malley's order, showing that we had won. Instead, the prick just re-set the hearing for January 22nd.

I guess Stucky never entered his appearance in that case, so the notice came to me as his lawyer of record.

So that's what brought me down to court today. That's why I'm here, right now.

~ Chapter Thirty Three ~

ANNIE FAIRBROTHER:

Mr. McNaughton was the one who alerted us to the plan. Alleged plan. Conspiracy, I should say. I mean, really, that's all it is. Alleged. There's nothing that can be proved. Nothing certain. Nothing that even remotely reaches beyond a reasonable doubt.

But something that bears looking into, nonetheless.

That's important to me, since I'm now serving as the U.S. Attorney's representative on the Special Commission that's reviewing the matter. The matter of the court's security protocols, that is. Several were breached that day, the day of the Million Man March.

True, the Special Commission got started late on its investigation, but with the government shut downs, everything sort of came to a halt here in D.C.

However, I can report that the Commission has made progress. We've already determined that the gun that Detective McCoy was telling you about, the one that was smuggled into court that day, it came through a Styrofoam take-out dish, that kind of thing that dozens and dozens of people bring into the building with them every day. None of these packages, it turns out, are ever x-rayed, and none of them go through the metal detectors. People usually just plop them on the table next to the metal detectors and then pick them up once they get through the machine.

It was my view, or rather, the Commission's view, that at a minimum, the court security officers should actually examine such packages, or have the people pass through the metal detector carrying their food packages or whatever. We even considered prohibiting outside food, but that got shot down pretty quick.

The Commission's Report is presently with the Chief Judge, and we certainly hope that he takes some action on it. Several other security measures were breached that day, but I'm not really at liberty to discuss them.

So you'll have to forgive me, I have no comment on the matter of Mr. Stancil's death being ruled a suicide.

What I can tell you about is this so-called Heyward Shepherd Conspiracy.

If you don't mind me referring to my notes. So I don't leave anything out.

Let's see.

It all started early *this* morning, when Mr. McNaughton came to my office in a panic. He told me that he needed my help to evacuate the St. Nicholas' School for Girls "right away."

I have that in quotations, so that must have been *exactly* what he said.

He told me that on his way to court this morning, as he walked down Constitution Avenue, he passed hundreds if not thousands of young teenagers, young white children, marching in the opposite direction.

(He used the word "white," I have that quoted as well).

It was the national Right to Life March, of course. Happens every year at this time.

But what alarmed Mr. McNaughton, as I recall, was how so many of these marchers, these young people, had come up to him to give him an invitation to the Abstinence Now! rally in the auditorium of St. Nick's.

Mr. McNaughton said he saw hundreds of these flyers scattered on the ground. He said it seemed that everyone had one in their hands.

The flyer, which Mr. McNaughton provided me, stated that the event was to commence at nine o'clock sharp.

On the other side of the flyer, were these words:

Whoso sheddeth man's blood,
by man shall his blood be shed:
for in the image of God made he man.

And that's when Mr. McNaughton said he remembered what Greek Fire was. He said his father used to teach him about ancient weaponry, things like – I have it written here in my notes – things like catapults, siege vehicles.

(Whatever that is).

You know, things that a seven or eight year-old boy might be interested in. Anyway, Mr. McNaughton remembered that Greek Fire was a legendary weapon used by the Athenians thousands of years ago. Greek Fire was a liquid compound. Once ignited, Greek Fire burned even hotter when mixed with water, sort of like modern-day napalm.

According to Mr. McNaughton, the Greeks would load this compound into pumps and spray it at the enemy's ships. Then the Greek archers would ignite the liquid with fire arrows and the flames would engulf the enemy fleet and its sailors. Mr. McNaughton said there were never any survivors.

Truthfully, I was happy that Detective McCoy showed up at this point. I was starting to believe that he – Mr. McNaughton – had lost his mind. I've seen lawyers do that, you know. It can be a very stressful job.

So, yes, I was happy to see it was McCoy knocking on my door.

But McCoy looked like he had seen a ghost.

He told us he had just received the unclassified Department of Justice report about the one-armed man. The one who had fallen to his death inside the courthouse on day of the Million Man March.

That's when I realized that Mr. McNaughton's theory had to be taken seriously.

McNaughton said he had learned from a client – he didn't say who – that the one-armed man had somehow planted some sort of bombs in the auditorium at St. Nick's, set to go off sometime after this morning during today's youth rally.

Mr. McNaughton thought that these devices were designed to start only small fires, nothing more than a sparkler really, but large enough to trigger the fire sprinklers, fire sprinklers that were rigged up to spray Greek Fire all over those poor children.

Mr. McNaughton says *this* is the Heyward Shepherd Conspiracy. He explained that Heyward Shepherd was the first person killed in John Brown's raid on Harpers Ferry.

Mr. Shepherd was a former slave who had purchased his own freedom.

Mr. McNaughton says that the children at the school were to be sacrificed in the manner of Heyward Shepherd – that just as John Brown's raid was supposed to start a civil war that would free black men like Heyward Shepherd, this killing, this slaughter of these young pro-life children from Pennsylvania and New Jersey and Ohio, this mass murder would start a war – a second civil war – to be fought over the practice of abortion.

§ § § § § § § § §

JAMES McCOY:

I showed AUSA Fairbrother the FBI file of Thomas Wayne Keith, a 48-year-old meth addict from Buffalo, New York.

He had spent much of his life in prison, including a fifteen year robbery sentence in New Mexico, during the time of the prison riot there. According to the FBI file, his sentence was partially commuted due to his cooperation during the negotiations to take back control of the prison.

And there's some suggestion in the file that he continued to cooperate with the FBI and the U.S. Marshal's Service after that, infiltrating several violent prison gangs, mostly in the upper mid-West, over the last ten years.

But he'd escaped while on a work detail and was rumored to have joined a survivalist group known as the Life Jihad out in the woods of North Carolina.

The Life Jihad was recently implicated in several anthrax-hoaxes sent to a number of abortion clinics in southern Virginia. That's what pieced it together for me.

A few months ago, on the day of the Million Man March, I found literature from that same group all over that closed-down church over by Stanton Park. The one with the Swastika-looking thing on its sign. I had followed the man I knew to be Bennie Grimes to that church.

To be honest, I followed him all over town that day, from the courthouse, through the Mall, up South Capitol, and then back to the church.

Unfortunately, that's where I lost him. He must have ran *out* of the church as soon as I ran *in*. There's only so much one cop can do. I searched the whole place, but he was undoubtedly high tailing it down Maryland Ave. toward Hechinger Mall.

Oh well. I don't know who he is, but I know what he did. I have his fingerprint. He can't hide forever. And as for this Heyward Shepherd Conspiracy, I'm inclined to believe Mr. McNaughton.

Though trust me, I was plenty skeptical at first.

§ § § § § § § § §

LIAM McNAUGHTON:
So when I told McCoy and Miss Fairbrother about the conspiracy, McCoy immediately offered to take us in his police

car so we could race over to the school. But it was already eight fifty-five by this time, and he doubted we would make it, so McCoy said we should call out a SWAT team to evacuate St. Nick's, but he wanted Miss Fairbrother's blessing, on account of his recent troubles within the Department.

Glaring at *me*, Miss Fairbrother said, "O.K. Call them! Call them right now!"

As McCoy radioed for the police dispatcher, Miss Fairbrother told us to follow her up the back stairs. She thought we might be able to see the school from the roof of the U.S. Attorney's building.

I don't know who was more startled, the snipers or us when we came barging through the fire door and onto the roof. The snipers took their guns off us only after McCoy showed them his badge. He then explained the situation, and one of the snipers – the one in charge, evidently – handed him a pair of high-powered binoculars.

That's when I realized that these guys were cops too.

So I asked if I could borrow a pair, too, and this lead sniper asked me who the Hell I was. I told him I was the lawyer, the defense lawyer. After that, he pretty much turned his back to me.

One of the other snipers came over and handed me his binoculars, however. He was younger than the other two, much younger. You know, face-covered-in-pimples young.

McCoy, meanwhile, was relaying to us the radio communications he was hearing.

"Several squad cars are already on scene," he was saying. "Confirmed large congregation of children in the auditorium. Waiting for further orders."

McCoy looked at Miss Fairbrother, and she looked at me.

"What about the SWAT team," I asked. "What about the evacuation?"

And I remember Miss Fairbrother saying, "Do it, McCoy! Call out the cavalry!"

But then the dispatcher wouldn't relay McCoy's command to evacuate the place because she said that *he* lacked proper authority.

Miss Fairbrother took the radio from McCoy and started screaming at the dispatcher, telling her that *she* was acting under the authority of the goddamn Department of Justice, but the dispatcher told her to get off the line.

Finally, the leader of the snipers took the walkie-talkie, said something very quietly, and the order went out over the radio: "Evacuate the building! Haz-Mat to respond!"

We began to hear the chime of church bells ringing nine times, and I remembered Ponytail's words to me: "On the appointed day, *three hours after sunrise*, our sacrifice will reveal itself to you." I mean, I didn't know what time sunrise was, but if anything was going to happen, it was going to happen soon.

But as the minutes passed, we all began to wonder if we'd really done the right thing.

At one point, McCoy shrugged his shoulders and said, "Better safe than sorry, right?"

Miss Fairbrother looked at him and replied, "We're all out of a job if we're wrong. You know how much it costs the city to call out the Haz-Mat?"

Then she glared at me, just like the first time I had seen her in court.

The day I first met my client Mal Stancil, may he rest in peace.

Finally, the report came that the SWAT team had arrived and that the auditorium had been successfully evacuated. But McCoy said that the bomb sniffing dogs hadn't alerted to anything yet in the auditorium.

In fact, he said the team was heading towards the basement, near the boiler room, because the dogs had picked up on something there.

I could hear the voices on the radio laughing through the static, "Supercop, what kind of wild goose chase do you have us on now?"

That's when the leader of the snipers asked to speak to Detective McCoy and Miss Fairbrother. "Alone," he said, meaning out of the presence of *me*, the lawyer. He made some sort of hand signal and immediately the young sniper – the one who had leant me his binoculars – told me to follow him to the other end of the building, as far from McCoy, Miss Fairbrother, and the other two snipers as possible.

I complied, even though it was clear that the lead sniper was getting McCoy and Miss Fairbrother together to figure out a way to pin the whole thing on me.

Following the young sniper to the southwestern corner of building, I stared out across the Mall and the Potomac River, and I swear I could see with my naked eye the building that Julianne lived in. Just past the Pentagon. I even thought I could pick out her balcony.

But when I tried the binoculars, we were just too far away. I couldn't see anything.

I felt kinda disgusted with myself, at that moment, trying to see into her apartment, trying to find out what she was up to. Why do I keep scratching that itch?

Julianne is a mystery I'll never solve, I guess. It's sad that love can end that way.

I remember feeling real shivery just about then. You know, on top of the U.S. Attorney's Officer there? It's cold as shit here in January, and I left my coat – my overcoat – in Miss Fairbrother's office. You see, I was wearing my new seer sucker suit that day – I know, I know, why am I wearing a

395

summertime suit in January, but all my other suits were still at the dry cleaner, since I didn't have enough money to...

Anyway, back to this morning. I began walking along the side of the building, looking over the edge, wondering how far down it was. And I was shivering like crazy, my teeth chattering.

The young sniper was following me, and I hadn't really noticed it before, but he had been talking to me the whole time, asking me things like, "Where's the best place to pick up chicks round here?" and "How come y'all keep electing Marion Barry as your Mayor?" but I was pretty much tuning him out 'cause I was in my own little world.

I was looking through his binoculars again, this time from the northwestern corner of the building, where I had an incredible view of the Cathedral, Howard University, and what looked to be a lake or a reservoir maybe. This lake or whatever was surrounded by these brick silos, I guess you could call them, and I suddenly realized that these were the Bins I had heard so much about. They looked like a bunch of mini-nuclear reactors.

These binoculars, by the way, were amazing. The detail, the focus – I was watching this bunch of homeless crazies pouring out of the fenced-in area where those silos, the bins, I guess, were situated and I swear I could even make out that dude Hip Hop – that homeless guy who used to prowl my neighborhood – and he looked terrified.

I was scanning the area, trying to find out why all the dudes were abandoning the Bins in such a hurry when the young sniper came up from behind and snatched his binoculars from me.

"You see that?" he asked, pointing towards the fenced-in area, right where I had been looking, and even without the binoculars, I could see the black smoke just billowing out of one of those brick silos.

The young pimply faced boy from Kentucky or Mississippi or Alabama or wherever put the binoculars down and turned to me and asked, as if I was the voice of authority, "Y'all really got volcanos up here?"

§ § § § § § § § §

You know, the thing I admire about lawyers – trial lawyers – is that no matter the situation, no matter what's said, they always have some witty comeback. Red. Mo. All the Murder Lawyers. Hell, even the Fifth Streeters. They'd know what to say when a guy asks about volcanos.

Me, all I could do was tell him the truth. I told him, "Those are the Bins, man. That smoke's coming from two dozen matchboxes, all going up in flames."

"And it's my client that put 'em there," I said. "He really did save the children."

You see, when I was a kid, I was real into comic books. You know, Spiderman, Daredevil? Anyway, as I was saying, the only thing to ever come out of the ghetto in comics were victims and the common criminals – purse-snatchers, pimps, pushers. But not the villains, and definitely not the heroes.

But in this case...?

I tell ya, the one thing I am certain of is this: every good trial lawyer has a good war story. Now that I've had some time to think about it, I wish I could find some way of making this one mine.

www.ingramcontent.com/pod-product-compliance
Lightning Source LLC
Chambersburg PA
CBHW060343260626
47160CB00006B/2195